FINDING HOME

A TIME TRAVEL HISTORICAL ADVENTURE

CHRISTY COOPER-
BURNETT

Black Rose Writing | Texas

ISBN: 978-1-68433-709-5
PUBLISHED BY BLACK ROSE WRITING
www.blackrosewriting.com

Printed in the United States of America
Suggested Retail Price (SRP) $19.95

Finding Home is printed in Calluna

*As a planet-friendly publisher, Black Rose Writing does its best to eliminate unnecessary waste to reduce paper usage and energy costs, while never compromising the reading experience. As a result, the final word count vs. page count may not meet common expectations.

For my son Mychael, thank you for always encouraging me.
To Cynthia and Nancy, my best friends of forty-five years,
for all that you do.
Special shout-out to my Chino Chicks for always believing in me.
You know who you are.
To Karen and Paula, who will be forever missed and in my heart.

"*Finding Home* is a highly recommended time travel
story, filled with everything you could want:
action, suspense, romance, and wonderfully-described
characters and settings."
– *Sublime Book Review*

FINDING HOME

PROLOGUE

Christine Stewart time travels for a living. She works as a transporter for the Cyber Criminal Enforcement Agency, Los Angeles division, or the CCEA, as people commonly call it. Twice a week she escorts convicted cyber-criminals back in history as a sentence for their crime, and after eleven years she is comfortable traveling different timelines in the United States regularly.

At least she used to be. Then in spring of 2070 she went on routine transport to Piedmont, Oklahoma, in 1867. Everything changed after that.

The CCEA stranded Christine there with a malfunctioning transponder and no idea how to survive. She had no choice but to hide in plain sight until the government rescued her, or she found her own way back. What she did not know then was someone had sabotaged the system, and on the day her equipment crashed, the same glitch trapped dozens of other agents all over the world wherever they exiled inmates.

A local man, John Harding, took Christine in after her prisoner abandoned her, leaving her with nothing but the clothes on her back and her useless transponder. If not for that farmer, Christine's chances of survival were slim. She met another displaced transporter from the Chicago sector after her arrival, who transported to Boonesville, Arkansas in 1867. Annabelle Harris made her way to Piedmont, where the two women formed a powerful bond and a lasting friendship.

When their devices showed signs of working again after six months, they were relieved, and thought they were finally escaping 1867. But before they could leave, Indians captured Annabelle, and Christine had to make the difficult decision to transport to base without her, knowing her best chance to save her was with help from the CCEA. But she did not go home as planned. Instead, she was flung even further back in time to medieval England. She landed in 1335, in a camp of four other agents, Ethan, Thomas, Aidan and Estera, and Ethan's prisoner, Malcolm.

Shortly after arriving in England, Christine discovered the creator of the CCEA time travel program had sabotaged the system, tech billionaire Jonathan Hoyt. He recruited two of the transporters in a scheme to steal a fourteenth century astronomer's writings. While doing research on the treatise, he identified a connection between extreme weather, planet gravitational pull, and pandemics. When his software predicted a devastating pandemic for 2072, he needed a missing manuscript from it to complete his analysis. The only way to access the information was to reach back in history for it.

Frightened and unsure who she could trust, Christine wasn't convinced the other agent's story was true, but she was unwilling to risk a worldwide pandemic. She gambled on her instinct and teamed with Ethan under the condition they confront Hoyt once they were home. They completed the mission with the support of the retrieval unit sent to find the lost agents, led by Christine's supervisor and friend, Frank Rhoades. Her son Michael was also a member of the same group who successfully located Annabelle in Oklahoma before arriving in England.

Christine and Ethan met with Hoyt after they returned to their timeline, and determined they made the right judgment call, as his investigation prevented a catastrophic global pandemic. They agreed to work with him on future disaster prevention using their positions as transporters, and Hoyt's ability to hide their travel from the enforcement department, the division who monitors all agents and exiled convicts.

After arriving home, Christine and Ethan began dating. Her friendship with Annabelle strengthened, and her world was slowly returning to normal after her trauma. But as so often happens in life, just when you think things are running smoothly, fate throws a wrench at you. And turmoil is certain to follow.

ONE

London, England, 2070

Malcolm collapses onto the tattered sofa, the springs creaking as he kicks the coffee table out of his path. The blow nicks a piece of wood off the edge, and he throws the SmartTech remote at the fireplace in frustration.

Not that he cares about the furniture. He doesn't. It came with the flat and the letting agent is going to toss him out of here when he can't pay his lease, anyway. Besides, he has never liked this place. It's dingy and damp and smells of mold and curry from the previous tenants, no matter how often or how thoroughly he cleans it. He peers around the small room and considers picking up the empty food cartons, but decides he cannot be bothered with it. Why should he? The chair in the room's corner has a permanent stain that looks like something you would see waiting for the rubbish bin. Everything appears worn, tired and stained. The only decent thing in here is his laptop. He glances at a pile of computer components he has spread across the desk where he is rebuilding an old Dell from scratch as a hobby. It was difficult to locate parts, but he found them online and has been working on it for a few weeks. It is his primary source of entertainment, pitiful as that may be.

He shakes his head, forcing him back to focus on the present. He has bigger problems to solve. The IT company where he was employed for the past ten years made him redundant today. After all his loyal service. He rarely called off sick, worked hard, and kept to himself. And this is what that loyalty earned him. So, he took their pink slip and told them to sod off after he erased his entire computer memory. That was an impulsive move, very unlike him, but he can't help but think they got what they deserved. They summoned him into Human Resources and instructed him to pack his desk, telling him they would deposit his wages by the end of the day.

Now he just wants to drink the full lot of Guinness he has stashed, get pissed and sleep it off. That would be the easy thing to do. But he needs to concentrate, and he cannot do that if he isn't thinking clearly.

He has no funds to speak of, a little over three hundred pounds in his bank account. And his final paycheck. But that will not stretch far. Not here, where everything is overpriced, and a full English breakfast costs you sixty quid.

Malcolm sits in the dark contemplating his next step until his head hurts. After a while he accepts defeat and gives into temptation. His bare feet land on something sticky as he makes his way to the kitchen for a pint, reminding him he cannot recall the last time he mopped the floor. Or cleaned anything in the flat, to be honest. The thought passes quickly though, and he resumes his crusade to the fridge.

He pushes worries of his financial state out of his mind as he works on the old computer. He drinks until the beer is gone, and within a couple of hours he is asleep on the couch.

Still sprawled on the settee with his legs dangling over the edge the next morning, the telly drones the BBC news in the background. He forces his eyes open as the rare sun-filled day wakes him. As he sits up, the pounding in his head causes him to wince. The sound of traffic wafts into the room, horns honk and a siren blares as it races by the street outside the lounge. He blinks against the harsh light; the brightness threatening to worsen the pummeling in his skull.

He'll never get back to sleep now. His brief reprieve from the nightmare that has become his world is over, compelling him to confront the issue at hand. Such as what to do for capital. Finding employment in this job market could take weeks, maybe months. He knows he does not have that kind of time. His landlord will evict him straight away if he does not have the rental payment by tomorrow. He might stall him for a day, but no longer than that. He curses himself for not putting a plan together. If he had any foresight, he would have saved money each month, knowing the company was downsizing. It was stupid of him not to prepare for it. As he runs through options and comes up blank, despair sinks in again. He has no family left, only a cousin in Leeds, but they aren't close. There is no one he can turn to, and the realization is crushing.

Movement draws his gaze to the mantel, where a digital picture frame loops through a slideshow of photos. He remembers when he and Katherine found the antique in a thrift shop and she loved the retro look of it. Now it taunts him as it displays scenes of them in happier days, their faces grinning at the camera. He picks up an empty beer can and throws it toward the fireplace, missing the image.

The first blow to his world came two weeks ago when she moved out. She left him a note to say she couldn't stay any longer; the relationship was not working, and she was moving in with her friend Maggie. She took all her things, leaving him no reason to reach out and have a civilized discussion about it. He has not spoken to her since then. She made her choice and he will never beg her to come back. If she isn't happy, let her move on. He is fine with that. He never fancied her all that much, anyway. She was more of a distraction to his depressing existence than a partner. At least that is what he tells himself. But if he is being honest, it hurt a lot more than he admits, even if he wasn't in love with her. After a year together, it was a punch to the gut he never saw coming.

Then things spiraled further downhill from there. He has been drinking more; he recognizes that. But after losing his job, who would blame him for knocking back a few pints? He considers filing a grievance against his former employer, but that takes months to resolve. And then what? They can appoint anyone redundant whenever they want to, making the entire process a massive waste of time. And that is the one thing he does not have. But he cannot shake the fact that no severance pay was just not fair.

He tries to recall the moment his world shifted. He doesn't know what happened, not really. His life has always been fine. Maybe that's the problem, he realizes. He struggles to remember when he resigned to accepting his existence need not be anything more than *fine*. When had he given up on life? His head hurts too much to dissect it now, but the notion refuses to leave him alone.

His rumbling stomach rips him away from his thoughts, and he makes his way across the sticky floor to the kitchen. The choices are limited, so he settles on a cheese and onion butty before flopping on the couch to flip through the television channels. He quickly gives that up after finding nothing but news and talk shows. Malcolm is never home during working hours, and he is not sure what to do with himself, so he putters around the place restlessly. He's not in the right frame of mind to work on the vintage computer. That would require a considerable amount of concentration, and two pain relievers have done little to ease the pounding in his brain. He taps the chip in his earlobe to activate his phone. As he stares at the wall for a few minutes, he realizes he has no one to call and rests his head on the sofa, closing his eyes again. Within minutes he sits straight up all at once, the restlessness finally becoming more than he can bear. He cannot stay in this cramped flat for another minute, so he grabs his jacket and steps outside to the noisy street. The air is frigid as it is most of the year in England, but at least it's not raining. He turns up his collar and walks the neighborhood before venturing further into downtown, following the crowds like a herded animal. He stops for chips and vinegar from a run-down food truck, waiting in the queue even though he's not hungry. He's only killing time while he thinks.

As he wanders through London aimlessly, he finds himself in Trafalgar Square, perched on the edge of the fountain to people watch. Malcolm feels a disconnect to this city lately. Almost as if he is living someone else's life, not his. The hackney carriages maneuver through the traffic, the black cabs still a British tradition even after all their years in service. He can spot the locals easily. They scurry through the center with heads down, oblivious to their surroundings. The tourists snap pictures and point at Big Ben and Parliament Square. They rubberneck at the National Gallery, the busiest attraction, with hundreds of sightseers coming and going every hour.

He is torn from his reverie when a woman sits down next to him, and he glances over at her. She is about his age, not bad looking in an unremarkable way. Plain, with a forgettable face. She smiles at him and he returns a quick half-hearted smile before he looks away, not keen on a chat.

"Those chips look lovely. I adore the kind they make on the food trucks. Not like the frozen crap they pass off in the shops."

"Hmmm," is all he can muster up, but he holds the carton out to her, offering some.

"Oh, thank you, I think I will," she says giggling. "Do you live nearby?"

"No," says Malcolm. He feels a twinge of guilt, knowing his curt answer is rude, but how else is he supposed to respond to that? Give her his address? He is still not in the frame of mind for a chat. That is his problem, not hers, but that doesn't make it any less true.

"Oh. I stay just round the corner. My flatmate has a date over, so I thought I'd take a stroll. Allow them some time on their own, if you know what I mean. I don't have a boyfriend, so nowhere to go, really."

Malcolm tunes out her chatter as he studies the crowd moving through the square. He loses himself in people watching when she leans in front of him, clearly expecting him to react to something she said. He tilts back, reclaiming his personal space as she giggles again. She has an annoying laugh which grates on his last remaining nerve.

"Were you listening to me?" she asks, frowning at him.

"Apologies, I was daydreaming for a minute there."

"I asked if you fancied having a pint with me. I know a pub nearby. It's top notch."

Malcolm looks at her and blinks slowly, wondering what to say that will not make him seem like a complete twit. He has no intention of going anywhere with her. Not now or ever. She has not stopped talking once since sitting down.

"I don't mean to be impolite, but I came here for some alone time."

"Alone time? In Trafalgar Square?" she asks, something between a laugh and a bray escaping her.

He gets up and leaves the chips, walking away without a word. Normally he would not be so unpleasant to a stranger, but right now he just doesn't have the inclination to be disturbed by it. He needs to figure out what to do, and the last thing he wants is some woman jabbering non-stop to him.

He takes the long route home, arriving as the sun sets. As he approaches his residence, he sees an envelope tacked to the door. He hopes it is only a notice for an upcoming service, but already knows he is not that lucky. Besides, maintenance would notify him via the SmartTech program, not a piece of paper taped to his entry. He opens the sheet to an eviction directive and his stomach twists. The landlord is a cranky old geezer who insists on leaving hand-written evictions on doors. He's seen them on other flats, but this is the first time he has ever received one. He steps into the flat and crumples the demand, tossing it on the desk.

As he looks around the place, a scheme forms in his mind. A brilliant plan, something he would never have considered yesterday. But today is a new day, and with his problems mounting by the hour, desperation takes over. He toys with the idea for a minute before he convinces himself it is a solid concept. He will transfer funds from the business who made him redundant to a dummy account under a fake name. He's a programmer, he can always create an alternate record with a false identity. Getting past the firewalls should be easy. Hell, he wrote them. He paces the room, wavering between guilt and anger.

He cannot do this. Can he? Why the bloody hell not? They owe him as far as he is concerned. They will never know it was him. He'll only take enough to start over, maybe move nearer to Leeds, where he spent his days as a lad. Yes, closer to the only family he has left. Before he changes his mind, he boots up his workstation and navigates to the corporate website, trying to convince himself this is only the severance he deserves. With a few keystrokes, he is in their bank account. He pulls up the second screen, opens an account under a fictitious name, and begins the process to transfer the money, careful to cover his tracks. Or so he thinks.

The progress bar spins for a couple of seconds before it freezes, and with that his world shifts. The machine locks, and a message lights up the monitor.

This device is under the control of, and owned by, the CCEA. This computer is the property of the British Government. Do not reboot by order of HRH. Tampering with seized equipment will cause immediate action, up to and including termination.

Code scrolls while he stares at it, panic welling inside him. He realizes it is copying the files, and he tries to turn the laptop off, but it refuses to acknowledge the command. He works to override the system with no luck as the severity of the situation sinks in.

He struggles to work out how they traced him. They must have added more safeguards in anticipation of all the redundancies they planned in the preceding months. A security enhancement he was not aware of. Of course, they would have done that. He isn't thinking clearly, or he would have expected this.

Malcolm's eyes dart around the room, his body unable to react swiftly enough. His hands tremble as the dread creeps in, and he blinks and tries to refocus, snapping out of his daze all at once. Knowing he must get out immediately, he grabs his jacket off the armchair and gives the place a final scan, thinking about what else he should take with him. He touches his pants pocket to confirm his wallet is there and pauses for a split second as he considers going to the wardrobe for extra clothes. But that will burn too much precious time. An overwhelming sensation floods over him, as he realizes escape should be his only priority. As he moves to leave, the sound of breaking glass causes him to spin to the window just as a drone crashes into the lounge. It flies over him to the entry door where it ejects a boot lock, securing him inside.

All this for an unsuccessful attempt at embezzlement. It seems harsh now that he is on the receiving end of the government sanction. But with the extreme prison overcrowding because of cyber-crimes, the CCEA makes no exceptions regarding punishment. In this highly technical society, all network-based violations are punishable by exile, successful or not. It is easier to be rid of the white-collar offenders by extraditing them to history. They don't dare send violent criminals back in time. That would be a timeline nightmare waiting to happen. Those prisoners are jailed for life, no parole, no probation, no plea bargaining. One would assume the possibility of being abandoned hundreds of years in the past would be a deterrent to criminals. But most people convicted are inexperienced nobody's who fancy themselves hackers and are convinced they are smarter than the system. Malcolm shakes his head before letting it drop into his hands. He cannot believe he was so stupid to think he could pull this off. He fell into the same trap as the other convicts, and he will pay dearly for that miscalculation.

"That's it then, isn't it?" he murmurs to himself.

The CCEA officers should arrive any minute. As he crumples into the stained recliner, he understands life as he knows it is over as of this moment. They will convict him of a cyber-crime, and with that comes a mandatory sentence. Then the courts send him hundreds of years into the past, somewhere in Britain, sometime between the dawn of mankind and

1900. He will live the rest of his existence there alone and probably in constant fear, with no hope of ever going home. And at only thirty-two, that may, or may not, be a very long time—depending on when and where they assign him.

He sits with his head in his hands. Within one minute, the agents show up and use their master key to unlock the boot and take him into custody. He does not resist as he sees no point in it. They shove him into a unit and drive him to the government holding building where they process him. As they pass Trafalgar Square, he glances over to the last place he was to enjoy his freedom. The edge of the fountain where he sat next to the woman with the irritating laugh.

TWO

Cotswolds, England 1335

In less than an hour Malcolm Aldred will travel forward in time from the countryside of the Cotswolds, in 1335, to 1867, Oklahoma. Which is a significant upgrade to his current plight. Although at this point he would go anywhere and do just about anything to leave medieval England—no matter the cost.

Seven months ago, he was in 2070 London, when they arrested and exiled him here as a prisoner of the CCEA. Now he is battling a path through the gloomy night in the English countryside, fleeing from guards at Beverston Castle.

He trails the people in front of him into the pitch-black woods, the only noise the group's footfall on wet leaves. They trudge single file into the forest in silence when a piercing cry shatters the calm, making him flinch.

"Wait! Don't leave me! I'm a transporter! Don't leave me!"

He recognizes Thomas' voice. Of course, he would rear his head at the most inopportune time, the tosser.

The group halts at the sound of the shouts, causing Malcolm to collide with the person in front of him. The man turns to peer around him.

"I've got this. Cover me and I'll get him," Penn whispers to Gray, another man further down the line.

The two men hurry to stand in position at the edge of the forest, the rest of them watching and waiting. One of them races across the field they cut through only minutes before, back toward the castle on the hill.

We should leave his arse here, Malcolm muses to himself. He considers voicing his opinion to the others, then thinks better of it. If they ship Thomas to base, at least he will pay for his part in their friend Estera's casualty. Death by medieval guard is too respectable for a bastard like him.

Penn runs towards the shouts, and Malcolm sees two figures drop as shots ring out. Gray uses his night vision and fires again. Penn reaches Thomas and pulls him further into the safety of the woods, arrows flying around them. He forces him into the cover of the trees and pushes him along as the procession moves deeper into the woodlands. Malcolm quickens his pace, closing the gap between himself and the man ahead of him.

"What the hell, dude? How did you escape those guards?" says Penn, shoving Thomas forward, not waiting for an answer. "Get moving, asshole."

Thomas is breathing heavily, struggling to catch his breath. His hands are in flex cuffs behind him, making it difficult to balance, and he stumbles and falls. Penn grabs him by the shirt and yanks him upright.

"They were trying to kill me," he says, gasping for air.

"I don't blame them. You're a train wreck, man, get going. I won't go back for you again," hisses Penn, still urging him onward.

Malcolm imagines he could strangle Thomas and feel not an ounce of remorse for it. He is a virus someone needs to eradicate, and right now he is slowing them down when every second counts if they are to avoid capture.

Gray hikes further into the woods, the group following closely. They tramp through the darkness, guided only by the lights on the retrieval team's helmets, finding their encampment a short time later.

They move in silence, breaking down the camp. Frank, the rescue team captain, gets right-to-work gathering MREs and vials of antibiotics.

"Okay guys, here's the food and medicine we promised you. I suggest you leave now. The guards might not find us tonight, but they'll be here by first light."

Frank offers the goods to the local men who came through the woods with them. They stare at him for a long moment without responding until he picks up an armful of the MRE's and thrusts them forward. Finally understanding what he is trying to convey, they each grab a stack.

"Where will thou go? How shall thou remain hidden from them?" the local asks Frank.

Frank shakes his head, eyebrows raised. "Talk about a communication breakdown. Don't worry about us, pal. We'll be on our way home shortly. We will be just fine. Remember what we told you about the medicine; you only need one tablet per person. You can crush it in their food if you think they won't take it. Also, remove the meals from the wrapping or it could mean trouble for you. Fill the packets with rocks and sink them in the lake. Good luck guys." They look at the modern day MRE's and antibiotics and nod wordlessly.

Frank cuts the flex cuffs off the few locals they held as detainees during the mission, shaking hands with all of them. The men mount their horses and ride off south, away from town and the castle, their goods hidden safely in their packs.

Ethan, the agent who brought Malcolm here and with whom he spent the last seven months, pours water on the fire, and leaves the handmade spears he carved the day before propped against a log.

"Malcolm, are you ready to go? You're still firm on Oklahoma?" he asks.

"Yes, America it is. Thank you all for agreeing to transport me there. I am thrilled to leave this place," says Malcolm.

The CCEA scheduled Ethan to drop Malcolm off and return at once to his timeline in 2070. But Ethan's transponder failed and trapped him here. Frank Rhoades heads the American retrieval team here to rescue them. The only reason they are here is to pick up Christine Stewart, the transporter who landed in their camp two weeks ago because of another system glitch. Malcolm and the British transporters have the great fortune of being with Christine, or who knows when their people may have found them—if ever. Estera Bargeron was a French agent who joined them several months before, the same way Christine did; their transponders signals crossed somehow. She died of the plague when they had no antibiotics to give her, thanks to Thomas stealing Malcolm's supply. Now Ethan and Frank have agreed to transport Malcolm out of England as a thank you for him helping them complete the mission tonight. An operation he wanted no part of, but they needed his help. He is certain their involvement in the scheme was a bad idea, but that is no longer his concern, and currently ranks right at the top of the least of his worries.

Malcolm follows Frank to the shelter and exchanges clothing with him, Frank's are garments much better suited to America in 1867. Back with the others, he moves through the group, shaking hands and wishing them well. When he gets to Thomas, he pauses.

"Estera would be alive today if you hadn't stolen my survival pack with the medication."

He punches him, and Thomas goes down like a sack of potatoes. He struggles to rise, but Ethan holds him down with his boot, and Malcolm smiles at him. He was never supposed to be friends with Ethan. The CCEA assigned him as his escort guard here, but despite the fact he was Ethan's prisoner, he likes him. He is a decent guy, and they have had no issues in the time they survived here together.

Frank prepares to send Malcolm to the same coordinates Christine transported to in Oklahoma seven months before, but not before he gives him a vial of antibiotics.

"I put these aside for you since that asshole over there stole yours." Malcolm shakes Frank's hand and pockets the pills, knowing these may save his life someday.

Christine hugs him next, asking him to deliver a message to John Harding, the man who took her in and saved her while trapped in Oklahoma. She wants him to know she is safe and how thankful she is to him for helping her survive there. She assures Malcolm John will help him, and he needs to go straight to his ranch when he arrives in 1867.

He faces Frank, bracing to transport, and reflects on the past several months. The government has tossed his life about like a rag doll the last year. And it is about to become more unpredictable in the next few minutes. He is not sure going to America is the right move. That remains to be seen. But he is certain it must be a better choice than medieval England.

Although he cannot repress the wave of doubt and fear that washes over him as he fades to black. He is on his way to 1867, America—alone.

THREE

Piedmont, Oklahoma 1867

Malcolm's first impression is the melody of bird shrill as he fights his way back into consciousness. Loud birds. And lots of them. Their singing reminds him of warm summer days spent in his grandparent's garden in Leeds, in the north of England. He used to sprawl out on the grass, listening to them sing to each other, eyes closed, the sunlight warming him. He loved visiting their house, planting flowers and vegetables with them. His grandmother would bring him iced lemonade while he worked side by side with his grandfather. Those working summers taught him the pride of a job well done. Watching the plants grow over the season and eating food you grew yourself was a feeling he never forgot. He did not have any outdoor space at his flat in London, a patch of dirt in the city was too rich and too much real estate for his budget. His grandparents died when he was a teenager, and there is not a day that goes by he does not miss them. He was closer to them than his own parents. He wonders what they would think of him now, exiled as a convicted criminal. And in America, no less.

He shudders as the chills sweep over him, pulling him forward to the present. His eyes drift open, and he takes in his surroundings without bothering to sit up. He blinks against the sunlight filtering through bare branches, highlighting thousands of floating dust motes in the air. He watches them swirl and dance away as he clears his mind. Dead leaves and walnuts litter the ground, still damp with morning dew that soaks through his worn clothing. He sits up and leans against a tree, struggling to shake the disorientation while willing the dull ache in his head to pass.

So, this is Oklahoma. He is not sure what he expected but is slightly underwhelmed as he peers around the immediate area.

It could be a dozen other places he has been to, even though it is at the other end of the world from home. He closes his eyes, savoring the stillness of the location, but that peace is short lived. The dread lies in his stomach like a brick as he realizes it is too late to change his mind now. He is here, no matter how unprepared. Indian territory in America. An inhospitable land, at best. It occurs to him he may not have thought this through completely—maybe this was not his smartest choice. He is an Englishman from 2070 in the 1800s, who understands little of this era. He only knows what Christine told him and what scant information he gleaned from school years ago. Which is not enough. British curriculum does not devote much time to American history. But he reckons almost anywhere is safer than medieval England in 1335.

He rises and stretches his limbs, glancing upward at the sky. It looks to be late morning as he plans to start for John Harding's property, which should be three miles from here if he has transported in at the proper coordinates. There should be a small river nearby, and he knows this because Christine reviewed the lie of the land with him while they were in England. He begins his search for that first, his thirst driving his priorities. It does not take him long to hear the water, and he clambers down the embankment, dipping his hands into the stream. Thankful for the cold liquid, it soothes his throat and helps ease the pounding in his brain. He is careful to drink only a few sips since he cannot purify it.

The prairie grass sways and sighs in the surrounding breeze, whispering in its hidden language. The gentle rustling elicits a calming effect on him, and his anxiety dwindles to a manageable level. Once he climbs up the river's bank, he searches for the boulder Christine instructed him to find, the one he will use to orientate his whereabouts. He knows he needs to go north but has no idea which direction that is. Without a compass, the landmark is his only guide. He remembers reading somewhere it is possible to navigate using the sun and stars, but he has no sense of how to do that. He finds the site, the only of its kind, and stands in front of the large rock, scanning the area. Turning left to a ninety-degree angle, he stares ahead to his route, straight across the plains toward his destination. He shields his view against the sunlight with his hands and peers out over the horizon, thinking it is nothing exceptional to look at. All he makes out are rolling hills and meadows as far as the eye can see. He hopes there is more to this place than that, as the land appears isolated and downright bleak.

He allows his exhaustion to get the better of him, and relaxes against the rock, telling himself he is only resting his eyes. The warmth on his face is so relaxing, he fights against the fatigue, but loses the battle and dozes off. He does not realize he has fallen asleep until he wakes with a start to the cry of a low-flying crow squawking as it moves overhead. He springs up to see the sun ready to set behind a hill, cursing himself under his breath for wasting the day. It is too risky to attempt finding John's ranch in the dark, so he will have to stay here overnight. Settling in for the night seems the only logical, safe option.

As he stretches his legs out, a rustling sound draws his attention. His senses go on high alert as he scans his surroundings. After a minute he thinks he must have imagined it when movement in his peripheral vison startles him. He spins to the right to see a native crouching next to the river, an arrow aimed at him. Like many people, he sometimes wondered how he would react if confronted with the threat of violence. And like most people, he thought he would never find out. His heart jumps in his chest as he locks eyes with him, realizing his assumption was incorrect. Neither of them moves, the tension between them palpable. Malcolm takes this as a positive sign, thinking if he were a hostile warrior, he would have killed him already. He lifts his palms slowly, raising them above his head to show he is not a threat. The Indian maintains his pose for what feels near forever to Malcolm, but is only seconds. Then he lowers his weapon and backs away, disappearing into the tall grass at the river's edge.

A moment later a horse neighs as he gallops off. He sighs with relief, and sucks in deep breaths of air, trying to steady his heartbeat to normal. He crouches against the rock for another ten minutes while he calms down. Once he deems it is safe to move, he makes a dash for the trees. That was too close, he thinks to himself. He cannot let his guard down like that again if he is to survive here.

He remembers Christine stayed in a large tree overnight while here, so he intends to do the same. He finds a substantial one with branches sturdy enough to support him; at six foot two inches and one hundred eighty-five pounds, he will need something strong. As he settles back onto the branch, he once again second-guesses his decision to come here. He has only been here a few hours, and already he has had an encounter with a native. And although he came out of it intact, he does not like his odds for the next time. Then he recalls how the group he was part of struggled in medieval England. And he works to convince himself this place is much more hospitable than that option—even with the threat of Indians.

As he listens to the crickets, he stares up at the cloudless sky, the stars twinkling brightly. The air smells fresh, of grass and cut wood, unlike the mold and perpetual dampness he grew accustomed to in England. The weather is mild too, much nicer here than in the Cotswold's countryside. It was damp and frosty when he departed there last night, and even though it is a little chilly here, it is significantly warmer than across the pond.

His hand reaches into his pant pocket out of habit, making sure the antibiotics are still there. Although he received inoculations before being sent to the year 1335, this is another country, five-hundred years ahead, with different diseases. These pills are his insurance policy against them.

He rests against the tree limb and closes his eyes, remembering the sequence of events that brought him to this time and place. His months in England were the most difficult of his life. Learning to endure hundreds of years in the past was no simple task.

After Ethan's device failed, he promised Malcolm he would transport him elsewhere if he helped him repair his faulty transponder. Even though he could not fix it, he stayed with him to increase their chances of survival, hoping Ethan could eventually make good on his word to him. Then other transporters, Thomas and Aidan, found them after they had been there two months, and the four of them set up camp together. Things went all right for a while. They survived, anyway. Then it got complicated.

While working to repair Ethan's transponder, it linked with another one. That sent agent Estera Bargeron to their encampment, who was stationed in Versailles, France in 1710, before arriving. Three months later it happened again, when Christine Stewart transported to England from 1867, Oklahoma.

He was ill prepared for what he would go through in medieval England. Things spun completely out of control when Thomas left camp, stealing Malcolm's store of antibiotics. That resulted in Estera's death from the Plague.

Well, at least they assumed it was the Plague. History says the Black Death was not introduced to England until 1348, but Estera had all the known signs, and there were clusters of the same symptoms in the area they were stranded. They will never know for certain, but Malcolm realizes details often fade or are translated incorrectly through the centuries. Records get lost or destroyed, and people make errors. Maybe the disease reached England in a small quantity earlier than originally thought? Or perhaps the supply of antibiotics they left in 1335 squelched the spread of it until thirteen years later when a seaman from Gascony brought it to Weymouth, Dorset? Or possibly it was a different virus with similar traits, an unknown strain of some sort? The CCEA do not vaccinate agents like they do prisoners who are there for the long term. Which made them vulnerable to infections and every illness of the era. And they never counted on their operation being sabotaged, trapping them around the globe for months. Malcolm's presence in 1335 was to be only a minor blip on the map, something that would never affect history. But once the transporters were stuck there who knows what lasting effects they may have had on the timeline?

Christine planned to turn Thomas over to CCEA Internal Affairs for his role in Estera's death, and Malcolm is hopeful she could do so. But now he cannot see them again, so he will not know what happened.

After hearing Christine's stories of America, he thought this was as safe as anywhere and decided if he could ever transport out of England, he would come here. She was convinced John would help him when he arrived here. Malcolm is not so sure, but it's worth a try. He has no other option. And the worst that can happen is John will tell him to bugger off and he'll be on his own. Which puts him no worse off than he is at this moment.

As he clings to the branch, alone and without a friend in the world, what seemed like a brilliant plan yesterday is fast losing its appeal. He pounds his fist into the tree in frustration. He knew what committing a cyber-crime would cost him if caught. Maybe he wanted to get captured, he muses. He had all but given up on getting his former life on track in London and had nothing to lose.

Reclining against the tree, he closes his eyes and again reflects on the people he left behind in England. He hopes they made it home safely. He owes Frank big time for giving him more antibiotics and Ethan for agreeing to send him here.

As his thoughts drift back to his current fate, he silently prays he can carve out a decent existence for himself here. But he cannot shake the uneasiness his luck has run out and his outlook here is tenuous, at best. He knows without a doubt this is his last chance to make it—no matter what timeline he is in.

FOUR

Los Angeles, California 2070

Hannah Cole finishes applying her mascara and leans back in the dressing chair, staring at her reflection in the mirror. Her eye color matches her green blouse, her wavy chestnut hair, long and silky. She is an attractive woman with full lips and a narrow nose. But the dark circles under her eyes that seem to be permanent now make her appear older than she is. And she rarely smiles anymore. Her resting face is a sad, defeated expression even she sees. Anyone who knows her can tell there is something wrong.

The timer on the oven dings, letting her know the steak and scalloped potatoes are ready. Her gaze wanders to the clock, and she curses under her breath. She dashes to the state-of-the-art kitchen to take dinner out of the vintage appliance and set the table. She glances over at the ChefAid and grimaces. Chad insisted on buying it. While it is convenient, she prefers to cook the old-fashioned way, preparing meals herself. The outrageously expensive hunk of steel will prepare anything you want, but it always has that processed chain restaurant taste to it she hates.

She is running late and hurries to get Chad's dinner out, worried she won't have the chance to put on a skirt before he gets home for his break. He likes her to wear skirts, not the jeans and sneakers she has on. She is so preoccupied she does not hear the police unit pull into the driveway, and flinches when she hears a beep as Chad punches the code into the front door. The sound of his footsteps in the entry makes her stomach clench. If she moves fast enough and runs to the bedroom right now, she might have time to change.

No such luck. He rounds the corner as she sets the bottle of sparkling water on the table. He peers at the meal but says nothing while he takes his utility belt off and hangs it over a dining chair before sitting down. The gun rests in the holster, the weight pulling it over the back of the seat unevenly. Hannah pulls her gaze from it and plasters a smile on her face.

"How is your shift going today?" she asks, doing her best to sound cheerful.

He glares at her before grabbing his fork and knife. "Great. I just love dealing with the crème de la crap of society. It's my dream job."

"I only meant, you know, nothing out of the ordinary, no gangs or anything to deal with?"

"Hannah, please, I don't come home on my break to talk about my shift at the P.D. I eat here to have a little peace and quiet without having to watch my back, okay?"

She studies the man she once loved, but now only fears. When had things gone so wrong? He used to love her. She is sure of it. He returns her stare with disdain and shakes his head as if she has no right to speak to him. He cuts into the meat and drops his utensils on the plate, the clang causing Hannah to flinch.

"How many times do I have to tell you I like my steak medium rare? I paid a fucking fortune for that ChefAid, and it can't even cook a damn slab of beef correctly?"

"I, I didn't use the ChefAid, I cooked it myself, in the oven after I browned it. I think the char is better. And I can get the seasoning just right then," she replies shakily.

"Yeah, well, you didn't do it worth a shit, because it's overcooked. This is medium, not medium rare. How am I supposed to eat this crap? How you screwed up a simple steak is anyone's guess."

Hannah knows she cooked the steak to perfection—one thing she is certain she does well is cook. He is just looking for a reason to fight with her. He came home in a foul mood, and she knew the moment he walked into the kitchen he would find some way to blame her for his anger. He rises and launches his plate into the sink. The crash makes her jump, and she feels the tears run down her cheeks.

"So, thanks for nothing, as usual. Now I'll have to pick up some fast food. What the hell do you do here all day, anyway? Watch TV and spend my money?"

She squeezes into the space between the desk and the pantry, trying to make herself smaller.

"And look at you! Dressed like a sloppy housewife in jeans and runners. Is it too much to ask that you be presentable? Jesus, Hannah, you're lucky I haven't divorced your ass, no one else would ever want you," he says, his anger escalating with each word.

"I'll program a steak in the ChefAid for you, it will finish in ten minutes," she suggests, tears beginning to slip down her cheeks.

"Are you seriously that stupid? I don't have time for that! I swear you do this to piss me off. You make me do this to you!" he hisses, as he advances toward her.

Her hands instinctively rise to cover her face as she recoils, squeezing her eyes shut while she slides to the floor. He reaches her in three long strides, and she realizes what is coming without looking at him.

"Chad, please, no!"

He drags her from the opening she has wedged herself into, striking her, over and over, while she curls into a ball and tries to protect herself. She knows better than to fight back, it will only make it worse. And she can't take a risk like that, especially when he has his service weapon hanging on his duty belt only a few feet away. She can never be sure what he is capable of when he's in the middle of a rage, it's almost as if he blacks out. After a few minutes, he is panting, spittle flying from his mouth as he shouts at her. When he finishes, he collapses into a dining chair. He downs the bottle of sparkling water, making a comment that at least she got that portion of dinner right.

Hannah lies curled on the cold stone floor, droplets of blood dripping onto the tile. The first thing she thinks of is that if he cut her lip, she cannot leave the house for several days while it heals. When had she gotten to where that was her worry? Not the fact he beat her up, but that she cannot leave the house now. She feels pathetic and weak. But worse than that, she is helpless and alone. She does not dare move until he leaves, paralyzed with fear. She watches him strap his utility belt on as his radio squawks to life with the dispatcher's voice.

"Nine Lincoln eighty-nine."

"Nine Lincoln eighty-nine, 10-2."

"Nine Lincoln eighty-nine, what's your 10-20?"

"Nine Lincoln eighty-nine, I'm 10-7, but can go to 10-8."

"Affirmative nine Lincoln eighty-nine. Two Bravo seventy-five requesting 10-25 for assistance with a 10-91. Proceed to channel one four for further instructions."

"10-4, switching to channel one four, stand by."

He lowers the volume on his HT radio and turns around to face her.

"Get yourself cleaned up, you disgust me," he sneers at her.

She does not make eye contact with him. Chad is not a man who apologizes and then feels remorse for beating up his wife. He believes she is his property, which gives him the right to torment her.

The sound of his boots echoing on the stone floor confirms he is leaving, and the house falls silent as the front door slams shut. She sighs with relief, knowing he'll be at work until after midnight. She understands police code. Before he was the monster he is now, he used to teach them to her. Another officer wants him to transport someone in custody for them. That means it will tie up Chad up for hours, checking him into jail and doing the report. She pushes herself up and her fingers gingerly touch her bottom lip. He definitely split it open again. She rises unsteadily to clean the mess in the sink, wincing as her shoulder spasms when she reaches for the ice. She needs to soothe her jaw before it becomes too swollen to move.

* * *

Christine Stewart is in the briefing room at CCEA headquarters observing the fresh batch of prisoners. They have assigned her to transport a twenty-six-year-old woman to Baton Rouge, Louisiana, to 1803. Another day, another dollar, she thinks to herself. She has only been back on the job for a week. Although technically, she has been off duty for almost eight months. Most of that time she spent in Oklahoma in 1867, and then in the Cotswolds in England, in 1335, when the government trapped her there. It was the most traumatic experience of her life.

There was some good to come out of her being stranded, though. She met Annabelle Harris, her best friend, while in Oklahoma, and found a new love interest while in England. Ethan Ward is a transporter from London, and they have officially started dating. He is transferring to the Los Angeles unit soon. Anabelle works out of the Chicago division, and since they have all agreed to help Jonathan Hoyt with future disaster prevention, they plan to work together regularly.

Christine sits through the tedious orientation with her prisoner, wrestling to stay awake. The nondescript room is depressingly bare and does nothing to inspire her from drifting off. There is a long table with basic chairs for prisoners, and the same hard plastic seats fill a row for transporters against the back wall. A large metal desk is positioned to face the prisoner seating, and a worn wood podium in front of that. An old analog clock above the door completes the look. They wasted no money on décor. It is all about intrinsic functionality. That's the CCEA way.

She shakes her head and straightens up in her chair. Anything to remain attentive. She has sat through so many of these orientations she is certain she could recite every word of Frank's monologue. Most of her job is monotonous, babysitting inmates through processing, and writing endless reports. Although the transporting part livens things up. You never know what could happen. Stranded in history for seven months as she was is the perfect example of that.

Traveling back in time is risky, and there is never a guarantee of safety. She has often considered her job description as continuous stages of complete and utter boredom, interrupted by fleeting moments of stark terror. That is what the CCEA should tell new recruits. At least it would be an honest definition of the position. As she blinks several times, attempting to win the battle against her heavy eyelids, the group of detainees stirs and the agent next to her rises. She daydreamed her way right through orientation. Today may be shaping up to be okay after all.

Once her boss clears her and the prisoner, she drops her detainee at the History Lab and goes to the cafeteria for her two free hours while her inmate receives instructions on how to behave in her new timeline. She sits near the window browsing her tablet, then texts Annabelle and Ethan; she misses them both more than usual today.

Her thoughts stray back to the previous year as she gazes outside to watch the traffic on the 101 freeway. It is still hard for her to believe how drastically her world has changed since then. Her son Michael works for the CCEA and was with the retrieval team who rescued her in England. He moved into his own place with his girlfriend Maddie after their return, who is also employed by the CCEA in IT. The empty nest experience is not one she has enjoyed so far, but she does not let him know that. She has not lived by herself for several years, and most nights she battles to stay entertained. That surprises her because all of her adult life she has preferred her alone time to other people. But her stint trapped in the past changed that. Now she craves companionship. Maybe all that company lowered her tolerance level. She once read to make something a habit, you repeat the behavior for fourteen days. Seven months of it must turn it into a permanent lifestyle conversion.

She hears a faint chime in her ear, signaling an incoming call, snapping her forward to the present. The programmed voice tells her it is an unknown number not in her phone bank, but gives the name Chad Cole. Why is he calling her? He is with the LAPD in the cyber-crime division. She knows who he is, their paths cross professionally occasionally, but she doesn't deal with him regularly. He always comes across as narcissistic, the cop who has an ego bigger than the biceps he clearly works so hard to maintain. She isn't in the mood to take on a personality like his right now, but she answers out of professional courtesy and sheer curiosity.

"Hello?"

"I'm calling for Christine Stewart, please," says an unfamiliar female voice.

"This is she. Who's this?"

"Christine? Hi, this is Hannah Cole. I'm not sure if you remember who I am? You probably don't. We were introduced last year at the state law enforcement dinner in Sacramento. I am married to Chad Cole, he's a sergeant with LAPD."

Christine struggles to recall Hannah's face, even though she knows she has met her a couple of times. She does not want to sound rude and admit she can barely conjure up an image of her, so she plays along.

"Sure, hi Hannah."

"Sorry to bother you, are you available to chat for a minute?"

"Okay. What can I help you with?"

There is silence on the other end of the phone while Hannah gathers her thoughts.

"I'm doing a freelance piece for a local website about the time travel exile program. I remembered you are a transporter, and I wondered if we might get together to ask you a few questions?"

"Um, okay, but wouldn't you rather talk to my captain, Frank Rhoades? He's been with the CCEA a lot longer than I have and has clearance to speak to the press."

"No! I mean, I'm comfortable with you, so I'd prefer to meet with you if that's all right? Besides, I wouldn't call myself a reporter. Or even a journalist. Just a freelancer."

"Well, I suppose so," she says, not interested in pressing the issue any further. "Although my clearance level limits what I can tell you. I'm uncertain how much help I will be. And I cannot reveal anything about my time during the system failure, or any of my experiences while stranded, just so we're clear on that point."

"That's fine. I appreciate it Christine, more than you know."

"No problem. I have a free hour now if you want to talk."

"Can we speak in person? Is that okay?"

"Sure. I'm available this evening if you are?"

"That would be great! Chad is working tonight. How about Giraldo's on Wilshire at six o'clock?"

"Sure, I'll see you there later."

"Sounds good. Thank you again, Christine. And please, don't mention this to anyone. I'm not at all certain this story will publish, so I'd rather not tell anybody yet."

"Right."

Christine ends the call and frowns. That was a strange and unexpected request. She hardly remembers Hannah, and she knows her husband is friends with other transporters he could refer her to. Maybe because Christine is high profile after her rescue appeals to the sensationalism of the article. But she will divulge nothing about the system outage. She signed a confidentiality agreement and may not speak about her experiences in the past. Freelancer acquaintance or otherwise.

She pushes the conversation to the back of her mind, focusing on finishing her workday. Normally she would be scheduled for travel today to transport the prisoner she is guiding through orientation, but the program is undergoing a last-minute unscheduled maintenance procedure. So, they postponed the actual transports until first thing tomorrow morning. But the brass decided the transporters should take prisoners through the normal on-boarding process as planned to save time. Which means she is clear to meet Hannah later and answer the few questions she can for her article.

She completes the rest of the workday with her prisoner and heads home to change into jeans and a blouse for her meeting. At least she has something to occupy her evening, she thinks to herself. It beats another night of mindless television. This empty nest thing is messing with her head. She had her son Michael young, when she was only nineteen years old, and they have always been close. She and his father divorced when he was eleven, and it's just been the two of them since then. And although she has dated here and there, she has not had a serious relationship until she met Ethan. She tells herself to snap out of it and stop being so pathetic. Michael only lives ten minutes from here, and she sees him almost every day at work. The pep-talk to herself makes her feel better, and she leaves the house in a pleasant enough mood.

It does not take her long to reach the restaurant. Giraldo's is quintessential vintage Hollywood, a dimly lit piano bar rumored to host the occasional celebrity, that still uses waitresses. She checks her reflection in the rearview mirror before going in, thinking she looks good for a forty-year-old, pathetic, empty nester. Her blue eyes are clear, her cheeks flushed, and her shoulder length dark hair frames her oval face nicely. Her nose is slightly upturned and freckled, giving her a youthful appearance. She applies a quick layer of lipstick and exits the car, handing the keys to the attendant. The valet ticket goes into her purse as she pulls the door open, stepping into the dim lounge.

She peers around the restaurant, waiting for her vision to adjust to the darkness, and finds Hannah in a secluded booth in the room's corner. As she draws closer, she feels maybe she is mistaken, and it's not her. As she remembers the law enforcement event where she saw her last year, she recalls her with the most beautiful, long chestnut hair that set her apart from the crowd. Today it looks dull and even a little dirty, pulled back in a simple ponytail at her nape. The bags under her eyes stand out from ten feet away. Despite all that, she is still an attractive woman. She wears a plain tee shirt and faded jeans with flip flops. Not the attire she would expect an emerging journalist to show up in, especially to Giraldo's. Perhaps she was trying for casual, but it comes across as sloppy.

"Hi Hannah," she says, extending her hand.

"Christine, thank you for meeting me." Hannah's palm is clammy, and her glance darts to the front door.

"Sure, no worries."

Hannah swirls her wineglass, her gaze never reaching Christine's.

"May I buy you a glass of wine or a beer? Or do you prefer a mixed drink?" Hannah asks, while rummaging in her handbag nervously but coming up empty-handed.

"I'll join you in some wine," she responds, sliding into the booth.

Hannah waves the waitress over to take Christine's drink order, and requests a plate of Vegan Nachos, whatever those are. The thought of nachos with fake vegan cheese or kale is wrong on so many levels it kills any appetite she might have had. She watches Hannah after the bartender leaves, waiting for her to begin the conversation. She appears fidgety and nervous, and when she does not speak right away, Christine takes the lead.

"So, what can I tell you about the exile program, Hannah?"

The server returns to place the drink in front of Christine and walks off, leaving the women alone again.

"I just have some general questions. Nothing important, really. For instance, what type of cyber-crime does an individual have to commit to qualify for the time travel exile program? Is it only financial crimes that guarantee a spot in the program?"

"Qualify? You make it sound like the Olympics. I'm uncertain the exiled inmates would agree with that analogy. I think it's more accurate to say we have caught them cheating. But to answer your question, no, it includes more than just monetary violations. We deem any crime classified as cyber-based suitable for exile. Although the courts decide what meets that criteria."

"Understood. So, let's assume they convict somebody and appoint them for extradition. Can that be repealed? Would they ever sentence an inmate and allow them to remain here?"

"No, unless there was overwhelming evidence of their innocence, I can't imagine a conviction being set aside. I've only heard of one occasion where a case was reconsidered. But I could be wrong, there might be more. That's really a question for the courts, not me. But I know if convicted, they would never live in this timeline once assigned to the program."

"Okay. Then once they assign them, and presuming they exile them, is there any way for someone to discover where they have gone? For example, a family member?"

"No, the inmate is not aware of their destination until the time they ship. In fact, neither is their transporter. We all find out together during orientation. They have no contact with anyone other than their four selected visitors on travel day when they say goodbye to those predetermined guests."

"But what if they disclose it during the visit?"

"We monitor them the entire time. If they reveal their destination, the transporter reports them at once. The system reassigns the detainee, and they would start the full process over again—orientation, historical training, wardrobe, everything. And they would also be ineligible for a second family visit before transporting."

"I understand."

"Aren't you supposed to be taking notes or something?"

"Um, yeah, yes, I guess so."

Hannah digs around her bag again and pulls out a pen and a scrap of paper that appears to be a receipt, jotting a few lines on it. Christine stares at her, thinking this conversation is getting stranger by the minute. Who still uses a pen?

"So could a law enforcement officer, for instance, find out where a prisoner exiled? Could they call out a favor and get the information? Which leads me to my next question. Could a convicted spouse follow their husband or wife back in time? Would it be possible for someone with connections?"

Her expression twists into a frightened frown, and her breath is coming quickly. She stares intently at Christine.

"First, no. No one, including anyone in law enforcement, can identify where we transport an inmate. CCEA employees are the only individuals with access to that information. We would never assign a family member or even a friend or acquaintance to the same location or timeline. Never. The program will not allow it. The system reviews all known data on a convict before assigning their exile destination. And believe me, we are thorough."

"The transporter knows where the prisoner went. What if someone got to them? Or what if they bribed a CCEA employee? That's possible, isn't it?"

"What if they got to them? Hannah, do you want to explain what this is really about? These questions are way out of line for a periodical about the time travel exile program. Do you suspect a CCEA agent of leaking intelligence about an inmate or divulging a prisoner's whereabouts?"

Hannah's eyes dart to the front door before settling on Christine again.

"Hannah? What is going on with you? You call me out of nowhere and ask me here for an interview, then scribble some half-assed notes on a store receipt as an afterthought."

"Nothing. I thought people might have an interest in what happens to a prisoner after they enter their exile. I'm a little nervous is all, this is my first article, and I forgot my tablet."

Christine raises an eyebrow and tilts her head. "Fair enough, only you haven't asked me a single question about anything other than how someone can reach a convict once they're gone. So level with me before I walk out of here. What is this really about, Hannah? Does Chad know you are here?"

"No! Please don't tell him!" Her hands tremble as she picks up her wine.

"Hannah, calm down." Christine touches Hannah's hand and guides her glass back down to rest on the table, afraid she is going to spill it, she is shaking so badly. The waitress approaches the booth with the food, and just as Christine suspected, the nachos look inedible. Broccoli and peas have no place in Mexican cuisine. Hannah keeps her gaze lowered until the server leaves. When she looks up, the tears flow.

Christine sighs and works to soften her tone. "I give you my word, I will not talk to Chad. I don't even know him. He's only another cop I've met a few times through regular channels at my job."

Hannah lets out a deep breath. "Thank you, Christine. I haven't told him I'm trying to pick up a gig with this online magazine. I prefer not to disappoint him if it doesn't happen."

"Oh, come on, Hannah. I think we both know that's not why you're here. Is there something I should be aware of? If you have information about a CCEA agent, just tell me. Maybe I can help."

Hannah drops her head, and the tears start again. The dim light casts a shadow across her face, highlighting the lines and dark circles under her eyes. This is not the same woman Christine met a year ago. She appears ten years older and is undeniably hiding something.

"Hey, you can trust me. I'm not going to report back to Chad. It's obvious you're upset and need some guidance." She reaches across the table to cover Hannah's hand with her own.

Hannah glances up to meet Christine's stare. Her shoulders sag as she tries to formulate an explanation but comes up with nothing. So, she goes with the truth. The ugly, appalling truth. Including every heinous detail. And the facade she worked so hard to keep up crumbles.

"I'm not sure you or anyone else can save me anymore. He's going to kill me soon, and there isn't a damn thing I can do to stop him. My life is a ticking time bomb. And it's about ready to explode."

FIVE

Piedmont, Oklahoma 1867

Malcolm climbs down from the tree and stretches, raising his face to the morning sun peeking over the horizon, soaking in any warmth he can. He plans to find John Harding's land today, and he only has a general idea of where to go.

Realizing it may take him most of the day to locate it, he starts to the river, making as little noise as possible. His run-in with the Indian yesterday is still fresh in his mind, and even though he spared Malcolm's life, given the choice, he prefers to avoid any further confrontations altogether. Once he confirms he is alone, he scales down the bank for a drink. He crouches in the mud to sip the chilly water and splash his face. The icy liquid numbs him. He pulls up the hem of his shirt to dry off when a fish jumps a few feet away, making his stomach growl at the thought of food. He would do just about anything for a good fish and chips.

He understands the faster he gets to John's place, the more likely he is to eat, so with that in mind, he climbs the embankment to the boulder to confirm his route. Out of habit he moves to grab his belongings then realizes he has nothing to bring with him. At the moment, the only items he has to his name are the clothes on his back and the antibiotics in his pocket. Not much of a beginning for someone starting over. He turns in a circle, examining his surroundings a last time before he inhales deeply and jogs off.

Malcolm runs until the trees thin out and the landscape gives way to grassy plains and hills as far as the eye can see. The dry grass swaying in the breeze, and a lonely crow somewhere in the distance are the only sounds other than his gasping as he catches his breath. It is eerily desolate, and it seems as if he is the only person on earth. Maybe he is. He allows that thought to take root and wonders if it is conceivable for the system to experience another glitch and propel him even further back than 1867. The possibility sends shudders through him and prompts him to move faster in search of John's homestead.

The countryside is so different from the thick forest he is accustomed to, the wide-open prairies a stark contrast. After alternating between walking and jogging for what feels like hours, he fears he is headed in the wrong direction. But when the flat plains yield to patches of trees after a mile or so, he is more confident he is on the right track based on the description Christine gave him.

It is still early morning when he crests a small hill to see a modest house in the canyon below. This must be it. There is vegetation snaking through the valley, a certain sign of a river. That should be the source Christine mentioned, the creek that provides their drinking water. Which means John's ranch is dead ahead, and beyond that should be the town. Or rather, what will one day be the official city of Piedmont. Now it is little more than a settled area in the middle of nowhere. He begins the walk to the cabin, apprehensive because he is approaching it from behind. He is careful to keep his palms visible and away from his body as he advances; he does not want to make John nervous if he sees him. Natives and gunslingers, some hostile, rule the old west, and that fact is not lost on him.

"Here goes nothing," he whispers to himself as he clears the gate and walks onto the property. A dog races toward him from around the barn, barking furiously, while chickens cluck and goats bleat in the pen next to him. So much for a stealthy entrance.

"Bugger off, you mutt," he mumbles, trying to shoo it off with his arms.

The front door swings open while the hound continues to bark and snap at him. A man steps out to the porch, rifle aimed at Malcolm. Great. Not the way he hoped this would play out. His heartbeat kicks into overdrive as he raises his hands in the air.

"Who the hell are you?" he demands.

"John? John Harding? My name is Malcolm Aldred. I am a friend of Christine Stewart's. I was with her in England, and she told me where to find you here. She thought you would help me."

He stares at Malcolm, his eyes narrowing. "Help you what?"

"Get settled. Get a meal, I don't know. Just point me in the right direction, I suppose. I'm new to the area and I've nowhere to stay, no money and no food."

"Christine went to California, not England, halfway around the world. I do not believe for one minute she knows you are here, and if you aren't off my land by the time I count to three, I will blow a hole in you."

"Please calm down, John. She was in England with me and sent a message for you. She wanted me to tell you she made it home, she is with her son and she thanks you for finding her in the grove and taking her in. She wants you to know she cannot thank you enough for what you did for her and Annabelle. Annabelle is back too. If you doubt me, she told me you were angry with her the day before she left. You stayed away all night, and she and Annabelle were here alone. She said only you, Annabelle, and she would be aware of that. She asks that you look at the floorboards in the far corner near the fireplace. One is loose, and she used to store something important to her in there. I've never been in your house, John, so I couldn't know that unless Christine shared it with me. You can go check if you want to, I'll wait right here. See, I have no gun," he says, pulling his shirt up to reveal a bare chest and empty waistband.

John leaves the door open and backs into the cabin, his weapon still trained on Malcolm. He walks to the room's corner and taps the butt of the rifle on the hardwood floor surrounding the fireplace. He finds one hollow board, and crouches to lift it. Inside is a piece of worn cloth. He picks it up, recognizing the fabric from Christine's dress. He holds it against his chest for a moment, the memories flooding over him.

Malcolm watches as John appears in the doorway again, his weapon now relaxed at his side. John looks at him and nods his head, then retreats into the cabin, leaving the entry clear. Malcolm takes this as his invitation to enter and walks onto the deck, entering the small home. It is a one-room cottage, with only the basics—bed, table and chairs, and a few shelves. The fire crackles, the warmth comforting him. He is cold even though he walked three miles to get here. Fear does that to a person.

The dog has finally stopped trying to attack him but lies at John's feet, ready to pounce again at a moment's notice. John sits at the table, head bowed, hands folded in his lap. He glances up at Malcolm, using his boot to push out a chair in an invitation to sit. Malcolm grabs the seat facing John, unsure of what to say and how to start the conversation.

"Why was Christine in England? I thought she went home to California."

"She is in Los Angeles, with her son. It's a lengthy, convoluted story of how she ended up there. One I won't bore you with."

"Just like Christine, you don't give up any secrets. And why are you here now?"

"I'll be staying in this area. I'm looking to settle in and get on with my life. Whatever existence I can create for myself, anyway. We hoped you would help me with that process. Point me in the right direction."

"And why would I do that?"

"Because she thinks the world of you. And I'm convinced you feel the same about her."

John drops his gaze, studying the table. When he looks up at Malcolm, his expression softens.

"You can bed down here until we settle you. But while you are here, I expect you to work and earn your keep. I'm not offering charity. This is a working ranch, and I could use the extra hand."

"I would expect no less, John. I will do everything possible to help you. Thank you."

"Please don't tell me you know nothing of farming or livestock, like Christine."

"I'm familiar with tending a vegetable patch, mate. As far as the animals, you may have to give me a few pointers in that area."

John sighs and shakes his head.

"We'd best start then. Daylight is burning."

Malcolm spends the rest of the afternoon trailing John while he tends and feeds the livestock. He helps groom the horses and weed the garden. John takes him fishing, and to get water and more firewood. By the time the sun sets he is dragging. Every muscle aches and he is starving.

His exile to 1335 provided him the experience for dinner preparation, at least. He cleans the fish and impresses John with his competence at the task. John serves it with fresh peas from the garden and apples with cinnamon and nutmeg, and it is a welcome meal after a long day. Malcolm mashes his vegetables into a pate to resemble the mushy peas side dish he used to eat in England. John doesn't comment, but looks at him with distaste, reminding him of their cultural differences. After supper he makes a bed of thick blankets on the hardwood by the fire and is asleep almost at once after climbing into his makeshift mattress.

The next morning, it starts all over again, awake before dawn, tending animals and doing various chores. They maintain this schedule for many days. Up before the sun, home at dusk and early to sleep. Most nights they talk or play faro, a betting game with cards.

John has questions, but Malcolm dodges most of them with vague answers and fabricates everything else to fill in the blanks. It is obvious John still misses Christine. He talks of her often, and when he does, his face relaxes, and he smiles more. Malcolm never alludes to the budding romance he witnessed between her and Ethan. That would only hurt John, and he has grown to like him.

Over the next month John teaches him to hunt deer, elk, wild turkey, and geese they find at the river. He learns to butcher, preserve and smoke the meat, and enjoys eating something other than rabbit and fish, which was his staple diet while in England. When John trades two goats for an enormous pig to a local farmer, they roast it and make salted pork, and Malcolm is pleased to gain another skill. They trade some for buffalo and beef, and when winter sets in they have a variety of dried meats and preserved fruits and vegetables.

One frosty morning as they chop firewood, John casually mentions to Malcom he can claim land next to his. All he needs to do is build a home and farm it for five years according to the Homestead act of 1862.

"That would be brilliant John, but I don't have a clue how to construct a house."

"You're a coot Malcolm, I will help you. You can't raise a cabin alone."

"I would be indebted to you. But why are you only telling me this now? This is an important piece of information I would expect you to mention before today."

"I had to be sure I wanted you for my neighbor, and I needed to be certain you could learn how to manage a homestead."

Malcolm laughs. "Of course. Fair enough, mate."

They shake hands and seal the deal. They will build a small house and settle him near John's ranch. Malcolm is content here, and he and John have formed a friendship he values. At night, before sleep comes, he imagines his new life and hopes he can be comfortable, if maybe not altogether happy here. Genuine happiness seems an elusive target, one he has resigned to never reach. But he soldiers on, vowing to carry on a day at a time and open himself to whatever fate has in store for him.

SIX

Los Angeles, California 2070

Christine stares at Hannah, unnerved as things become clear. She realizes she does not have information about a CCEA agent, this is much more personal.

"What are you saying, exactly? Are you suggesting Chad would harm you?"

The last of Hannah's resolve shatters as the tears gush. She swipes them away and collapses against the booth.

"Yes, I mean Chad. And I'm not just suggesting it, I'm confirming it. I can't get out Christine, I don't see what else I can do."

"Oh God, you cannot be serious? You want to exile to the past to escape a lousy marriage?"

Christine drains her glass of wine and considers ordering something stronger. Is Hannah crazy? This is insane, and she plans to tell her so.

"Do you have kids, Hannah?"

"No, no children."

"Then leave him. Move away, out of the country if you have to. There is no need to exile to shed a creep like Chad. Women get out of miserable marriages every day."

"It's more than that. He is physically and mentally abusive. And you don't get it. I know things. I wish I didn't, but I do. I appreciate this is a risky move, but I have no other option. This is my only choice."

"What do you mean? You know what?"

"I overheard Chad and some of his cop buddies one day. I wasn't supposed to hear their conversation, and it wasn't intentional, but I heard them, nonetheless. They have an operation in place where they manipulate evidence, they seize it and sell it. It never gets on the record. I asked him about it later, and he went ballistic."

"So, turn him in. There is always a way, Hannah. What you're proposing is so extreme, you have no clue. In today's society there is no reason for you to take such radical steps to elude an abuser and a thief."

"You don't understand, and I can't expect you to. This was never about my choices. There are none for me. This is about the type of man Chad is. Either I disappear or I die. It's that simple. I can't turn him in. This enterprise runs deep, and I have no idea how far up the chain of command it goes. But I do know some brass is involved. If I leave him, I am nothing more than a loose end to him. I am not willing to take the chance they wouldn't convict him. And I couldn't live my life looking over my shoulder forever. I'd never be safe." She pushes her tee-shirt sleeve up to expose dark black and purple bruising along the top of her arm, the sight of it causing Christine to gasp.

"What are you suggesting, exactly?"

"I'm saying it wouldn't be a huge leap for them to get rid of me. I'm pretty sure they've done it before. They could never allow an ex-wife to go, not knowing what I do. That would be far too risky. Right now, I'm under his eye and he has control, so he's not worried. But the minute I leave, I'm at risk. I could bring their entire enterprise down. Do you think they are going to just let me walk away? This isn't only about the money their operation generates. Manipulating evidence means it affects the outcome of criminal sentences. Every one of the cases this touched would be thrown out and retried. If they would even retry them. The convict's attorneys would see to it that all those verdicts were overturned, and they'd be acquitted."

Of all the possible reasons she had expected to hear about why Hannah can't turn Chad in, this was not one of them.

"Hannah, you're talking about murder and corrupt cops here. Something like this would be a nightmare for the District Attorney and the courts. This is no joke."

"You think I don't know that? Why would I want to give up everything I have ever known to live hundreds of years in the past? Leave the only family I have left? This wasn't my first choice, Christine. But it's the only one that will ensure my safety."

"Why now? When were you aware of what they are doing?"

"Not long, three months. I needed time to figure out what to do. I wanted to contact you two weeks ago. But I had to wait until the split lip and black eye he gave me healed enough for me to leave the house. He did that to me because he said I overcooked his steak one night. Any minor thing sets him off now. I can never predict when he will blow up. If I wear clothing he doesn't approve or cook a meal he isn't in the mood for, he becomes violent. If he has a stressful shift at work, it's even worse. And to top it off, I'm convinced he's cheating on me. Not that I would ever confront him about it. His anger is intensifying, and something has changed. I don't know what or why, but he is stressed out, and I'm sure it's because of his illegal activity. Maybe they are pressuring him to deal with me, who knows?"

"What? How? How does he get away with this? He's a police officer, we hold law enforcement to a higher standard!"

Hannah scoffs and finishes her wine while she signals the waitress for another round.

"Don't be naïve, Christine. That's how he gets away with it. When he leaves marks on me that will show, he doesn't allow me to see anyone. He holds the power because he realizes his buddies in blue have his back. Perhaps you hold law enforcement officers to a loftier code, but Chad didn't get that memo. They've hidden their operation this long, I'm sure they have no intention of giving it up now. We are talking about a lot of money in this scheme they have going."

"Maybe his inner circle would support him, but surely his lieutenant or the captain can do something about this. Just because he's LAPD doesn't mean he's above reproach."

Hannah laughs and shakes her head.

"Oh, please. That's precisely what it means. I tried talking to the watch commander once a few months ago, right after I found out. He informed me with no direct proof they won't pursue it. And believe me, he wasn't very troubled about it either. He summarily dismissed me like I was a hysterical, jealous wife. It was probably a huge mistake for me to tell him about the evidence operation. Things changed after that, and Chad's anger escalated. I'm too afraid to press charges for the abuse, and it would be a waste of breath, anyway. He has an exemplary service record, and I'm sure they cover their tracks well. Besides, the supervisor didn't keep our meeting confidential as I asked him to, so I think he's part of the organization. He told Chad the very same day I was there that I had been to visit him. Then the guy lectured him about keeping me in line and getting his house in order. When he discovered I reported him, he went ballistic and informed me in no uncertain terms I should shut my mouth and forget what I heard if I know what's good for me. He broke my arm, shoving me into a wall. Not to mention the dislocated shoulder and concussion. I lied to the emergency room doctor and told him I was in a car accident. Chad said he was driving behind me when it happened and drove me to the ER himself. He claimed he would file the report because he had the other car's information. They accepted everything he said with blind faith because they see him in there all the time through his job. They think they know him, and they trust him because he's a cop."

"Hannah, you cannot let him continue to hurt you or get away with stealing evidence!" she says, shuddering in disgust at the thought.

"What am I to do, Christine? He has the upper hand, and he knows it. Chad controls the finances. I have zero money of my own. He will not allow me to work anymore. Last year he agreed I could take a job, but he called and showed up so often they fired me after only a month. And believe me, he made it clear I was not to work again."

The tears return and she leans forward, elbows on the table, speaking in a low tone.

"This is the perfect solution. If I am exiled into history, he can't get to me. If you exile me, then I know he won't find me, because I trust you to do the right thing and not give in to his demands."

She studies Christine with pleading eyes.

"You're wrong, this makes no sense at all. The system assigns transporters, I have no control over who I transport. I mentioned to you before, they don't reveal who my prisoner is or where or what timeline I'm traveling to until the day I leave. There must be someone else you can turn to for support. Family or friends?"

"There is no one," she says, her shoulders sagging. "I have no one except a sister in Texas. She's a single mother with two girls struggling to stay above water herself. She is in no position to help me. And I wouldn't bring this to her doorstep, anyway. Besides, he would look for me there first. He knows I have nowhere else to go. I'm isolated from any friends I once had. Anyone we socialize with now are his colleagues at the department and their wives. I am far from close to them. And I could never entrust them not to talk to their husbands and risk it circling back to Chad."

"Okay, but why me, Hannah? No offense, but we don't know each other. Like at all."

"I understand. Call it intuition, I guess. You impressed me as sincere when I met you. Maybe you don't remember. But the group of people we were chatting with at that dinner included that senator who dodged a prison sentence for fraud on a technicality. You weren't afraid to voice your disdain for that, even when everyone else congratulated him for his victory. I agreed with you and wished I had the guts to say so, like you had."

"Are you telling me a conversation a year ago made you look me up now?" she asks, raising an eyebrow.

"Well, not exactly. I read the story online of the missing transporters and saw you were one of them. I followed the reports, and I knew you would make it home. I guessed someone with your tenacity would be fine. And you were. So, when I heard you made it back, something clicked for me. It triggered me to consider the time travel program as a means out of my situation. I figured you were the person who would save me. Was I right, Christine? Are you the somebody who will help me out of this nightmare? I have nowhere else to turn at this point."

Christine sighs and drains her second glass of wine. She would much rather sprinkle her purse lint over the vegan nachos and eat them, than become mixed up in this. But she also cannot walk away now that she knows what Chad is doing. She waves for the waitress and orders two more glasses, waiting until she leaves before speaking.

"You're asking me not only to put my job on the line, but to break the law. And what makes you think I could pull this off, anyway? You do not realize what I'd have to do, Hannah."

"That's not true. I'm fully aware of what I'm suggesting. It was hard for me to call you and even ask for this meeting. But I thought if anyone could help me, it was you. If you can't or won't, then I understand. But I am going through with this. I would just feel far more secure if I had your cooperation. I know Chad will extract my location from another transporter. Let's be real, everyone has a price and a breaking point."

"Well, I don't. I always thought Chad was an asshole. I wouldn't mind seeing him go down, to be honest."

"Then you've just proved me right. I'd be in expert hands with you, and at risk with anyone else. And I understand you say he cannot transfer back there to come after me, but you don't know Chad like I do. He'll figure out how to get to me. He might pay off a convict to do it. Promise them to look after their family here, or turn the transporter, or allow the prisoner to smuggle drugs on his exile. Whatever. He has connections and is very resourceful and very persuasive. And he is patient. He will wait for the right opportunity and I'll never see it coming. I can either stay here and let him beat me to death or arrange an accident for me, or live in the past and try to blend in and hide. At least back there I'd have better odds, the lesser of the two evils. I stand no chance if I stick around here."

"I think you're giving Chad too much credit. With you exiled, he would presumably give up and continue on with his life. He doesn't strike me as a guy with the character or perseverance to see that kind of project through. With you in the past, you pose no risk to their operation here. But let's assume for a moment that he could bring a CCEA employee on board. That would involve waiting for them to assign an inmate near your same location and timeline. Someone he can talk into going after you. The odds of that happening in a reasonable timeframe are slim. Besides, if you really believe he is cheating on you, you must realize he would likely focus on her and move on. I don't mean to sound insensitive, but men like Chad, they are creatures of convenience. And I'm sure you get what I'm suggesting."

"Well, you do not know Chad. He is a cruel man who will consider me leaving him to be an enormous blow to his ego. Not to mention the risk of allowing me to live with the information I have on him. No matter what timeline I go to, I am still a loose end. He would never let that pass. And time will only fuel his anger. Eventually, he'll work it out I did this to get away from him, and he'll spiral into a rage of epic proportion."

She drops her head into her hands and cries again. When she peers up at Christine her eyes are red and swollen, and she looks as if she has the weight of the world on her shoulders.

"What would you do in my position? I see no other path out. If I stay here, he will kill me. He'll get away with it too. And there's no one to care or do anything about it. They will help him cover it up, and we both know it."

Christine leans forward across the table where she looks at Hannah for a long moment.

"I'm not promising anything but allow me a few days to check on some things. I don't know if I can help or not. Or if I'm even willing to, to be perfectly transparent. But I'll be in touch either way."

Christine slides out of the booth, leaving her third glass of wine untouched. She tosses money on the table and walks to the door without looking back. Once in her car, she calls a familiar number.

"I need to talk to you tomorrow before I transport. Can you set aside time in the morning? Good, I'll meet you at seven o'clock. No, nothing's wrong, I want to run something by you, is all."

Christine sets the car auto pilot to home and rehashes the meeting in her mind on the journey there. She considers what she is about to put into motion. She can help Hannah escape. That part is the simple matter of transporting her. Covering her tracks and hiding her is more problematic. But isn't that what she, Ethan, Frank and Annabelle agreed to do with Jonathan Hoyt? Take on operations to sidestep disasters? This qualifies as a potential disaster, albeit on a much smaller scale than intended. But it still fits the bill. She only hopes they see the situation that way too. She needs to find out if Frank will go along with this. If not, then she dreads lowering the boom to tell Hannah she cannot save her.

SEVEN

Piedmont, Oklahoma 1867

Over the next several days, Malcolm and John spend daylight hours chopping down walnut trees, splitting logs for the cabin, and doing chores on John's ranch. Malcolm has never been in better physical shape. The endless hard work is exhausting but gratifying, and he has a tremendous sense of accomplishment at the close of each day. It surprises him to find he prefers this era to the timeline he is from. This uncomplicated lifestyle thoroughly suits him.

John takes Malcolm into Piedmont a couple of times for supplies and to learn the lie of the land. It is a pleasant enough burg with a general store, a saloon and one-room schoolhouse. The town doctor has a small office, and the hotel, reminiscent of a bed-and-breakfast, includes a modest restaurant for travelers. He still feels he is in the middle of nowhere, that this is all that exists of the world. And this is all there is for him. He cannot travel outside this area or the CCEA enforcement team could cast him further back in history and to wherever the system determines he should go. Malcolm does not want that to happen; he is finally settling here, and the possibility of being sent somewhere else on his own is more than a little daunting. He is not sure where his specific cut-off boundary is, so he errs on the side of caution and sticks close to home. With John helping him secure property and erect a cabin, for the first time in a very long while he has a future to look forward to. One that he is excited about, and he has no intention of jeopardizing it.

He has a successful solo hunt and celebrates by trading the deer and elk he gets for seeds and building supplies. In the spring he and John intend to plant a garden with corn and beans, and later in the year Malcolm will add pumpkin, sweet potatoes, and zucchini. Between hunting and his vegetable plot, he only needs to buy coffee, flour, cornmeal, salt, sugar, and spices. Walnuts are free for the taking along with apples, pears, plums and apricots. The fruit trees are a morning's ride beyond the walnut grove, but it is worth it to have fresh produce in the summer.

He produces his own lard now, and plans to trade meat for hens to get eggs, and maybe a goat and a pig. Cattle are too expensive for him, but he is hopeful he can afford one, eventually. John has taught him how to prepare bread and biscuits using a baking powder called saleratus that causes the dough to rise, and although they are not the best he has ever tasted, they are at least edible, and the closest thing to scones he has seen here.

His progress here pleases him, and they should settle him by spring if all goes according to plan. He smiles, thinking soon he will be king of his castle. Not yet, though. Right now, he has nothing more than a patch of rock-hard dirt and a pile of split logs. But his vision of what could be spurs him onward.

He falls into a routine with preparations for the house; they build basic furniture from the wood they cut and start framing on the dwelling. John teaches him everything he knows about constructing a cabin, and while his knowledge does not meet modern standards, the structure is strong, and it will stand.

He is, however, anxious about completing the shelter before the cold season arrives. The weather is frigid with no snow yet, but John assures him it is coming. Although the climate here is downright cozy compared to England, he knows this territory is unforgiving. Then one morning soon after, almost as if he conjured it himself just by worrying about it, he awakes to a white blanket covering the prairie. John tells him it is rare for snowfall before Christmas, but the winter freeze lies as far as they can see. They postpone further effort on the build until after the powder melts.

While they wait for the inclement weather to pass, most nights they play faro around the fire, and Malcolm teaches John scabby queen and gin rummy. During a break from cards one evening, John makes coffee and sits across from Malcolm, looking serious.

"What's on your mind, mate?"

"Where are you from?"

Malcolm blinks slowly. "What do you mean? I've told you I'm from Leeds in the north of England. Doesn't my perfect queen's English give that away?"

"That's not what I am asking. First Christine comes here, and I find her alone in the woods. Then her son shows up to get Annabelle after Christine disappears, and now you arrive. None of this feels right. They would never talk to me about their past. I don't understand what you're all hiding."

Malcolm considers John's question for a minute as he watches the flames dance in the fire. He runs through the options in his mind and decides there are only two—lie or reveal the truth. He concludes John is his friend, maybe the only real ally he will ever have again, and he does not want to deceive him. What harm would it do to tell him? He is here until his death. That is a fact. John can either believe him or not. And if not, at least it will be cathartic to confess to someone, to unburden himself from this secret. And if he believes him, well, all the better, and he can open another world to him.

He clears his throat before speaking and turns his attention back to John. "What I am about to reveal to you is going to be tough to accept. It may seem a fairy tale to you, but I give you my word, it's accurate."

He speaks quickly, the words running together as he attempts to tell his story.

"I was born in Leeds but am most recently from London. They arrested me there for a felony I admit I committed. Not a violent transgression, what we call a white-collar crime where I am from. A financial misconduct. I met Christine after they sentenced me to my prison time, for lack of a better term. She arrived in England and literally landed in the camp I was in with four other people. One was from Britain, two from Scotland, and the other came from France. We were together in that encampment for several days before I asked to come here. Christine, her son Michael, and Frank, the man she works for, went to Los Angeles. Ethan, Thomas and Aidan, the others I was with, proceeded on to England. Frank sent me here because I helped them steal a set of priceless writings from a fourteenth century astronomer. The catch is, we were all in 1335, England. They traveled forward to our present timeline in 2070. Everyone but me, that is. I am a convicted cyber-criminal, so my government exiled me to the past, which is standard practice for convicts of my classification." He stops to refocus his thoughts, trying not to get too ahead of himself.

"I realize you don't know what a cyber-criminal is. It's someone who breaks the law by entering another person's business or personal records without authorization. There are thousands of us in timelines all over history, and all over the world. They will not allow me back in my timeline to 2070. The others were all transporters, people who work for the government and escort criminals like me to their exile destinations. They were stranded in the past when our time travel system failed, but they were all lucky enough to go home. Frank's team showed up to rescue them, and he and Ethan took pity on me and agreed to send me here. I came here because Christine told me about her life here, and I am safer here than in medieval England. So here I am, done and dusted."

He takes a deep breath and reclines in his chair, waiting for a reaction. John sat wordlessly throughout Malcolm's narrative, eyes narrowed at him. Now he stares at him in disbelief for several long moments before speaking.

"I see you want to beat the devil around the stump, Malcolm. Do you think of me as addle-headed?"

"No, I absolutely do not. I realize this knowledge is a lot to digest. But I can tell you about inventions you cannot even begin to imagine," he says, rising from the chair as his arms sweep in front of him in a grand motion. "In my generation there are enormous machines that fly through the sky called airplanes, carrying people as passengers. You travel from Los Angeles, over the Atlantic Ocean, to England in two hours. Cars, which are horseless carriages, take you across country and move quicker than any horse at top speed. We have computers that prepare our meals. That's a device you enter data into. The closest thing you have here is a telegraph, but our processors are far more advanced. We have a cooker we call a ChefAid. You order foods you want from a supplier, and they bring it. Then you ask it to cook your food for you. Voila, it spits out your meal, done to perfection. We have the internet, a colossal information center at your fingertips, anything you wish to know is in there. And you type in whatever you need to buy from online stores, and they deliver it to your home. We implant cell phone chips in our earlobes, which allow you to talk to anyone, anywhere in the world at the tap of a finger. Of course, the government removed mine when they arrested me," he says, dropping into the chair, his elbows on his knees. "Those are only a few details from 2070. There are so many things to share with you."

John shakes his head and glares at him. "Malcolm, I don't know if you are cracked or a snake in the grass. I suppose when you are ready to confess the truth, you will. Until that day comes, I'll hear no more talk of machines that fly or ride over land faster than a horse."

"Bollocks, John! I am telling you the facts. Listen, I understand why you don't believe me. I have many qualities John, some of them not always good. But I am not a liar," he replies exasperated, leaning forward in his chair.

"Then our discussion ends here."

John takes his coffee to the chair by the fire and does not speak to Malcolm the rest of the evening. The exchange strains their friendship, and John only acknowledges him when necessary in the days that follow.

Over the next week, the snow thaws and they resume production on Malcolm's home. They have no interaction with each other, except related to the build. The only sound all day is the crunch of their boots on the melting slush, along with hammering and sawing. Malcolm's confession has divided them, and it is difficult for him to focus. He endures this silent treatment until he can no longer stand it.

Malcolm glances up to the late afternoon sky, then back at John, his breath blowing out in icy puffs as he speaks. "Looks like the weather will hold for a few days."

When he gets no response, he tries again. "I realize you are angry with me, but I am being honest with you about my former way of life. I understand this is hard to accept, but that's the only story I have because it's the truth. Have you not wondered how Christine made it home alone? Or why she disappeared into thin air one day? Or how she came to be here in the first place? She told me you had to teach her how to do just about everything here. And now you've had to instruct me. Does that not strike you as odd? We do not know how to survive here because we are not from this era. This lifestyle is bloody foreign to us."

John glowers at him and puts his saw down on the makeshift work bench.

"I won't listen to this nonsense."

He storms off toward his ranch, following the well-worn path between the two cabins, leaving Malcolm looking at the pile of logs that still need to be split. He gives John some space and does not return to the homestead until just before dark. John maintains his silence, which is deafening in the small shack. Malcolm wishes nothing more than to forget this and backtrack to the way things were before he opened his big mouth. Going back in time is something he has done so much of lately, yet on the one occasion he really wants to, he can't. So, he tries to put it right with John again.

"Truce, mate," says Malcolm, as he holds his hand out to John.

John glances at Malcolm's extended palm but makes no move to shake it.

"I will help you complete the ranch, but after that you stay on your property and I'll remain on mine. I don't enjoy being taken for a fool, Malcolm."

Malcolm wants to respond, but John turns his back on him to pursue cleaning his gun, not interested in anything more he has to say.

The silence from John carries on into the next day, and Malcolm goes hunting and shoots a deer and a wild turkey. Borrowing John's rifle seems an imposition now that their friendship is nonexistent, and he decides to buy his own. He ventures into town alone, walking by cabins and ranches scattered across the prairie on his route there. Some houses are little more than dugouts carved into small hills. He wonders how those people survive. It saddens him to imagine what life must be like for them, and he gives a silent thanks John helped him when he got here. But he's certain John means what he says, and that help will come to a screeching halt once his house is finished. He curses himself under his breath once again for his mistake in trying to convince John about his past. It was stupid of him to think someone from this timeline would understand or even be able to fathom time travel is possible.

Once in town, he barters the deer for an old rifle. He trades some other dried meat, and some salted pork, along with the promise of vegetables in the summer, and in exchange he gains a mare who appears as if he has ridden her hard and put her away wet. Not the best animal available, but it is a starting point, and he looks forward to riding home rather than walking. And if he will be on his own, he needs a weapon for hunting and defending his land, and a horse for transportation.

He rides his new mare to the cabin, unable to stop thinking about how steeped in irony it is that he craves nothing more than to go back in time and prevent himself from revealing where and when he is from to John. But that will not happen. Just as he did in London, he acted on an impulsive decision that has come around to haunt him, and now he must live with it.

He feels lonelier than ever without John for company, and he is certain fate has condemned him to be lonely for the rest of his existence. He made a friend and lost him in one fell swoop, and all at once his promising future here fades before his eyes.

EIGHT

Los Angeles, California 2070 / Baton Rouge, Louisiana, 1803

Christine raises her palm to the screen mounted at the back entrance of the CCEA building.

"Entry approved," coos the programmed voice.

The door clicks open, and she steps into the noisy hallway. People shuffle around her, noses buried in their handheld screens. She feels the agitation creep in and tries to force it down as she waits for the crowds to straggle by. She did not sleep well last night. Her mind raced with worry about all that could go wrong if she helps Hannah with her plan to exile to the past. Stranded in Oklahoma and England for seven months, she is acutely aware of the struggles Hannah may encounter. It will be more difficult than she imagines, but that she would ask to enter the program voluntarily is a testament to how desperate a position she is in.

Christine's furlough into history was a journey of self-awareness, and she is proud her temperament has evolved, and she developed the ability to be vulnerable. But this morning her lack of sleep is trying her patience in every form imaginable, and that progress seems to lurk somewhere in the distant past. She even resents Hannah a little for involving her in this plot. The last thing she wants information about is someone's marriage issues, or worse yet, to have any inside knowledge about a criminal syndicate—particularly with a couple she does not know. But because Chad is mistreating Hannah and embroiled in an illegal evidence racket, that takes things to a new level, and she has an obligation to help. She cannot turn her away now that she knows what is happening. She just hopes Jonathan and Frank agree.

When she arrives in Frank's office, she can no longer control her annoyance, and the irritation shows all over her face. She drops into a chair and frowns at him.

"Who pissed in your cereal this morning?" he asks with a smirk.

"I didn't get much sleep last night, Frank, don't start with me." She grabs a protein bar off his desk, fighting with the wrapper.

"Give me that, before you hurt yourself," he says, snatching it out of her hand. He tears open the package and hands it back to her, his chair creaking as he settles further into it. "How do you stand those things? They taste like I imagine dried bark and cardboard does. Linda makes me eat them because they're supposed to be healthy," he says, curling his lip and rolling his eyes. "So, what's keeping you up at night? You pining away for Ethan? Had a little sample of romance and now you miss it?" he chuckles.

Her glare is laser-sharp as she bites into the snack, her face puckering at the flavor.

"No, it's not Ethan. I, or rather we, have a bigger problem. Do you know Chad Cole? The Sergeant with LAPD?" she asks, swallowing the bite of food that feels like sawdust stuck in her throat.

"The clown with the cartoon arms assigned to cyber-crimes? The asshole who thinks he's the cock of the walk?"

"Yep, that guy. Well, his wife called me yesterday and asked to meet me. Some nonsense about writing an article about transporters for an online paper. Surprise. That's not what she wanted. Chad is abusing her. Not only that, but she found out he is mixed up in an illegal evidence ring with several other cops."

"Okay. What does that have to do with us? We'll call his superiors if she is too scared to do it and have his ass incarcerated. End of problem."

"Yeah, that's what I said too. She has another idea. Hannah wants me to exile her as a prisoner of the time travel program. She thinks he'll find her if she stays here, and his buddies at the P.D. will support him. She is beyond terrified of the guy, and she has no family or friends to turn to. He won't allow her to work either. And Frank, it's really serious. He's physically abusive, and she has good reason to believe he may want to eliminate her because of what she knows. And this evidence ring goes up the chain of command. She isn't sure how far, but it involves at least his immediate supervisors."

Frank scoffs, as he leans further back in the chair, folding his hands behind his head. When she doesn't respond he sits up straight again. "Wait, you're serious? She thinks he is going to try to kill her? And she actually said she wants to exile? I didn't realize you were friends with Cole's wife."

"I'm not, I hardly know her." Christine tells him how she and Hannah met a couple of times, how she followed Christine's story on the news, and about her recent meeting with Hannah. She recounts the details of their conversation and everything she knows about Chad's crimes.

"I want to help her, Frank. I'm sure Jonathan would suspend the system for the duration we need to take her somewhere safe."

"Oh, we're calling him by his first name now are we, Jonathan? No way, Christine. We cannot risk that. Anyone who goes through the process without authorization gains the attention of the enforcement team. Even Hoyt can't prevent that."

"Then let's send her there through the right channels. Let them convict her, and once she is in the system, we'll ask Hoyt to tweak it so she transports with me. He can assign her to Piedmont. She'd be safe there with Malcolm. Ethan trusts him. And that way if Chad ever sent someone after her, at least she would stand a chance in the fight."

"Wow, Christine. You have this all worked out, don't you?"

"I told you, I couldn't sleep last night. It gave me the opportunity to think. This is what we signed up for, right? To save lives? When you, me, Ethan, and Annabelle agreed to work with Hoyt using the time travel program, we vowed to prevent future disasters. Well, trust me, this is a catastrophe waiting to happen. He will kill her Frank unless we help her get away from him. Besides, as CCEA agents we are law enforcement too. We're supposed to aid and assist, aren't we?" she says, tapping her finger against the badge patch on her chest.

"I don't know, Christine. It sounds too risky to me."

"And suspending the operation for disaster prevention isn't? We would travel for much longer to do that. I'm only asking for Hoyt to cover me while in Piedmont to visit Malcolm for a few hours. Then he can tag Hannah to me when she is ready to transport. We don't have a choice, Frank. We have to do something."

"I am not suggesting we ignore the fact he needs to be stopped. You just haven't convinced me this is the right way to handle it. Besides, I think you have overlooked one thing. How is Cole's wife going to commit a cyber-crime? Does she have the knowledge to hack into a system or steal money? You said she doesn't work. How can a housewife pull off a violation significant enough to have them extradite her into the time travel program?"

Christine laughs and tosses the snack wrapper and uneaten portion of the bar into the waste basket.

"Frank, that's the easy part. We have the perfect person to help us with that—Maddie. Did you forget Michael's girlfriend is an IT specialist here at the CCEA?"

"And you expect she will want to involve herself in this mess?"

"I think she has tangled herself up plenty with my son and our previous excursion into history so she won't hesitate to give us a few pointers. Besides, she too, signed on to become a card-carrying member of team Hoyt."

"Yeah, I guess she did. You've clearly got your mind made up. I've known you long enough to realize what a waste of my time it is, lecturing you about this. But I don't like it, Christine. We can talk to Hoyt and see if he will agree to it. He might not cooperate, you know. I'm sure he was considering larger scale projects for us. And to be honest, it won't disappoint me if he says no. If he can't help, then we drop any plan to exile her. We'll turn him into the DA's office anonymously and let them do their job. They'd love to hear what he's up to, especially right before the upcoming election when an arrest like that would be a huge check mark for them. Agreed?"

"Fair enough. I'll call him and set up a meeting for after I return from my transport in two days."

"Fine, let's get you to Louisiana," he says, standing up.

They separate at the elevator as Frank leaves to prepare the pods for departure while Christine goes to the locker room to change into her period clothes. She steps into the skirt, adjusting the bodice where she keeps her transponder. This is her least favorite aspect of the job—wearing the clothing. The costume is hot and difficult to move in. Her dislike for the apparel only grew worse when she had to wear this attire for seven months when stranded in the past.

This is her first transport since coming home and she is apprehensive, although she tries not to show it. She dictates Michael a last-minute text message before tossing her tablet, uniform, and employee ID into the compartment.

54

Hey son, traveling today, be back on Thursday. Would like to take you and Maddie to dinner on Friday night. Let me know if you are free. Don't worry, I promise to come home this time! Hahaha. Too soon to joke about it? I love you! -Mom

Hopefully, Michael and Maddie can meet her. She misses her son, but she's also eager to talk to Maddie about the Hannah situation. She doubts Hannah has sufficient expertise to infiltrate a government website and get herself arrested. But Maddie, on the other hand, is an IT whiz who can access anything. The more she considers it, she realizes that without Maddie's guidance this is never going to work. They need to be sure whatever Hannah does, no one ever traces it back to Maddie or Christine. And it must be legitimate enough for the courts to accept Hannah orchestrated it herself, or some slick defense attorney may win her an acquittal. The details make her head spin. She needs to ask Maddie if they can even pull this off. But first, an appeal to Hoyt will determine if she should bring the subject up to Maddie at all. If he cannot help them, then the entire plan is off.

Another transporter strolls into the locker area, pulling her back from her daydream, and nods at Christine before disappearing around the corner. She has stalled long enough. It's time to leave. Stepping into the hall, she makes her way to the jump room. After a deep breath, she crosses to the holding space to claim her prisoner and check-in with Frank. Twenty minutes later Frank secures them in the pods. As she wipes her damp palms on her skirt and concentrates on controlling her breathing, she glances over to her prisoner's pod. The woman looks as if she may hyperventilate. Christine knows how she feels; she did not expect to be this tense on her first transport after being rescued. She closes her eyes, trying to focus on inhaling and exhaling, while Frank recites the countdown to Louisiana in 1803.

* * *

Christine regains consciousness before her prisoner. She sits up, resting against a tree with moss dangling so low from the branches it nearly brushes the ground. She smells the swampiness of the place all around her, almost as if it is penetrating her skin. There is a small body of stagnant water a few hundred yards away, and a murky lake directly in front of her. She rises quickly, remembering large reptiles are prevalent here. She has no idea whether this is freshwater, saltwater, or perhaps even brackish, a combination of both. Not that it makes a big difference to her, crocodiles live in seawater and alligators in fresh, and she doesn't care to run into either species.

She dreads waking her prisoner, based on her behavior in the pod. If she freaks out, Christine must leave her without completing the on-site walk through—that is CCEA policy. It is dangerous for an agent if an inmate becomes hysterical. Frenzied, emotional people make terrible decisions, and those judgment calls are hazardous for both of them. She watches the woman sleep, thinking this is the last peaceful doze she will enjoy for a long time, maybe ever. As she stirs, she feels sorry for her. Her life is never going to be the same. From this point forward, it is all about survival—nothing more. She comes awake with a start, sitting straight up to gasp.

"Oh my God, are we here?" she asks, sucking in ragged breaths.

"Yes. Try to calm down. You'll make yourself sick. Take a moment and just breathe. After that we'll go over your plan, okay?"

"My plan? What plan? I don't have any damn plan! I'm in 1803 hillbilly country! What the hell kind of plan am I supposed to have?" she shrieks, grabbing the tree trunk for support as she stands.

"Quiet down, Elizabeth. Let's not attract any unwanted attention, human or otherwise," she says, thinking of the reptiles lurking in the swamp nearby. "Do you want me to review your survival items with you one more time?"

"What? No! Those aren't 'survival items', that's just bullshit trash to keep me alive for a few days, a week, tops. How do you live with yourself, doing this to people?" she cries, as she paces between two trees, dangerously close to hyperventilating again. She stops and glances down at her shoes in disgust, the muddy ground sticking to the bottoms of them, before she resumes her pacing.

This is not a promising sign. She is losing control and anyone within a one-mile radius will hear her shouts. A year ago, her remarks would not have meant much to Christine, just another inmate unhappy with their sentence. But since she has lived what Elizabeth is about to, she sympathizes with what she is facing, and her words hit home. How *does* she live with herself doing this job? The truth is, not very well lately. It's becoming increasingly difficult for her to justify it to herself. As she considers that, Elizabeth's crying is getting louder by the minute and jars her back to the issue at hand as she struggles not to rise to the same level of exasperation.

"Elizabeth, get it together. Sit down and let's talk."

"I am done talking. There's nothing else to say. Please, I am begging you, let me go home. I can disappear and no one will ever hear from me again, I swear to you," she pleads, wringing her hands and taking a step closer.

"You know I can't do that. But I'd like to give you some advice and pointers so you survive this. It's important you listen to me. I can help you. Here, take this," she says, holding out a mini lighter.

Elizabeth takes it, rolling it over in her palms. She looks up at Christine, tears streaking her face as her breathing slows, and her hiccups subside. Once she composes herself, Christine talks. And she does not stop until she tells her all she knows about surviving an exile, and as much history about her destination as she can. Although Baton Rouge has been settled since 1721, the Louisiana purchase has just been completed, so she warns her about upheaval from the indigenous natives. She helps her gather moss, leaves and tree branches to make a shelter, and right before she is ready to go, she slips her a hunting knife and a drawstring bag full of coins.

"What is this," asks Elizabeth, her eyes widening at the sight of it.

"Add these to your pack. This will help you get started. You can lodge at an Inn or rent a room with the silver. But eat your MREs and remain in the woods for a few days. And whatever you do, do not camp near the water's edge. Stay back some or the alligators might become curious. Acclimate to your situation, and when you're more self-assured, venture into town. Just remember what I told you, act as if you belong here. The knife is for protection. Don't hesitate to use it for that if you need to. Do you understand what I'm saying to you?"

"Yes, I think so. Thank you. Sorry I yelled at you earlier."

"No worries, I know you're stressed. But I have to go now. I've been here longer than I should already, and they will wonder where I am at base."

And just like that, she panics all over again. "No, please don't leave me here," she sobs, as the floodgates open and the tears flow.

"I have to, Elizabeth," she states, standing up. Christine had relied on logic, thinking Elizabeth would remain calm. Now she realizes what a mistake that was. There is nothing logical about the exile process—it is all about emotions.

Elizabeth grabs the hem of her dress, lunging for Christine's transponder. At that moment, Christine knows Elizabeth stands little chance of surviving here. Her panic and inability controlling herself will not serve her well. Christine takes two steps backward and programs her device to take her home. The last thing she sees is Elizabeth scream and grab for her again as she fades to black.

NINE

Los Angeles, California 2070

Christine arrives in the jump room on Thursday as scheduled and lets out a sigh of relief when she realizes she is back safely. The trauma of the previous eight months has taken a toll on her, and it manifested with this transport. This was not an ideal prisoner for her first trip, and that did not help matters. Elizabeth Wilson berated her for doing her job, and she cannot blame her for that opinion, either. It will be a long while, if ever, before she is comfortable in her profession again. She considered leaving the CCEA after they rescued her, but what else would she do? She has worked here for eleven years, makes a decent living, and is a good agent. At least when she is not permitting the fear to control her. And the guilt. That's new. Although not an uncompassionate person, she experienced no remorse or thought much about the exile program and its impact on prisoners until it sidelined her in history. Now her prisoner's words resonate with her, cutting her right to the core. After experiencing it firsthand, she understands how cruel it is to abandon them in the past.

Her pod opens as she shakes her head to clear her thoughts. She goes to the decontamination chamber and strips her period dress off, dropping it in the hazardous waste bin. That simple act gives her extreme satisfaction when it lands at the bottom of the container, as it was by far the most uncomfortable article of clothing she has ever worn. The bodice pinched her in all the wrong places and the bustle in the skirt was just annoying.

She passes through a decontamination shower, slipping into a fresh uniform, and the preventive medical tech scans her to confirm she did not bring any diseases or bacteria home with her. They release her half an hour later and she continues to her locker to retrieve her tablet and ID. She checks her messages to find a reply from Michael.

Hi mom. Sure, we can meet for dinner on Friday. How about six o'clock at La Vida? And yes, WAY too soon for jokes about your time missing! Jeez, mom, really? Love you too.

She is relieved to know part of the plan is in place. She sits on the bench in front of her locker, head in her hands, having trouble pushing Elizabeth Wilson out of her mind. She cannot help but wonder if she is even still alive considering two days have elapsed. When you travel through time, you always lose a day, so when Christine makes it to base it means Elizabeth has been on her own for forty-eight hours. She feels better knowing she did what she could to improve her chances of survival, she only hopes she heeds the advice. If anyone were to discover she gave her prisoner extra supplies such as the silver coins, knife and lighter, losing her career would be the least of her worries. But the guilt and culpability she experiences now when exiling inmates are stronger than any fear of being found out.

She peers around the locker room to confirm she is alone. Trying to distract herself from Elizabeth's plight, she says Jonathan's name to activate her cell chip. She is about to disconnect when the familiar voice answers.

"Jonathan Hoyt."

"Jonathan, it's Christine Stewart. How are you?"

"Christine, what a nice surprise. I'm doing very well, thank you. How about yourself?"

"I'm fine, thanks. Just home from a trip to 1803, Louisiana. Listen, I was wondering if you are available to meet with Frank and me in the next day or two?"

"I can see you later this afternoon if that will work for you? I am off to Dubai tomorrow for several days to complete a deal, so otherwise it would need to be the week after."

"Today is fine, I don't think this will wait that long."

"That sounds ominous. Is anything wrong I should concern myself over?"

"No, no, nothing about our agreement. I have something I require your support with is all."

"Fine, let's say four o'clock in my office?"

"Done. We'll see you there."

She hangs up and goes in search of Frank to give him the news. They plan to drive to Hoyt's together and meet at Frank's car at three thirty. Christine dives into the transport report. She needs to get finished but dreads it. Because Elizabeth wasn't cooperative, and became hysterical once they were in Louisiana, she must inform the CCEA of her welfare. Her statement sends a red flag to the enforcement team and they monitor the inmate to be certain she remains in compliance. Which is the best thing, considering her state of mind when she left her. Although the government gives them supplies, Elizabeth was right—it is not suitable to keep them safe. They furnish them with no weapons and only enough food and water to sustain them for a few days. The vaccines and antibiotics they receive before departure are the most valuable items they bring with them. The past is no place to become sick, and without modern medicine, they stand little chance of survival. So she intends to take a few extras with her on each trip. If she decides the inmates need additional support, she will slip them supplements like she did Elizabeth. It's not as if they are coming back to this timeline to expose her, and she views this as a victimless crime, anyway. That is how she justifies breaking the law to herself.

The time passes by quickly, as she catches up with some overdue reports and prepares the information on her recent transport. She looks at Elizabeth's picture on her laptop screen. She is pretty and young, only twenty-six. Not much older than her own son. She probably doesn't have sufficient life experience to survive in 1803. Few people would at her age. Christine accepts she cannot save the world, cannot even spare a small percentage of the criminals arrested and assigned to the program. But if she can provide them a boost, she will. Whether they use it or not is up to them. She clicks the send button on her tablet, sealing the fate of her prisoner and saying a silent prayer she survives there.

At three o'clock she gathers her things and starts for the locker area. After changing into street clothes, she applies lipstick and mascara, not sure why she does it. She's not trying to impress Jonathan Hoyt. There must be some old-school part of her that believes she should be made-up in public. Since the CCEA does not allow transporters to wear any make-up or perfume when transporting, this makes her feel more like herself.

She arrives at Frank's automobile to spot him already waiting.

"Let's go, I don't want to be late for supper. Linda ordered steak and potatoes."

"Glad to know your priorities haven't shifted, Frank."

He rubs his stomach and grins.

They arrive at Hoyt enterprises right on schedule and security escorts them to the fortieth floor where Hoyt's personal assistant greets them and shows them in.

"Frank, Christine, how nice to see you both again." Jonathan Hoyt crosses the room, extending his hand.

"Thanks for squeezing us in Jonathan, I realize how busy you are," says Christine, returning his handshake.

"Good to see you, Hoyt." Frank shakes with him and sinks into an expensive upholstered chair near the ceiling to floor windows.

"Can I get you something to drink? Water, coffee?"

They both decline, and Hoyt takes a seat across from them. Christine cannot help but notice his suit, which is definitely designer. His shoes are shined to perfection, and even his socks appear expensive. His silk tie matches the pocket square on his jacket. The quintessential image of money. And plenty of it. Oodles of it, actually.

"Tell me how I can assist. Christine, you said you need my cooperation. I am happy to help if it's anything within my control."

Christine tells him about Hannah, the abuse she is suffering at the hands of her husband, his involvement in the crime ring, and their plan to exile her in the time travel program. When she finishes, she leans forward in her chair, nervously awaiting his response.

"I can cover your tracks in Piedmont to visit Malcolm, no problem. Just make certain you are out within four hours. Any longer than that and the system will flag it. I won't be able to prevent that, it's a precautionary measure I built in when I wrote it," he smirks and shrugs. "I had no clue someday I would need to transform my software to accommodate surreptitious time travel trips."

"Sure, who could blame you for not knowing *that* was coming?" says Frank, turning to peer out the window.

Christine flashes Frank a look, but he ignores her as he admires the view of Los Angeles. She knows him well enough to pick up the sarcasm in his voice, but when she glances over to Hoyt, he seems unaware of Frank's derision, so she turns her attention back to him.

"So once Hannah is in the register, is it possible to arrange the system to assign her to me for transport? Can you tweak the destination, so it schedules her to Piedmont?"

"Yes, I can manage that without fear of discovery."

"Perfect, that's what we need. I'll ready things on our end and notify you once they have arrested her," replies Christine.

"Are you certain you can pull this off and no one will detect it, Hoyt? I prefer not to take any chances with my livelihood," asks Frank.

"Nor do I, Frank. I risk my entire company and everything I've built when I do this. So yes, I am positive I can execute this with no repercussions."

"All right, I'll be in touch. Thanks again for meeting with us, Jonathan, and for helping." Christine extends her hand and turns to leave, Frank following her out of the office.

Once they are alone in the lift, Christine twists to peer at Frank. "Okay, that's settled then. I will talk to Maddie tomorrow. I'll call Hannah and let her know we are working on a plan and make sure she hasn't changed her mind."

"Yeah, you do that. And I swear Christine if we get caught and this costs me my retirement, I will never forgive you and I'll drag Hoyt down with me."

"Oh Frank, stop being so paranoid. You heard Jonathan. He has far more to lose than we do. He wouldn't go through with this if he wasn't sure he could do it."

Frank grunts and faces forward again.

"I hope you're right, Christine. I miss the days when the CCEA was just my career and not a way to save the world or exploited women."

"We're almost done, everything is going to plan. I can see the light at the end of the tunnel."

"Yeah. Or maybe, that's the train heading straight for us? Did you ever think of that?" he says.

Christine chuckles and loops her arm through his. "Frank, it's so endearing when you worry about me. Except for times like this when it's really irritating as hell. Don't stress, I'll get Hannah back to Malcolm in one piece."

"That's exactly what I'm afraid of."

"Seriously, you are so dramatic sometimes for a middle-aged man."

He snaps his head toward her, frowning. "Who the eff are you calling middle—."

The elevator door closes on their conversation as it whisks them down to the lobby.

TEN

Los Angeles, California 2070

Christine enters La Vida, her gaze sweeping around the crowded room. A Friday evening anywhere in the city is busy. She does not see Michael and Maddie there yet, so she gives her name to the hostess to lessen the delay once they arrive. This is one of the few eateries in Los Angeles, along with Giraldo's, who still has an old-school wait staff. Chain restaurants are all digital with minimal human contact, and industrial version ChefAid's process the food. Christine prefers this place precisely for the atmosphere and service. Plus, the cuisine is far better when prepared by an actual person. Places like this use real chefs, not a hunk of stainless steel to prepare your meal.

Ten minutes later, her son walks in holding hands with his girlfriend.

"Mom, hey, how are you? How was your first transport back at work?"

She smiles and shrugs at him, not eager to talk about her trip to Louisiana.

"Hi Christine, thanks for asking us to dinner. We've been too busy to order food at home and we're out of everything, so it was perfect timing."

"Hello, you two lovebirds, I'm glad you could make it," says Christine, giving each of them a hug. "I added our name on the list. It will be a few minutes," she peeks at the small pager to be sure it has not alerted her.

They use the time to catch up and chat about their recent vacation to Aruba. When the monitor lights up, Christine sprints to the hostess stand ahead of them.

"Hello, our device lit up, so I guess our table is ready," she says, holding it up to show her. "I need somewhere with a little privacy, please. If we have to wait longer, we can."

The girl studies the computer screen in front of her and smiles at Christine. "I have seating for you near the fireplace, it's secluded."

"Thank you so much," she responds, as she waves them over.

Christine orders a glass of wine for herself, and beer for Michael and Maddie, and they continue to make small talk until dinner arrives. Once finished, Christine is ready to reveal her idea to them.

"So, you remember how Frank and I agreed to help Jonathan Hoyt with future disaster prevention using the exile program, right?"

"Mom, I think it's great, making the world better, and all that kind of stuff," says Michael.

"Yeah, so do I," says Maddie.

"Well, I have a project in mind, and it requires your expertise, Maddie."

"Me? Really? How exciting!" Maddie claps her hands together once and leans closer to the table, all her attention focused on Christine.

"Whoa, you need Maddie's input, Mom? But she's in IT."

"I understand that Michael, it's not as if anyone is asking her to transport anywhere. I could use her technical guidance to get someone arrested."

"What? Oh, I don't know about that, Christine," Maddie says, the disappointment clear in her expression. "That might make me an accessory to whatever law they break." She leans back in the booth, her excitement from a moment ago gone.

"No Maddie, I would never ask you to be an actual part of anything illegal. We just need some advice with setting her on the correct path. She is a novice at IT, so we have no idea where to start."

"This sounds a little crazy mom, who is it, and why are you caught up in this?"

Christine tells them about her encounter with Hannah, the abuse, Chad's involvement in the crime ring, and her plan to exile her. After recounting her meeting with Frank and Jonathan Hoyt, she stops talking and glances between them, waiting for their reaction.

"What a creep. That sucks for that poor lady. I'll help you, no worries," says Maddie as she bites into her dessert.

"Hang on a minute. This guy sounds like a class A asshole. I don't think you two should get involved in this," Michael states. "Plus, he's LAPD. He has a certain amount of power. I'm not saying he should, but that's how it is."

"So, you're suggesting because he is an idiot and a cop, he gets a pass? No way, Michael. I make my own decisions, and I want to help," says Maddie, folding her arms across her chest and twisting to face him.

"Okay, time out. I didn't mean to cause an argument between you two. Maybe Michael is right. I should not have involved you Maddie, I'll think of another strategy," says Christine, not wanting to press the issue with them.

"Uh, no you won't. I already said I would help, and I want to," says Maddie, still staring at Michael, braced and daring him to challenge her again.

He holds his hands up in surrender. "I'm not trying to tell you two what to do. Believe me, I get there is no use in me doing that. And Maddie, I'm only concerned about your and my mom's safety, that's all. But Mom, I trust your judgement, and I feel Frank and Ethan always have your back. My first reaction was just that the dude is trouble. He won't ever find out either of you had anything to do with it, right?"

"I realize you worry Michael, but no, he will never get access to the information. Hoyt can cover me. And I like Malcolm, Michael. Hannah would be safe with him. Besides, Ethan trusts him, and he spent seven months camping with him in medieval England. If you don't know someone after that, then I can't imagine when you would. And honestly, I'm not looking to hold her hand through this process. I plan to transport her back and that's it."

"Excellent fact about Ethan trusting him. But Mom, seriously, you are all about handholding. It's what you do with everyone and everything," he says laughing.

"Okay smarty, I was only trying to make a point is all."

Maddie grins and snuggles closer to Michael, the squabble forgotten.

"I'd like to move on this as quickly as possible, Maddie. I don't guess Hannah has much time to waste. Tomorrow is Saturday, do you two have any plans? If she is available, can you be there?"

"Sure, we aren't busy until six o'clock," says Maddie.

"Great, thank you. I'll call her when we leave and see if she is free. I'll shoot you a confirmation or cancellation, either way."

They finish their dessert in good spirits, and before they say goodnight Christine promises again to contact them as soon as she hears from Hannah. She dictates a message to her when she settles into the car.

Hi Hannah. Can we meet tomorrow afternoon sometime? I have something to discuss with you. Let me know ASAP.

It's still early when Christine gets home, so she draws a hot bath. She rests her head on the edge of the tub while she soaks in the steaming water. She closes her eyes, thinking about her upcoming girl's weekend with Annabelle, and smiles to herself. In two weeks, they have plans to attend a concert and spa day, and she is looking forward to it more than anything she has done in months. Before Annabelle, she had not had a best friend since junior high school. When they met in 1867, they only had each other to talk to. Only they knew where they were from, who they really were. Initially, Annabelle irritated Christine. But to be fair, almost everyone did at that stage. She learned to lean on Annabelle for support and came to trust her, and by the time the system glitch sent Christine to England, she trusted Annabelle with her life.

Her phone signal chimes softly in her ear, tearing her from her thoughts. It's Hannah, so she taps the chip in her earlobe to accept the call.

"Hi Hannah."

"Christine, I got your message. Chad is at work, so I'm free to talk."

"Good, can we get together tomorrow?"

"I think so, Chad is golfing with his friends and has a ten o'clock tee time. I can see you after he leaves. Are you going to help me?"

"Not over the phone, Hannah. We can discuss it in person."

"Okay, where do you want to meet?"

"Let's plan on my house at eleven o'clock so we don't worry about anyone eavesdropping on our conversation. I'll send you my address."

"Sounds good. I'll be there. And Christine, thank you. Just. . .thank you."

"Right. No reason to thank me yet, I've done nothing. We're only talking."

"I know, but you've already helped more than most people would."

She disconnects the call and steps out of the bath, grabbing a towel from the cabinet. "I guess this is happening," she mutters to herself, not at all convinced it is one of her best decisions.

* * *

Christine jumps when the doorbell rings, which causes the dog to bark furiously. The house is so quiet with Michael not living there; she thinks she will never grow accustomed to being alone in it. A moment later she hears the beep of the door pad as someone punches the access code in and realizes it must be Michael and Maddie. Max leaps from the couch and rushes them as soon as they enter, moving between them, jumping and whining to get their attention.

"Hi, you two. I guess Max misses you," she says laughing.

"Hey buddy," Michael picks the dog up, scratching behind his ears.

"Hannah isn't here yet, but should arrive any time."

The three of them sit in the family room and chat about work and a couple of Michael's friends when Max barks again. He hops off the couch and darts to the entry, running circles in place when he gets there.

"That's got to be her," says Christine, as the doorbell chimes. She opens it to Hannah, who looks tired and nervous.

"Hi Hannah, come on in," she says, holding the door open.

She walks in, and her gaze immediately lands on Michael and Maddie. She stops in her tracks, eyes darting between them, then back to Christine.

"Hannah, this is my son Michael and his girlfriend Maddie. I asked them here because Maddie agreed to help."

"You said nothing about anyone else involved in this. This was a mistake. I have to leave." She spins toward the door and takes a step before Christine stops her.

"Hannah, please don't go," she says, putting her hand on her arm. "You can trust us. We need Maddie's skills. She works as an IT specialist at the CCEA. She has just as much to lose by assisting you."

Maddie stands and goes to Hannah, extending her palm. "Hi Hannah, I'd like to help you if you'll let me."

Hannah gazes at Maddie's hand, finally taking it in hers. She steps to the chair across from them, sitting on the edge of it nervously.

"Hannah, I can exile you if you still wish to go through with this. But I caution you to be absolutely positive this is what you want, because once you commit to it, I cannot reverse what we put in motion. Once you cross that threshold, it seals your fate. I don't mean to sound melodramatic, but I need to be certain you understand this is a permanent decision. Once the courts banish you to the past, you will remain there for the rest of your life. You will be no different from every other inmate in the program."

"I realize that, and I am going through with this." She lifts the hem of her blouse to reveal deep purple bruising on her side.

Maddie gasps at the sight of it and Michael turns away, shaking his head.

"He did this after I met you at Giraldo's. He came home for his dinner break early, and when I wasn't there, he went ballistic. I forgot to take my phone, so he couldn't reach me. He could smell that I'd had wine and convinced himself I was out with another man. So, he 'taught me a lesson' and then carried on with his night and finished his shift, as if nothing happened."

Tears fall down her cheeks, and she lowers her eyes, ashamed to meet their stare.

"I can work this out, Hannah, trust me. I'll teach you how to hack into a prohibited government system. That is the easiest and quickest way to ensure they arrest and convict you of a cyber-crime," says Maddie.

"I have little experience with computers. Chad never wanted me to have a proper job, and I dropped out of my first year in college when I met him. I only know the basic stuff you learn in school."

"That's a solid start. I can walk you through it and then create a step by step written manual. It will be super easy for you."

She smiles at Maddie and glances over at Michael.

"I'm here for a reason, Hannah. I work in prisoner control at the CCEA. We will make sure you wind up on my unit to keep you safe. I trust the

Correctional Officers I serve with and I will be there, too. They house all prisoners in separate cells, but with you on my floor it means an added safeguard. Plus, I can relay messages to you from my mom, so it provides a means of communication."

"Hannah, we will get you away from him, somewhere you'll be safe, and he can never hurt you again. I give you my word," says Christine.

"Okay, thank you. Thank you all for what you're doing. I don't know where I'd end up without your support."

Christine sighs. "I have an idea where you'd end up, and it's not good. Let's get to work. We should start this as fast as possible."

ELEVEN

Piedmont, Oklahoma 1867

Once the snow melts, production on Malcom's house resumes. Malcolm spends a full day building a four-poster bed and gathers straw and feathers for a mattress. When he constructs a table with chairs and a simple dresser, his confidence soars. He is not convinced installing greased paper for the windows is a good idea; it seems inefficient, but John insists it works. Glass is far too expensive and limited for him to access, and the paper provides a diffused light source and helps prevent insects and small animals from breaching the cabin.

He knows flies and fleas will invade in the summer, but he decides to deal with that nuisance when it gets there. He remembers his mother using rosemary to repel fleas when he was a child, so he makes a mental note to search for that before the weather is too hot.

Malcolm's routine now is to ride to town alone twice a week to sell meat and fur hides for supplies he lacks. He stockpiles dried beans, rice, oatmeal, coffee, salt, sugar, flour, candles, and molasses. He smokes and salts pork, turkey, and deer, enough to last the winter. He is not a fan of elk, so he trades away most of it. The township is not large, but it provides him the chance to interact with new people, which is a welcome distraction.

He glances over at the jail as he passes, vowing never to see the inside. He has seen no law enforcement here, but assumes there is a marshal somewhere if there's a cell. The general store is modest and carries only basic supplies and feed. The interior is so small they stack overflow goods in barrels outside near water troughs where horse-drawn carts are parked, and children run between them, giggling and chasing each other. There is only one street through the center of Piedmont comprised of a thick layer of mud in this winter weather. He imagines in the summer months it must be as dry as a dust bowl here. But it's a quaint little town and has everything he requires.

As they near the end of the year, they complete the cabin, and Malcolm moves into his new home. His first night there he finds it comfortable and stays warm with the fire burning around the clock, but he is lonely. He stands in the doorway where he has a view of John's ranch from his front porch. It's a constant reminder John is there, and he still feels terrible about the state of their friendship.

Most days he dedicates his time to improving his home in any way he can just to pass the hours. After a week of living alone, he walks to John's asking if he needs an extra hand with chores. John tells him he will manage, slamming the door in his face. Malcolm tries the same tactic several times, and the result is always the same. John refuses to talk to him.

One day, as Malcolm is tending to the animals, a stray dog shows up at the ranch. The mutt becomes his only company, besides his trips into town. He names the mongrel Buddy, and the hound follows him everywhere. Buddy is a reliable early warning system; he lets Malcolm know when coyotes are sniffing around the livestock.

By week two, the loneliness is too much for Malcolm to bear and he decides he needs interaction with other people. He stops by the saloon as Christine asked him to. The prisoner she transported here is named Marcus Simpson. He is a young guy who was over-confident, a dangerous disposition when in exile. Although he abandoned her here when he realized she was stranded, she still wanted Malcolm to look in on him. Even though he disagrees with her compassionate attitude toward Marcus, he gave Christine his word. So he intends to follow through as promised. He scans the room for someone that fits Marcus's description, but finds no one. Thirty minutes later, he has no trouble spotting him as he saunters in. Something about his manner gives him away immediately. He is probably going for swagger, but he cannot pull it off and it just comes across as immature arrogance as he strolls in acting as if he owns the place. Malcolm didn't like Marcus before he met him, and his first impression has only solidified that initial opinion. He follows his path through the tavern, thinking about how he refused to leave Christine any water when he ditched her. That was a crap thing to do, and it tells Malcolm all he needs to know about him.

He cannot help rolling his eyes as he watches Marcus ramble up to the bartender. He cannot be any older than twenty-five or twenty-six, but acts as if he is in charge of everyone in the saloon. He sits on the stool next to him and Malcolm doesn't even attempt to mask his disgust and he looks him up and down. Not surprisingly, when Malcolm tells him Christine asked him to check on him, he insists he needs no advice and does not understand why she is concerned. Which is fine with Malcolm. He thinks Marcus is a smug asshole and is glad to be done with him. He did what he pledged to do, which is look in on him and offer a helping hand if needed. When Marcus laughs at him, unable to suppress his inflated opinion of himself, Malcolm has had enough, and orders him to bugger off. He is almost sorry for the poor, misguided youth. Almost. He's too naïve to realize that fate has a way of screwing with us at the most inconvenient times, and he wishes he could be there to witness it when life slaps him down a peg or two.

He soon forgets about Marcus and returns to work on his modest ranch, trying to prepare his garden for spring, but the ground is as hard as concrete, and requires heavy plowing. Every time it rains, he devotes hours to tilling the earth while it is soft, and to trap the moisture underneath. He catches rainwater in a barrel for the animals and continues to haul creek water home for drinking and cooking. He filters and boils it well, knowing his body cannot tolerate it the same way people born into this era can. Because he is not immune to the bacteria, he wants to take no chance of contracting dysentery or anything else that could make him sick. Using his supply of antibiotics for an illness he can avoid by taking sanitary precautions would be foolish.

He worries about the outdoor loo and spreading germs and disease that way, especially with no real soap or running water. By the point he completes the outhouse, he has yet to master adapting to the bathroom facilities. During inclement weather, it is horrible, at best. He can only imagine what will happen when it gets warmer and the pest population increases.

When they started on the house, John suggested Malcolm build a dugout in the side of a little hill. He did not think of that, unaccustomed to survival on the plains, and he feels more secure knowing he has somewhere to go in case a tornado or dust storm strikes. Both of which John assures him happen here with regularity. Tornadoes terrify him, and he does not want to experience one without a safeguard in place. Not that dusters are on his bucket list either. This land is unrelenting, and anything he can do to make it more bearable, he approaches with enthusiasm. He lines the shelter with logs to prevent the dirt from brushing off, and he constructs a removable door of more wood, grass, and mud. John chose the spot for the cellar, dug into the hillside in the back of the cabin, and they built the home in front of the bluff to provide some protection from the wind. He creates the structure to hold three people and a few days supplies, although he does not know why. Chances are, he and Buddy will be the only two ever inside it.

Life goes on this way for a month. He continues improvements on the house, trading meat to townspeople for other supplies, and spending nights in front of the fire with his dog. He finds a copy of *Walden; or, Life in the Woods* by Henry David Thoreau at the general store in town and immerses himself in it. It is not exactly standard British literature, but he relates to the author's circumstances, existing in solitude as he is now. He comes to think of his new reality as a pioneer as his own 'experiment in simple living', just like Thoreau.

Then one morning, as he tills the soil after a rainstorm, he watches John approach the ranch. Wiping the sweat from his forehead, he rests on the handle of the iron rake.

"Cheers, mate," he calls out, waving at John.

"I am going on a hunt tomorrow and came to see if you want to join me."

"Hot damn! You know I will, friend!"

And just like that, they restore their friendship. Or at least they are on the right path to repair it. He spends the rest of the afternoon gardening in the best state of mind he has been in for weeks.

The following morning, they are off early on the hunting trip. Malcolm doesn't dare ask John what prompted his change of heart, not wanting to jinx his good fortune. He smiles as Buddy and John's dog yelp and run in circles at their feet, excited to go with them. They ride in silence to the river, but Malcolm does not mind the quietude. He is content with just having the company.

They dismount near a cluster of trees, tying the horses there. As they unpack their rifles Buddy growls and the fur on his back stands on end. Malcolm looks toward the water but sees nothing. John's dog bares his teeth and emits a low rumble. John raises his rifle, staring in the same direction. Malcolm continues to stare at the river when a flash of something moves in the grass. John aims his gun and fires, then shifts to the left quickly. At first, he thinks John has bagged an animal.

But a moment later he understands what is happening as an arrow lands with a dull thud where John stood only a second before. Malcolm stands frozen in place, watching it reverberate in the ground. Before he can react, an Indian emerges from the tall grass, another weapon positioned in the quiver. It is the same native he saw his first day here. The one who spared his life as he slept against the boulder, defenseless. When John lifts his rifle in the Indian's direction, Malcolm does not think, he just reacts. He crosses in front of John, preventing him from firing. But John moves around him. The two men stand ready to fire at each other. Malcolm shifts to block John's line of sight again, and remains rooted between them, stunned into silence. He knows he cannot let John shoot him. The Indian allowed him to live, and now it is his turn to repay that debt. He holds Malcolm's gaze for a brief minute before looking back to John, then lowers his bow and retreats backwards into the reeds, hidden from view. A moment afterward they hear his horse galloping away and Malcolm follows John to the river's edge where John searches to make sure there are no others.

"Why were you trying to shoot him?"

"Because he would scalp us and leave us for dead if he had the chance."

"You don't know that, John!"

"I do. There is more than one type of savage in these parts. He was probably Cherokee. Some are friendly, but I'm not taking any chances. It's kill or be killed here, Malcolm."

"Savages? You're not serious, John. You fired at him first. He was only defending himself. You can't predict what he would have done, maybe nothing. This isn't right. That would have been murder and I'll be no part of it," Malcolm says.

"You weren't going to shoot him, I was. But you need to be sure not to hesitate again. You see a savage, you open fire. The sooner you learn that, the longer you'll stay alive here. There is no time to waste, unless you want ten more of his friends here with rifles," says John, ignoring Malcolm's rage.

The revulsion settles in Malcolm's stomach. He does not tell John he has seen the native before, he is uncertain how he would react to that, and they have only returned to speaking terms today. He understands this is what survival means in this untamed era, this is the existence John and everyone else here tolerates as normal. But to him, it is barbaric and unjust, and he refuses to accept it. That man did nothing before John shot at him, and that he is American Indian does not rationalize an unprovoked attack on him. He has experienced firsthand the native is not hostile. But what if he were? Would Malcolm have the nerve to execute another human being? Self-preservation is the strongest instinct man has, but he knows he would still hesitate to take another's life.

In that moment, he understands exactly how far out of his element he is in this timeline. Until now, he was complacent. He went along, this lifestyle inconvenient, but not intolerable. However, this experience made him realize the changes he must make to blend in here, and it shakes him to his core. He longs for the naivete he had when he arrived here, but that point has long since passed.

Over the next few days Malcolm puts the incident at the river behind him as best he can, although he vows to never forget it. He realizes the day will surely come when he must defend himself and his home, as this era is not without hostiles and outlaws. Some Indians here are a threat, that is a fact. However, he also worries about all the other ways this place might take him down. Tornadoes, lightning strikes, dust storms, insect swarms, other emigrants, starvation, injury, grass fires, snakes, the possibilities go on and on. So, he focuses on doing as much as possible to minimize the risk from the lengthy list of things that could harm him. Eventually, his worry about the native fades and he falls back into his routine, and life returns to normal, such as it was.

Until early one morning, as the snow melts and the promise of spring is around the corner, something astonishing comes with a knock at his door. A turn of events that will transform everything and lead him on a path he could never have imagined.

TWELVE

Los Angeles, California 2070

The group gathers around the dining table, watching Maddie as her fingers fly across the keyboard. She stops typing and takes a deep breath.

"Okay, this should do it. I figured out how to get into the site. I will create a step-by-step instruction manual of how to break into the Department of Energy. Not a branch of government that would land you in a federal prison or earn you a death-sentence, but important enough to convict and exile you. I can capture screen shots of the process for you too. Once you have access, burn the guidebook. I'll wipe my history and remove it from my memory, but you cannot leave those directions behind. I'll make a list of websites for you to log onto, so your search record shows you were there. They are black web sites that talk about how to hack and stuff like that. The CCEA wants to know how you infiltrated a secured federal website. They need to prove you did this, even when they catch you in the act," says Maddie, stretching her arms over her head.

"I understand," says Hannah.

"Let me get this together for you. We'll do a test run and take it right up to the point of entry. That way I can answer questions and support you if you become stuck on something. I'll have it complete for your practice round. Are you available tomorrow afternoon?" asks Maddie, looking at the others around the table.

"Chad goes into work at two o'clock, he works swing shift for the next week, covering a vacation shortage. So, I am free after that. But he'll be home for his dinner break, so I need to be there by seven o'clock."

"Why don't we reconvene here at three o'clock then? Maddie, how long do you think it will take for a practice run?" asks Christine.

"A couple of hours tops, and that includes any obstacles we may encounter."

"Okay, that should work then. I will be here tomorrow. Thank you again, all of you," says Hannah.

"Hannah, go home and sleep on this tonight. No one would blame you if you changed your mind. I will take you to confront Chad's supervisors, to have him arrested if you decide to do that instead. This is a major life transformation. I mean major. I don't want to discourage you, but you're probably nowhere near prepared for this. This isn't some fairy tale romantic jaunt back in time, like some fantasy movie. Do not make this decision lightly," says Christine.

"I know what I'm getting into."

"No, you really don't Hannah. I plan to post you to 1867, in Piedmont, Oklahoma. There is a man there, his name is Malcolm Aldred. I met him while in England. I trust him and he will help you adjust to life there and keep an eye out for you. It won't be an easy transformation, but having an ally there means all the difference. And because I was there for six months, I can provide you with lots of information on the era."

"All right, I will go online after Chad leaves for work and assemble as much material as possible on the area."

"No, don't do that. The CCEA will dissect your search history as part of their investigation once you're arrested, and we cannot have them find any reference to Oklahoma. If they do, that will prevent you from being exiled there. Besides, remember, it is not Piedmont in 1867, it's only a settled area near where the modern-day city is founded a couple of decades later. And it's in the middle of Indian Territory. But I'll tell you everything you need to know," says Christine.

"Understood. I'd better take off. I don't want Chad to find out I was out today."

Christine walks her to the door, and it surprises her when Hannah turns to hug her before leaving.

"I hope you realize what you're doing," she mumbles after Hannah as she watches her disappear into her car.

The following afternoon they assemble in Christine's dining room, ready for Hannah to try her skill at accessing the government site. Maddie reviews the printed instructions with her, and Hannah boots up her laptop. Her hands quiver slightly as she types in her password. She takes a deep breath and glances at Maddie before pulling up the website.

"You can do this, Hannah. I'm right here in case you need me. Remember, this is only a trial run and I'm here if you have questions. This will alert no one at the Department of Energy or the CCEA. Until you actually hack into their system, you are just another person logged onto their public site. Breathe and do exactly what your instructions say."

Hannah looks at the sheets of paper laid out on the table. She works on the laptop for thirty minutes, and Maddie nods every so often as she successfully completes the phases. Once she finishes everything except the paragraph typed in red, the last step, she stops typing. She exhales slowly and studies Maddie. Maddie grins and holds her hand up for a high five.

Hannah smiles and slaps Maddie's palm. "I did it!"

"You did very well. You've got this."

"Christine, I'm doing it tomorrow, while Chad is working. Is that too soon? I prefer to get it over with before I change my mind."

"I need you to think about this again tonight, Hannah. If you have even the slightest bit of uncertainty, you should not move forward. I cannot stress enough to you that this is permanent. Once you enter that website, this process is a fast-moving train I cannot stop."

"I know. I don't have any doubts, just scared. I guess that's normal, huh? But I'm going through with this. I will send you a text the minute it's done, to confirm."

"No texting. No communication from this point forward. I want nothing to trace back to us. In fact, give Maddie your phone password and she'll delete the other texts I sent you, and do the same for mine. She can manage that from the carrier website. Let's assume you carry on with this tomorrow as planned. If for whatever reason this doesn't happen, then notify me."

"All right. Thank you all. Michael, I will see you in a month or so. After my trial."

Hannah leaves without another word, and the others remain at the table.

Christine looks from Maddie to Michael. She hates that this involves them. But it will require all of them to pull this off and not get caught by the CCEA. Or worse yet, by Chad.

* * *

Hannah's hands shake as she sets the supplies on the dining room table. The laptop is open and booted up; the instructions lying next to the matches. She wants everything ready so she can move quickly, once finished. She plays it over in her mind one more time. Follow the directions on the cheat sheet, take the papers to the sink and burn them. Rinse the ashes down, then use a towel to dry the basin. Unlock the front door, sit on the couch, and wait for them to come. She orders wine from the ChefAid and drinks straight from the bottle. She may not get the chance to wash a glass, and Chad does not like dirty dishes left undone.

Hang on a minute. "Screw him", she mutters to herself, laughing. This is her home too, and if she uses *all* the glasses, then so what? The rebellion feels reckless but empowering as she reaches for their best wine goblets and pours one to the brim. Hannah leans against the counter, sipping the drink as her pent-up anger boils to the surface. She loathes her husband for forcing her to do what she is about to. Exile is an extreme measure, but she has no other choice. No thanks to him. This will push him into such a rage when he finds out what she has done. The thought makes her chuckle again, the power almost consuming her. Something inside her comes alive with the prospect of freedom, the knowledge she no longer answers to him after today. She has the ChefAid prepare her lunch, and what she does not eat, she tosses over the side of the table. Before she can stop herself, her sneakers grind the food into the stone. She despises the color of this flooring. Chad selected it, and it reminds her of dirty dishwater.

She punches the computer panel on the stainless-steel monstrosity, ordering more red wine, then kicks the appliance. She detests it even more than the floor. She strolls through the kitchen clutching a bottle in each hand, alternating between swigging the liquid and pouring it on the tile, the upholstered chairs, and counters, knowing it will destroy them.

Next, she moves to the living room where she splashes it on the cream-colored couch, the same sofa Chad is always bitching to her to keep pristine. The image of the last time she sat on it flashes before her. She dropped a piece of popcorn on it, one single kernel of unbuttered popcorn. He became unglued, yelling she could do nothing right. He called her a slob who only wanted to ruin the expensive things his money paid for. The memory makes her stomach twist. She drains the remaining wine over the furniture, but not before taking a final gulp, fantasizing about what she would say to him if he were here.

"Sorry Chad, but I'm not sure this stain is coming out," she says out loud, giggling to herself as she flings the empty bottle over her shoulder.

After trashing the sofa, she moves on to his closet with a newfound sense of fearlessness. She tears clothing from the hangers, hurling them onto the bed in a rage where she spends a while cutting them to bits, the alcohol buzz spurring her on. She laughs when she sees the shreds of material strewn across the mattress, on the floor, even hanging from the headboard. Now this is how you go out, she thinks, tossing a handful of cloth scraps into the air.

After an hour the exertion drains her, the adrenaline crash pulling her back to reality. She wanders to the kitchen, numb, before a state of shock overtakes her as she inspects the damage. Chad will be livid when he discovers this. Thinking about it makes her smirk, and she cannot stop the feeling of satisfaction spreading over her.

She sits at the table and types, referencing the instructions. Half an hour later, she stares at the laptop and hesitates. Her fingers tremble as they hover over the keyboard. She doesn't dare use the voice activation setting as she normally would. Maddie told her they could retrieve the recording to play in court, and she knows her speech will give away her fear. She can't chance that happening. This must go as planned. The courts cannot have any doubt she did this deliberately and with malice, so they assign her to the exile program. Hannah inhales sharply and seals her destiny with the final keystrokes. Once she finishes, she leans back in the chair, a fresh drink in her hand, and waits. It does not take long, maybe forty-five seconds at most, until her screen seizes, just as Maddie said it would.

This device and all records contained in it are now the property of, and under the jurisdiction of the CCEA, by the authority of the United States government. Do not attempt to reboot the system. Tampering with a seized device will cause immediate action, up to and including termination.

There is no turning back after this. It's over.

She takes the printout to the basin and touches a match to the corner, rinsing the ashes down the drain and drying the sink. Then she unlocks the front door and rests on the stained couch to stand by for the agents. The bright red stain of the wine spreads out behind her like some macabre murder scene. She stretches her arms along the top of the sofa, palms up, both hands in plain sight. Just as Chad taught her to do if ever confronted by law enforcement. No reason to provoke them into using their tasers or shooting her.

A moment afterward she hears the sirens. She grins as she considers the responding officer may be someone she knows. Wouldn't that be the coup de grâce? Chad would die of embarrassment. The CCEA agents enter the residence, guns drawn, at the same time the LAPD does. Typical overkill. Hannah offers no resistance. A minute later Chad races across the threshold, stopping short as he surveys the scene before him. He stares beyond her to the kitchen, and his eyes widen at the sight of it. He must have heard their address on the scanner—every cop's nightmare. Well, the joke's on you, honey. Her smile never leaves her face as she follows his gaze.

"What have you done? I'll kill you, you bitch!" Chad screams, as an agent who looks vaguely familiar snaps the cuffs on her. Two LAPD officers hold him back as he struggles to get to her.

She peers around her home one last time, ignoring the surrounding chaos. It is difficult for her to grasp that at thirty-one years old, she has committed herself to live the rest of her existence in the very distant past. The reality of it sends a fresh tremor of fear and dread through her. All because she allowed the moron shrieking at her to gain control of her life. Never again, she vows to herself, as the agent leads her from the house that has been nothing more than an upscale prison to her for all these years. Never again.

* * *

Hannah has not been paying much attention to her own court case. She is struggling to muster enough enthusiasm to be troubled. She spends most of her days in session daydreaming about what liberation from her abusive husband will be like, numb to the surrounding proceedings. Hannah realizes she should feel *something*, and that people expect her to be more despondent. She is going through a traumatic, life-altering experience, after all. But despite anyone's opinion of her, she cannot invoke the emotion. She should be falling apart. She has evidence to take down a crime ring run by LAPD officers who she is certain want her out of the picture. She is on trial for a cyber-crime and about to be sentenced to live the remainder of her existence in the 1800s. All her trust has been placed in a woman she really knows little about. She should be a mess. But she isn't. She has more control of her future and her emotions than she has had in the past ten years. Being arrested and incarcerated has given her the first sense of freedom she has had since marrying Chad.

The attorney insists she plead not guilty, but she is not getting out of this, so she goes along without a fight. The more legitimate her defense is, the less anyone will suspect she planned this. They will convict her, she is sure of it, and that is all she cares about. Most days she is bored while in court and doodles on the pad of paper her lawyer gave her to take notes on. Chad is in the courtroom every day and whenever she twists to look at him, he glares at her. His face flares red with indignation, but she always smiles at him in response, only because she realizes it further confuses and enrages him. She is powerful and protected while out of his reach. He has tried several times to speak to her via the inmate video visiting system, but she has refused each request.

The attorney nudges her, compelling her to focus on what the judge is saying. She stares back at him blankly, hoping he will recap what she missed while distracted.

He leans over to her, cupping his hand over his mouth for privacy. "He wants to know if you wish to grant your husband a no-fault dissolution before they assign you to the exile program," he whispers to her.

"Oh. Yes, absolutely. I want nothing to do with him," she replies, leaning in closer to him.

"Yes, your honor, my client will concede to a no-contest termination of the marriage."

Chad springs from his seat. "No!" he shouts. "I am not giving her a divorce. I forbid her to go into exile for sentencing." Spittle flies from his mouth as he yells, so incensed he cannot control himself. The judge looks outraged at Chad's outburst. Hannah's numbness is replaced with fear for a brief moment as old anxieties and self-doubt rise to the surface. She faces forward and tamps down the uncertainty, forcing herself to concentrate on breathing.

"Sergeant Cole, sit down immediately before I direct the bailiff to remove you from this courtroom—permanently! You have no choice in this, and your opinion is not relative to this case. This court remands Mrs. Cole to the CCEA for incarceration to the time travel exile register, and the dissolution of your marriage stands. Control yourself or I will hold you in contempt and call your commanding officer to recommend they suspend you. That will be all ladies and gentlemen. Thank you for your time and service to the Los Angeles County Superior Court. This matter is closed, and I hereby order the defendant remanded to the custody of the CCEA to carry out the court's sentence."

Her apprehension gone, Hannah grins widely at her lawyer, who shakes his head. She can tell he thinks she is ten minutes away from a complete mental breakdown. He tries to get her medically released by telling the court she cannot grasp the repercussions of her acts. She does not blame him for trying. That's his job. But she puts the kibosh on that when she interrupts him to inform the judge she is fully aware of her actions and the consequences. Then she spins around in her chair to lock eyes with Chad. His face twists into a mask of rage, and she recognizes this as the moment he understands she is leaving him the only safe way she can. And it infuriates him beyond belief. He rises, glowering at her before he storms out of the courthouse. The doors slam behind him, causing her to flinch, but she recovers quickly. It serves no purpose to feed the fury in him, but after years at the hands of his abuse, she cannot help but gloat as she wins back a tiny fragment of control. And it felt every bit as good as she imagined it would.

THIRTEEN

Los Angeles, California 2071 / Piedmont, Oklahoma 1868

Today is the day Christine leaves for Piedmont to visit Malcolm and John, to tell them about Hannah, and when to expect her. She is uncertain how John will react to seeing her again, but she has no choice, she needs to talk to Malcolm. Walking into the transport area, Frank is waiting for her, pacing with a furrowed brow.

"Ready to break the law, compromise our retirement and potentially sacrifice our freedom?" he asks, as he hands her a mouth guard and nods his head toward the jump room.

"Stop Frank, please. I'm already nervous, I don't need you to add to that. Turn around while I change clothes."

Frank turns, squeezing his eyes shut. She removes a pioneer style dress out of her backpack, one she purchased online from a civil war reenactment company. It was the best she could do on such short notice. Wardrobe only issues costumes to transporters when they exile a prisoner, and she cannot travel to 1868, Oklahoma, in her street clothes or uniform. And she also can't take the chance of discovery by changing in the locker room.

"Okay, you can swing around, I'm dressed."

She secures her transponder in the dress's waistband, where she cut out a small pocket to hold it. She learned to sew when she was in Piedmont, never imagining it would be useful after leaving there. Before then, she had never threaded a needle. Why would she? No one in 2071 sews anymore unless you work in a factory producing clothing. And even then, they automate most of that. Frank snaps his fingers in front of her face, pulling her back to the present.

"Did you hear anything I said?"

"Sorry, no."

He holds out a women's wristwatch. "Put this with your transponder. Remember, Hoyt said in and out within four hours, Christine. Don't stay longer than you have to."

She turns the watch over in her palm, inspecting it. "Where on earth did you pick up a timepiece? I haven't seen one since I was a kid in my mom's jewelry box."

"It was Linda's grandmothers. She dug it out for you. I guessed it would be less conspicuous than anything else you could take with you. You know your cell chip won't operate in that timeline, so you need to track time somehow. And really, does it matter where I got it? Watch the clock, that's the point. I swear you focus on everything but the important things sometime."

"Oh, can it, Frank. I was just curious. I should have known it was your wife. You wouldn't have thought to bring me one," she says, rolling her eyes at him jokingly.

He curls his lip at her as she moves to leave, then touches her shoulder. She twists to confront him, and he surprises her when he pulls her into an embrace.

"Be careful, Christine. Don't take any chances, if it's not safe, transport home."

She stares at him for a moment before she smiles and plants a kiss on his cheek.

"Honestly, Frank, you are more drama than a teenaged girl. I'll be fine. I'll be back here before my four hours are up, I promise."

He straps her in the pod, and it's his turn to roll his eyes as she blows him a kiss goodbye.

* * *

Christine wakes up in the grove of walnut trees, just as she did almost a year ago. Panic sweeps over her in a flash at the memory of it, so she turns her transponder on to be sure it is operational. The device boots on, and she sighs with relief.

She sits against a tree, waiting for the vertigo to subside and her head to clear more. Transporting is perpetually like this. It takes a huge toll on your system, resembling jetlag on steroids. But she's grown accustomed to it, and ten minutes later she feels well enough to start the trek to John's land. She pauses at the river and dips her hand in for a drink, careful to sip just a small amount to quench her dry throat, unwilling to take a chance with bacteria. A pouch of emergency water would be convenient, and she makes a mental note to herself to bring one on her next trip.

She squints against the sun as she inspects her surroundings, marveling at the wildflowers blooming in the prairie grass. She forgot how beautiful this place was. The early spring flowers paint a canvas of yellow, purple, and orange for as far as she can see. She did not realize how much she missed the serenity here until now. The bird songs are the only sound she hears.

Christine inhales deeply and jogs in the ranch's direction in a slow, steady stride, lost in thought for a while before she checks the watch. Only a little over three hours remain before she needs to transport home. Picking up her pace, she finds her rhythm quickly. It is difficult to jog at a good speed with the grass so high, but she makes it to the final bluff before John's place in decent time. As she crests the hill, she halts in her tracks. There is a structure about a half mile from John's homestead. That is new since she was last here. She is not sure why this shocks her—people claim land and build here often. There are homes scattered all over from here to town. But she did not expect John to have a neighbor this close. He likes to keep to himself, so it surprises her he would tolerate someone building so near to him. She moves further away from the unknown house, maintaining a straight line to John's. She catches her breath as she approaches the back of the ranch, bent over, hands on her knees. It does not take the dog long to know she is there, and he tears around the side of the barn, ready to protect his property. He stops short, whining when he sees her, then crouch crawls toward her, tail wagging. She bends down and holds her palm out. He sniffs it and jumps to her, licking her face as he recognizes her scent.

"Hey puppy, I missed you too," she says, scratching him behind the ears and laughing. "C'mon boy, let's go see John." She pats her side, and the hound follows.

She steps onto the porch, smooths the waistband of her dress, and knocks. The dog sits beside her, panting and whining for more attention, tail still wiggling wildly.

John swings the door open wide. He stands there for a few seconds before it registers with him who he is looking at. His rifle slides through his grasp, the butt hitting the floor with a thud.

"Maybe you should steady that gun before you drop it completely and accidentally shoot one of us, John?" she says smiling.

He looks down at the weapon as if he only now realizes he is holding it, leaning it against the wall. His mouth hangs open, although he has not uttered a word.

"May I come in?"

"Christine, I. . .I'm sorry. I'm just stunned to see you. Please come in." He embraces her tightly before releasing her and backing into the cabin.

"I realize it must be a shock for me to show up unannounced like this, and I apologize for that. There was no way to send you an advance message."

"Don't be silly, I'm delighted you're here, just surprised is all. Come and sit down. Do you want coffee?"

"No, I'll pass, I was never a fan of the sludge you all call coffee here," she says grinning.

"How, why are you here? I don't mean to say I'm not happy you are, just confused."

"I have a friend of mine here, Malcolm Aldred. I need to speak to him, it's urgent I find him and relay some information to him. I only have a few hours before I must leave again. Has Malcolm contacted you? I asked him to, I hoped you would help him settle in and acclimate to the lifestyle here."

"Yes, he came to see me when he got here."

"Oh, that's wonderful news. Do you know where he is?"

"I do. I can take you to him. How did you get here, Christine? I didn't see a horse. Did you ride the stagecoach to town and walk here?"

"It's a long story, John. And I apologize I don't have the time to tell you about it now."

"It always is with you, Christine. But I suppose I should expect that with you by now. Let's go, I'll bring you to Malcolm."

"I'm sorry, John, I never intend to be secretive with you."

He nods wordlessly as he leads them outside and through the gate.

"Do we need to get the horses?" she asks, glancing at the barn.

"No, not this time."

He starts to the rear of the property and the unfamiliar house she saw on her way here.

"That's Malcolm's place?"

"Yes, we built it together."

"No shit? Well, I'll be damned," she says chuckling.

John snaps his head toward her, brows furrowed.

"I'm sorry, that just slipped out."

She and Annabelle had a difficult time restraining themselves, using present-day words and phrases when they were in this timeline. It was an issue for their first few months here. John had never been around a woman who routinely used foul language, and Christine's stress level had her swearing like a sailor. She eventually learned to think before she spoke, a novel concept for her. She had no choice if she wanted to remain incognito. A female cursing, speaking her mind or giving honest opinions did not go over smoothly in the mid-nineteenth century.

They step onto the deck of the modest home and John taps on the door. Christine stands behind him, off to the side where she hears Malcolm yell to hold on from inside. A moment afterward the door swings open, revealing a shirtless Malcolm in buckskin trousers. His hair brushes his shoulders, and from the state of it, he has not been awake long. He looks irritated about the early morning intrusion until his glance shifts to Christine.

"Oh my God, Christine! What are you doing here?" He pushes past John without acknowledging him and embraces Christine. She returns the hug and holds him out at arms-length.

"Pioneer life agrees with you, Malcolm. You look good. Healthy and well fed."

"Are you trying to say I've fattened up?" he says laughing.

"I mean that in the best way, my friend."

"Can we come in Malcolm? Or must we stand on your porch all morning?" asks John.

"Yes, of course, I'm so sorry. I am just gobsmacked to see Christine and forgot my manners."

He steps into the cabin and a yellow mutt retreats to the room's corner. John's hound follows and wiggles into the bed with the other dog. Malcolm pulls a shirt on before he grabs the kettle to boil water, adding another log to the fire.

"Tea, anyone?"

"I'd love some, thank you," says Christine, as she takes a chair at the table. John waves his hand in a motion to decline.

"Christine, I thought I'd never see you again. What happened when you went home? What did Hoyt say? How is Ethan? What about Thomas and Aidan? Did you prevent the pandemic?"

"Slow down, I'll get to all that in a minute. I know you weren't expecting me to show up here. I didn't foresee myself here either, trust me. But something has come up. Frank and I need your help." Her eyes dart to John for a second.

"You may as well tell us both, Christine. I told John the truth about where and when I'm from. He doesn't believe me. But whatever you say might convince him I did not lie to him."

Christine stares at Malcolm, dumbfounded. She blinks a few times before continuing.

"All right. First, let me answer your questions. Everything was fine when we got home. The press was relentless, but I expected that. Ethan went to London, and then we met in Los Angeles the following week. Aidan was right about Hoyt, he repeated almost verbatim, what Aidan had told us in England. Hoyt had studied Richard of Wallingford's research about planet gravitational pull, how that causes extreme weather, and the link to pandemics. He uploaded all the information into software he wrote, and it predicted a global pandemic for two years out. He needed the missing documents, the portion lost to modern day history."

She doesn't mention that two years later is the year 2072, not with John present.

"Wow, so he was honest with us. That's brilliant. What did you and Ethan do?"

"We gave Hoyt the writings, he added the research to his software, and he submitted his analysis to WHO. They used it to ramp up the current vector control and stock antibiotics and create a vaccine. They are still working on all the details to warn the public, but they have a year before it hits, so they'll have the chance to squash it before it escalates into a pandemic."

"And what about Aidan and Thomas?"

"Aidan returned home and resumed life as normal. Ethan and I turned Thomas into Internal Affairs for his part in Estera's death when he stole your antibiotics. We all know she could have lived through her bout with the plague if not for him. He will go to trial for it. I imagine they'll convict and imprison him."

"Good, he deserves it. And Ethan? What's become of him? And Frank?"

"Ethan is transferring to the Los Angeles unit. Frank is fine. Same old Frank. Gruff on the outside, soft on the inside."

"That's Frank all right," he laughs. "Ethan is moving to Los Angeles? Does that have anything to do with you?" he asks with a smirk.

John looks between the two of them, lost and confused. Christine shakes her head at Malcolm, sending him a look that suggests he change the subject. Picking up on her cue, Malcolm turns to John and smiles. "Tried to tell you, mate, we aren't from here."

Christine casts a glimpse at Malcolm, her eyes narrowing. "Listen, I'd love to sit here and catch up with you all day, Malcolm. But Hoyt tweaked the program, and I have to be back to the unit within two-and-a-half hours or the system will flag me. And if that happens, Frank and I are history, no pun intended."

FOURTEEN

Piedmont, Oklahoma 1868

Malcolm leans forward on the table.

"What's going on, Christine? It must be important for you to come here unauthorized and risk your career."

"It is. Frank and I are risking more than just our careers. If they discover me here, they could arrest us for misappropriating the government program for personal gain. That's why I want to be back well before my due time. Hoyt can cover me for four hours, but beyond that he can't offer any protection."

"Right, let's carry on with it then. What can I assist with? I owe you and Frank both my life, so you know I'll do anything you ask."

"In ten days, I'm bringing a woman here. Her name is Hannah Cole. I need you to take her in and watch over her. Help her assimilate. She is escaping an abusive relationship, and she may still be in danger. She was married to an LAPD cop, and she is convinced he will bribe an incoming prisoner scheduled to transport somewhere near here to kill her. At first, I thought she was paranoid, but the more I learn about her ex-husband, the more I feel he is capable of that. She has information about some illegal activities he is involved in."

"Wait, how do you know she'll be here in ten days? And why are you certain you are transporting her?"

"Hoyt rigged it. I'll be her transporter, and the timeframe is already set. Frank will send us to the same coordinates you and I arrived at. Will you meet us at the grove so I can hand her off to your care? She has become a friend to me, Malcolm, and I need to know you'll protect her. Ethan, Frank, and I trust you. We're sure you can keep her safe."

"I will. Any friend of yours is a friend of mine. Tell me everything, and I'll ready the cabin to accommodate another person."

"Thank you, I knew we could count on you."

Malcolm fills Christine in on what he has been doing to stockpile supplies and how he has learned to hunt and care for the animals. In turn, she tells him about how Hannah approached her, the story of Chad's abuse and part in the crime ring, and how she came to be in the exile program.

"What is happening, I don't understand any of this," says John, head swiveling between them.

"John, I appreciate this is difficult to comprehend, but Malcolm told you the truth. I trust you John, as does Malcolm, or he would not have shared this with you. Annabelle and I could not explain while we were here because we weren't clear about what held us here. With our equipment malfunctioning, we couldn't be sure how long that would last. We only kept things from you for your own safety."

John stares at Christine and breathes deeply. It scares her he might hyperventilate as this is a tremendous revelation for someone in 1868. The concept of time travel is not a subject she expects him to accept in stride.

"I realize it seems as if I've come unhinged John, but I'm perfectly sane, I assure you."

"I don't know what to think, Christine. It's hard to imagine any of what you and Malcolm have told me. I'm not saying you are untruthful, but it sounds like a tall tale."

"I understand that, I really do. I'm sure Malcolm can fill you in because I'm out of time."

"You're taking this better from Christine than you did from me."

John glances at Malcolm and nods wordlessly.

"He thought I was lying to him, Christine."

"I never said you lied," says John.

"Well, you strongly implied it, mate."

Christine looks between the two of them, frowning.

"Guys, please. I'm short on time. Maybe you can resume your discussion after I take off?"

"Apologies, Christine. To be honest, I don't hate the prospect of having some company. I'm quite keen on having a fresh face around here. No offense, John, but you're the only person I've had any prolonged contact with since arriving."

"It's settled then, I'll be back in a little over a week with Hannah. I'm not sure what time. Will you come to the walnut grove early and hang out until we arrive?" asks Christine.

"I'll be there. And don't worry Christine, I've got this. She'll be safe."

"I know Malcolm. If I didn't have faith in your ability, I wouldn't be here. Thank you, my friend, I'm grateful for your help."

"Oh, before you go, I spoke to Marcus. The nicest way I can put this is he was not open to advice from me. He seemed offended that you asked me to check on him."

Christine rolls her eyes and sighs. "Why am I not surprised? That kid is his own worst enemy."

"I can't say I disagree with that. Now, let's bring you back to your drop site and get you home before your time runs out."

"I need not be there to transport. I can go from here since I'm not on the books on an official trip."

She peers at Malcolm with a questioning look, and he nods his head and smiles.

She grins back at him. "Fine. You sang like a canary, so I'll leave you to clean up this mess with John."

"What do you—"

The rest of John's sentence turns into a gasp as Christine removes her transponder from her waistband and activates the transport function. She fades from view in front of his eyes, leaving him dumbfounded. He spins to face Malcolm, mouth ajar, but once again unable to speak. His expression is the perfect personification of shock and confusion.

"Now do you believe me?" asks Malcolm, as he slaps John on the back. "Sit down, I have a lot to tell you. Make yourself comfortable. This may take a while."

* * *

Christine opens her eyes and blinks several times as Frank helps her out of the pod.

"Get changed and through decon as fast as possible. The conference room has some electrical issue, and they moved the supervisor's meeting up here in an hour."

"Great. Of all days, huh?"

"Yeah, that's how our luck runs. No transports scheduled for today, so no one can find you here."

"Be back in a flash," she says, stepping into the decontamination chamber to shower.

She walks back in fifteen minutes later in a fresh uniform.

"How did the trip go? Did you see Malcolm?" asks Frank.

"Yes, everything went to plan," she says, folding her dress and stuffing it into her backpack. "He's more than willing to help. John helped him build a cabin and plow an area for a small garden, so he definitely has the means to take her in. He has food and supplies for stockpile. Turns out Malcolm's quite a hunter with a rifle, and he's been trading meat and hides."

"So, everything's set then?" asks Frank, as he finishes shutting down the equipment.

She dreads telling him what Malcolm did, but knows she must. She takes a deep breath, squeezes her eyes shut and braces for the onslaught.

"Yep. There is one point, though. Malcolm told John the truth about where and when we're from."

She opens one eye to see Frank spin around to face her, mouth ajar. "What? Please tell me I didn't hear that correctly," he says, working hard to maintain his composure.

"I know, I know," she says, holding her hands up in a gesture for him to calm down. "That wouldn't be my initial choice either, but he had already done it before I arrived. There was nothing I could do."

"Well, did you at least inform John that Malcolm is crazy and try to damage control?" he asks, pacing the small room.

"Not exactly. I transported home while he was there, so he would believe Malcolm."

"What the hell, Christine!" he shouts, stopping short to face her.

"Frank, calm down. John is an integral part of this arrangement and more to the point, he needs to trust Malcolm."

"What if he tells someone? What if this affects history somehow?"

"John will disclose that to no one. Count on that. He doesn't have any close friends. I know this man Frank, I understand that you don't, but I lived with him for six months," she says, taking a step closer to him. "He would not jeopardize telling someone and have them think he was mad. You need to trust my judgement. Sorry, but it's done."

"It would be nice for you to consult me first, Christine, just once. This is my risk too."

The silence stretches between them for several long moments until she sighs and casts her eyes downward in resignation.

"I apologize, Frank, but it was a fluid situation, and I made a field call. You know I would do nothing to jeopardize either of us deliberately. But I was short on time and wanted to get out of there. And since you now have this unexpected meeting, it looks like matters worked out for the best. And I promise, I will resolve to be more discreet."

Frank grunts and she follows him out of the jump room. If a manager shows up early, that could be a disaster. She cannot let anyone catch her here when she is not on the schedule to transport. Hoisting her backpack over her shoulder, she glances at him in time to see him retreat to his office, his face etched with worry.

Frank is not happy with her decision to confirm Malcolm's story to John, but it is too late to change things now. He paces in front of his desk as he silently prays this never reaches back to haunt them.

* * *

The next ten days drag on for Christine, as she longs to have Hannah's transport complete in the worst way. Only Michael can speak to her now that she is in custody. No one must find out she shares any connection to Hannah, or they will pull her as the assigned transporter. She gets a message to her through Michael, telling her she has set things up with Malcolm and everything is in place.

Chad still tries daily to talk to Hannah, but she refuses all video visits from him. The CCEA does not grant prisoners in person guests until the day they transport, when they allow their family goodbyes. It is just as well, thinks Christine. Let the jerk stew in his own juices. Any communication with Hannah at this point may rekindle his anger or whatever other feelings he has for her. Best to have the relationship end with no contact. With any luck, he will give up and move on once she exiles, although she cannot shake the feeling that he is every bit as persistent as Hannah says.

The weekend before Christine transports Hannah, Ethan flies over from London to visit, which is a welcome diversion. But the CCEA schedules him to complete the interview process for his Los Angeles transfer on the same day she will transport Hannah. Which only provides them a couple of days before she leaves. They make the most of it by taking a trip to the mountains, and she books them for a hiking trail. They spend their time together walking the pathways with the dozens of other people who have the same idea, and her romantic plans wither with the crowds.

Her parents used to walk the state trails without reservations whenever they chose to. They even went camping sometimes. Now California only allows overnight stays with a lottery system, but it is so crowded it is hardly worth the effort. The environment is so protected they post rangers every mile and cameras all along the route, so no one picks a flower or disturbs any wildlife. When did squirrels and racoons become an endangered species, she wonders to herself? She strolls the path, her hand in Ethan's thinking about how it saddens her and really dilutes the nature experience. But it is better than not being able to hike at all. That is definitely a perk of living in history she misses. The freedom it offered. She saw some unbelievable scenery, and it was so pristine. There was no pollution, no trash littered about, and with no cars or airplanes, it was completely serene. She sat at the edge of a forest and admired a beautiful castle with Ethan in 1335. The memory rushes back to her as they stroll through the San Gabriel mountains. A little over seven-hundred years later mankind has ravaged and spoiled many of nature's resources, and there are times she wishes she could just live in the past. The people she loves are the only thing keeping her here. Well, that and indoor plumbing.

By Sunday evening, she is steeling herself for another workweek and is apprehensive about Hannah's move. She does not share her unease with Ethan; he has enough on his mind with his upcoming interviews. She kisses him goodbye early Monday, faking her confidence as he promises to catch up with her before she departs for Oklahoma.

Later that morning Christine is in the employee lounge completing some backlogged reports when Ethan finds her.

"Hello, gorgeous."

"Hey you. I thought you'd be tied-up until this afternoon with interviews and testing," she says, as she rises to give him a quick kiss.

"I assumed so too, but they sprung me early. My unit in London sent over my latest physicals, so no need to retake them here."

"Already? It's only nine o'clock. Damn. It figures on the day I travel you have a free period."

"I was thinking the same thing. You lot are fairly easy to deal with over here, I was in and out in no time. I'll wait for you to get home before heading back to London, if that's fine by you?"

"It's more than all right, handsome." She wraps her arms around his waist and looks up at him. "Annabelle is flying in next weekend."

"Oh, don't worry, I wouldn't dream of impeding on your girls' agenda. You ladies carry on as planned. I'll fly home on Thursday and start packing up my house."

"Sounds good. Have I told you how excited I am that you're coming here?"

"You may have mentioned it a time or two. I feel the same," he says, as he tightens his embrace around her.

Christine's phone alarm chimes in her ear, signaling her to the orientation room. Her stomach twists at the sound of it, knowing what she is about to do. None of them are out of danger until she takes Hannah to Oklahoma, and this entire business is behind her. There were many times over the preceding weeks when she second-guessed her involvement in the plan. But they are all in far too deep to turn back now. No matter how this plays out, she is along for the ride—like it or not.

FIFTEEN

Los Angeles, California 2071

Christine reluctantly pulls herself from Ethan's embrace.

"I've got to run. I'll meet you at my place in two days, yes?"

"Count on it. Be careful today, don't stay in Oklahoma longer than you must. Do not offer anyone a reason to view this transport as anything other than normal. I know under the circumstances it might tempt you to stick around and make sure she's okay. But promise me you'll come right back so nothing appears abnormal."

"I will, scout's honor. I'll get in and out."

He kisses her forehead and brushes her hair away from her face. "I'll take you at your word, even though you're not a girl scout. I wish I could see you in that cute pioneer dress. Reminds me of when we first met."

She gives him a playful slap on the shoulder. "Oh stop, those costumes are horrible, and you know it. It's still hard to believe you fell for me while dressed like that and camping with you in medieval times. You're a brave soul."

"Well, you clean up rather nicely, Ms. Stewart."

She kisses him and picks up her tablet. "Ditto. See you in a couple of days."

He acknowledges with a nod, and with that she is off to the elevators. She is alone for the ride to the eleventh floor and takes time to control her breathing and steady her nerves. This is just like any other day, she tells herself, repeating it in her mind several times before the elevator reaches her destination. She steps from the lift, concentrating on inhaling and exhaling. When she enters the orientation room, she finds Frank and a few agents milling about and chatting. She grabs a chair in the back while Frank walks over to her.

"You okay? You look a little pale."

"I'm fine. I just want to get this done."

"That makes two of us. I'm ordering them up in a few minutes."

"Do you think anyone will notice I'm going to Piedmont? I worry it's too soon and the agents might take note."

"They probably will. It's only been a few months since we stranded you there. But as far as they know, the Midwest is a common drop-off zone and timeline, and the program selects locations randomly, based on inmate algorithms and family history. They would have no reason to assume you had any part in the transport selection process. On the contrary. No one would guess you want to go back there, especially this soon."

She nods at him and settles into her chair as he makes his way to the head of the room.

"Okay people, I'm calling the detainees up, have a seat ladies and gentlemen and let's get this moving," says Frank as he types the release authorization onto his computer screen.

The other transporters sit in the rear row with Christine. Sherry Blacklock is next to her, and Christine sees her staring at her in her peripheral vision. She turns toward her, and Blacklock smiles.

"Your first transport since getting home?"

"No, I went to Louisiana last week. With a very vocal prisoner, so that was fun."

"Oh God, they are the worst, aren't they? And the reports take forever, too. Well, good luck and safe travels today."

"Thanks, same to you," says Christine, smiling back at her.

The door opens and five prisoners shuffle in. She sees Hannah and makes a point not to look at her. The guards deposit them at the table, where they sit watching Frank. Hannah remains face forward, without acknowledging Christine. Perfect. She told her to ignore everyone until she came to get her. Frank steps behind the podium and clears his throat.

"Good morning, ladies and gentlemen, and welcome to orientation. Today you transport to your assigned destinations. I will run through the plan for the next several hours, provide you your exile posts, and then you'll watch a film before moving on to phase two. Questions so far?" asks Frank.

When none of them responds, he continues with his spiel. "Good. Your transporter escorts you through the various stages before your departure. After you finish here, they will take you to the Historical Lab where your coach reviews etiquette and language for your placement. Once that is complete, it's off to Concessions, where they distribute the supplies you bring to your exile. From there you go to the Health Division, where you receive inoculations against diseases for your new timeline. Next is your one-hour family visit. The final stage before transport is wardrobe, where you change into your period attire. All female inmates see a hair technician, and we may assign a male to a consultant if your hairstyle needs any modifications."

The prisoners stare at Frank wordlessly.

"Please do not give your transporters a hard time. They cannot alter your agenda. The system determines your exile location and timetable. They don't design your clothing, and they have no say about what goes into your survival supplies. They have no influence over any of the other departments you visit. If you feel the need for a sedative, tell your transporter and they can help you by arranging medical to issue you one. If, however, you are uncooperative, violent, abusive or belligerent, we will sedate you without your consent. I would suggest you avoid that at all costs. If that happens, you are unconscious when you arrive at your destination, and you remain that way for several hours, unattended. The agent cannot wait for you to wake up. That means you are alone and relinquish your on-site assimilation."

An inmate lifts his hand to ask a question. "Yes?" Frank says.

"How long do our transporters stay with us when we get there?"

"As long as it takes for a final review of your survival supplies and to make sure you have directions to the nearest town. Maybe twenty to thirty minutes."

"That's it? And then we're on our own?"

"Yes. You will spend today preparing for that."

"That doesn't seem like enough time. How are we supposed to know what to do? This is crazy to leave us there alone that soon!"

The other prisoners nod and mutter their agreement. Everyone but Hannah, who remains silent, looking straight ahead.

"You're going to amass a lot of information today on how to survive. Stay alert and you'll have no issues. Don't get yourself sedated for bad behavior and that increases your survival rate."

"But I—"

"Any further questions on the subject, review them with your transporter," says Frank, cutting off the rest of his sentence.

Blacklock leans over and whispers to Christine, "How much you want to bet I end up with that inmate?"

Christine chuckles and nods.

"Moving on, you will all receive an outline of your individual exile area. Study this map and familiarize yourself with it while here in orientation after the film. The graph does *not* leave this room with you, so pay close attention to it here. This is vital to your continuity."

Frank touches his computer screen, and a sample chart projects onto the wall.

"This is an example. There is an 'X' that marks your drop site. There is a sizeable portion shaded green around that spot. That is your safe region. The yellow section is a caution zone, and the red highlighted areas are where your restricted range begins. The scale at the bottom shows you each area in miles. You are free to travel anywhere in your green section, no restrictions. If you wander into the yellow zone, the system notifies the enforcement unit you are nearing your confined boundary, and they monitor you until you reenter your sanctioned space. If you enter a red territory for any amount of time at all, it flags you within seconds of the breach. When they confirm you are in an unauthorized sector, they will transport you away."

Frank steps out from behind the podium and perches on the corner of the table.

"I want to be very clear about what that means. The enforcement team monitors your movements twenty-four-seven, three-hundred-sixty-five days a year. At the time of your sterilization, we also inject you with a tracking device. We insert this chip into an undisclosed area of your body you cannot access yourself. On the off chance you were to locate it and recruit someone to remove it. . .well, just don't. We imbed it in a way so only we can extract it with a specially designed instrument compatible with the apparatus. If you try to expel it on your own, the wound will probably become infected, and you risk serious illness and even death. And you'll still have your tracker. Don't waste a valuable antibiotic on an infection you can avoid altogether."

The same prisoner who spoke up earlier raises his hand again. Frank nods at him.

"Why didn't we know this before now?"

"The CCEA has no obligation to disclose that to you. You're a detainee of the US government, and we chip all inmates with trackers. That's just the way it is. I'm telling you now, so you are aware of the consequences. The enforcement unit does not play around, so don't test them."

The prisoner shakes his head but does not respond. He folds his arms across his chest and slumps further into his chair.

"If I may continue? If the enforcement team confirms you are in a red zone, they exile you further away in time with no warning. One minute you are there, and the next you are elsewhere with only the clothes on your back. And they always move you further backward. You need to be certain you remain inside your authorized area. This rule is in place to avoid any disruptions to our current timeline. You must never do anything to effect that. Even though we assign you to areas where no known relatives of yours live, you cannot travel to contact any family members. Follow these guidelines and you'll be fine. Let's take a five-minute break and then I'll get to your transporter assignments."

Christine gets up to stretch while the prisoners mill about, getting water and talking to each other. All except Hannah, who stays in her seat. Christine realizes either she is in shock or trying to adhere to the rules she gave her. She really hopes it is the latter. Five minutes later Frank calls the room to order.

"Okay, grab your seats please, let's get to the assignments."

He reads off the prisoner names and their assigned transporters, and Christine is the fourth assignment read.

"Cole, Hannah, you are with Officer Stewart, transporting to Piedmont, Oklahoma in 1868."

Frank does not flinch, his performance worthy of an Oscar, but Christine hears the loud gasp from Blacklock as her head snaps in her direction. She sees Steve Goebel, another transporter, lean around Blacklock to peer at her. So much for no one noticing. She ignores it and keeps her focus on Frank. As Frank distributes the maps to the prisoners, the other agent leans toward her.

"Are they serious? How frigging ballsy is that? They are sending you to where they stranded you for six months? I'm certain you can have that changed, Christine."

"It's all right. It had to happen eventually. May as well get past it now," she replies, still staring straight ahead.

"Well, you're more understanding than I would be," she scoffs, and turns to Goebel to whisper something to him.

"Okay, your transporters will spend a few minutes with you going over your graph and we'll watch the film afterwards."

Christine rises as Hannah swivels in her seat. She waves her over and they sit across from each other, out of earshot of the other agents and prisoners.

"Are you okay?" asks Christine.

"Yeah, I think so."

Hannah's hand trembles as she holds the map. Christine reaches out and wraps her hands around hers.

"It'll be fine. I promise. I'm here with you every step of the way. Malcolm will take over from there. You are not alone."

"All right. I'm trying to calm down, I really am."

"Study your outline during the film. Malcolm didn't receive a map like this since he came from 1335, England. This is an extra the CCEA recently added. They used to just hand out pamphlets with certain events you couldn't travel within one hundred miles of. The old system confused prisoners. It resulted in many of them leaving their safe zones and being exiled further away. The charted technique is more concise, and it is essential. If either of you pass into the red zone, I cannot stop the enforcement team from exiling you somewhere else. Or get you back once they do. Do you understand?"

"Yes. Shouldn't I see the documentary, though?"

"Skip it, it's brutal. I will review it with you later. The map is more significant. Commit it to memory."

Christine pulls her hands away as Blacklock glances over at them. As predicted, they assigned her the mouthy inmate. She rolls her eyes as he gestures wildly, arms swinging around in front of him. Blacklock looks like she would rather be almost anywhere but here, negotiating with her entitled prisoner and his list of grievances. He clearly has more complaining to do. Christine smirks at her and returns the eye roll in what she hopes shows as a gesture of solidarity.

"Okay, let's settle down and I'll start the documentary, find your seats please," says Frank.

He opens the file on his screen, then stands at the podium.

"This film outlines an important topic, and you need to take it seriously. When you exile, you go to a time in history where individuals mistrust you and they are superstitious. If you tell someone you are from the future, or reveal yourself somehow, they will probably kill you. They won't accept or appreciate your confession. I warn you—this documentary is going to upset and enrage most of you. But it is imperative you realize why we show it to you. We are working to save your lives. They shot this footage with a transporter's hidden camera in a brooch on her period costume. This inmate outed herself and her transporter as coming from 2061. They arrested her, hung her until dead, and then cremated her on a pile of wood. That was in 1692, Massachusetts, and it sparked the Salem Witch Trials."

The prisoners murmur while looking around the room.

"I know that sounds harsh. It isn't easy to see a person die, especially when they are an exiled inmate, just like you. But you will never forget it, and that is the point. We need to impress upon you how very important it is not to reveal your origins to anyone. You will presumably make friends where you're going, maybe even find a partner and enter a relationship. This complacency will tempt you to trust someone, and you'll want to confide in them. Do not do it. Don't take that chance. And believe me, that's exactly what you would do—gamble with your life."

The inmates squirm in their seats, the stress beginning to show on their faces. Frank lowers the lights and starts the documentary as Christine settles into her chair and closes her eyes. She does not have the stomach today to see the film she has seen so many times. So, she decides not to. She will have no choice but to listen to it, but they cannot make her watch it. This minor rebellion makes her feel more in control, and she smiles to herself as she mentally flips the bird to the upper echelon of the CCEA. It could be possible she still harbors a slight bit of resentment for them stranding her in history.

SIXTEEN

Los Angeles, California 2071

The film starts as the narrator explains the documentary. The canned voice rehashes how the inmate made a fatal mistake when she confessed to locals she and her transporter were from the future. They searched the transporter's hotel room and cleared her of suspicion. However, they accused the prisoner of being a witch, and arrested her when she produced a lighter she smuggled back with her. When she lit a man's jacket on fire in the crowd, it proved to be her undoing. They convicted her of witchcraft, hung, and then cremated her. It reports the experience with unedited, merciless detail. The idea is to convince prisoners it is imperative for their safety and to preserve the current timeline, they do not reveal to anyone where or when they are from. And it is effective. The brutality of the outcome stays with a person. They did not edit out the death, and it is a barbaric, sickening thing to see.

This group of inmates reacts no differently from others before them. The documentary shocks and angers them. Christine has seen it many times, but never becomes desensitized to it. Watching someone die, and knowing it is real and not a movie, is very jarring. She keeps her eyes closed through the entire documentary. When the lights come up, she sits up straight and blinks rapidly to adjust to the brightness.

"I realize that film is not a pleasant experience, but the message is important. Tell no one where or when you are from. I cannot stress this enough. I guarantee they will panic. And frightened people are dangerous. You would be smart to remember that. Do not put yourself in a situation where you must deal with it," Frank tells the inmates.

The prisoners all look stunned by what they viewed.

"Okay, let's take the next thirty minutes to study your maps. If you have questions, please let your transporter know."

Christine makes her way to the head of the room to speak to Frank.

"Hey, how is our girl?" he asks.

"She's doing all right, I guess. I can tell she is nervous, but I've done my best to relax her. I don't blame her, though. I'm not certain she fully grasped what she signed up for until today," says Christine, glancing back at Hannah.

"Yeah, I'm sure she didn't. She'll be in excellent hands with Malcolm."

"I know. She doesn't realize that yet. But she will."

Christine sits with Hannah to examine her map and the half hour goes by quickly. Frank calls the room to order and announces the guards will be up shortly to shackle them. As always, they meet this announcement with disapproval. We do not permit prisoners off this secured floor without wearing shackles for everyone's safety. Statistics show this is the most likely stage a prisoner will attempt to escape, although Christine never understood why they would choose now to try to flee. They are in a protected government building alarmed to the hilt, full of correctional officers and agents. Maybe as reality sets in and it grows closer to their transport point, desperation takes over.

The guards arrive right on schedule and cuff the detainees, and Hannah looks as if she may be sick. Christine grasps her by the elbow and leads her from the office to the elevator before another transporter can join them. Once inside, she breathes a sigh of relief.

"How are you feeling?"

"Not great. I'm more nervous than I thought I would be. I've been all right until now," says Hannah, her breathing ragged.

"I understand that, but do your best to collect yourself and calm down. We go to the Historical Lab next. You'll be there for two hours and then I'll be back for you."

"You can't come in with me?" she asks, her face twisting into a grimace.

"No. Transporters don't stay in Historical. You'll be fine. They will review customs for the era, appropriate manners, and language. It's only to give you a head start on how to blend in."

Hannah inhales a deep breath and releases it slowly, trying to steady herself.

Christine registers them when they report to Historical a few minutes later, and as soon as the coach calls Hannah to the back, she leaves for the employee lounge. She uses the opportunity to check in with Annabelle. Annabelle knows better than to mention Hannah's name over the phone and keeps her side of the conversation generic.

"Hey girlfriend, how's your day going?"

"Oh, you know. I'm hanging out in the break room waiting for my detainee to get out of Historical."

"How's that going?"

"Good so far. I should leave in a few hours. You still planning on flying in this weekend?"

"You know it! Joe is taking the girl to visit his mom, so that'll occupy them, the way grandma spoils them. When does Ethan return to London?"

"End of the week. He says he wouldn't dream of encroaching on our girl's time."

"Smart man, that one," she says.

"Yes, he is. I just wanted to check in. So, I'll see you on Saturday."

"Yes, you will. And Christine?"

"Yeah?"

"Be careful on your transport. Don't make me come after you."

"Hilarious Annabelle. I've got this, not to worry," she replies, glad that Annabelle unearthed some levity in this situation. Because she is having difficulty finding any amusement in what she is about to undertake.

She disconnects the call and checks the time. Another hour until she needs to pick up Hannah. She pays some bills on her tablet, and sends a message to her sister, Kat. Just before Hannah is due out of Historical, she starts for the lab. When she steps inside, Hannah is already waiting for her in a secure lock-up. She motions for the guard to open the enclosure and leads her out to the hallway.

"Let's get over to Concessions. How was your session?"

"Um, interesting, I guess. The 1800s aren't very female friendly, are they?"

"No, they aren't. But it's not that bad. You're going to a sparsely populated territory, no one will bother you in Piedmont. Malcolm will make certain of that."

Hannah nods, but seems unconvinced.

Concessions have a few people ahead of them, so Christine logs in, and they wait. Ten minutes later the clerk calls them up and hoists the leather pack onto the checkout table, pushing it toward Christine.

"Survival equipment for Cole, Hannah, inmate number 090291, transporting to Oklahoma, 1868. Next in line," she announces, unceremoniously shoving the bundle to the end of the counter.

Christine heaves the duffel bag over the countertop and directs Hannah to a nearby table where she opens it.

"Okay, let's look through this stuff." She leans in closer to Hannah, lowering her voice. "You have an immense advantage going into this because Malcolm has supplies stockpiled. He and John built a cabin and prepped a small patch of land for a garden. Frank gave Malcolm antibiotics before he left England, so between the two of you, your reserve should be more than adequate."

"Are you certain Malcolm wants to share all he's amassed with me? He's never even met me, Christine."

"Yes, I'm positive. He's a kind man, Hannah. He didn't give me a moment's hesitation when I spoke to him about bringing you there. Accept his help and don't feel bad. Also, he told John the truth about where he is from. So, prepare to deal with that."

"What?" Hannah whispers to her. "Why would he do that? That could endanger us! Didn't he see that documentary too?"

"I don't think so. That film is about an American transporter. Remember, he exiled from England. They have their own orientation process. I trust John, and you can too. I suppose you should also know I transported home with him in the cabin. There's no retracting what Malcolm told him."

"Good to know," scoffs Hannah, rolling her eyes.

Christine ignores Hannah's sarcasm, attributing it to her nervousness. She empties the contents on the table, separating the supplies into piles.

"Okay, first we have emergency water pouches. We layer them with a fast-acting biodegradable coating, so bury the container in about a half an inch of dirt and it will completely degrade within thirty days. A stream runs behind Malcolm's cabin that provides drinking water. He knows to filter and boil it when used for cooking or drinking, but just so you understand, if you don't, you *will* contract dysentery, or worse. Most people think boiling it is enough—it isn't. You need to strain it first, then heat it to a rolling boil for several minutes. There is a roll of very fine cheesecloth type material in your backpack for filtering. I'm not certain our bodies ever build up a tolerance to the bacteria, so be sure to use it. I never took the chance when I was there. I filtered and boiled any liquids I ingested. John's stomach can handle drinking from the untreated creek. You and Malcolm, not so much. But because you are there for the long term, you might consider ingesting a slight amount every day. That would be a way to introduce it to your system slowly, to see how you tolerate it. We give you purification tablets, which I would suggest you save. If there is ever an occasion when you cannot sanitize water for whatever reason, these work instead. Your LifeStraw purifies water from its source. Questions about any of these?" asks Christine, packing the products back into the knapsack.

"No, I understand."

"All right, next are the meal replacement capsules. One of these a day is equal to twenty-five-hundred calories and has all the vitamins, nutrients, and supplements you require. We include several high calorie protein bars too. You also have a piece of flint, which Malcolm will be glad to see. They have invented matches in your new timeline, but they are not in wide use yet. They still have some kinks to work out and can be dangerous in 1868. There is also a wool blanket, which always comes in handy. The MREs are self-explanatory. Last, we have a supply of two-hundred, one-dose broad-spectrum antibiotics. I'm sure you recognize how valuable those are."

"I do, yes. I'm thankful to travel somewhere where there is a house set up for me, because I cannot imagine doing this with only these supplies and nowhere to live."

Christine nods, the helpless feeling of being stranded with nothing but her failed transponder all too familiar to her. The memory causes her to shudder, but she recovers quickly and returns the items to the backpack, swinging it over her shoulder.

"Let's drop this off in the jump area and then we'll grab some lunch. Order something good today. 1868 limits your meal choices. I recommend anything with cheese or pasta. And chocolate. Just a suggestion."

Christine steers Hannah to the bank of elevators, and they ride to the transport floor. She ushers her to the inmate staging space, where she secures her in the cage as she walks to the departure rooms. After placing Hannah's supplies in a locker, she closes it and selects a new code.

They arrive in the cafeteria a few minutes later and stand in the queue with the rest of the lunch crowd. Christine watches the other agents with their prisoners, the inmate plates piled high with processed food and desserts. They all received the same advice from their transporters—order your favorite foods now, you may not get them again in your lifetime. She studies Hannah as they move closer to the service station. She has that deer-in-the-headlights look about her. She smiles at her when she glances her way. Hannah does her best to return the smile, but all she manages is a quick grin that looks like she may be sick at any moment. She frowns as she eyes the trays, and Christine cannot help but notice her fidgeting. She is becoming annoyed at the sound of her cuffs clinking together. She touches her shoulder, and Hannah stops squirming her hands.

Hannah notices the other inmates ordering with reckless abandon. She is uncertain she can stomach any kind of cuisine at this point. Then she sees the macaroni and cheese and decides she should take Christine's advice and try that. It is her favorite comfort food from childhood. She gets a slice of cheesecake for dessert and a diet Coke, her one vice, to wash everything down.

They sit in silence, both lost in thought. Christine eats her chicken salad thinking about the transport while Hannah pushes pasta around her plate, hardly touching it. After a while she shoves the meal aside, giving up. Christine raises her eyebrows and peers at Hannah's uneaten lunch.

"You're finished?"

"Yeah. I'm too tense to eat anything."

Christine puts her fork down to focus on Hannah. "You shouldn't be, you know. Your experience will be far more pleasant than most inmates."

Hannah glances around the room, wondering what will become of these prisoners. She realizes she has much better odds than them, and she feels guilty about it. But she cannot let that affect her. This is her only chance to escape Chad, and she knows it with every fiber of her being. The realization fuels her with new resolve, and she vows to do nothing to jeopardize that now. Not when she has come this far. She slides her plate in front of her to eat again, despite the knot in her stomach. She's sure she will regret passing up the opportunity for what is surely to be considered a luxury food later. They dine in silence as Hannah mentally steels herself for what is coming.

SEVENTEEN

Piedmont, Oklahoma 1868

John never moves a muscle. He continues to stare where Christine stood only a moment before. Malcolm is not sure he even realizes he has slapped him on the back or spoken to him. He appears to be in a trance.

"Okay, let's sit you down, mate," he says, guiding John to the table.

John does not resist, allowing him to lead him to a chair where he collapses, his gaze never leaving the spot Christine transported from.

"But I. . .I don't understand. She was here, and then she, she wasn't," he says, as he gawks at the empty space.

Malcolm pulls a seat up to face him. "John, look at me," he says, snapping his fingers in front of him to grab his attention. John turns his head to focus on him.

"That's better. I tried to explain I was telling you the truth. I realize this is a ton of information to digest, but try to stay with me here. Time travel is possible. At least where we come from. Do you understand?"

"I, I don't know," John stammers.

Malcolm pours both himself and John a finger of whiskey and sits down to explain as much as he dares to at this point. He does not want to overwhelm him, although judging by John's hypnotic state, that ship has already sailed. They continue to take shots of the liquor while he talks for the next few hours. John asks a question every so often, but mostly he just listens, enthralled by all he shares with him. When the alcohol causes Malcolm's head to spin, he takes a break and prepares strong coffee. Then, as the day gives way to evening, he makes them a simple supper of rice and deer meat, and they dine in silence. John leaves for home shortly after dinner, still unusually quiet, and Malcolm arranges to come over in the morning to discuss how to best prepare for Hannah's arrival.

It was a shock for Malcolm to see Christine, and he was astonished to hear she would bring a friend here to settle. He did not know the American transporters had agreed to work with Hoyt until she told him today, and all he knows about the woman is she is an acquaintance of Christine's fleeing an abusive and criminal husband. He shakes his head as he thinks about that. He has never understood men who abuse women; he is not wired that way.

Malcolm is pleased Christine trusts him enough to bring her here, and he will do all he can to protect her and keep her safe. Plus, the prospect of company thrills him. He has had a lot of alone time since arriving here. Even in medieval England, he lived with others and misses being around people regularly. He adds kindling to the fire and climbs into bed, pulling the blanket up to his chin. Tomorrow he starts comfort improvements on the cabin, and he falls asleep eager to begin.

As he rounds the corner to John's place early the following morning, he sees him already outside feeding animals. Malcolm waves, and John gives him a quick wave back. He lets out a sigh of relief as John looks less stunned by yesterday's events. If he engrosses him in today's chores, perhaps that will speed his acceptance, his mind focusing on the task at hand.

"Good morning, John. Are you feeling better?"

"Morning. I'm fine. Really not fit to talk about it yet. I'd rather just do our work, and when I'm ready, we'll speak of it again."

"That's bloody good with me. The first thing I need is another bed. I'm smart enough to realize she probably won't be willing to sleep in mine. I thought we could build a screen to separate the areas for her too. It will be hard for her to live with a stranger. She has so much to adjust to, and I don't want her to feel as if she hasn't any privacy."

"Agreed."

They spend the morning sawing wood for the bed frame and screen. They use the long, sturdy grass from the river's edge and weave it between the framing to create a matt for the shield. By afternoon the furniture is complete, and they fill the cushion with hay and feathers. Malcolm uses the same cotton material he did for his own bedding to hold the stuffing, and while not a modern-day mattress, it provides a semi-soft surface to sleep on.

Malcolm stands back to admire their handiwork. "Not bad, if I say so myself."

John sits drinking coffee and nods his approval. "Tomorrow we should start on the garden. We must till the soil further down. Use the rainwater today so it soaks in overnight."

They eat together and then play cards until the whiskey runs out. John asks Malcolm a few random questions about his timeline, but other than that is strangely quiet regarding Christine's visit. When Malcolm can stand it no longer, he places the deck on the table and looks at John.

"John, you have said little all day about Christine's appearance, and more importantly, her departure yesterday."

"I am still unsettled she was here. I'm sure it's no secret to you, or maybe to her either, that I care about her. More than that, actually. I was getting over her absence, and then she showed up, and here I am, right where I started from months ago. It's frustrating. I don't want to feel like this, but I cannot shake the feeling."

"I understand that sentiment. I've been in the same predicament myself. Women are the bane of our very existence, my friend. That's been the case since the dawn of mankind. And it will never change. My advice to you is this—the best way to get over a woman is to find a new one."

John scoffs and twists away from Malcolm. "I don't realize if you've noticed, but this place does not offer a wide choice of wives. I would take a wife if there was a suitable possibility within one-hundred miles of here."

"What about the schoolteacher? She seems to be a fan of yours. She makes a production of saying hello to you whenever we're in town."

John's face reddens, and he gazes into space, considering Malcolm's words.

"Maybe ask her if she would like to join you for dinner at the inn next time you see her," he suggests.

John waves his hand in a dismissive motion and rises to leave. "I'll see you tomorrow to help you plow," he says, as he grabs his hat and leaves without another word.

Early the following morning they are up to feed the livestock and work on the garden. The weather is mild, and they plant the seeds Malcolm was saving. It takes most of the day to till the earth far enough down to satisfy John, but once they finish it provides Malcolm with a tremendous sense of accomplishment.

He thinks about how to improve the latrine for Hannah and has already collected used newspapers from town. The usual method of using an old corn cob or shells for personal hygiene seems inadequate, and Malcolm has not grown accustomed to it either. He only imagines how Hannah will feel about it. He trades a deer hide for some dried eucalyptus leaves and other herbs and spices, and the plant covers the stench some, but not sufficient to bring it even close to tolerable. But he does not dare leave the door to the outbuilding open to air it out for fear of attracting unwanted creatures. Many of the local wildflowers are fragrant, and he plans to pick them to arrange around the cabin and outhouse. For whatever little that does to disguise the odor further.

For their next project, John helps him build a small platform to help Hannah mount a horse as he expects she has no equestrian experience. Few people in 2071 ride horses anymore, and he has no reason to believe she may be one of the rare ones who has done so. He spends the following days stocking as many supplies as possible, and John works with him to store the extras for maximum shelf life. He also makes sure the dugout is stocked in case they must ever use it.

The rest of the week passes slowly as Malcolm tends to minor details around his home, equal parts anxious and excited about his upcoming visitor. He fishes, then barters them for fabric at the general store. He wants Hannah to have the materials to produce new clothing if she chooses to. Although he assumes she does not know how to sew, she will have to learn at some point if she aims to stay here. He had a few items made, but the resident seamstress is ill and is no longer taking orders until further notice.

Two days before Christine is due back, Malcolm goes to the river alone to hunt turkey, his favorite meat. Crouching in the reeds at the river's edge, he finds the perfect hiding place. He is not there long when he hears movement to his left, but when he turns, he sees no one. Before he can react further, something large sprints through the grass. In the next moment, the same Indian he encountered twice before is in front of him, an arrow aimed at him. He lowers his rifle to the ground slowly to show him he is not a threat.

"I mean you no harm."

The native narrows his eyes but says nothing. Malcolm rises to his feet to face him, leaving his gun on the ground. It is disturbingly quiet, the grass gently swaying between them and the occasional croak of a frog the only sounds. They stand staring at one another for a few minutes, and when he does not respond Malcolm touches his palm to his chest.

"Malcolm," he declares, patting his ribcage.

"Kanuna," states the Indian, lowering his bow and arrow. Malcolm notices he keeps it in the ready position at his side.

"Kanuna," repeats Malcolm smiling.

"Kanuna," the native replies, pointing at an enormous bullfrog, then at himself.

Malcolm extends his palm to the Indian, who peers at it but makes no move to shake it. He slings his quiver over his shoulder and walks away, leaving Malcolm's hand hanging in the space between them.

"Okay, baby steps. This is progress. I didn't have to shoot anyone, and his arrow hasn't pierced my heart today," he mutters to himself.

He watches Kanuna mount his stallion in one fluid move and trot off, glancing back once before cresting the hill and riding out of sight. He is upbeat about this exchange, hopeful he and the Indian will at least maintain peaceful relations, if not be friends. He is curious and wants to know more about him. So, he decides to hunt here near the river more regularly, as this is where he always sees him. Kanuna must recognize this is the best hunting spot too. They already have that in common. He muses the more he is around the Indian, the more he will come to trust Malcolm. He lifts the only turkey he got onto the horse with him and heads home for the day, still contemplating ways to establish a friendship with the native.

EIGHTEEN

Los Angeles, California 2071

Christine and Hannah sit in the medical wing, waiting for them to call her in for vaccines. Hannah scans the handout listing the pharmaceuticals she is about to receive, trying to distract herself from thinking about the transport.

The CCEA has assigned you to the year 1868. Inmates appointed to this timeline are given the following immunizations:

Scarlet Fever, Tuberculosis, Typhus, Small-Pox, Measles, Chicken Pox, Cholera, Whooping Cough, Yellow Fever, H1N1, Avian Influenza, Acute Coryza (common cold). Vaccinations are mandatory, and all detainees are required to participate in the vaccine program. The CCEA will retain any inmate refusing inoculations for compulsory medical treatment.

She crumples the sheet, balling it in her fist. She is not looking forward to the injections. Even though they no longer require needles, it is still something she is not fond of. A hold-over from childhood when they did use them. Or maybe she is tense because the closer she gets to transport time, the more uncertain she feels. She questions her decision a hundred times, reminding herself there is no turning back. Chad would kill her now if given the chance. She tears off tiny pieces of the crumpled paper, making confetti until Christine grabs it from her and tosses it into the wastebasket.

"Sorry, nervous habit."

"I gathered that. Try to calm down. I'm here, and I will be here the entire trip. I've done this a thousand times, it's perfectly safe," she assures her.

"Yeah. Unless they strand you for six months without prior notice."

"Touche´. But that isn't going to happen this time."

"Cole, Hannah, inmate number 090291," calls out an aide, interrupting their conversation.

They follow her to a cubicle where a nurse stands ready to inject Hannah. After her vaccines, the RN explains she must stay in the holding area to monitor her for allergic or adverse reactions. They are not alone in the waiting room, so Christine works on her tablet while Hannah studies the pattern on the carpet tiles. A male inmate in the row of chairs across from them is staring, but Christine hopes her stink eye is enough to deflect his interest. Apparently, it is not.

"Where are you going, sweetheart?" he asks, his eyes never leaving Hannah.

Hannah's gaze meets his, but she does not answer. His transporter says something to him Christine cannot hear from across the room. Good, get him under control because I am in no mood to, she thinks to herself.

He waits a beat before trying again. "I asked you where you were going, bitch."

Christine signs off her device and leans over to Hannah, "Don't engage him," she whispers.

Hannah stares directly at the inmate.

"Piss off, jackass. Do you really think there is any chance I'd tell you?" she scoffs, raising her eyes to meet his.

He tries to rise, but his agent is faster and pushes him back into his chair. This triggers the prisoner to fight, and Christine dashes across the room to help him subdue his detainee, who now resists like he is a champion cage fighter.

Christine snaps her head toward the receptionist. "Don't just stand there, call for backup!" she yells while grappling with the combative man.

The receptionist's eyes widen as she engages the paging system.

"999, assistance needed in medical 204. 999, assistance needed in medical 204," her voice rings out over the speakers before she collapses into her chair, watching the scene in front of her unfold.

One of the male nurses rushes out from behind the check-in counter to help them contain the inmate until the guards arrive. A moment later security pins him to the ground while the aide administers him a sedative. His transporter leads him from the office after giving Christine a chin lift as a thank you for the support. It is the only thing he can do with both hands wrapped around his now sedated prisoner. She returns to her seat and glances at Hannah, who appears to be in shock. They are alone with the receptionist out of sight, talking in hushed tones to her coworkers, so Christine swivels to face her.

"I told you not to talk to him."

"I know. I'm sorry. I guess something in me snapped. I am tired of men calling me a bitch," she says, dropping her chin to her chest.

Christine chuckles and pats Hannah's hand. "Good girl, that's the first step to regaining your power."

Hannah beams at her and sits up straighter, feeling more like her old self than she has in years. "Yeah. I will never allow another man to speak to me that way ever again."

"Well, that idiot just made his trip a lot worse than it needed to be. He's not the shiniest penny in the piggy bank," says Christine, rolling her eyes.

Hannah nods, lost in her own thoughts.

Fifteen minutes later, medical releases them to Hannah's family visit.

"Is your sister here today?"

"Yes"

"Anyone else?"

"No. She's all I have. There is no one else."

"All right. You'll have an hour with her. This will not be easy. For either of you. If you stay calm, it'll help her accept what's happening. I'm required to remain in the room with you, and once the visit is over the guard releases you and we continue to wardrobe."

Hannah does not respond, but her eyes fill, and she bites her bottom lip nervously.

"Hey, stop it, Hannah. Don't make this worse for you or your sister. Remember why you are doing this. Focus on that."

She takes a deep breath and wipes her tears with the back of her hand. The sound of the shackles jingling is an unsettling reminder she is a prisoner of the CCEA. They step off the elevator and a correctional officer steps forward to usher them into the visiting room holding area. Her dread grows by the second. She does her best to push it aside as Christine nods to the guard and leads Hannah through the next door. A petite woman with long hair the color of Hannah's sits on the couch, springing up when they enter. She bursts into tears at the site of Hannah in her inmate jumpsuit and shackles. She runs to hug her while Christine moves discretely to the room's corner.

"Hannah, are you okay?"

"I'm fine, I promise."

"I cannot believe you did this! You should have left him and moved in with me. What were you thinking? Why would you hack into a government website? How do you even know how to do that?"

"I just learned, that's all. And no, I could never move in with you, Heidi. You know he would only follow me. I wouldn't do that to you and the girls. Plus, I have no money of my own. It would never work."

"You think I would worry about money, Hannah? You're my sister! I love you. Your nieces love you. I would do anything for you."

Hannah takes her sister's hands in hers, "I know you would. And that's precisely why I could not burden you with my problems. Chad is my issue, not yours. You don't deserve all my crap dumped on your doorstep. Consider your girls, Heidi."

"You're my sister, dammit! Don't tell me what I can handle and what I can't. What you've done is permanent, and you made this life-changing decision without even considering me or my feelings!"

"That's not true. I thought it over and spent many nights agonizing over this. You and my nieces were the only reason for me to stay. And ultimately, I couldn't base my choice on that. It wasn't fair to you, and it's too dangerous. It would be self-indulgent and neglectful of me to do so. Do you get that?"

"No, no, I don't. What's selfish is you leaving me, the only family I have left."

"I hope one day you'll understand why I had to do this. I had to, for me. And for you, too. He would never stop coming for me, and you would be in jeopardy. All that would do is put you in the same pathetic situation as me. We would all be in danger, and I refuse to bring that to you. Your girls deserve better than that. Now listen to me carefully, Heidi. I withdrew half of his cash from our savings before I, you know, did what I did. It's enough capital for you and the girls to move, or put aside, or whatever you want to do. It should last you a while. I made a bank check out to you and it will be delivered tomorrow. I also sent moms jewelry and all of mine. Sell it, pawn it, I don't care. It means nothing to me. He bought it all for me, so it's tainted as far as I'm concerned."

Heidi buries her face against Hannah, sobbing. She reaches her cuffed hands over her sister's head, wrapping her arms around her and rocks her while she cries.

"I don't want you to leave," Heidi says, raising her head to peer at Hannah.

"I know, sis. Please try to understand how much I care about you. That's why I must do this. I love you more than I hate him. I need to get away to protect you and myself. I only hope this makes sense to you someday."

"This will never make sense, Hannah, never," she says, crying harder.

They hug and talk while Hannah gives her more details about what she left for her. Then the guard comes in. That rekindles the sobbing to its previous level, and the sisters force Christine to pull them apart. Heidi shrieks, and Hannah continues to cry. Christine whispers to her the visit is over and escorts her out while security holds her sister back. She flails her arms, trying to get past him, but Hannah never looks back. Out in the hall Hannah cries softly, and the scene she just witnessed affects Christine deeply.

"Let's go take a break for a minute, okay?" suggests Christine.

Hannah nods, and Christine leads her to the women's room where she locks them in after checking to make sure they are alone. Hannah runs to the nearest stall, slamming the door shut behind her, where she gets sick.

"Are you all right?" asks Christine, tapping lightly on the metal frame.

"Yeah, I'll be okay. Just give me a minute."

She walks out of the cubicle looking no better than when she went in. Her face is pale, and her forehead is beaded with perspiration.

"Take a moment and collect yourself. Sit here and settle down for a bit."

They perch on the sink counter silently, but for Hannah's sniffling.

"I'm sorry, I didn't expect her to behave like that. Hell, I didn't think I'd react that way either."

"Yeah, I know. That is the hardest part of today, trust me."

Hannah closes her eyes and inhales a deep breath. "God, I hope so, because that was brutal."

"Are you feeling better? Ready to go up to wardrobe?"

"Ready as I'll ever be, I guess."

"All right. Blow your nose and splash some water on your face, okay? I don't mean to sound crass, Hannah, but suck it up, girlfriend. You will only make this more difficult unless you get your act together."

"I'm fine," she says, sniffing and standing up. The cold water is refreshing, and she rinses her mouth. She stares at her reflection in the mirror for a minute before blotting dry with a paper towel.

"You're going to be fine. I promise. Hey, look at me."

Hannah looks up at her with red eyes. "You don't know everything will work out, but I appreciate you trying to reassure me."

"Hey, even a broken clock is right twice a day. I've done this a long time, and I'm telling you, it's gonna be okay," says Christine.

"A broken clock? That's what you want to compare your accuracy to? Is that the best you can do?" she says, frowning.

"I never said I was a philosopher. That's all I've got, sorry. Come on, we'd better get going before someone comes looking for us."

She tosses the crumpled napkin in the waste basket and follows Christine out, head held high, trying desperately to resist against the panic threatening to overtake her.

NINETEEN

Los Angeles, California 2071

Christine leads Hannah through the entry to wardrobe and logs onto the screen on the wall. Shortly after, a woman waves them over to check-in.

"Stewart, right? Inmate Cole?"

Christine nods as the clerk reaches under the counter to grab a pile of clothing.

"Okay, here you are. Cole, Hannah, number 090291, traveling to Oklahoma in 1868. You have a dress, apron, boots, shawl, sun bonnet and dress jacket," she says, handing the bundle to Christine.

She ducks under the tabletop again and slaps a plastic-wrapped package on top. "This has your bloomers, chemise, stay, or corset as they're also called, pantalets, petticoats, and stockings. You can forgo the stay if you choose while doing chores or manual labor, but I recommend wearing it at all other times, as is the custom of the era. Wear at least one petticoat under the dress. You have two dresses in here. We cut one a few inches higher, and it has weights sewn into the hem. It's shorter to protect it from the mud and dust, and we placed the ballasts there to prevent improper exposure on a windy day. These items are all clean, but all your outerwear and the boots we create to look worn, so you blend in. You always wear your chemise and pantalets under your outerwear and wear your apron to keep your dress clean. Wear your stockings when you receive guests or when you leave the house. I'm sure they reviewed all this with you in Historical."

She holds out the handheld computer to allow Christine to sign for the clothing. She scribbles her signature and grabs both bundles, directing Hannah to a makeshift dressing room. A female guard unshackles her, and Christine follows her behind the privacy screen to help her change.

"I realize this appears to be a ton of stuff to put on, but you'll adapt. They aren't as bad as they seem at first, they just require some getting used to," she whispers as she tightens the smock around Hannah's back and holds out a waste bag for the prison attire.

"It seems like a load of crap, actually. Why can't I keep my own panties and bra?"

"Because that's not how pioneer women dress in 1868, America. You need to be authentic. Remember the old saying to always wear clean underwear in case of an accident? Well, think of that. If someone were to discover modern-day unmentionables on you, you would be in trouble. The devil's in the details, Hannah," she says, standing back to study her handiwork.

"Well, my undergarments are hardly lingerie, they're standard prison issue. They couldn't possibly be any more generic or unattractive," she says, dropping them into the bag Christine holds. "But I know what you mean. Although I do not intend to let anyone see me in my bra and panties. God, this historical clothing is just frigging uncomfortable," she complains, pulling up the stockings and slipping the boots on.

"Trust me, I get it. But our current style undergarments are not what they wear in your new timeline. Even standard prison issue underwear. You never know where you might find yourself, so no sense in taking an unnecessary chance. Okay, let's move over to the cosmetology area."

Christine steps around the divider and nods to the guard to secure Hannah. They walk across the office to the short line of men and women waiting to be transformed. One of the stylist's waves them over and gestures for Hannah to have a seat in the beautician's chair.

"Is this your natural color?" she asks, running her hands through her hair.

"Yes," she replies.

"Lucky you. That makes my job much easier. I had to put hand-dyed permanent plugs on the last guy here, and that took hours," she says, rolling her eyes. "Yours is quite long, though. I can trim it up to be more manageable if you want me to. It might be hard for you to style, like this."

"Can I keep the length? I've never had a shorter haircut, and it's all I have left of my former self. I'll watch you and I expect I can recreate whatever you do."

"Sure. So first I'm going to brush it back and secure the bulk at the base of your neck. I'll take the remaining hair and continue twisting until it's an upturned bun at your nape. Maybe your transporter will hold this, so you can observe me. This style should be easy to do yourself later if you follow me now," she adds, handing Christine a hand mirror and spinning the chair.

The stylist takes fifteen minutes to complete Hannah's new look as she talks her through each step. When she finishes, it is a huge transformation. With the dress and her hairstyle, she looks like a different person.

"Your hair is pretty in an updo. Too bad they won't let me do any make-up on you. Just for fun, you know? I could make you into a model. Do you think you can recreate this style? This would be a typical pioneer hairdo," says the stylist.

"Yes, it shouldn't be an issue. Thanks for showing me what to do."

"No problem. You can always twist a ponytail into a bun at the top of your head if you don't want to mess with it. Or braid it. You'll see hairstyles the other women in your timeline wear and copy their styles. Best of luck to you," she says, smiling as she rotates Hannah's chair back toward the large mirror at her station.

When Hannah sees her reflection, the woman staring back at her is unrecognizable. A stranger. The change is shocking, and even more peculiar, she feels different.

Christine taps her shoulder and Hannah rises to leave with her, adjusting her apron. She stares at herself in the mirror for a moment longer before locking eyes with a man behind her in a 1700s period costume and powder wig. He studies her, his expression a mixture of sadness and fear, before dropping his gaze to the floor as his transporter leads him away.

"I prefer to make it to the transport room before everyone else starts arriving, lets hustle, okay?" says Christine, snapping Hannah out of her reverie.

Hannah hastens her stride to stay in step with her.

"What's the rush? These boots are hard to walk in, they're really narrow."

"I get it, truly I do. But try to hurry, please."

They move straight to the transport zone where Christine secures Hannah in the holding cage.

"Sorry about having to do this, but I can't leave you unattended. That would raise several questions, and everything has to appear completely routine," she says, as she lifts the duffel bag from its compartment.

"I understand. I forgot about that thing," she replies, gesturing toward the pack.

"That's why I wanted to arrive early. I have some things to add to your survival kit. It will make the load heavier than everyone else's, so try not to show that when you pick it up. I have a bottle of shampoo and body wash. It's the super-concentrated stuff that only needs a drop or two mixed with water to lather up. They're enormous bottles, so it should last you a very long time. I included triple antibiotic cream, deodorant for both you and Malcolm, several travel toothbrushes, toothpaste, and a couple of packages of one thousand wet wipes. I added pain medication too. I know they reviewed hygienics and sanitation with you in the Historical Lab, and these luxuries won't last forever, but at least this will ease you into the latrine hygiene situation. I gave you the products I missed the most when I was in Oklahoma. I also reproduced some money. I laser printed pictures of it from the 1800s on linen paper. No one there will realize it is counterfeit, it's an exact copy. I copied five hundred dollars of it. That's a ton of cash for that timeline, enough to get you everything you need."

"Wow, thank you, Christine. That was very thoughtful of you."

"Don't worry about it. I'm going to go change and I'll be back shortly."

Christine walks to the changing room and grabs the costume hanging on the outside of her locker. She changes clothes, stuffing her uniform into her container with her tablet and employee ID. Grabbing the shrink-wrapped items and dropping them into the backpack, she clears the code and slams the metal door shut. As she glances around before hoisting the knapsack over her shoulder, her stomach lurches at the thought of being caught. Just as she nears the double doors, Blacklock rounds the corner, lifting her chin in a greeting. Christine stops short, the other agent blocking her exit.

"Hey," says Christine, smiling as her heartbeat escalates.

"How's it going?" she asks, squinting at the satchel. "You're here early, Stewart. Why do you have your girls pack in here?"

Christine glances over her shoulder, trying to appear casual. "What? Oh, I already pulled it, and I forgot to take my earrings off. It was easier to run in here and toss them in my locker than have to secure this behemoth again."

Those are the words that come out, but she fears her face tells a different tale.

"Sure, well see you out there," says Blacklock, frowning and stepping aside.

"Yep, catch you in the jump room."

Christine darts away without looking back. Dammit, that was too close, she thinks, trying to slow her pulse to normal. They prohibit a prisoner to take anything to their exile other than their sanctioned survival pack. It was stupid of her to risk it on this, of all transports. If they catch her, this entire plot would be over, along with her career. The CCEA would convict her of a crime, and she would unwittingly drag Frank down with her. And probably Hoyt too, even though neither of them knows she stashed extra supplies for Hannah. She balls her hands into fists to hide the trembling and proceeds to the staging area. She sees Hannah peering at her with eyebrows raised in a question. Christine nods and continues toward Frank to check them in.

"How're things going," he asks.

"Fine. I'm ready to leave. The faster we get out, the better."

"You're up third to launch today. I didn't mess with the prearranged schedule. Didn't want to give anyone a reason to audit anything about today's transport. You're in staging section five."

"Okay, I'll bring her over, and we'll be in place as soon as you're ready for us."

Twenty minutes later Frank straps them in their jump pods. Christine glances at Hannah, who looks terrified.

"Don't fall apart on me now, Hannah. We'll be fine. Remember, I've done this twice a week for the past eleven years."

Hannah does not reply, but nods her head nervously and squeezes her eyes shut. In the next moment, the room darkens as Frank counts them down to transport. She concentrates on breathing as sparks of light spin around her, and vertigo overtakes her as she fades to black.

* * *

Malcolm is up before dawn. Sleep evaded him last night. He might have gotten an hour's rest as he lay awake, thoughts of Hannah's impending arrival threatening to consume him. Has he managed all he can to prepare? He is nervous about meeting her. What if they do not hit it off? He does not worry much about himself; he gets along with most everyone. But what happens if she is some high-maintenance diva who cannot adjust here? His mind spins with a thousand questions, but no answers. It is no simple task to land here from two-hundred years forward in time and create a life, all while hiding in plain sight. It is more dangerous for a woman, and Malcolm hopes Christine prepared her for what lies ahead.

He gives up on sleep and rides to the river as the sun promises to peek over the hills, the grass sparkling in the light with the morning dew. The view steadies his nerves as he sits on the boulder near the water eating his breakfast of dried turkey and a stale biscuit. His black coffee is now lukewarm, and he does not mind the bitterness because he is saving the sugar to have more when Hannah arrives. Not clear why he feels so obligated to make certain she has all she needs, he convinces himself it is because Christine asked him to look after her. But he knows what truly excites him is the prospect of company, and someone to chat with besides John. Someone from his timeline. With her, he can talk about things John will never comprehend. He moves to the edge of the grove, tying the horse to a tree, and watches the sunrise while waiting for his guest to arrive.

* * *

Christine blinks and tries to shake the disorientation. She looks at Hannah curled up on the ground to her right, out cold. She moves nearer to her and shakes her lightly.

"Hannah, wake up. We're here."

Hannah's eyes flutter open to peer up at her, struggling to focus.

"Huh?"

"We're in Oklahoma."

Hannah sits up, blinking rapidly, her hand going to her head as she sways. She glances around and then springs to her feet. She takes in her surroundings and breathes deeply as she leans against the tree for support.

"Shit. Oh my God, what have I done?" she cries, twisting to face Christine.

"Calm down, Hannah. It's normal to experience a little anxiety at first. Remember why you wanted to do this. Sit down and inhale some deep breaths," Christine gently guides her back down to a sitting position while Hannah tries to suppress the panic.

"I need a minute," she says, gasping in air raggedly.

"Take your time. But control your breathing before you hyperventilate. It's going to be fine. I promise," she says, taking a seat beside her.

They sit under the tree for several long moments as Hannah calms herself and steadies her nerves. After ten minutes she has composed herself enough that her hands are no longer trembling like a leaf in the wind and her breathing is stable.

The sunlight filtering through the trees creates an ethereal feeling in the grove, and Hannah has never heard so many birds singing in all her life. Just when she thinks her anxiety level has returned to her normal baseline, she jumps and squeals when a walnut falls from the tree above her, bouncing off her head and startling her. Christine laughs and holds it up to show her.

"It was only a nut, see? Let's rest for a few more minutes before we search for Malcolm," suggests Christine.

"He's coming here to meet us?"

"Yes. I cannot go to the farm with you. Because this is an official transport, they monitor my tracker so I can't leave this immediate area. If I do, it will flag the system at base. They'll probably do a forced exit to get me home, thinking someone has taken me hostage. They'd also send you elsewhere as a safety precaution. We need this to be routine, to keep you protected and not draw any attention to you."

"Okay. And you're sure you trust Malcolm?" Her eyes fill as she speaks.

Christine takes Hannah's hand in hers. "You asked me to help you and I have done all I can to make certain you are as safe as possible here. I trust him. Ethan and Frank trust him. You'll be in excellent hands with him."

Hannah leans over to hug Christine, crying into her shoulder. "Thank you for everything. I owe you my life. I still can't believe you've managed all this for me. And I have no means to repay you," she says, pulling away and wiping her eyes.

"Take care of Malcolm for me. Create a decent life here, that's how you repay me. Deal?" she replies, grinning.

"I'll do my best."

"All right, then. Let's go find your new roommate."

Hannah lifts the heavy supply pack. Everything she owns now fits into the bag she carries. The thought depresses her as she follows Christine out of the grove. When they reach a clearing, she spots him. He is facing away from them, grooming his horse. As they step closer, he hears them and spins around, dropping the brush he is using. He grins when he sees them, and Christine meets him halfway where they embrace. Hannah stands where she is, watching the reunion, feeling like a third wheel, and more nervous than ever to meet Malcolm.

He is a striking man with an athletic build. His dark hair brushes his shoulders, and his beard and mustache are neatly trimmed. His blue eyes are the color of denim and light up when he smiles. Hannah is not sure what she was expecting, but this was certainly not it, and her reaction is almost visceral. She feels her cheeks get warm, and averts her gaze, chiding herself for even thinking about how attractive he is. She hopes he does not notice her blushing.

"Wonderful to see you again, my friend," says Christine.

"And you, Christine." He plants a quick kiss on her cheek, grinning at her.

Malcolm peeks around Christine to Hannah. He walks toward her, beaming. "You must be Hannah," he says. "Malcolm Aldred. I'll be your tour guide for the year 1868, and years thereafter. Welcome to your new home, Hannah."

She extends her hand, and he scoffs and draws her into a hug. She cannot help but smile at him. His grin is infectious, and he seems so warm and friendly. Her nerves settle as she realizes she need not have worried about meeting him. She sighs with relief as he grasps her hand in his and gives her a reassuring squeeze.

"Don't worry, I have the house ready for you, and we are pretty well stocked. We will be bloody fine, I assure you."

"You're British," she blurts out before she can stop herself.

She did not mean to announce that aloud, it just slipped out. And it is a ridiculous thing to say. She knows he is a Brit. Christine met him in England. But it still surprises her to hear his accent when he speaks, it makes everything he says sound so lovely. He could read her a phonebook if they were still around and make it sexy, she thinks to herself as the heat spreads across her face again.

"I am, yes. I hope that's not an issue. Our countries are allies," he teases, smirking at her.

"No, not at all. I didn't mean it that way. I, I had forgotten, is all," she stammers, completely flustered.

"I'm taking the piss with you, just being cheeky," he laughs.

Her eyes widen, and she glances at Christine. "He means he's joking. You'll become familiar with his British phrases. I only understand him because Ethan talks the same way."

"Oh, okay," says Hannah, "I'll try to catch up."

"Hannah, I need to transport out in a few minutes. I will leave you in Malcolm's very capable hands."

She moves to hug Hannah goodbye. "Will we ever see you again?" asks Hannah.

"I honestly can't say. If I can make it back, if Jonathan can tweak the system, I'll check on you two if possible. No guarantees, but I'll try."

Malcolm hugs her next. "Give Ethan and Frank my best and send my thanks again. And tell that lad of yours to stop messing about with his girl and lock that down."

Christine chuckles. "I will pass that along to them, but I'm not sure I'm ready to tell my son what to do about his love life."

She smiles at them for a moment. "I wish you both the very best, I really mean it," she says, before she turns to walk into the woods. She pauses when she reaches the edge of the trees and turns to wave to them.

Hannah watches her until she is out of sight, unsure about what to do next.

"Have you ever ridden a horse before?" asks Malcolm, as he heaves her heavy bundle up.

She shakes her head, eyeing the animal warily.

"Well, don't be frightened, I'll be driving. You just hang onto my waist and enjoy the ride."

He mounts the mare, adjusting the pack in front of him, and pulls Hannah up to sit behind him in the saddle. He reaches back to find her hands, wrapping them around his midriff before nudging the animal forward with his heels. She tightens her grip on him as the horse trots away.

She decides in that moment that rather than be fearful, she will embrace the experience and give this unfamiliar place a fair chance. She turns to look at the grove that represents the last remaining shred of her old existence, then twisting around she peers past Malcolm as she rides into her new life—full of apprehension and a dash of promise.

TWENTY

Piedmont, Oklahoma 1868

Malcolm jumps from his horse and offers his hand to Hannah to ease her down. She falls into his arms, and he sets her down gently, but not before his eyes meet hers and linger for a moment longer than they should. She shakes her head to break the spell and pulls away from him as she looks across the land at the plowed ground, the animal pens, and the modest home. She cannot allow herself a distraction now, not after she has come this far. She needs to focus on surviving here and flirting with a stranger will not accomplish that.

"Wow, you've managed all this in only a few months?"

"I did have a helping hand. I couldn't have accomplished it without John. I'm sure Christine told you about him?"

"Yes, she did. Even with his help, this is a lot to get done."

"I didn't have much else to do," he says, grinning.

"I wasn't expecting this though. It's really impressive, Malcolm."

He beams at her and removes the pack from the horse. "Shall we have a go at unpacking and then show you about the place? Follow me and stay on the dirt path, snakes hide in the grass."

"All right," she replies, scanning the ground at her feet and hurrying after him into the house.

He raises the grease paper covering the windows, and the sunlight streams in as she peers around the one-room cabin, taking it all in. There is a large fireplace on the far end with a table and chairs positioned in front of it. Cooking utensils hang from a split log which serves as the mantel, and a pot hangs on an inside hook over the fire. Barrels and burlap bags line the wall with what she assumes are stores of flour, cornmeal, and other dried goods. Wooden shelves above them are filled with a few tin cups, plates and bowls, a black pot, and a kettle. Jars of rice, oats and coffee sit on a shelf and what looks like salt or sugar below it. Three oil lamps are on display beneath them, the glass cloudy and the frames rusty. There are candles stacked beside them, next to bottles of various spices. The other side of the room has two beds separated by a standing divider. One bed has a crate at the foot with blankets folded over it.

"This is your bed, over here," says Malcom, moving toward one of them. "I built this privacy screen for you, and a trunk for you to store your belongings. I realize they don't allow you to bring much, but I figured you might need some space of your own for items you acquire. Clothing and such."

"This is very cozy. Thank you for being so thoughtful."

"It was my pleasure," he says. "You know, on second thought, it's a beautiful morning. Do you want to see the property and we'll unpack afterwards?"

"Sure. I'd love to, yes."

Malcolm tosses her rucksack on the bed and leads the way outside. Their tour takes her to the livestock first, and she pinches her nose at the goat pen.

"You'll become used to the odor after a while," he chuckles.

"That is highly doubtful. That smell is terrible. I guess we get spoiled in our timeline. We aren't around live animals often, except for pets."

She studies him as he shows her to the dugout and explains this is their go-to in case of a tornado, dust storm or other emergency that drives them from the house. Since April and May bring the most tornadoes, he wants to be confident she is prepared and knows how to reach safety.

She gives him her full attention as he tells her about life on the prairie. Callouses cover his hands, no doubt a result of the manual labor during his months here. He catches her looking at him and she averts her eyes, pretending interest in the latrine. She cannot help but eye it with a frown.

"I've done all I can to improve the loo situation, but it remains dodgy despite my finest efforts, sorry."

"Yes, Christine warned me. She did send some creature comforts with me, though."

"I shall look forward to seeing those."

With the tour complete, they go inside again and rummage through her survival pack together. Malcolm is elated with the extras Christine sent them.

"This is top notch stuff. I have all the antibiotics Frank gave me when I left England. Between us, we have enough to last a lifetime. Our vaccines are protection from most of the diseases that circulate here, so we should be in great shape. I feel we should save the money for any emergencies or large purchases. What do you think?"

"I agree. It will serve as a safety net in the event we ever need it. It looks as if right now you have things very well under control here. But are you sure you are okay with me being here, Malcolm? I realize you don't know me, and this is a lot to take on, having another person here."

He puts the vial of antibiotics down and positions himself on the bed, facing her.

"Never think you are a burden, Hannah. I told Christine I was pleased to have you here, and I meant it. I owe that group my life. I would do anything to help them. And to be very honest, I look forward to the company. Especially since we are from the same timeline. I have felt very isolated here as the only person from the future."

"Thank you for making me feel so welcomed. I'll do my best to be an asset here."

She holds up the last item and smiles. "This is a surprise Christine didn't tell me about."

"Fresh drops? Bathroom deodorizer? That woman is the bee's knees. I shall no longer fear the outdoor loo," he says, laughing.

Hannah chuckles and says a silent prayer Christine's good karma circles back to her soon.

"How can I contribute? I don't have a clue about how to run a ranch."

"Neither did I. But I'll teach you. Your help with the animals will be appreciated. We need to feed and water them, gather eggs, brush the horses, and tidy the pens. Once we finish planting the garden, we need to be sure insects and weeds stay out of it. The rest we'll muddle through together and master it as we go."

"I can do all that. The day Christine told me where I was going, I went to random internet stations all over the city to study this timeline. Because

I knew where and when she was taking me, I made it a point to learn all I could."

"That will come in handy, I'm sure. Do you sew or cook at all? Can you fish?"

"I cook, and I'm pretty decent at it, too. But I've never sewn or fished."

"Well, I'm glad one of us knows their way around a pot and pan, I struggle to do even the basics in the kitchen. I will teach you to fish, but I'm afraid stitchery of any kind is not in my skill set. I also think it is vital for you to handle a rifle efficiently. There are wives who meet in town to quilt and sew together. It would be brilliant if you joined a needlecraft group. We cannot afford to have clothing custom made at the tailor shops just yet. And if something happens to me, or I cannot work, I want to know you'll survive here on your own."

Hannah stares at him with wide eyes and shudders. "I cannot be here alone, Malcolm. Seriously, I won't make it."

"I'm not planning to go anywhere, but you still need to master how to endure here. That's just smart preparation on our behalf. If we are to thrive here and not only exist, then we need to be as skilled as possible. And remember, John is here too, so he can help. But it would be remiss of me not to equip you for some unforeseen event. I am committed to helping you flourish here, and part of that is to ready you for any situation. And I intend to do that, Hannah. Now don't worry, nothing is going to happen to me."

She nods her head and folds her hands in her lap. "Do you expect those women can tutor me on how to make sweatpants and sweatshirts? Anything more practical than this garb?" she says, sweeping her arms in front of her, motioning to their clothes.

"Oh Lord, I hope so," he says, chuckling.

They spend the day chatting and getting to know each other as they drink coffee by the fire. Hannah spoils Buddy with belly rubs, and he takes to her immediately. Malcolm finds her to be the most charming women he has ever met. Not only is she beautiful, but smart and kind. But nothing good can come of developing a crush on her, he thinks to himself, so he pushes the thought away, not wanting to add any awkwardness to their new friendship. They review their plans for the ranch and agree to start her coaching the next morning. He suggests she rest after her transport in, as it elicits such a toll on the body, and she happily accepts the invitation.

Hannah wakes from her nap refreshed, stretching as Malcolm putters in the kitchen area, preparing them an early supper of smoked ham and beans with biscuits. The two of them chat well into the night while she catches him up on news from around the world. As predicted, it thrills him to talk to someone from his own timeline. Although they grew up half-way across the globe from each other, they have plenty in common and he laughs more than he has in months. More than before his exile, even. He loves how her face lights up, and her nose crinkles when she laughs. She loosens her hair, and it cascades across her back, swaying in the firelight as she moves. When she tucks a loose strand behind her ear, it is so mesmerizing he takes a moment to recover and does not notice when she speaks to him.

"Malcolm, did you hear me?" she asks, snapping him back to the present.

"I'm sorry, did you say something? I was absent there for a minute."

"I asked if you would mind if I turned in for the night? It's been an endless day for me, and I guess I've hit the wall."

"No, of course not. Please make yourself comfortable. This is your home now, too. I'll move the screen in place for you and let you get settled. Call me if you need anything. Will it bother you if I stay up and play solitaire?"

"Not at all. When I was a child, I always thought I was safest if I fell asleep while my parents were still awake. Isn't that silly? Not that I consider you a parent," she chuckles.

"I understand. It made me very secure too. My folks died when I was eleven, so believe me, I get it."

"I'm so sorry. I didn't mean to evoke a painful memory."

"Nah, it was a long time ago. You get some sleep Hannah, tomorrow you begin your journey to becoming a pioneer woman."

"I'm not quite sure how I feel about that yet, but I'm pleased you're willing to help me."

She wrinkles her nose at him and disappears behind the divider. He forces himself not to look in her direction, although it requires all his resolve not to do so. Oh yes, he could be in real trouble here with Hannah Cole.

* * *

Hannah stirs when she hears Malcolm moving around the cabin. The smell of coffee pulls her from her drowsiness, and the aroma of bacon causes her stomach to rumble.

The first day of her new world awaits.

Yesterday went better than she had expected, and Christine was correct about Malcolm; he is an outstanding man. She is already at ease with him. She is looking forward to today; it will empower her to learn how to run the farm. Chad never involved her in any important decisions or allowed her any shred of respectability. Before she met him, she was independent and competent. Over the years, his verbal and physical abuse chipped away at her self-esteem until he stripped her of all confidence.

The very thought of him causes her stomach to twist. She shakes her head trying to clear her thoughts of him. He is nothing but an awful memory. Her world is here now, and she intends to make this life as good as it can be. She pushes her ex-husband out of her mind as she follows Malcolm outside. The morning fog lifts just after sunrise, when he shows her how to feed and water the animals and brush the horses.

He brushes the horse until she shines, then grabs the saddle. "The mare will be yours. I plan to purchase a stallion for myself. We both need our own horse eventually, a two-car family is a necessity."

"I guess they are this century's main mode of transportation, aren't they? Well, I must confess, yesterday was the first time I have ever been on a horse in my entire life, passenger or driver. It's hard to imagine controlling such an animal on my own." The horse nuzzles her hand and neighs as if to reassure her.

"It's not as difficult as it looks. I find it sort of fun, to be honest. But what bloke doesn't like to play cowboy?" he says, tipping his hat to her before strapping the saddle on.

"I'm willing to give it a go. I'm sure it won't be the last new thing I try here."

She strokes the horse's sleek mane, marveling at what a beautiful creature she is. She has never been this physically close to an animal this large before, not even as a child. She has been to a zoo, but the animals there are so far away from the visitors. This is a new experience, and it surprises her to enjoy it so much.

After feeding and grooming the remaining livestock, they leave for the river. She rides with Malcolm, after he suggests they postpone teaching her to ride on her own for another day. The weather is cool and mild, perfect for fishing. When she hooks her first fish, she jumps with excitement and experiences a surge of pride. An hour later they have several on a string and break to eat. Buddy naps next to her, stealing bites of deer meat, and Malcolm jokes that he only likes her better because she is spoiling him.

Hannah is relaxing on the blanket in the shade when movement catches her attention out of the corner of her eye. She sits up to look past Malcolm, freezing in place as her eyes widen and her face pales. He looks at her curiously and turns to follow her gaze. He rises slowly and raises his palm in a wave.

"It's all right, Hannah, he's peaceful," he says, his eyes never leaving their visitor.

Hannah has still not moved, frozen with fear but for her heart beating wildly in her chest. The dog lets out a low growl, the fur on his back standing straight up.

"Kanuna, hello," says Malcolm.

"Malcolm," says Kanuna, raising his palm. "Malcolm, Agehya," he adds, pointing at Hannah. Malcolm cocks his head and Kanuna tries again. "Malcolm, woman."

"Yes. Hannah," responds Malcolm, twisting to glance at her.

"Hannah," repeats Kanuna.

Malcolm gestures for him to join them, holding out the jerky to him. Kanuna squats, balancing on his heels next to Malcolm, chewing the meat while studying Hannah. She remains motionless, unsure of what to do. He both fascinates and frightens her.

Kanuna nods toward Buddy, who growls at him. "Gihli"

"Dog," replies Malcolm.

"Agi'a," says Kanuna as he eats, motioning with his hands using the universal sign for eating.

143

"Eat," answers Malcolm.

Kanuna points to the water, "Ama."

"River."

The native shakes his head. "Ama. Water."

"Ama. Water," repeats Malcolm.

And so begins their friendship. A few words traded in each other's language, and the mutual respect of each having spared one another's lives at some point. Kanuna grunts and rises, taking a pendant off and handing it to Malcolm. He stands, takes the necklace, and offers his hand to Kanuna. This time he grasps Malcolm's hand before walking away. A huge smile spreads across Malcolm's face as he watches him disappear over the ridge and out of sight.

Hannah releases a deep sigh, and her shoulders relax. She folds her hands in her lap to conceal the trembling.

"I didn't know what to do," she says.

"You did quite well. I've met him before. He means no harm. He is Cherokee, and no threat to us. There are Indians here who are not friendly, and to be fair, I don't recognize the difference yet myself. However, I know he is not dangerous. This is the most verbal communication we have ever had, so that's a good sign."

"I have never felt so helpless. I have no weapon, and the truth be told, I am completely inept at defending myself," she says, dropping her head.

"We'll fix that, Hannah. I will make you a leather belt to carry a knife. You can use that blade throughout the workday, but it will also double as protection."

"Okay. That would make me feel slightly safer, I suppose. Although I'm just as incompetent with a blade as I am in a fight."

"That will change, I promise you. The more you use it, the more comfortable and confident you will be with it."

Hannah is relieved when they gather the day's catch and picnic supplies and start back to the ranch. Once they are home, he teaches her how to clean the fish, and she watches him do a couple before she attempts one herself. She does not do too bad at it and by the time she is working on her second one, she has the hang of it. She cooks two of them for their dinner with rice and winter squash from John's garden.

"This is delicious, Hannah. It far surpasses anything I've cooked. I don't know how you seasoned it so well with the meager spices I have."

"Thank you. I have always enjoyed cooking. Many people don't do it anymore, it's a lost art. The ChefAid made that obsolete. But my grandmother taught me how, and I spent summers with her in Texas as a young girl where she let me cook with her. It will serve us well here because she never used modern techniques. I learned to bake from scratch, and Lord knows, there are no shortcuts here."

"Very true, there are few conveniences here. None that you and I are accustomed to, anyway. We have both had very urban existences until now, but I'm afraid those days are over for us."

Hannah nods wordlessly, thinking about all she will need to learn to survive here.

They spend the evening in front of the fire talking as they have every night since her arrival. The topic of conversation is always the same. They discuss their pasts and plans on how to thrive in this timeline. She tells him about her childhood in Texas with her and her sister spending time with their grandmother, and they trade stories while Malcolm insists he be the one to clean the dishes and make tea. He fascinates her with his tales of growing up in England and the differences in their upbringings. It amazes them at how much alike they are in their beliefs and core values. She is even more astounded at how at ease she is with him. Hannah never relaxes with a stranger, particularly not a man. Chad had seen to that. If she showed any interest or attention to another male, he became enraged. It did not matter there was no romantic intention or attraction on her part, anything would set him off. She was seasoned to years of avoiding dialogue with men, so it was surprising how quickly she overcame that with Malcolm. There is something about him that makes her comfortable and secure. She can be herself around him without fear of ridicule.

As the flames in the fireplace die down, Malcolm rises to stretch. "I'm knackered, you?"

"What? I'm not sure what that is."

"Knackered. It means tired," he says, smiling.

She yawns, and a giggle escapes her. "I guess I am too. Pioneer life is exhausting, to be honest."

Malcolm adds logs to the fire and turns to her. "I'm glad you're here, Hannah."

"So am I. Thank you for making this such a smooth transition for me. I cannot imagine being here alone. I owe you and Christine everything." She crosses the room to give him a soft kiss on the mouth.

"Goodnight, Malcolm."

He stands there stunned into silence. Then, just like a lightning bolt, it hits him. He falls for her at that moment. It sounds ludicrous, he knows. The sane, rational half of his brain reminds him he has only known her a few days. The entire thing is reminiscent of some ridiculous chick flick movie plot. But the idealistic, impractical part of his brain does not seem to care how illogical it is.

He stands looking after her, unable to move for a minute. She turns to smile and winks at him before she disappears behind the divider to her bed. He reaches up to touch his lips, beaming from ear to ear.

She steps to the cover of the screen, shocked at her behavior. What is wrong with her? She just kissed a man she has known for less than a week and then winked at him in the most outrageously flirty move ever. She tries to be mad at herself but fails. All she knows is she is brave and impulsive around Malcolm, newly awakened emotions for her. She slips into bed, still smiling but a little unsettled, promising herself to get in check and stop acting like a teenager.

TWENTY-ONE

Los Angeles, California 2071

Christine comes awake with a start in the jump pod. As her mind clears, she sighs with relief. She made it home. Hannah is with Malcolm.

She opens the door and heads to the decontamination zone. The spray douses her, and she proceeds to the changing area where she tosses her clothing into the hazardous waste container. She passes through the second shower and goes to the dressing room where she rips the plastic wrapping from her fresh uniform.

When she walks to the next chamber, the medical team is ready for her. They administer her an antibiotic injection and take her vitals, then secure her in a scanner to give her a more thorough check. After receiving an all clear, they release her to the general transport section where Frank waits to usher her aside.

"Everything go okay?" he asks in a low voice.

"Perfect. No hiccups at all."

Frank's shoulders relax as the relief rushes through him. "Excellent. Let's not chat much here. No need to make people suspicious this is anything other than a normal day. I'll swing by after work today."

"Sounds good. I'm going home to get some things done around the house. Annabelle flies in on Saturday, so I want to clear up my weekend."

She snatches her tablet and employee ID from her locker. Ethan left her a message he got called to London to complete his final transfer exit interview early this morning. She's disappointed, but he'll be here soon enough. She makes a mental note to call him on the way home. She is almost clear and out of the building when Blacklock walks in.

"Hey Stewart, how was your trip? I see you made it back okay."

"It was fine, thanks, routine transport," she says, thinking that once again, Blacklock's timing is the worst.

"You're forgetting something," she says, tilting her head.

"Huh?"

"Your earrings. You forgot to take them off before, and now you didn't put them on," she says, tugging at her earlobe.

"Damn," says Christine, her hand reaching to touch her ear. "Oh well, I'm in a rush, I'll get them tomorrow."

She walks away before Blacklock can comment further, pushing the button for the lift. Riding the elevator to the ground floor, she steps outside to the parking lot, her focus on Ethan moving here in two weeks. She does not make it far before she hears her name. As she spins around, she squints against the sun, trying to determine who called her.

"Stewart, wait up," shouts a man.

She sees someone in uniform jogging toward her but does not recognize him until he is halfway to her. His polo shirt bears the LAPD insignia and stretches across his biceps, which are ridiculously large. His gun holster and other equipment bounce on his hips as he jogs closer. He stops a few feet short of her, catching his breath.

"I'm Chad—"

"I know who you are. What do you need, I'm in a hurry?" She does not even attempt to disguise the distaste on her face.

"Right to the point, I see. I'll return the courtesy—I want my wife back," he states, eyes narrowing at her.

"I have no idea what you're talking about," she says, turning to her automobile.

He grabs her arm, twisting her toward him. "I think you do, Stewart. And you're going to tell me where she is."

She glances down at his grip on her. He is considerably stronger than she is, and his fingers dig into her skin.

"Listen, Chad, I've heard the rumors about your wife's conviction like everyone else. But I have no clue where she went. What makes you think I have any knowledge about her whereabouts?"

"You assume I haven't established connections in every law enforcement agency in this city? Well, you're wrong. I've done this job for a long time. Don't insult me, Stewart."

"I'm not telling you anything because there's nothing to tell," she says, glaring at him while she struggles to pull herself loose from his grasp.

His hold on her tightens as he leans in closer. "I know you transported her. I *will* discover where she is. Whether it's from you or someone else. I'm not a man who gives up. And when I find out, I'm sending the first available inmate after her ass. You're familiar with the old saying if I can't have her, no one can? She will be sorry she ever considered this a good way to leave me."

Christine freezes as she realizes he knows Hannah planned this. He smirks and does not hide his amusement as she controls the impulse to gouge his eyes out with her free hand.

"Oh, it surprises you I figured out why she did this?" He laughs and shakes his head. "I'm not stupid. And that bitch underestimated my tenacity. She is my wife, and she will pay for what she did. And anyway, I know she'll regret her decision. She's weak and she'll beg to come crawling back. Women like her always do."

"She's your ex-wife, asshole. And by the way, she's not going to tolerate you calling her a bitch anymore. Plus, I hardly think anyone, least of all her, is interested in your take on the state of her mental health. Now get your sleazy hands off me," she hisses, twisting loose from his grasp as a group of agents walk toward them from around the building, distracting him. Blacklock is among them and waves when she sees her. Christine recognizes the irony she is the one who provides her getaway, considering she has practically sprinted from her twice in as many days. For once, Blacklock's timing benefited her.

She buzzes the car open. Jumping inside, she hears the automatic door locks engage and punches the autopilot for home, leaving Chad glaring at her. Once out of the parking lot, she changes her mind and switches it to manual. She rarely takes control of the vehicle like this, but she needs to do something with her nervous energy. Her hands tremble, not from fear, but anger. She always considered Chad a moron, and this abrupt encounter has only reinforced that assumption. But the most pressing issue remains some corrupt CCEA agent must have told him she transported Hannah. The good news is he does not know where—yet. Which eliminates transporters she worked with that day. They are all aware of where she took Hannah. It was someone who looked up the files before her travel point, when the report would only show Hannah's assigned transporter, but not her destination. The system does not clear inmate destinations into the archives until after the transport is complete.

She pulls into her driveway, still in a foul frame of mind. Max greets her at the door with his usual enthusiasm, but it does nothing to improve her disposition. She promised Hannah Chad could not get to her, and now her shark of a husband is circling the waters. She is determined to do whatever she has to, to prevent him from finding her.

Frank arrives an hour later, and she scowls as she swings the door open.

"Oh wonderful, you're in a pleasant mood," he deadpans.

"Yeah," she scoffs, "You will love this."

She tells him about the confrontation with Chad and her theory on who might have shared the confidential information with him.

"You're right. It had to be an employee who only has connections before the transport date. But that doesn't help any. It could be anyone. There are hundreds of employees with access to that intelligence. And if we report it, they will investigate. We do not need the enforcement team poking around and asking questions. If they were sharp and searched long enough, they'd uncover something to implicate us. Hoyt tweaking things isn't foolproof."

"Yes, I considered that too. So, what do we do?" asks Christine.

"I'm not sure we can do anything. We can't stop him from trying to determine where she went, and unfortunately, he'll probably get the information. The best we can manage is to warn Hannah and Malcolm to be hyper-vigilant."

"Yeah, I came to the same conclusion. So, I guess I should contact Hoyt and let him know what's happening so he will suspend the system and I can go back to tell them."

"Yes. But we have some time. I won't release the report yet. The archives don't even transfer to records until I clear the transports. I can put that off for a few weeks since I'm working on the quarter end statistics and I've been told that's a top priority. Enjoy your weekend with Annabelle and call Hoyt on Monday. Ask him to schedule the system freeze as close to three weeks from now as possible. The longer apart these blips register with IT, the better."

"Okay. That makes me feel a little less stressed. But what if he gets to an agent from that day? They all know where I exiled her. And they also know when. Everyone in that place noticed because it was Oklahoma. Sherry Blacklock even commented on it, suggesting I request a change of destination and timeline. She wasn't the only transporter who gave me a look when you announced my transport site. Goebel looked at me like I had sprouted a second head or something."

"He would already know where she was if he had gotten to any of them. I realize that's not exactly solid intel, but it's a chance we must take. If Hoyt programs another glitch too soon, it could catch IT's attention. That's all we can manage, Christine."

"As much as I don't like that, I agree. I trust Malcolm to keep her safe," she says, although she finds it impossible to sustain the brief comfort the thought brings her.

After Frank leaves, Christine is restless and eager to find somehow to distract herself from her racing thoughts. Once she finishes dinner, she watches a movie and checks in with Annabelle to get her flight schedule for the next day, then calls Ethan. She putters around the house, unable to stop thinking about waiting three weeks to notify Hannah about Chad's intentions. She says a silent prayer she and Malcolm remain safe.

* * *

Chad stands facing the man in a dark corner of the bar where a country song plays through the speakers above them. The place smells of fried food and cigarettes. He would never normally enter a dive like this, but that is the point. The chance of him running into anyone he knows here is next to none.

Chad leans in closer to the man and lowers his voice. "I need her exile destination. The source I thought I could tap isn't cooperating."

"That kind of intelligence won't come cheap."

"I don't care. I have money. Once you have her whereabouts, monitor the transport schedule and alert me when the CCEA appoints a prisoner anywhere near her."

"I suppose you also want me to devise a plan with that inmate once we find them?"

"Well, I'm sure not going to do it. I need to keep my hands clean, that's why I hired you. And this project has to be wrapped up as soon as possible. Before she vanishes in the wind."

"I'll do what I can."

Chad grabs him by the collar, thrusting him against the wall. "You'll do more than that, or I'll make your pathetic life more miserable than it already is. Do you understand me? You'd be smart not to forget who I am or what I'm capable of. You're kidding yourself if you think I won't deliver on that promise."

The man nods, shaking loose as Chad shoves him away and turns to leave. He watches him fling the door open and stomp out. That guy has some serious anger management issues, and he just wants to complete this job and never see him again, he thinks to himself. He taps his cell chip and calls a familiar name.

"I need information, and my client will pay a premium for it. Can you meet me tonight? This requires expediency. He's looking to find out where the time travel program sent his wife. Yeah, I trust him. He's a cop, he has more to lose than we do."

He ends the call and lights a cigarette. It was a mistake to get mixed up with Chad Cole, but he's in too deep now, and he needs the money. His guilt about what he is going to unleash on Cole's wife is overridden only by his greed. He pushes the remorse and any fragment of conscience he has left aside as he exits the bar.

TWENTY-TWO

Piedmont, Oklahoma 1868

Malcolm and Hannah spend the next few weeks planting and tending the new garden, and they hunt and fish several times a week. Malcolm and Kanuna form a friendship, and while Kanuna's English is minimal and Malcolm's Cherokee is even worse, somehow, they learn to communicate. They see each other often, trading supplies and tracking animals together.

Hannah brings him homemade bread, and he gives her beeswax for candles, honey, and cane baskets. Kanuna and his tribe hunt bison and share meat with them occasionally, although it is not a favorite of theirs. The buffalo are hard to capture because of their size and the number in a herd, and it takes a team effort for a successful kill. Malcolm and his lone rifle could not take one down easily, and they feel better leaving them to the Indians. Hannah knows the bison population is declining, and by 1890 fewer than six hundred will remain in North America. They both agree the natives had their land taken unfairly, and she regrets how her government handled it. She tells Malcolm of the history between the native Americans and the pioneers, and they both want to do whatever they can to maintain a friendly rapport with Kanuna. Relinquishing one of their chief food sources seems an excellent start.

Malcolm brings Hannah to Piedmont once a week to trade and pick-up supplies, mostly just to get her off the ranch, as he can easily go to town alone. But she is still learning how to ride a horse, and they both concede it is not safe for her to be on her own yet. He knows all too well it is a tough transition, going from living in an enormous city such as Los Angeles in 2071 to a small, settled area in 1868. Although she doesn't indicate she is unhappy, he understands she is adjusting. They visit with John almost every day, who takes an instant liking to Hannah. But who would not admire her? She is kind, strong, and beautiful. She never complains about the work here. In fact, she asks Malcolm to take her to the inn today to inquire about joining the women's sewing and quilting group that meets there. He cannot help but respect how she has immersed herself in this lifestyle with no complaint.

Malcolm often wonders at how he cannot imagine his life without her, even though she has only been here a short time. He does his best to tamp down his attraction and growing affection for her, but soon realizes it is no use, and he no longer tries. She is the most wonderful woman he has ever known. But he keeps his sentiments to himself, careful not to step over the line and make her uncomfortable. Besides, he has no clue how she feels about him. He convinces himself if they remain only friends, that will be enough. But deep inside, he recognizes he wants more with her. However, he is a patient man, and he knows she is worth waiting for. He is happier than he's been before, despite being hundreds of years and thousands of miles away from his former existence. And the realization stuns him.

Hannah meets with the women in the sewing group and they accept her with no hesitation. She makes a friend in a local woman named Anne, who teaches her how to prepare butter and preserve and can fruit and vegetables. They see each other regularly, and she and her husband come to supper one evening. They assume Hannah and Malcolm are married, and they play along, even holding hands. There is no other explanation to give them other than them being husband and wife—unless they were to pretend to be family members. A man and woman cannot live together unmarried in this era—it is simply not done. As they chat with the other couple over dinner, Malcolm obsesses over Hannah's hand in his. She glances over at him from time to time, giving him a little squeeze. He smiles back and tightens his grip. Even if it is only for their company's benefit.

Malcolm knows he cannot hide the way he looks at Hannah, and he does not try to anymore. One day while she is at her sewing circle with Anne, John stops by for a visit. As the conversation progresses, John blurts out what is really on his mind.

"So, when are you planning to wed her, Malcolm?"

"What?"

"Hannah. When are you going to ask her to marry you?"

"I'm not John. Don't be daft, mate. And I'd appreciate it if you say nothing to that effect in front of her and embarrass her. She has only been here just over a month. That's a tad too soon where we are from."

"Embarrass her? I believe she is growing tired of waiting for you to court her. And why is this too quick? I'll remind you, Malcolm, you are no longer 'where you come from'. You share a cabin with her. Might as well make an honest woman of her. Who knows how long you'll live?"

Malcolm frowns at John with his mouth agape. "Well, thank you very much for your vote of confidence in my survival skills."

"Don't take offense. Just a fact, Malcolm. Life offers none of us any guarantees. No one can be sure when time will run out for them. Maybe consider that. Do you not notice how she looks at you? You're about as balled up as a man ever was if you don't see it."

Malcolm scowls at John but considers his words. He struggles between his emotions and logic but remains silent. No, John can't be right. He has not seen Hannah look at him the way he does her. Has he? Maybe he has just not noticed before. There have been lingering touches and gazes, sure. But he assumed he was reading more into it. He is so caught up in his own feelings for her, he never stopped to consider she may reciprocate those sentiments. It certainly wouldn't be the first time he missed a cue from a woman, although he definitely plans to pay attention now. He tells John goodbye and leaves to pick Hannah up from her sewing lesson.

Malcolm rides to town under cloudy skies, thinking about what John said to him. As he approaches the hotel, he sees her standing on the sidewalk chatting with Anne. She has her hair gathered at her neck, the chestnut waves tumbling loosely down her back. Anne spots him and whispers something to Hannah, who spins to face him, beaming. His heart skips a beat, and at that moment, he realizes he stands absolutely no chance. He belongs to her, and only her. This is a complication he did not expect, but there is no backpedaling now.

She walks to him, still smiling. "Malcolm, you won't believe it. I started a quilt, and I did it myself!" she says excitedly.

"Well, good on you. You're becoming quite a pioneer woman, aren't you?" he says, holding his hand out to pull her up on his new stallion. They both freeze, hands interlocked, their eyes fixed on each other before Hannah breaks the silence when she realizes what they are doing.

"Yes, I'm getting very efficient at this, I must admit. I will be able to can fruit for us for winter and craft a nice warm quilt too." She answers, clasping his palm firmly as he boosts her up.

"Goodbye Hannah, I'll see you here in two days," Anne calls out from the walkway.

Hannah waves and wraps her arms around Malcolm, leaning her head against his shoulder. The weight of her against him is reassuring, and he smiles as he clicks his tongue and taps his heel on the horse's side.

They ride home in silence, but not an awkward quiet, a comfortable one. She snuggles closer to him and breathes in his scent. She pulls her shawl tighter as a shiver moves through her when a gust of wind hits them. The sky is overcast, black clouds threatening rain. But she knows she is safe with him, as if nothing will ever hurt her. Her feelings for him are changing, becoming more than just a crush, and she does not fight it. She sees how he looks at her, and it doesn't bother her. To be honest, she likes it. And she is sure she is falling for him too. Her thoughts drift to when she met Chad. She felt she was in love then, but in retrospect it was only youth and lust. Never did she have this feeling of contentment and security with Chad. Her relationship with Malcolm is so much more of *everything*. It is deeper than she can articulate, the complete trust she has for him is comforting. She is lost in her daydream when Malcolm stops the horse and twists in the saddle. She shifts to see what he is looking at, and the sight makes her stomach lurch. An enormous tornado looms on the horizon, spinning in their direction.

"Malcolm, we need to get to the cellar," she says shakily.

"It's several miles off, we'll be all right."

"They shift without notice Malcolm, and they travel fast. I know you don't have tornadoes in England, but trust me, they are unpredictable. I grew up in Texas, at the tip of tornado alley, but we are smack in the middle of tornado country here in Oklahoma."

As she finishes her sentence, they watch as the twister takes a sharp turn toward them.

"Okay, I believe you know what you're talking about. Let's get to the house. We'll run to the dugout if we need to. Hold on tight, we are going in record time."

Malcolm runs the horse at top speed, Hannah hanging onto him as tightly as she can. The wind whips her hair into her face and stings her eyes. She turns to check the position of the twister, only to find it maintaining its course straight for their homestead. She buries her face against Malcolm's back and says a silent prayer they make it to the shelter in time. They approach John's seeing him start the climb into his cellar. John is yelling something at them, but the clamor of the approaching tornado drowns out all other sounds around them. It is as loud as a freight train moving right for them. John waves at them frantically, motioning them to his dugout. Malcolm guides the stallion to the opening of the basement and lifts Hannah down. He slaps the horse on the hindquarter, and it runs for shelter behind the house. He grabs Hannah's hand and pulls her toward the hatch, pushing her in first. The sound of the cyclone grows louder as he scales down the ladder and secures the hatchway. Hannah huddles in the corner, covering her ears with her hands and looking terrified. John climbs up, positioning himself just below Malcolm. They hold the door shut with the attached rope pulley as it shudders with the power of the wind. The noise increases as lumber is tossed about like it were matchsticks across the top of the cellar. Then it passes as fast as it came on, leaving an eerie silence in its aftermath. John climbs down, allowing Malcolm to descend and reach Hannah.

"It's over, we're safe," he says, embracing her.

He feels her trembling as he wraps his arms around her, and she rests her head on his chest. "I never want to go through that again," she says, a slight sob emerging from her.

"I don't think that's possible," says John. "Spring brings them every year. You'll grow accustomed to it."

"I doubt I will ever get used to that," she says, wiping her eyes.

"Let's go inspect the damage. I suppose there's no way around that," says Malcolm.

John is the first out of the dugout. Hannah gasps as she surveys the surrounding destruction. Parts of the fence railing are strewn about, tree branches are everywhere, a limb poking through the window of John's cabin. The animals are still in a panic, pacing their pens and making a commotion. Malcolm's horse is in the cabin's rear yard, prancing nervously. They turn in a circle, taking in all the devastation when they see a portion of the barn's roof is missing. The water trough is several feet away from where it normally sits at the edge of the property and is now upside down next to the barn.

"Not as bad as I expected. It looks as if it hit the corner of the barn, and part of the fence is all. Passed right by," says John.

"This is it passing us by?" asks Malcolm. "Good God, I've seen nothing like it in my entire life. Let's check our place, and then I'll help John clean up as much of this as we can today. John, I have lumber left over from my build. We'll use that to reconstruct the railing and the barn roof tomorrow."

Malcolm runs down the horse and calms it enough to bring it home, as he and Hannah hold their breath when they round the corner to their property. The twister did not hit their house, and they sigh with relief. They are quiet as they climb the porch to the cabin, neither of them wants to talk about the tornado, even though it is heavy on both their minds. It was a stark and frightening reminder of how inhospitable this land is. Malcolm gives Hannah a hug before leaving to begin the cleanup, holding her longer than he normally would.

As Hannah unpacks her quilting and gathers things for dinner, she is still shaken from the experience. She tries her best to concentrate, but her thoughts keep wandering back to *what if.* Today could have ended up much worse than it did. As the sun sets behind the hills and she readies the table for supper, Malcolm comes home exhausted, but satisfied with the cleanup progress at John's.

He spends the entire next day helping John rebuild the damage to his property. When he arrives for lunch Hannah tries to lighten the mood and shows Malcolm the quilt she started, so proud she is learning how to sew. The vibrant colors of cloth are cheerful and will create a charming addition to the cabin's décor. Not that there is any existing theme. Now that spring is here, she can pick wildflowers for the house, that will at least add some color. She plans to sew a tablecloth and curtains with gingham fabric so they can remove the grease paper from the windows—or at least cover it so they do not have to look at it. Her mind races with all the ways she aims to make the cabin a home, and she smiles at the thought. That takes her by surprise because she never expected to be happy in 1868, Oklahoma. She imagined she could tolerate being here, perhaps even come close to content with a little luck. What she had not planned on was Malcolm being so wonderful. They have a pleasant life here, albeit somewhat inconvenient. She misses running water, and a proper bathroom, but she enjoys the cooking, gardening, and sewing, and focuses on the positive side of living here.

Malcolm has just returned home, an hour before the sun sets, drained after another full day of physical labor.

"I smelled dinner all the way outside. What are you cooking?"

"I made meatloaf with minced turkey and pork and mashed potatoes. I also cooked up some squash John gave us. I experimented with grinding the meat, using some inspiration from our timeline. Everyone loves meatloaf, right?"

"Well, I do," says Malcolm, lifting the lid on the roasting pan to peek in.

"Hey, hands out of that, it's not done yet," she says, slapping his hand playfully. "I was thinking today, maybe I can find some denim and make us both a pair of jeans, since I'm on the road to becoming a master seamstress."

"Oh, I would be forever indebted to you, lass. These pants are fine, but what I wouldn't give to kick around in some good old jeans."

"Me too. This is the most cumbersome clothing I have ever worn. I can make myself a pullover shirt, and we can wear jeans here at home. We shouldn't be seen in them in public, but at least we'd be comfortable while we work. We could wear them for hunting and fishing too."

"I'm all for that. See what you can find, and I'll sell some meat and hides in town this week. Perhaps we should see if there are any hackberries tomorrow? It's too early for pears and plums yet, but we may snag a few hackberries. We could bring lunch and make a day of it if you'd like?"

"Sure, that sounds great," she says, beaming at him. "Go feed the animals then wash up for dinner, it will be ready by the time you get back in here."

"Yes ma'am," he says, saluting her.

When he walks in again, John is trailing him. "I found this starving man in our garden."

"You're always welcome for supper John, grab yourself a plate."

"Thank you kindly, it smells delicious."

They eat the meatloaf and potatoes, the men going back for second helpings. As Hannah clears the table, John motions for them to be quiet. He listens for a minute, and waves for them to get down. Malcolm grabs his weapon and crawls to the window behind John. John uses his rifle barrel to move the grease paper aside an inch and peer out.

"Indians," he whispers.

"It's probably Kanuna," Malcolm whispers back.

John shakes his head and turns to Hannah. "No, these aren't friendlies. Hannah, get under the bed with your knife. If anything happens to us, stay there. Do not come out. Pull the blanket over the side so you're covered."

Hannah looks from John to Malcolm, confused. "But I—"

"Do it, Hannah, now!" hisses Malcolm, as he moves to the other window.

Both men position at the windows, rifles aimed as she scrambles beneath the bed. She pulls the blanket over the side as she hears the horses neigh and the dogs bark furiously, scratching at the door to get out. A shot rings out from somewhere outside, causing her to gasp and push herself further toward the wall. An arrow whistles through the open window where John has taken a stand and pierces the back of a dining room chair with a loud *thwack*. John instructs Malcolm to fire, and the blast in the enclosed space is deafening. She covers her ears and sobs, still clutching her knife. Her entire body shakes and her stomach lurches at the prospect of what could happen next.

All at once the shooting stops, and John motions to Malcolm to follow him outside.

Malcolm glances back toward the bed, and whispers to Hannah. "Stay hidden until I come for you, do you understand?"

She nods to herself, unable to speak, her whimpering the only sound she can manage.

"Hannah!" Malcolm calls out again.

"Yes," she answers, choking the word out.

The front door opens, and another bullet shatters the quiet. The noise makes her jolt, and she cries out. She slaps her hand over her mouth, and the silence after seems to last forever. She trembles in her hiding place, clinging to the blade like a lifeline. After yesterday's tornado scare, this is more than she can tolerate, and her stomach twists with fear as she has never known before.

The voices coming from the yard terrify her. The yelping sounds like an animal—but she knows it is not. Gunshots ring out, and she hears Malcolm shout something to John she cannot make out over the turbulence. She makes herself as small as possible, pressed against the wall, weeping softly as images of what might happen outside flood her. Hannah prays for Malcolm and John's safety as she imagines what they are facing just beyond the cabin door. This is the thing she feared most—an Indian attack. She squeezes her eyes shut and tightens her grip on the knife. If something happens to them and she is left here alone, what will become of her? Then she realizes perhaps the Indians know she is in here. She cannot allow herself to complete the thought. It is too terrifying to imagine.

TWENTY-THREE

Piedmont, Oklahoma 1868

The scene outside is chaotic. Malcolm takes shelter behind the outhouse, John, on the side of the cabin, their weapons trained on four Indians on horses. They wear face paint and chest plates made of beads or bones—Malcolm cannot identify which. Their quivers are slung over their backs, and they hold rifles instead of the bows and arrows he expects them to brandish. One native has a goat who belongs to Malcolm tied to a short rope and secured to the back of his horse. The animal bleats loudly and struggles against the restraint in the turmoil. The yelping sounds they emit as they raise the guns over their heads add to the unnatural sight playing out in front of him. Even with all he sees, he doesn't know why he can't bring himself to fire. They are attacking his home and stealing his livestock. Yet there is something so fascinating and majestic about them, an overwhelming feeling prevents him from shooting.

John no longer has an open shot from his hiding spot, and firing would only make him an easy target. Malcolm, however, has a clean line of sight. But he stands frozen behind the outbuilding, weapon poised, but unable to pull the trigger. If they move toward Hannah, he knows his instinct will override everything, and he will kill every last one of them where they stand. But he cannot execute a man over a goat. What feels like several minutes has really been only seconds, as he watches them from the protection of the structure. One of the Indians shouts in a language he cannot translate, and for reasons he does not understand, he steps clear of his cover. He lowers his rifle to the ready position at his midsection. Three of them turn to him, weapons raised, but the native who shouted raises his hand to stop them from shooting. He glares at Malcolm for a beat before letting loose a high-pitched yelp. He turns and rides off; the others following him.

The sound of a galloping horse draws Malcolm's attention to the rear of the property, where he sees Kanuna ride into view. As the attackers crest the hill and disappear over the horizon, Malcolm remains rooted in the same spot, staring in the direction they rode. John runs from around the house and joins Kanuna at Malcolm's side.

"You had a clean shot, Malcolm, why didn't you take it? They will be back now to make off with whatever they want, whenever they choose," says John, obviously upset. "They came to steal from us, thinking we would be unprepared after the tornado that blew through yesterday. And you have proved them right!"

"No. Malcolm has honor and is brave. That is why warriors leave. They not come back," declares Kanuna in his broken English.

John scowls at Kanuna, the disbelief written all over his expression.

"I don't know why I didn't shoot John. If they had gone after Hannah, I would have taken action, that much I'm certain of. But it seems all they wanted was food, the goat. I choked, I guess. It was surreal. Like a scene from a movie."

He frowns at Malcolm. "A what?"

"Never mind, I'll explain movies another time. I need to get Hannah. She must be terrified."

"Kanuna went to check on her. Help me put the other animals in their pens before you wind up losing all of them."

Only then does he realize Kanuna just crossed the threshold and is in the cabin. He helps John herd the livestock and secure them before heading to the house.

* * *

There has been no sound from outside since the gruesome yell moments before. Hannah's heartbeat seems to echo in the room, and she is convinced her ragged breathing will give away her hiding place. She hears soft footfalls and sees the lower half of Indian moccasins. Adrenaline surges through her veins as she grips the knife with white knuckles, poised to attack. The blanket pulls up, and she takes a minute to realize someone is calling her name.

"Hannah."

First a hand appears, then a familiar face peeks under the bed.

"Kanuna," she says, with such relief it escapes with a sob.

"Come." He reaches under and she allows him to help her out.

She rises and stares at the open door, tears streaming down her cheeks. "Malcolm," she exclaims, twisting to run.

"No," he says, grabbing her arm.

She spins to face him, her expression pleading. "He good," says Kanuna, nodding.

She lets her breath out, not realizing she was holding it until then.

Malcolm jogs through the entry at that moment, moving straight to Hannah. He wraps his arms around her, and she buries her head in his shoulder, sobbing.

"It's all right. It's over."

She lifts her eyes to meet his. "What happened?"

"Four natives trying to steal livestock. They fired on us as soon as they saw our rifles. Once we returned their fire it was dodgy, but they left. They got one of our goats."

He can't bring himself to tell her how he froze during the battle. Not yet, anyway. He cannot explain his lack of action and wants to think about his behavior before he defends it to anyone else.

"Oh no! Is John okay?"

"He's fine. Just checking his place. Kanuna heard the firefight from the river and came to help."

Malcolm offers Kanuna his hand, and he shakes it. "Friend, Malcolm," says Kanuna.

"Yes, friend," replies Malcolm.

Once Hannah composes herself, she packs the leftover meatloaf and potatoes for Kanuna and insists he take it as a thank you. He holds it up in a gesture of appreciation.

"No atsadi Nvda."

She cocks her head at him, and Malcolm translates. "He doesn't have to fish tomorrow with the sun. He has food now."

She smiles shakily at him and he turns to leave. He is a man of few words, but somehow, he and Malcolm have built a close trust for each other and she values his friendship today more than ever.

Dusk is in full swing as Malcolm leaves to check on John. She sits at the table but peeks out the window every few minutes until he returns, too shaken up to do anything more. Malcolm checks the ranch a final time for the evening and puts Buddy on the porch for the night as a precaution. After getting the dog settled in a blanket, he joins her, hoping to sooth her uneasiness.

"Well, that broke up the monotony, didn't it?"

She meets his stare before they both burst into laughter. Then her eyes fill again. "I can't understand why I'm laughing at this. I've never been so scared or helpless in my entire life."

"Hey, we're all right. They won't come back here. Kanuna thinks our honor and bravery toward them means they have respect for us now." He smiles as he says the words, not entirely believing them. He knows the Indians are going to return at some point, and he had better be ready for them when they show up.

"Okay," she sniffs. "Would you care if we took the screen down tonight? Just so I can see you? It would help me feel safer if it wouldn't bother you. First the tornado and now an Indian attack. I'm on edge."

"Of course, I don't mind. Keep your weapon next to the bed too."

"I wish I had one, Malcolm. Well, besides my knife, which I have no intention of letting go."

"Actually, you do. I intended to surprise you with it when we went hunting again. But I suppose after this, you should have it." He crosses the room and reaches behind his headboard, where he draws out a rifle. "She's not fancy, but she will get the job done."

"Wow, I can't believe you did this! When did you sneak this past me?"

"Come on now, I can't give away all my secrets."

She picks up the rifle and tests the weight in her hands. "I've always shot handguns at the range back home, but I've used one of these a couple of times. It's perfect. Thank you, Malcolm," she says, giving him a quick kiss on the cheek.

His first instinct is to grab her and return the kiss, but he stops himself, still uncertain how she feels about him. Instead, he puts more wood on the fire and grabs the cards from the cupboard.

"You continue to impress me, Hannah. I had no idea you knew how to shoot. You up for a game before bed?" he asks, holding up the deck.

"Sure, I can win again, if you want to play," she says, trying to hold back a smile. "I was married to a cop, remember? His version of a rare date night was going to the shooting range."

"Card challenge accepted," he teases, narrowing his eyes at her playfully. "Your ex-husband sounds like a true romantic."

"He was, is, an egotistical idiot. Let's not talk about him, he isn't worth our time."

"Agreed."

Malcolm shuffles the deck while they each have a shot of whiskey to take the edge off the events of the past two days. When Hannah yawns after they play a couple of games, he gathers the cards and insists she get some sleep after all the trauma. As he folds the divider and stores it in the room's corner, he tries not to let on how thrilled he is to have it down. He twists around while she slips out of her dress and under the blanket, and she turns to the wall while he undresses and slides into bed.

He rolls over to face her. "Goodnight, Hannah. Sleep well. And please don't worry. You're safe, I promise you."

She smiles at him and pulls the cover up to her chin. "I trust you, Malcolm. Goodnight."

Those three words, 'I trust you,' ignite a fire deep within him and he makes a pledge to himself right then—he will protect her by whatever means possible. He smiles to himself as he looks at Hannah, the firelight dancing and casting shadows across her face. He has never been closer or more connected to a woman before.

* * *

Malcolm wakes before Hannah and watches her sleep for a minute before putting water on for coffee. Her long hair fans out over the bed and she has kicked part of her blanket off to reveal her bare leg up to her thigh. He looks away, not wanting to humiliate himself or embarrass her by gawking like some lovesick adolescent. He feels the heat spread across his face and shakes his head.

"Blimey, get it together, man," he whispers to himself.

Once the coffee is brewing, he has his behavior in check, and the aroma draws her from her slumber, just as he knew it would. She sits up in bed, her gaze going straight to the coffeepot.

"You are a saint, Malcolm. That smells great," she says, rubbing her eyes.

"It's a beautiful spring morning. Let's go pick hackberries after breakfast."

"I'm game. Give me a moment to wash up. I wish I had jeans or something else to put on. I'm sick of this long dress," she adds, glaring at her clothing hung over the edge of her bed.

"You're welcome to wear a pair of my cotton trousers and a pullover shirt if you prefer that to the skirts? They're not pretty, but I washed them with the soap Christine sent us."

"Oh yes, I would like that. I'll be much more comfortable picking fruit and riding if I'm in pants."

"Done. I'll go tend to the critters and you wash up and change clothes."

He goes to the chest at the end of his bed and pulls out brown trousers and a beige tunic. He grabs suspenders and a flat-brimmed hat and lays them out for her.

"Suspenders?" she asks, wrinkling her nose.

"These will never stay up on you without them."

She shrugs and glances at the clothing. Not exactly her style, but it is better than her usual attire. She wants to ride her own horse today to gain more practice, and the dress does not make that easy. As soon as Malcolm is outside, she washes her face and brushes her teeth, pinning her hair up.

She must roll the trousers up several times to prevent them from dragging. She draws the suspenders tight and cinches her belt with the knife pouch over the tunic. Rolling the shirt sleeves up as a finishing touch, she slips into her boots. She positions the hat and pulls it down, securing it in place.

She finds a cane basket Kanuna gave them, and packs a simple lunch of biscuits, jam, and dried ham. After including four emergency water pouches from her survival supplies along with the LifeStraw, she closes the lid. She starts for the door, then remembers something else. Someone at the hotel who hosts her sewing circle left a map of the area out when she was last there. She put it in her apron and forgot about it until now. The folded paper gets placed into the bottom of the basket, and she snatches her rifle from where it leans against her bed. She takes a quick glance around the cabin to make she sure she has everything they need and steps out onto the porch.

Malcolm is saddling the horses and stops to stare at her. The shirt is cinched tightly at her waist, showing off her curves, and loose tendrils of hair fall out from under the hat. He always sees her in yards of fabric in her dress with a smock, so this is the first time he has really seen her figure, and it renders him speechless for a moment.

"I know, it's not a fashion statement. This is the best I could do with what you lent me."

"Very posh. I think you look bloody fabulous, Hannah," he says, never breaking eye contact with her.

She senses herself blush as he stands smiling at her.

"You're such a great bullshitter, Malcolm. I'm uncertain if that should flatter or completely horrify me you would consider this get-up in any way attractive."

He laughs, and grabs the basket from her, tying it onto his saddle pack. "Take that as the sincere compliment I meant it as."

They mount their horses and ride off in a trot towards the river where they stop to let the horses drink and rest. The weather is mild, and a light breeze blows through the prairie grass, making it dance like waves—a perfect spring day. But Malcolm does not want to stay long. It is a three-hour trip to the orchard with the wild fruit trees. The days are longer now that summer approaches, but he wants to be back to the ranch before dark, still uneasy after the attack on them yesterday. They pick walnuts from the grove, storing them in their saddle packs, and continue over the plains and creeks, side by side. On the way they find a few persimmons left from the growing season, which Hannah can use with the nuts to produce sweet bread. She insists he forage from a patch of prickly pear cactus she discovers, telling him it spices up soup or fries nicely with onion.

"How did you learn about all these wild plants? I've never eaten cacti, and I have never heard of a persimmon."

"I told you, I had the leverage of knowing where I would exile. I took the time to research everything I could during my incarceration, and I ordered books on edible plants, nuts and fruits from the prison library."

"Well, lucky me. I get the benefit of that legwork."

"Too bad we don't have an oven. I could bake cookies and such. The pot and fire limit our menu choices."

"We can purchase one. We haven't used much of the money Christine sent with you. I know we are saving it for large purchases and emergencies, but that is a major acquisition, right? And it would make our lives easier. Especially for you, since you prepare most of our meals. I am always down for a good nosh up, so a cooker it is."

"Really? Do you think we could?"

"It will only be a wood-burning stove, but it seems as if that would be an improvement on the pots and fireplace we operate with now."

"Infinitely better!"

"Then consider it done. That is my next goal in improving our living arrangements. I intend to build a makeshift shower too. I can rig the barrels to a pour jug that pulls warm water over us a bit at a time and erect lumber around it for privacy. I'll situate it close to the house. I figure it will work. Oh, and John said he would help me construct a small barn for the animals during inclement weather. And eventually, I would love to save enough to replace the grease paper with real windows."

"Malcolm, if you locate me a stove and build us a shower, I will cook you anything you want for the rest of our lives! And I agree one hundred percent with the glass. We should order it next time we are in town."

"I will hold you to that cooking promise."

Hannah stops her mare, peering ahead. "Oh my gosh, I think that's a Pawpaw tree up there," she says, trotting her horse to a small group of trees.

"A what?" Malcolm asks.

"A Pawpaw tree. You won't spot many this far west in Oklahoma. They ripen quickly once picked, although these aren't anywhere near ripe yet. Maybe I can speed up the process by putting them in a barrel. The dark might help mature them. It's worth a try. They are like a fat banana. It's sweet and tangy and the same texture. We can eat it raw or I'll cook it into bread for some flavor. Or a fruit salad if we find apples. We still have honey left that Kanuna gave us, and that would make an excellent treat."

They pick a dozen and pack them away with the walnuts, prickly pear and persimmons. After two hours of riding, Malcolm tells her they are near the orchards where they search for another thirty minutes before they locate it. They walk the horses through the shady grove to look for anything ready to harvest. The peaches, pears and plums are blooming with small green fruit not yet ripe, but the hackberry trees are ready. They eat lunch sitting on a plot of grass under an enormous tree. Hannah opens a persimmon for Malcolm, who screws his face into a knot after tasting the tangy fruit. She chuckles and assures him the sweet tartness will be delicious in a cookie or bread.

Her mood turns serious when she pulls out the flattened map and spreads it open before them. She runs her fingers over the worn paper, showing him where their restricted zones start.

"We are just inside the yellow sector now. We shouldn't move much beyond this point."

"I had no idea where our secured area was. But of course, I wouldn't, arriving from England."

"Christine was very adamant we pay close attention to our unauthorized localities. She said she could not save us if we travel into a red territory and it flags the enforcement team. The only major historical event I could find near us is the Battle of Washita River, which occurs on November 27 this year. That takes place near Cheyenne, which is about one-hundred-twenty miles from the ranch, as best as I can calculate. General Custer attacks Black Kettle Southern Cheyenne camp, killing peace-seeking natives and many innocent women and children. We don't want to be there for that."

"No, we don't. I hope the Cherokee are safe. Kanuna and his people deserve nothing less."

"I agree. I know you aren't as familiar with American history as I am. I mentioned the government forcing the indigenous to give up their land. I want no part of that. Kanuna is our friend, and we should help him in any way we can as long as we're here."

"Agreed. I'd be gutted to see them mistreated."

After lunch they pick the berries, and Hannah climbs the low branches of a hackberry tree to reach the top fruit, while Malcolm stands below her, arms outstretched.

"Hannah, please come down. That isn't very safe," he pleads.

"I've climbed plenty of trees in my youth, I'll be fine."

"But you're not a young lass anymore, may I remind you."

"Are you calling me old?"

"Never! I'm a much smarter man than that, I promise you."

"Fine, I'll come down if it will make you feel better."

She starts the climb down and as she reaches the bottom branch two feet above Malcom, her boot slips, and she falls forward into his arms. He takes a step backward as he catches her at the waist. She gasps and wraps her arms around his neck for balance as she slides down through his embrace until her eyes are level with his. Their gaze locks, and Malcolm's heartbeat quickens. Her eyes are as green as a spring meadow. Loose tendrils of hair curl about her face, framing it against the sunlit sky. The breeze lifts the strands of stray wisp, allowing them to float in the air as if moved by some unseen hand. He is near enough to count the freckles on her nose and finds it impossible to pull away from her.

Hannah is instantly aware of his arms around her. She is so close to him she can feel the heat coming from him, and time seems to slow her every breath.

He brings his hand to her head and draws her toward him. She hesitates before she leans in to meet him halfway. Then he kisses her, and all her resolve shatters like fine china. Their kiss is gentle, as if they are both fearful this might be the only opportunity they ever have. She pulls back, staring at him. This is everything she imagined it would be, and she allows herself to melt into him for a second time. When he whispers her name, her heart flutters at the very sound of it on his lips.

Her touch is all Malcolm needs to realize how Hannah feels about him. It is intoxicating. The slow burn and passion that has been building in him for the past two months boils to the surface and he pulls her tighter to him. He places her tenderly on the ground, her eagerness for him only intensifying his own longing.

As they undress each other, their gaze never wavers, eyes locked on each other. Neither speak as they lower themselves to the bed of grass.

Malcolm is gentle, even though his desire for her is feverish. He wants to go slow and savor every moment with her.

Hannah has never had such a riveting encounter with a man. The intensity is like nothing she has ever experienced. He is tender and powerful all at the same time, and she gives herself to him with a passion she has not felt before now.

As they lie together afterward, limbs entwined, Hannah cannot help but grin. She breathes in Malcolm's scent and closes her eyes. How is this possible? That she would find this man and fall in love in 1868, Oklahoma, is hard to believe. But that is precisely where she finds herself. She turns to look at him, and he smiles. Reaching up, he brushes stray hair from her face.

"I love you, Hannah Cole."

"I love you too, Malcolm Aldred."

"If those are the last words I hear, I will die a happy bloke."

She kisses him again and pours a small bit of water from a pouch onto her palm. She runs her fingers through his hair, trying to smooth it. "You have a cowlick," she says, giggling.

"That means I need a haircut. I've had it since I was a lad. When it grows too long, it stands up in that spot and refuses to lie down no matter what I do."

He lifts her hand in his and kisses her palm, placing it on his chest. She rests her head on his shoulder. They talk for hours, confessing their feelings for each, sharing secrets and the stories of what drove them to their exiles.

"What led you here, Malcolm, to the exile program, I mean."

"I had a moment of poor judgement that would change the course of my life forever. I'm not a thief, I think I was just fed up at that point. Something in me gave way, for lack of a better explanation. But I shall never regret it. It brought me here to you. And for that reason alone, I can only be thankful," he says.

Hannah talks about Chad and the abuse she suffered at his hands. He draws his lips into a thin line, his eyes flashing with anger as she tells him the story of her marriage.

"It all seems like a lifetime ago. The memory fades more each day, almost as if it happened to someone else. I'm a different person, and I cannot imagine tolerating his maltreatment now. Pioneer living has toughened me up, I suppose, and given me my old confidence. And more importantly, I'm happy here with you, Malcolm, and I wouldn't give that up for anyone or anything."

"I feel the same way. I have waited for you my entire life, and it took going back in time two-hundred years to find you. But it was worth it all to get to this moment."

She looks at him with tears in her eyes. "I couldn't agree more."

After an hour of lazing in the grass, Malcolm reluctantly rises to dress, knowing they should start for home before it gets any later.

They run the horses part of the way, making a good pace, Hannah laughing at the feeling of freedom and the wind in her face. They arrive before dusk and unpack the fruits before Malcolm washes and feeds the animals. He takes some hackberries to John, insisting he will be fine with none of the persimmons. When he walks back into the cabin, he heads straight for Hannah. He wraps his arms around her, and they linger there for several minutes.

"Are you all right with this, Hannah? If you've changed your mind, I'll understand. I want to remain a couple, but not at your expense. I really hadn't expected this to develop. Don't misunderstand me, I wanted it to happen, and I'm completely chuffed it did. But I need you to be all in. So, if you have reservations about me, about us, this is the time to voice them."

"Oh, shut up, Malcolm. My dad used to always say stop talking after the sale. You sold me when I met you," she says, taking his hand in hers and leading him to the bed they would share every night from that day forward.

TWENTY-FOUR

Los Angeles, California 2071/Piedmont, Oklahoma, 1868

Christine's weekend with Annabelle is the distraction she needs. They attend a concert and dance like they are teenagers while drinking wine. On Sunday she barbeques, and Michael, Maddie, Frank and his wife, Linda, join them. The liquor and conversation flow, and when Annabelle's car service picks her up for the airport, Christine is exhausted, but happy. Once she is alone, she calls Jonathan Hoyt, not waiting until Monday as Frank suggested. She wants that done so she does not worry about it. He agrees to suspend the system for a few hours in three weeks to allow her to warn Malcolm and Hannah of Chad's intentions.

The next few weeks fly by. Ethan's upcoming relocation to Los Angeles occupies her thoughts, and she helps him with arrangements from her end. Although they are a couple, she has not agreed they live as one. She feels strongly they should each have their own space for now. Maybe some of that decision is her former anti-social-commitment-phobic-self rising to the surface, but she is reluctant to rush things with him. If they move in together, then it would force the relationship to accelerate, and she prefers it to develop organically. She knows she is in love with him, and he with her. However, she has not been serious with a man in ten years, and she wants to take it slow. Her trauma of being stranded in history all those months softened her personality and allowed her vulnerability to cultivate, but her newfound level of patience does not always transfer to mundane, day-to-day living—she accepts she is a work in progress.

As the covert date approaches, she and Frank construct a plan. She should wear her own period clothing, just as she did on the last stealth trip, and go for no longer than four hours. And they will follow all safety precautions upon her return. She cannot help but be nervous though, she puts everything on the line with each unauthorized expedition she makes. Hoyt assures them no one can detect anything when he adjusts the process, but she realizes nothing is ever foolproof. The moment she thinks they are impervious could be their first mistake. So, they plot and review every detail many times before she travels. On the day of her transport, she arrives in the jump room well ahead of the other scheduled agents. Frank reminds her to watch her time, handing her the antique wristwatch again. She places it in the pocket of her apron where she has stashed some envelopes of MiracleGro, and a large package of fruit and vegetable heirloom starters. The pack contains seeds for a wide variety of vegetables and berries, along with grapes and watermelon, and she stuffed some peanuts in there too. No reason she cannot bring them a little treat as long as she is going there, anyway.

"Be careful and get back here as soon as possible," says Frank. "And don't think I didn't notice what you have in your pocket, Christine. Aren't we taking enough chances without you smuggling goodies to them?"

"Take it easy, boss, it's not the end of the world. It's some seed packets and grow powder, that's all. They can shell the peanuts and plant them and at least make peanut butter. You don't realize what it takes to survive there, I do."

"A few peanuts, fine. But seeds and fertilizer too? What's next, a plow? Why not bring them an aquaponic kit too?"

She rolls her eyes at him. "So dramatic, Frank. It's Oklahoma. They need something to bolster plant growth in that dirt. Anyway, I'll meet you here before noon. Try not to fret and wring your hands like a little old lady the entire time I'm gone," she sighs.

"You know, if we weren't such established friends, I would take offense at about fifty percent of everything you say to me."

"Awww, I love you too. Now, get me out of here. Time's wasting."

He secures her pod and starts the transport, sending her to the one place she thought she would never visit again.

* * *

She opens her eyes to the recognizable landscape of the walnut grove. It is warm out with a gentle breeze blowing through the trees. She studies the wristwatch. She has burned thirty minutes of her four hours. She sits for a minute to allow the vertigo to pass and stretches her legs, planning to jog the entire route to Malcolm's, saving time. Christine runs almost every day and can do the three miles easily. She starts the now familiar trek to the ranch, finding her rhythm quickly. She passes the river sparkling in the morning sun and turns northeast on a straight path to the cabin. Once she crests the final ridge, she sees the house. Stopping to catch her breath, she wipes her forehead with the bottom of her apron and checks the watch again. It took her forty-three minutes to make it here. Not an impressive run, but she is wearing work boots and moving through tall prairie grass. An enormous difference to jogging on flat pavement with running shoes. She drinks from one of her emergency water pouches and takes off, reaching the porch a few minutes later to tap on the door. She hears Malcolm shout, "C'mon in John, just doing the breakfast dishes."

When she clears the threshold, she peeks around the corner, "Sorry to disappoint you, it's not John."

Malcolm drops the pot he is holding and twists toward her. Hannah is making the bed—the only one in the cabin. Isn't that interesting, she thinks to herself? She's fairly certain Malcolm mentioned building her a bed on her previous trip here. Christine notices this immediately but says nothing. Hannah squeals and runs to her, hugging her tightly. Malcolm is behind her, pushing his way into the hug.

"What are you doing here?" asks Hannah, "I'm so excited to see you!"

Malcolm stands with his arm slung over Hannah's shoulders, her head tucked against him, both beaming from ear to ear. Christine stares at them a moment, mouth open, eyebrows raised.

"Um, I, I have some things to talk to you about. . ." she trails off, still staring at them, Hannah now firmly grasping Malcolm's waist.

"Oh, this must surprise you," giggles Hannah, glancing up at Malcolm, who laughs.

"Well, I admit it's not what I expected. So, are you going to tell me about it?"

"Sit down," says Malcolm, pulling out a chair. "Can I get you some water or coffee? We have some nice mint for tea, if you'd rather have that?"

"Tea would be wonderful."

Malcolm sets a pouch of water from Hannah's supplies on the counter to start tea.

"I can drink creek water."

"No, no, we don't want to get you sick, we'll use this. We just used the last of our boiled water. No sense in taking a chance of an upset stomach."

"So, when did this happen?" she asks, motioning between the two of them, their entwined hands resting on the table.

"A little over a month ago, I suppose. It was inevitable. You sent the most fantastic woman in the world to me, Christine."

Hannah kisses the top of his hand and continues to grin.

Christine sits in silence watching them. She groans inwardly, knowing this will complicate what she is about to tell them even more than she thought. She takes a deep breath and treads lightly as she begins the conversation.

"All right, well, I cannot argue with that logic. Listen, I have little time here, and I need to warn you both about a potential problem. Given what you've just told me, you will like this less than I thought."

Before either of them responds, a knock at the door draws their attention. Malcolm reaches it in three strides and opens it to John. He steps in and stops when he sees Christine. She rises and John meets her halfway for an embrace.

"What are you doing here? Are you all right?"

"I'm fine, John. I just got here. I'm glad you're here, you should hear this too. I have some news to share."

"Christine, what's this all about?" asks Malcolm.

"Hannah, Chad confronted me about your transport."

"What?" she shrieks, rising so fast her chair topples over, her hand flying to her mouth. "What did he say?" Her mind spins with images of Chad on his way here to hurt her.

Malcolm rights the chair and guides her back into it. "Calm down, let's find out what she has to say and then we'll figure out what to do, okay?" She nods at him, water flooding her eyes. She swipes at the tears with her palm.

"He tried to convince me to tell him where you are. Which, of course, I didn't do. But he obviously has an informant in the CCEA who has disclosed I transported you. Frank delayed clearing your transport for three weeks so your destination would not go into the records right away. It was as long as he could postpone it."

"Okay, good. So, we have some time," says Malcolm, directing the remark to no one in particular as he paces the room.

"No, you don't understand. Chad came to me three weeks ago. The information goes into the archives tomorrow. Hoyt couldn't send me back to notify you until now. We must limit my visits here. When he suspends the system for me to come here, it shows as an anomaly. Within normal tolerance as far as IT is concerned. But if too many of those malfunctions show up spaced too closely together, well, that will raise a red flag."

"So, tomorrow he'll know where I am?" cries Hannah.

"Not necessarily, no. He didn't know your whereabouts, or he would never have approached me. We aren't sure if his mole has clearance beyond inmate assignment or if they can access the entire system for destination records. It could be any of hundreds of employees. We can't report him, or it will lead an investigation straight to us. And worse, to you. If they discover we planned this, they'll reassign you in a heartbeat. Not to mention they will arrest Frank and me."

"So, what, we just wait to see if he turns up?" asks Malcolm.

"Not him, an exiled inmate. He told me he would bribe the next prisoner coming anywhere near you to kill you. I'm sorry, Hannah. But there was no way to prevent this from happening. If he wants to find you and has the resources, he probably will. Frank and I wanted to warn you so you can take precautions."

"Precautions? What am I supposed to do? I can't run. If I enter the red sector, they'll send me somewhere else."

"Then we'll both travel outside the green zone. My tracker works. We'll leave and keep doing it and continue to time jump. He'll never keep up with us that way," says Malcolm, still pacing the room nervously.

"That won't work, Malcolm. Even if you run together, they'll assign each tracker elsewhere, independent of each other. They will move you to one place and Hannah to another. Your best bet is to stay put and remain cognizant of the threat."

"We'll be ready for anyone who tries to get to Hannah," declares John.

Malcolm runs his hands through his hair and stops pacing. "Damn straight we will. Starting today. I'll be damned before I allow that slimy bastard to dispatch someone to come into our home and harm Hannah! That bloke has really lost the plot if he thinks I am going to stand by idly."

Christine reaches for the watch, noting she only has an hour and a half to make it to base. "I have to leave soon, and I almost forgot. I brought you something."

She takes the packages from her apron pockets, placing them on the dinner table. "Fruit and vegetable seeds, MiracleGro and peanuts. The soil booster will help the plants thrive, especially the peanuts."

"Thank you, Christine. I'd be more excited if I hadn't just learned of Chad's plans, but we are very grateful for these," says Hannah, scooping the gifts toward her.

"I understand it's difficult to hear this. But Malcolm and John are right. You'll prepare in case anyone shows up. Don't forget, you have the advantage here. Chad and whoever he hired won't realize you are expecting them. Hell, maybe the prisoner will change their mind and move on. They may be too busy dealing with their own survival to worry about you. I'll check in with you in a month or two. That's the best we can manage, I'm afraid."

"We'll be fine, Christine. Thank you for warning us. I'll take care of her, I promise."

"I know you will, Malcolm. I wouldn't have sent her here if I believed otherwise."

She gives them each a hug goodbye, assuring them she will come back as soon as possible with any additional information. She transports away from inside the cabin, once again leaving John aghast as she fades into nothingness.

John excuses himself to go home, providing them privacy to absorb the news. Hannah wills herself to calm down and look at the situation through the eyes of an outsider, not her own, the woman Chad abused for so many years. First, he will have to find out where she is, then hire someone willing to harm her. That person has to locate her and then get past Malcolm. All of that will take time, the minor obstacles slowing his progress. Information is power, she reminds herself, and right now they have that advantage in their corner.

They sit at the table, neither of them speaking. They are both shaken by the report of Chad's plans, a palpable heaviness in the air. Hannah flinches when Malcolm finally breaks the silence.

"Are you all right?"

"I'm not surprised by this, not really. I knew he would be livid and never accept me leaving him. Chad is very vindictive. He'll continue at this until someone agrees to do his dirty work. That's just how he is."

"Hannah, I would appreciate it if you never say that man's name in my presence again. And I use the term man loosely here. I would call him a dog, but that would only insult Buddy. I give you my word here and now, I'll not allow him to spoil the world we are building together. I will move heaven and earth if necessary. Christine is right. We need to carry on with our lives as planned. We know there is a threat, and we will brace for it. It makes no difference to me how far off the trolley he's gone. You are no longer married to him. I refuse to let him disrupt our way of life," he says, slamming his fist on the tabletop.

Hannah shudders, then rises to slide onto his lap, wrapping her arms around his neck. "He can never ruin what we have, Malcolm. But I agree, we continue as usual and be careful. We have the power because we realize what he's up to."

Malcolm kisses her and untangles from her embrace. He stands facing her, taking her hands in his and looking into her eyes.

"Hannah Cole, I love you," he declares as he dips to one knee. "Do me the honor of becoming my wife."

Eyes widening, she stares at him in shock.

"Say something, please. I can't tell if you're too stunned to speak or attempting to let me down easy."

"What? Oh, yes!" she replies, giggling. "A thousand times, yes!"

In one fluid motion he picks her up, spinning her around while they laugh, planting kisses on her face. Malcolm runs to the door and flings it open. He stops on the porch with his arms spread wide. "She said yes!" he exclaims, shouting it over and over.

Within two minutes John and his dog run along the worn path between the houses and plow through the gate to see what is going on.

Hannah stands behind him, giggling as Malcolm grabs John in an embrace. "She said yes, John!"

"I worked that out, Malcolm," he hollers back over the noise of the dogs barking, the goat bleating, and the pigs squealing. "It seems everyone for miles knows, including all of our animals!"

Kanuna marries them two days later with John and Kanuna's wife Adsila as their witnesses. Hannah wants Anne there, but she already thinks they are husband and wife, so that would raise too many questions they cannot answer. Malcolm purchases a gold and ruby ring from John that belonged to his mother and gifts it to Hannah on their wedding day.

"But I don't have anything for you," she says, sitting on the edge of their bed admiring her ring.

"I can hire a blacksmith to make me a band. I wanted you to have a ring on your wedding day."

He slides the ring into his pocket, and they ride to their wedding site at the river's edge.

The ceremony combines American and Cherokee traditions as Kanuna incorporates much of his clan's rituals. They stand in front of three separate fires, a large one lit in the center. When Kanuna sings a sacred tribal song, they light the smaller fires that represent the bride and groom. They push them into the larger fire, which embodies the Creator and the marriage to burn as one, then end the service by drinking from a Cherokee wedding vase together. Kanuna tells them because they did not spill from the jar, they can expect a mutual understanding throughout their marriage. Malcolm slips the ring on Hannah's finger and lifts her, twirling her while she throws her head back laughing. Kanuna and his wife sing, and John joins in the celebration. Neither of them worries theirs is not a lawful union in the eyes of the state, or that anyone would ever challenge its validity. Why would they? Their commitment is what matters to them, and they are both devoted to each other. It is a wonderful wedding filled with joy and love, and they both forget about Chad and his plot to hurt Hannah, if only for a while.

TWENTY-FIVE

Piedmont, Oklahoma 1868

Life returns to normal as the weeks pass, and no threats materialize. They assume Chad cannot determine where she is or has not found an inmate willing to do his dirty work for him. But with the possibility of someone coming after her, coupled with the recent Indian scare, they both agree Hannah should learn to handle her rifle expertly. She practices every day, and after a month she is skilled enough that Malcolm teases her they would certify her as a sharpshooter if this era allowed women to qualify. He calls her his Annie Oakley as their own private joke, as no one will recognize her name until Annie joins the Buffalo Bill Wild West Show in 1885. She is proud of her progress and handles her new weapon with confidence.

Early one afternoon not long after the raid on their home, while Malcolm is at the river with John, Hannah is picking miner's lettuce in back of the cabin when she sees an Indian approach from the hill behind the dugout. She freezes, knowing he is probably one from the recent attack. He rides out of sight as she peeks around the corner. She watches him trot his horse to the side of the house, the stallion prancing excitedly while he studies the livestock pens. Although she is frightened, the anger boiling within her somehow overrides her fear. If he wants an animal, then he can have one, but she will be damned if he is going to terrorize her and steal from them. No man, including this Indian, will ever intimidate or threaten her again. She worries enough about that with Chad's potential ambush. She sneaks around the house and slips inside unseen. She mumbles angrily to herself as she tramps through the kitchen gathering items. Grasping her rifle in her right hand, she positions it at the ready aim, but angled downward for safety, just like Malcolm taught her. She grabs the hen off the counter she had planned to prep for dinner and tucks a bag of flour and a jar of jam under her arm. Stalking to the door, she takes a deep breath and steps onto the porch. Without hesitation, she marches outside and thrusts the food over the fence to him. She maintains eye contact with him in what she hopes conveys as confidence and fearlessness. His expression never wavers, as he watches her with a mixture of curiosity and shock as his horse paws the ground restlessly. He is much younger than she initially thought, no older than late teens. He is tall and lean, but muscular. His dark eyes never leave hers as he snatches the chicken and reaches down for the other food. He makes no move to go when she waves him off. After a tense moment while neither of them moves, she turns on her heel and stomps to the cabin, slamming the door after her.

Once safely inside, she collapses against the door, hands trembling while her heart beats wildly in her chest. She peers out the window to watch him turn and ride off the same way he came.

That evening when she tells Malcolm about what she did, not surprisingly, he is furious she risked endangering herself. She downplays the incident, telling him the native was only a child. In retrospect it was a very careless ploy no matter his age, but inwardly she is proud of herself for facing her fear. If she had not, they would continue coming back forever, and the next casualty might not be just a goat. She truly believes that at the center of it all, neither the pioneers nor the Indians want to fight. Everyone will be much happier if they get along. So, if she can help kick-start the trend, then so be it.

The following day she gets an idea, and has Malcolm construct a mailbox of sorts, a wooden box with a lid to keep birds and critters out. The next time the Indian comes, she clutches her weapon and walks out to show him what she left in the box for him. She never has to confront him again after that. He visits once or twice a week and gathers whatever she leaves for him, and they never speak to each other. The most she ever receives is a curt nod of his head. If Malcolm is home when he arrives, he always makes sure the native is aware of it. But Hannah knows he will not hurt them. She stocks the crate regularly with baked goods and bread, cookies, and dried meats. Once the crops are mature, she includes a wider variety of fruits and vegetables too. Malcolm complains what she is doing is comparable to a mob payoff for protection, but she does not care. It is a minor price to pay for peace.

Then one day after the native has picked up food for a few weeks, she opens the box to leave cookies and an apple pie to find something already in there. She pulls out a pair of stunning suede work gloves. They have fringe along the outer seams and colorful beaded butterflies and flowers adorn the top. They are small enough to fit her, and she slips them on. She beams as she admires the gift. They are a beautiful confirmation the Indian wants peace as much as she does, and she will treasure them for years.

As summer progresses, life on the prairie goes on as normal. They have their daily routine of chores and their existence is quiet, if not somewhat mundane. Chad no longer haunts her thoughts, and they both enjoy running the ranch without missing the hustle and bustle of big city living. John and Malcolm build a small barn for the animals which completes their homestead, and they concentrate on increasing their crop. But there is always something to do, and a day off now and then would be nice.

John's latest recommendation to improve their property includes stacking piles of firewood, grass and leaves around the land. It is a tedious task Malcolm does not particularly enjoy, but John tells him they will burn them if the insects get too bad, the smoke driving them away. Their garden is flourishing after they enlarge it, and they return to the orchards for peaches, plums, and pears. Hannah finds wild grapes and makes fruit salads and jams, giving them a wide assortment of foods to eat. Once Malcolm bought her the wood-burning stove, she used it every day. She gives Anne some of her baked goods, and other people request them. Soon after, she strikes a deal with the store in town to sell her creations there. She bakes bread with walnuts and pawpaw, persimmon cookies, caramel for the apples, pies, cornbread with jalapenos, and biscuits with candied currants and raisins. At home she treats Malcolm to his childhood comfort food, shepherd's pie with minced beef and mushroom gravy, adding peas and carrots from the garden. His favorite is her turkey pot pie and meatloaf, and she loves coming up with more recipes. She experiments with smashed tomatoes and basil and makes a marinara sauce and hand-rolled pasta. She even creates a pizza with flat bread, bell pepper, mushrooms and ham, using the tomato sauce. Decent peanut butter comes only after a few tries, because without a food processor, it is harder than churning butter. He scoffs when she mentions a peanut butter and jam sandwich on freshly baked bread.

"That is not a popular option where I'm from. Give me a ham sarnie, or a cheese and onion and I'm good," he says.

"I sure miss cheese. That's on my list to conquer soon. Once I perfect that, it will open a whole new world of cooking for me."

"Woman, you will make me fat if you continue with all this baking."

"It keeps me entertained. Besides, sales are picking up at the store. I think this era is ready for me to introduce some flavors to them. Maybe pasta and marinara, chile rellenos, chicken and turkey pot pie. Most cuisine here is so bland. They have everything they need to produce flavorful food. They just don't realize how to use it."

"Most can't afford it, I expect. The locals have large families, and that costs. We were lucky we had John to help and teach me to do things. And we have Christine to thank for most of the garden we still need to plant. And the money she sent with you saved us. Without that, we would not be nearly as well off as we are now. We would not have been able to purchase the cooker or glass windows for a very long time, if ever."

"It's also just the two of us. Most families here include six or more kids. That's crazy by our timeline's standards." She stares out the window for a moment before continuing. "Does it bother you the CCEA took away our chance to have a child, Malcolm? I resent it, if I'm being honest. I understand why we are sterilized before exile, if a prisoner has children while extradited, that offspring could be someone who changes history. But it still saddens me to know I will never give you a baby."

"Of course, it bothers me. I'd love nothing more than to raise a family with you, Hannah. But we have lots to be thankful for. We've created a decent life here. Better than most."

"That's true. But it makes me sad to consider these local children not eating enough. We can make a difference here, Malcolm. Maybe improve their lifestyle. What if I bring food to the schoolhouse to start? I appreciate people here are proud and may not be open to charity. We can't just drop by with a meal. That might offend them. But if I provide school lunches, perhaps ease into helping them?"

"I'm all for it. I'm happy to support them. And we need to get this food out of here once you cook it before I weigh too much to mount my horse."

With that, Malcolm excuses himself to chores as Hannah plans her menu for the schoolchildren. As she makes fresh peanut butter, he shouts her name from outside. The urgency in his tone causes her to freeze. He bursts through the door to grab her by the hand. As he pulls her over the threshold, she sees John racing toward them before she can ask what is happening. Then she hears what sounds like a heavy rain, but no rainfall comes. The next minute the sky darkens, and she instinctively looks up. Thousands of flying insects blot the sun on the horizon. Malcolm runs for the animal pens.

"Hannah, help me get the animals in the barn!"

She snaps out of her shock and moves quickly as John sprints to Malcolm to open the pig's pen, herding them to the barn. The men run to the piles of wood, lighting as many as they can. Once they finish, the three of them race to the dugout, the two dogs close behind, as the first locusts emerge on the edge of their land. Hannah shrieks as she feels them fly into her, tangling in her hair. She swats at them all the way to the shelter. They dive into the opening, John securing the door. Malcolm pulls the insects from her braid, smashing them with a rock as she continues to swat at her head and cry out when she entangles one. They cannot hear their own ragged breathing over the sound of the swarm outside. John got his animals into his barn but did not have time to light any of his leaves, like Malcolm did. He came to help them, knowing they would not know what was happening or what to do. They wait in the cellar for several hours until the throng has passed, then John retreats to his ranch with his dog as they survey the damage at theirs. The garden is gone, as if it were never there. Not even a bare stalk remains. Some railing on the fence has been eaten away, and the pests stripped the trees of bark. They completely consumed any hay not in the outbuilding. The livestock are unharmed but spooked, and they cannot coax them out of the outbuilding. They leave them there overnight, to calm down. Buddy bounds out after them, sniffing the ground, chasing any insect not fast enough to catch up to the horde. Both windows are cracked, and more than a few stray grasshoppers found their way into the cabin.

They cannot believe the amount of destruction the insects caused at both the homes. The fire piles helped curb the damage some, and later they learn this was only a minor swarm. It takes Malcolm and John a few days to ready the gardens for new vegetation and rebuild the fencing. One small tree dies and must be cut down, and the stump burned. It was a devastating ordeal, but they get through it, tackling one task at a time, and are more thankful than ever to have the seeds Christine brought them. They use fresh vegetables in the house to start seedlings, and combined with what they have from Christine, they replenish everything. The fertilizer is not only a produce enhancer, but a growth accelerator too, so the plants will mature within three weeks. They split the bounty of seeds with John as he lost his entire crop too.

Two weeks after the swarm, life is getting back to normal, and Hannah wakes with a renewed enthusiasm. She prepares peanut butter and jam sandwiches, and ham with tomato, in case the children dislike the peanut butter and jelly combination. She piles them in her basket with homemade potato chips and fried green tomatoes, using eggs, oil, vinegar and herbs to make a ranch dressing. It is not the best dip she has ever made, but it beats anything else this era has to offer in condiments.

She grabs the basket and goes to look for Malcolm. She finds him in the goat pen, covered in muck.

"What happened to you?" she asks, covering her nose with her hand.

"Gary the goat doesn't want to cooperate. He has taken to throwing a wobbly every day ever since the natives nicked Glenda. The locust plague didn't help him much either. I really must get him a new girlfriend. On a happier note, the shower is almost complete, just another hour or so before it's running. I'll be glad to test it after this mess," he says, stepping out of the pen and shaking mud from his hands.

"I made sandwiches for the schoolchildren," she says, jumping back to avoid being splattered with the sludge. "I want to bring them to the schoolhouse, so they have them for lunch today."

"Allow me two hours and I'll be fit to go."

"Malcolm, I can't wait that long. These sandwiches will melt in this heat. I'll be fine to ride into town alone. I'll be home by the time you're out of your shower."

"I'm not comfortable with that, we are on alert, in case you've forgotten. I can wash my hands and just nip into the shower. I'll only be two ticks before I'm ready to go."

"Oh, Malcolm, it's been a few months. Nothing has happened, and Christine hasn't even been back here. She said she'd let us know once she had any news. I assume Chad gave up or couldn't find out where I am. I'll be home in a few hours at most. We cannot maintain this level of vigilance and live our lives in peace. You said yourself we would not allow this to change our way of life. So, don't let it, then. Stay here and finish the shower."

Malcolm must admit, she has a point. There has been no sign Hannah's ex-husband has found her. It has been business as usual since Christine's visit.

"Fine, but don't stop and shop, come right home, okay?"

She gives him a quick kiss and picks up the basket of food. "I promise. See you later."

He watches her ride off over the ridge and sets to work on completing the shower.

She rides through town, reaching the schoolhouse within a few minutes, where she ties her mare to the tree. The children are playing on the swings as she enters the school where the teacher is straightening desks and humming to herself.

"Hello?

The woman spins toward her, hand on her chest. "Oh my, you startled me."

"I'm so sorry, I didn't mean to frighten you. I'm Hannah Aldred. My husband and I have a modest ranch outside town near John Harding's place. We have a sizeable garden, and we harvest more than we can use. Perhaps you have seen some of my breads and baked goods for sale at the store? It's just the two of us, we have no children, so we thought it might help if we shared some things with the youngsters. I made some bread with spread and meats, potatoes and fried tomatoes. I hoped they'd enjoy it for lunch today. I have cookies too," she says, smiling, careful not to confuse her and use the term sandwich. She had not heard anyone refer to a sandwich here, so she doesn't want to raise any questions.

She holds the basket up as the teacher walks to her. "That is very generous of you, Mrs. Aldred. I'm Claire Madsen. Some students only bring hardtack to eat, so I am certain they will appreciate anything you serve them. I will call them in if you wish to prepare the lunch."

"Wonderful! I'll get this set up."

Hannah unpacks the feast on a table under the window but leaves the persimmon cookies in the basket to bring out after the sandwiches, as the students shuffle in one by one to sit at their desks.

"Children, this is Mrs. Aldred. She is serving a mid-day meal for you today. Form a line and help yourself, one at a time. You may use your book bag if you need to, to carry the food. Fold it over to make a plate. Please be sure your lessons are not in there."

Hannah smiles as each child loads their makeshift plates with food. Before she knows it, everything is gone, and she hands out cookies to the group. They all eat like they haven't had a decent meal in days. She can't stop smiling, knowing how much they enjoyed it, but sad that they were so hungry. They all thank her, and she laughs when one little boy burps loudly.

Claire dismisses the youngsters to go play outside while she helps pack up the basket.

"That was delicious, Mrs. Aldred."

"Please, call me Hannah. Would it be all right if I came back tomorrow?"

"Claire," she says, extending her hand. "I'm certain that would delight the children, Hannah. I apologize for Jacob's ill manners. I fear that boy needs someone to teach him proper etiquette. He lost his parents and only sibling last year to illness, and he lives with his grandmother. She's too frail to handle him, so he is on his own most of the time."

"That's awful, he's so young. And his burp didn't bother me at all, honestly. In many cultures it is a sign of appreciation for the food. I shall think of it as a compliment. I'll see you tomorrow, Claire," she says, gathering her basket and waving goodbye.

She mounts her horse, feeling this is the start of something very fulfilling for her. Malcolm asked her not to stop in town, and she had every intention of not doing so, but makes a last-minute decision to make a quick dash into the store. She is delighted to find her goods have almost sold out, and she promises to return with more by the end of the week. Spending the pay the shopkeeper gives her, she purchases a set of small plates and tin cups, which she packs away for the kids tomorrow.

When she arrives home, Malcolm has the shower operational and has already completed the trial run.

"You clean up nicely, sir," she kisses him and smells his hair. "That shampoo Christine gave us is great. You smell fantastic."

"Would you like to try the new facilities?" he asks.

"I believe I will, thanks." She undresses and grabs the wool blanket she brought with her from Los Angeles, wrapping herself in it as she strides out the front door. The shower is a few feet from the deck, built on the side of the house facing the hill. That means no one approaching the ranch can see it, offering more privacy. Malcolm erected a wall of lumber around it, leaving a narrow entry. The floor is hand cut hardwood. Over time the boards will dry rot and need to be replaced, but for now, it is perfect. He installed a rope threaded through a barrel which houses the water, and by pulling it you control the amount of pour. It is not ideal, but sure beats bathing in a porcelain bowl. And if they want to, they can heat the water before adding it.

She finishes her shower and wrings the excess water out of her long hair. Wrapped in the blanket, she tiptoes through the grass and onto the porch. Malcolm glances up from cleaning his rifle when she steps through the door.

"My, my, Mrs. Aldred," he says, then whistles at her. She smiles and drops the makeshift towel, wet hair clinging to her. He admires her for a moment before pushing the weapon away and carrying her to the bed.

Over dinner she tells him about her day and the students she met. He is not crazy about her going back to the school, especially without him. But she plans to return as often as possible, despite his objections.

They settle into a routine in the weeks that follow. Hannah goes to the schoolhouse during the week, and Malcolm tends to the farm and hunts. She bakes and they bring food to their neighbors and continue to peddle goods at the general store. She spends more time with Jacob than any other child, knowing he has no one but his grandmother. He comes to their house after school most days, where he helps them with the garden and livestock. He eats dinner with them, and Malcolm brings him home afterwards, allowing his grandmother a break from the rambunctious boy. The woman's health is declining, she is seventy years old, which is very elderly for the timeline. Hannah suspects she will not live much longer. They already love Jacob as if he were their own, so when she passes, it is a simple decision, and he moves in with them. The woman left instructions with the doctor that Malcolm and Hannah were to receive all her belongings. Hannah spoke to her frequently, to assure her they would take Jacob in after her death, and the woman was grateful to know they would care for him. It takes some adjusting, as they have a lot less alone time, however, they both agree it is worth it to have a son.

Hannah now has a full collection of pots and pans, dishes and other kitchen ware, thanks to Jacobs grandmother, while Malcolm is thankful to collect three cows, two pigs, several chickens and a sheep. They find a buckboard wagon in her barn, which makes chores far easier, and allows Hannah to transport more baked goods to town to sell. They can also carry feed and supplies home without having to borrow John's cart. Their small ranch is growing by leaps and bounds, and if things continue at their current pace, they will be self-sufficient within a year.

Life is near perfect for Malcolm and Hannah. Until it's not.

TWENTY-SIX

Piedmont, Oklahoma 1868

Hannah and Jacob sit at the dining table while she reviews his schoolwork.

"Your work is fantastic. There is only one math correction you need to make. Your penmanship is spot-on, though. I'm so proud of you."

The boy beams and chews the last bite of his cookie. "Can I go play with Buddy?"

"Sure, but don't talk with your mouth full, please. And watch out for snakes," she says, tousling his hair.

He springs from the table and is outside in a shot, where he leaps off the porch, not bothering with the steps. She laughs at him before closing the door as he runs off to find the dog. She is so pleased with the way he is adjusting. He is thriving, and even Claire has noticed a difference in him at school. Hannah and Malcolm have hosted her and John for supper, and she can tell there is something brewing between them. Claire lights up when she is near John, and it is obvious to Hannah she would like their relationship to be more than friendly. Their weekend dinners have become a ritual. Hannah schedules this week's get together later than usual with the theory that if the sun has set when they finish, John will accompany her home. Knowing the romance requires a slight push in the right direction, she is determined to be the one to facilitate that. Malcolm sees through her tactic and tells her to leave it alone, it will happen on its own. She ignores his advice, and when Saturday comes around and John offers to escort Claire home, she shoots Malcolm a smug look that says I-told-you-so.

The following morning Malcolm gathers supplies, planning to hunt with John and Kanuna. Jacob begs to go, but Hannah talks him into staying behind this trip with the promise of a strawberry cake. She does not like the notion of a ten-year-old boy with a rifle—even if it is supervised. She realizes she will have to allow him to go sooner or later, both he and Malcolm will insist on it. In this timeline, boys grow up fast, shouldering responsibilities and burdens no child should ever bear. But Jacob need not do that, and she wishes to protect him and preserve his childhood for as long as possible.

Hannah tends to the garden, while Jacob plays with the dog and digs in the yard. She knows Malcolm will fill the hole in later, so she doesn't complain about it. Boys will be boys. Let him dig and get some fresh air, she thinks to herself. Once her weeding is complete, she goes into the cabin to mix cake batter, humming a favorite song from before her exile when she hears the front door ease open.

"Wash your hands outside in the shower before you come inside Jacob, I don't want dirt and mud all over," she says without turning around.

A warm breeze moves through the house, and when her only response is Buddy barking in the distance, the hair on the back of her neck stands on end. She turns and drops the bowl, batter splashing across the floor and onto the chair legs. Her blood runs cold at the sight of the man standing inside the cabin clutching a large knife.

"Jacob is a little tied up. Hannah Cole, I presume?" he asks, a smirk playing on the corners of his lips.

She does not answer him, just continues to stare, her breathing ragged and her heart beating so loudly in her chest she is sure he must hear it from across the room.

"I've had to wait awhile to catch you alone. But like your husband, I'm a patient man. He wants me to get rid of you quickly, but I've been watching you, and I figure why not have some fun first? Be a shame to waste this opportunity. The women here, well, let's just say they don't ring my bell, if you follow my meaning."

"Whatever he offered to do for you or your family, he'll never keep his word to you. Chad is only using you. We can help you and make your life here easier. But if you kill me, my actual husband Malcolm, will come for you."

"Sweetheart, your ex already did for me exactly what he promised. My cheating wife disappeared. And your most recent spouse won't be able to chase after us, not where we're traveling. After we spend some quality time together, you and I are going into the red zone to jump time. Adios to Oklahoma. See, Chad doesn't want you dead, he prefers you suffer. He figured you'd settle in here by now. And he pegged you perfectly. He said you'd have a lover or a husband, and he wants to take that from you. Simple as that. He didn't tell me I could have you first, but honestly, he seems *really* pissed off at you, so I'm sure he won't mind."

Hannah's eyes flash to the counter where her belt and knife lay, and then to her rifle propped against the wall, stalling while she contemplates her situation. She knows if unarmed, she stands little chance against him. He has a full foot and a hundred pounds on her. She silently curses herself for taking the belt off. The rifle is closer and will be her best bet, and she is not going down without a fight. She makes a dash for it, but he is faster.

"I don't think so, sweetheart. I'll take this." he says, snatching the weapon. "I'm sure I'll make good use of it wherever I end up."

He reaches her in two steps. She lunges for the knife, but he grabs her and drags her toward him, twisting her hands behind her back and tying them together. The rope cuts into her wrists, cutting off her circulation. She screams, but there is no one to hear her except Jacob, and she sobs thinking of him and Malcolm and what this will do to them. He pushes her through the door, and she stumbles down the stairs. He picks her up and lifts her onto his horse, Hannah fighting the entire time. But he is much stronger than her, and he climbs on to hold her in place. He walks the stallion out of the gate in no hurry. He is sure her husband and his friends are away for the day. No need to ride the animal into the ground. They will find somewhere secluded to spend the night, have some fun, and then tomorrow cross into the red sector.

* * *

Jacob struggles against the ropes, his wrists burning from the effort as the dog continues to bark beside him. As he peers through the slats in the dugout door, he sees the man lift Hannah onto his horse. He does not recognize him, but he knows he is dangerous, otherwise he would not take his new mom or tie him up like he has.

"Get away from my ma!" he screams out again.

He continues to twist, and after a minute he is free of the binding. Pushing the cellar door open, he runs out in time to see them crest the ridge and ride west. He knows what direction that is because she taught him that in their geography lessons. They are heading west toward Cheyenne—he remembers the name because it is like the Indians. He mounts the mare, not bothering to put the saddle on, and gallops her all the way to the river. When he does not find Malcolm there, he guides the horse into the grove of trees, where he spots John and rides up to him. He struggles to tell him what happened, talking so fast he is not making sense.

"Slow down, boy, I can't understand what you're saying to me. Now you've gone and scared all the deer off."

The noise draws Malcolm and Kanuna, and it startles Malcolm to find Jacob there.

"Jacob! What are you doing here? Does Hannah know you're here? I suspect not."

"He took her. A bad man grabbed her, and they rode west, toward Cheyenne. He knotted me up good and locked me and Buddy in the cellar. Then he tied her up and put her on his horse."

"What? Hannah left with a stranger?"

He nods furiously as the tears streak down his cheeks. "I couldn't help her, he tied me up."

"Jacob, you've helped her by coming to find me. When did this happen, how long ago?"

"Just now. I saw them ride off and came here to get you."

"Brilliant job, son." He looks to John and Kanuna. "It's Chad's guy, I just know it," he says, a sense of dread sweeping over him.

"Let's move," says John, already running to where they tied the horses.

"Pa, are you going to bring her back?" asks Jacob, his tear-stained face pleading with Malcolm.

"You bet we are. I need you to go to Ms. Madsen's house and remain there until I come to pick you up, do you understand? John and Kanuna will come with me. I'm counting on you, son."

He nods and hangs his head.

They move at top speed, and as they pass the ranch, Jacob cuts east to Claire's and the men ride west. Kanuna leads the trio and slows when they arrive at a thicket of trees, signaling them to dismount. He guides them into the woodland, stopping at a patch of grass that appears flattened.

"Here," he says, pointing to the spot. "We leave, hurry," says Kanuna, mounting his stallion in one fluid motion.

They follow him past the tree line and into the open prairie again. They run the horses, and before long, they make out a rider in the distance. They drive the animals harder, the other man oblivious to his pursuers. As they draw closer, Malcolm sees Hannah's long hair and recognizes her instantly. The man in the saddle is in no rush, trotting his stallion. Malcolm fires his rifle and both Hannah and the stranger twist to see the three of them advancing. Hannah tries frantically to warn them off. Her hands are bound behind her and she is tied to her captor. It is no use. She screams and bites the shoulder of her kidnapper who swats her aside like a fly.

He kicks the horse who takes off at a sprint as the others push their horses faster to catch up to them. They are still a half a mile off, and when Hannah turns to look back, she sees them pulling away from the men. She fights to get loose and distracts him enough that he doesn't notice when the animal slows. She twists around to see their pursuers gaining on them, and she feels a glimmer of hope they might rescue her. But in a flash, her faith shatters when her stomach roils and her head sways. At first, she thinks it is because of being bounced so violently as they galloped. Then a familiar tingling sensation starts in her legs and she realizes what is happening. He must feel it too, because he halts the stallion and turns to find the men approaching quickly. He unties the rope binding them at the waist and drags Hannah off, pushing her in front of him and holding the knife to her neck, her hands still tied behind her. The three men slow, and once they are within earshot, Hannah screams.

"Stay back! Malcolm. We're in the red zone! Malcolm, stay there!"

"Come any closer and I'll slit her throat right here and you can watch her bleed out." He shouts to them.

They remain where they are, Malcolm jumping from his horse. "Let her go! Please! I'll do whatever you want. Take me instead. Just don't hurt her!"

"Screw you! You're too late, they already know we've breached the red zone," he says, swaying on his feet.

Hannah's legs give way, and she crumples in a heap, her abductor sinking to his knees beside her. John aims and shoots him in the chest without hesitation, and his body heaves forward and collapses in the grass next to her.

She tries to stand but falls to the ground. Malcolm yells to John, suppressing his desire to rush to her, knowing he cannot save her himself.

"John, get her, I can't, or they'll transport me too! Please hurry! Grab her before it's too late!" Malcolm sobs, a wave of fear and panic overtaking him.

John drops his rifle. His chest heaves and his arms pump, racing to Hannah as she raises herself up to a kneeling position to let out a final cry.

Hannah's world tilts and shifts out of focus. "No!" she shrieks, her expression twisting into a tortured grimace as she fades from sight, a fragment at a time. Like a million small particles of dust lost to the wind.

Malcolm's shouts die on the air as he drops to his knees, sobbing. John stops, staring at the site where she kneeled only a moment before. His head bows, and his shoulders slump. He spins to face Malcolm, the regret written all over him.

Malcolm looks up, the torment etched on him, the tears flowing. John walks to the horse and leads it to Kanunu, who gapes at the barren ground where Hannah disappeared. John hands him the reins and places his hand on the man's shoulder.

"We'll talk about it when we get back to the ranch."

Kanuna drops his chin in a nod, too stunned to do anything else after watching Hannah disappear before his eyes. John tells Malcolm to get on his horse, and none of them speak as they ride. Every so often Kanuna mumbles something to himself in his language, using words neither John nor Malcom can translate. He is no doubt in shock over what he just witnessed. Malcolm is in a daze, allowing them to lead him home, not caring if he makes it or not.

Hannah is gone. He knows of no words to express how he feels. He can never find her if they have sent her further back in time. What will he tell Jacob? What will he do now? He cannot carry on her without her. Nor does he want to. If he loses her to the past, life is nothing but a vast, desolate void.

John goes to Claire's and arranges for Jacob to stay there for a few nights while Malcolm tries to adjust to losing Hannah. He remains in shock most of the afternoon, and to John's credit he doesn't force him to talk about it. When John finally leaves for home, unable to coax Malcolm into eating, he lights the fire for him and brings a blanket to the chair he hasn't moved from.

The following morning Malcolm awakens in the same spot, and for a moment he forgets the horror of the day before. He peers around the room before the memory hits him, taking his breath away. Willing himself out of the seat, he stares at the half-finished quilt slung over the dining table, the bright, cheerful colors a stark contrast to his dark emotions. The bowl of dried cake batter still lies on the floor, a grim reminder of what took place there.

Losing Hannah is a wrenching blow. Malcolm agonizes over every minute spent here, which means it is another spent away from rescuing her. And it is excruciating. It physically hurts to be separated from her, as if the fabric of his very soul is being ripped apart. He is completely gutted and unsure what to do with himself. Haunted by the image of her transport, the vision replays over and over in his mind. There is only one way to save her, and he knows it—Christine. And each day she does not show up is one more that Hannah is alone and in danger. The thought arouses a new resolve in him, and he picks up his rifle and whistles for the dog. He saddles up and heads to Claire's bringing their son home. He has to have faith Christine will come back. And he needs to be ready when she gets here.

TWENTY-SEVEN

Los Angeles, California 2071 / Piedmont, Oklahoma 1868

"Hello?" Christine taps her ear, bringing her phone alive.

"Hey, it's Maddie. Are you in the building?"

"Hi, yes I'm here."

"Can you meet me in the lunchroom?"

"Okay, is everything all right?"

"Yes. I just need to talk to you. I'm leaving my station now."

"See you there in a few minutes."

Christine walks into the cafeteria and scans the area for Maddie. She sees her sitting at a cramped table by the window and weaves her way through the seating scattered throughout the room.

"Hi," she says, pulling out the chair across from her. "You know, when my son's girlfriend makes a cloak and dagger phone call to me, it worries the mom in me. What's happening?"

"Oh no, sorry, this isn't about Michael. We are fine, better than fine, in fact. You asked me to keep an eye out on Hannah's records. So, I've been checking the file twice a week, and someone accessed it yesterday. It didn't show until today, but they were definitely in there. Whoever it was, they know where she is."

Christine sighs and nods. "Are you positive?"

Maddie cocks her head and raises her eyebrows, looking at her in disbelief she just asked that question.

"Right, sorry. Of course, you're sure. I already notified Malcolm and Hannah of the possibility, but I should check on them now that we know for certain. I told them I'd be back if there was any news, and this undeniably qualifies as news. Are you absolutely certain no one can tell you've been monitoring the files?"

"I'm positive. My activity cannot be traced. But whenever an employee outside of IT views a record, that goes on the operation log. We protect the inmate's whereabouts as securely as the Marshall's do the Witness Protection Program. Family members get crazy when they want to know where we transported their loved one."

She thanks Maddie again, and the two go their separate ways, Christine heading straight to Frank's office. Something on his computer has his full attention, and he does not notice her until she is standing in front of his desk.

"Good Morning. To what do I owe this unexpected visit?" he says, glancing up from the monitor.

"We have an issue," she says, closing the door.

"We seem to have several issues lately. What now?"

She tells him about her meeting with Maddie and her plan to go to 1868.

"You've already warned them, I'm not confident we should risk sending you there again," he says, leaning back in his chair and frowning.

"It's been a few months since I was there. We need to trust Hoyt can hide the trips. He wrote the software for goodness sakes, Frank. If anyone knows how to circumvent the process, it's him."

He leans forward and lowers his voice. "It just makes me uneasy. Every time you travel somewhere unofficially, it's another chance for them to catch us."

"I'm not nervous, and you shouldn't be either."

She works hard to maintain a neutral expression because she *is* apprehensive. Frank is right. Each trip is an opportunity for the CCEA to uncover what they are doing. But she has additional information, and she feels strongly that she needs to relay it to Malcolm and Hannah. Chad has found a staff member to access the reports. There is no other reason for anyone to read Hannah's file after they archive it. She must warn them, nervous or not.

The time travel program Hoyt wrote works very specifically. It moves you to any previous year in history, but always to the current month and day. Otherwise, she could reach back to a specific day to inform them someone would open the records and potentially locate her transport destination. But she isn't that lucky. When she transports to Oklahoma she will arrive on the same month and day as her own timeline, but to the year 1868.

Christine says Hoyt's name, prompting her phone chip to dial him. She explains the situation to him, and he agrees to suspend the system the following day.

"There, done. I don't have a transport scheduled for two days, so I can do this, no problem," she says.

"There are three transports on the schedule tomorrow, so be here at noon to travel after they leave," replies Frank.

She leaves Frank's office preoccupied with thoughts of her trip but manages to finish her workday even though she is distracted. Back at home, she packs her civil war reenactment dress into her gym bag when Ethan calls.

"Hey, beautiful."

"Hi. I'm glad you called. I was going to call you later. I've got to go see our mutual friend tomorrow. Someone accessed our new buddy's documents."

"Oh, that's not good. You're certain?"

"Yes. But don't ask my someday-daughter-in-law that question, she takes offense to having her job knowledge questioned."

"Ah, I see. Well, she *is* quite skilled at her work, isn't she?"

"Very. So, I'll be gone for a couple of days, then when I get back, I'm scheduled to transport the following day. Just wanted you to know I'll be incommunicado."

"Duly noted. I have to be honest, I'm not a fan of you going to see them, but I realize it must happen. I wish I were there. I'd go with you."

"Well, that's sweet, but unnecessary. I can handle it."

"Oh, I've no doubt about that. It would be strictly for selfish reasons. The opportunity to be a hero and defend my woman, all that he-man nonsense. You know how insecure we men are."

"Please do not turn into *that* guy," she says, laughing.

They talk for another twenty minutes before she promises to call him as soon as she is home from Oklahoma. They are careful not to mention names or places. Neither of them believes they are at risk of being recorded, but if the government issues a warrant, they can retrieve all phone conversations and listen to everything. Christine does not plan to get caught during any of their humanitarian missions, but she is also cautious to cover her tracks—just in case.

The next day she meets Frank and goes through the now familiar task of transporting when she is not on the schedule to do so. She is becoming too skilled at doing this, she thinks to herself. And she sees the same apprehension written all over Frank's expression. It worries him too. Neither voice their concerns though, and to an outsider it would appear as if she hasn't a care in the world as she transports out of 2071.

Once she awakens in 1868, she takes off in a jog to the farm almost immediately. She has less time here than her other trips. Transporters are due in the jump room late afternoon, and she cannot be there then, so this will be a quick excursion. She wore running shoes this trip and plans to make it to the ranch in record time. She checks the timepiece and starts out of the orchard. Her feet hit the dirt, slicing through the tall grass as she settles into a steady tempo.

When she crests the hill to the cabin, she stops to rest. She stands hunched over, hands on her knees, dragging air into her lungs. The wristwatch shows her she made it in twenty-six minutes. Not bad. A seventeen-minute improvement on her last run here, thanks to the shoes. She runs the final couple of hundred yards to the house, knocks and waits, her breathing slowed to near normal when John answers.

"Christine, you're here! Thank God, we've been waiting for you. Malcolm, Christine is here."

Malcolm flings the door open wide and embraces her. She is not clear why everyone has been expecting her, but it unsettles her.

He takes her hand and pulls her inside and to a chair.

"Does someone want to tell me what's going on?" She asks, looking between the two of them. "Where's Hannah?" she asks, glancing around the cabin.

"Chad's guy kidnapped Hannah. He took her into the red zone, and they transported her. John shot him but couldn't save her before enforcement activated her transport. Send me after her, Christine," Malcolm says, gripping her hands.

"You have to bring my ma back. We need her," says a small voice from the other side of the room.

202

She turns to see a boy of about nine or ten step out from behind the bed, his tear-stained face screwed into a scowl. She looks from the child to Malcolm and then John, confused.

"Okay, can someone please explain? Start from the beginning."

Malcolm tells her about the visit from the stranger, how he tied Jacob up and the ensuing chase over the plains into the restricted area. He fills her in on who Jacob is and how he came to live with them. When he finishes, the three of them look at her with pleading eyes. She glances at Malcolm across the table and nods her head in the boy's direction. He realizes what she is asking and sends him outside so they can speak more freely.

"We've told him nothing about where we are from. He doesn't understand what took place with Hannah. We may tell him when he gets older, but for now he's too young to comprehend what's happened, let alone something like his new parents are from the future."

"Uh, yeah, I wouldn't recommend it. It's enough that John is privy to it. No offense, John," she says, glancing at him.

"Kanuna knows too. He was with us for the pursuit and watched Hannah transport," says Malcolm,

"Who the hell is Kanuna? And what kind of name is that? This has gone all the way off the rails, Malcolm. We expect you to keep the fact you're not from here, confidential. Do they not review that with you in the United Kingdom for goodness sakes? The more people you tell, the greater the risk." She rises and paces the length of the cabin to help her concentrate.

"Kanuna is a Cherokee. He is a friend of ours. He assumes the Gods have taken her, or something, I don't know. Who knows what he thinks about it, honestly. But he's no threat."

She stops abruptly to stand in front of him. "I hope to hell not Malcolm, for your sake. Like it or not, you're a time-traveler now, so act as if you are. Do not discuss your point of origin with anyone else. You put all of us in danger when you do that."

She resumes her pacing, her brow furrowed. "Okay, returning to the more pressing problem. First, I cannot send you after her. The enforcement team would know you moved and program you for reassignment immediately. Second, I'm not sure I'm able to go after her as Hoyt can only hide trips for a few hours at a stretch."

"You have to help me, Christine!"

"Give me a minute and let me think, Malcolm. I mean, how did this guy even get to her? I warned you something like this was a possibility. How did this happen, you promised to protect her?" she says, the frustration evident in her tone.

Malcolm rests his head in his hands and when he lifts his face, Christine instantly regrets saying it. His suffering is as clear as anything she has ever seen.

"I'm sorry Malcolm, I didn't mean that the way it came out," she says softly.

"No, you're right. I became complacent and left her and Jacob here alone. I should never have done that. This is all my fault, and I accept responsibility. If something happens to her, it is because of my negligence, and I will never forgive myself," he says, turning away from them.

"No, it's my doing. I didn't get to her fast enough," says John.

"Stop this, both of you. Chad bears full accountability for this entire mess. No one else is culpable. Just allow me a moment to consider some options," says Christine.

She sits down, thinking about what to do, and feels the weight of the world resting squarely on her shoulders.

"The only solution I see is to ask Hoyt to cover sending me to wherever they've exiled her, pull out her tracker and bring her back here. That would be safer than removing yours and taking you there. And because someone accessed her records, the enforcement team is sure to investigate that. They will want to know why anyone would need information about where she is, and we can't risk them digging into this transport. If we remove her chip, and she registers as deceased, it will probably end any further inquiry. Prisoners are transported for zone breaches every day, and a good percent of them don't last long in their new locations. She'll appear to be just another inmate who ran into trouble and didn't make it out. Plus, who knows what the situation is like where she's at? And I can say for certain you could not take Jacob with you, so moving you there isn't an option."

"Then she has to return home. I couldn't care less what part of the world or what timeline we are in, just that we are all together. That's all that matters to me. Can Hoyt make that happen?"

"I have no idea, to be honest. Maybe. Probably. But I need to talk to him. She has not been gone long, so try not to worry. She's resourceful and she will realize we are working to bring her home. I'll be back as soon as possible with details and hopefully a plan."

She embraces them and tries to reassure them again before transporting to base. Once there, she scrambles out of the transport pod and hurries through the decontamination process. Frank is waiting when she exits, and she fills him in on the latest developments in Oklahoma. They continue to Frank's office to call Hoyt, where she reveals her idea for retrieving Hannah. He assures her he will do some quick overriding of the system mainframe to hide the trip and promises to ring her right back with Hannah's current location. They are both too anxious to speak while they wait for Hoyt to call. Christine paces while Frank fidgets until the call comes in.

"She's in Alexandria, Virginia. In 1790," Christine tells him after disconnecting. "He can buy us three days. That's not a lot of time, but better than none. I'm willing to try."

"Great. You cannot go there on your own. You'd never recover her by yourself. Alexandria is a large port for that era. I don't remember transporting you there before. Have you been there in any timeline?"

"No. I've been near, I went close to Jamestown in 1650 a couple of years ago, but not to Alexandria. But what choice do we have?"

"Great. It would have to be somewhere you've never traveled to, wouldn't it? You can't take her GPS out by yourself either."

"At this point I would welcome any suggestions, Frank. Any at all."

"I'll ask Adams and Gray to go with you. Adams is a medic, and Gray tracks better than anyone. You'll all go in costume, and Adams can bring the surgical extraction tool to remove her chip. That way, if we get caught, the three of you together are easier to explain away to a nosy transporter as a last-minute, high-risk VIP transport. You leave with a supply pack, but no weapons. There is no way we could justify a weapon if someone here saw it or it fell into the wrong hands in 1790."

"Do you think they'll agree to do it?"

"They helped you in England, didn't they? I'm confident they'll help again. That's the only way I'll concede to send you. I cannot drop you there by yourself, it's too dangerous. And it would be futile, anyway. You'll need their support to find her. You all go to Oklahoma, tell Malcolm the plan, then on to Virginia to retrieve Hannah and take her back to Piedmont. But you heard Hoyt, he can only offer you three days at most in Virginia. Every minute after that compromises our position. If you can't locate her, or she's expired, then you come home by the third day. Agreed?"

"Yes. There is no other option. It's worth a shot. Will you call them?"

Frank taps his cell chip and settles into his chair to call Adams and Gray.

* * *

The two transporters mill around the jump room, restless. It is six o'clock in the morning, and their eighteenth-century menswear is already beginning to bother them. They sport leather boots that reach just below their knees, tights, and breeches that tie at the top of their boot. Their ensemble includes a loose cotton shirt with oversized sleeves and a tricorne three-cornered hat. They both have toupees on with longer than normal hair. The wigs are undetectable, and they are clean shaven, as was the custom for the timeline. Their shirts look as if they slept in them. Christine steps out of the locker room wearing a dress with a full skirt and hoop, which is fit tightly at the bodice with three quarter length lace-trimmed sleeves. She is convinced the corset is slowly crushing her ribcage. A few days in this clothing will do nothing to improve her current state of mind.

Frank walks in and gestures for them to gather around.

"Adams has the surgical extraction device, along with protein bars, food replacement capsules, MREs and emergency water. I put waterproof matches and antibiotics in the pack in case you need them. There are silver coins so you can stay at an inn rather than camp out. No weapons, as we discussed previously. It's too risky. Remember, seventy-two hours, no longer. Your transponders are preset with your destinations. Oklahoma, Alexandria, Oklahoma. Do not deviate from that course. And for God's sake, be careful."

They all nod, and Christine's glance cuts to Frank.

"We'll be okay. This isn't the first time we've done this, Frank. We are all very competent. In and out, that's the plan," she states, placing her transponder in her dress's hidden pocket.

"You're all accomplished at transporting. Two of you have been on *one* retrieval mission. I wouldn't call that highly experienced. Just cover your backs and come home in one piece, please."

"Well, don't forget that one of us also survived seven months stranded in the past. We've got this. We'll be back before you miss us," says Christine.

"She's right, Frank. We've got this," says Gray.

Adams nods and hoists the backpack over his shoulder.

Frank scoffs and motions them into the transport chamber. Two minutes later the pods are empty, and he cannot help but worry whether they are the hunters or the hunted. Because at this point in the game, he feels it could swing either way.

TWENTY-EIGHT

Piedmont, Oklahoma 1868 / Alexandria, Virginia 1790

Christine awakens to Adams stirring next to her and Gray still out cold. Before they left, they agreed to send her to Malcolm's alone. The men's costumes would draw too much attention if anyone were to encounter them. Malcolm and John's cabins are fairly isolated with the nearest neighbors two miles away, but they do not want to risk the chance of being discovered. It would just be one more problem to deal with. And they are full up with problems.

Christine does not look forward to jogging there in her costume. It has a massive amount of fabric to it that is hard to move in, so she brought running shoes, because there is no way she is going three miles in her period footwear. They have a slight heel and pinch her feet, and it is bad enough she must walk all over Alexandria in them. Gray wakes up as she changes into her sneakers, and she tells them to expect her back within an hour. After she stretches for the run, she realizes that this route has become a habit for her, and that is definitely not a good thing. She raises her hand in a wave and starts her journey.

She makes better time than she expected to with the heavy dress slowing her down. She could not bring the wristwatch, so she is not sure of her time, but she knows it is nowhere near as fast as her last run. Jacob is outside when she arrives, and darts into the house to tell Malcolm she is here. The front door swings open as she reaches the first step.

"Christine! Come in," says Malcolm.

She follows him into the cabin to find John at the table and stops dead in her tracks when she sees an Indian in the seat opposite from him. She does her best not to stare, but her previous experience with Indians is not anything she wants to repeat, and her reaction is instinct.

"It's okay, this is Kanuna." Malcolm guides her to a chair.

"Hello," she says, maintaining eye contact with him.

He grunts and lowers his chin in a nod as an answer, his expression never changing.

John grins at her, grasping her hand in his. She squeezes his hand and smiles back.

"So, you must have a strategy if you're here, right?" asks Malcolm.

"Yes. Gray and Adams are in the grove waiting for me. We will find Hannah, remove her tracker, and transport her back here. That's the plan. We have three days to locate her. I'm certain you remember Adams is a medic. We'll do our best to recover her, Malcolm."

"Where is she?"

"She's in Alexandria, Virginia."

"In what year?" he asks shakily.

"1790."

Worry and fear pass over Malcolm's face. "Bloody hell. I'll go with you to the grove. I assume you all need to transport together? I'd like to visit Gray and Adams and thank them in person, anyway."

"Sure, that would be great."

Christine nods to Kanuna, who grunts at her again. She gives John a quick goodbye embrace and settles onto Malcolm's horse with him.

"Are you gonna bring her home?" Jacob's voice sounds small and timid, almost fearful of her response.

"I will try my best," she says, smiling down at him. "I have excellent trackers with me, so the odds are good."

He waves as they ride out of the yard.

Adams and Gray greet Malcolm with embraces. They have not seen him since their trip to the Cotswold's to rescue Christine, so they spend a few minutes catching up before she suggests they start for Virginia.

"Thank you for going after Hannah."

"We'll do everything we can, buddy," says Gray, shaking his hand and slapping Malcolm's back.

Christine hands her shoes to Malcolm.

"The pack's too full to take these to Alexandria, and I don't want to risk them being found later. Bury them, burn them, or whatever. I hate to lose a decent pair of running shoes," she sighs.

"Sure, I'll get rid of the trainers. You just concentrate on bringing my wife home."

He shoves the sneakers into his pack and mounts his stallion as he watches them disappear. He says a silent prayer they find her and get back safely. His entire world is now in the hands of the three agents he just watched travel seventy-eight years into the past.

* * *

Hannah feels herself awakening but resists it. Her right shoulder hurts, and her throat burns with thirst. Yet the thought of consuming anything, even water, makes her nauseated. She fights the consciousness as her mind swirls with confusion about why she is asleep and in pain. She tries to maneuver her arm to rub her sore shoulder but cannot get it to move. She gives up after a minute and slips into the empty dullness she craves.

Hannah stands on the wooden sidewalk, gazing across the dirt street. The breeze kicks up dust, blowing gentle gusts between the divide. She cannot believe she is here after all this time. Many years have passed since she was last here, since she last saw him. The memories rush back to her, flooding her with images of the past. Him looking down at her as they walk the same streets, dodging horses and people, his eyes the bluest she has ever seen. Her laughing as he pulls her close for a stolen kiss. She stood on this weathered walkway many times before, waiting for him to come out of the feed store. She is an old woman now, and the journey here was difficult. At her age, the hundred-mile trip on a wagon train had almost been the end of her. She had started out much farther away, making her way here over the years as opportunity allowed.

She glances at her hands; the skin stretched thin across her fingers, wrinkled with age. The ruby on her ring finger sparkles in the sunlight, evoking more memories from decades ago. Movement catches her eye, and she looks up to watch him exit the store. Malcolm loads feed and supplies onto the buckboard wagon behind the stallion, oblivious to her gaze. Her heart beats faster at the sight of him. Her love for him will never fade, not in this lifetime or the next. No matter how many miles or years come between them, it burns as brightly today as the day she fell in love with him.

He removes his hat, wiping the sweat from his forehead with the back of his hand. The cowlick in his hair stands up and her hand instinctively rises to smooth it down, something she has done a hundred times. She catches herself, letting her arm fall to her side. He mounts the wagon and pauses for a moment, then stiffens, sitting up straight. He seems to sense her stare and shifts to look at her. She smiles, her face angled downward, hidden by her bonnet. She does not worry he will recognize her; time and grief have changed her far too much. Even though it has been years for her, it has been mere months for him. He peers at her with a mixture of curiosity and confusion, then tips his hat and nods at her before snapping the reins to steer the horse away. As he rides off, he twists to glance at her one final time, and she raises her head and smiles.

This is enough now.

She had to see him once more. And now she has.

They will realize she is here soon. They will send her somewhere further away again, to a place in time that ensures she can never come back here. Far away from him. But it no longer matters to her. She is old. She is tired. She is ready to go. Let them do what they must. There is nothing left for her here. Or anywhere else.

Hannah watches until she loses him to the horizon, then uses her cane to hobble to the side of the walkway, settling against the bench. She runs her palm over the worn wood as she thinks of how they used to sit here together when the weather was mild. They had the world at their feet then. She found the love of a lifetime in him, hundreds of years from where she began her search.

Her hands folded in her lap, she rests her head against the seat and allows her eyes to drift shut. She sits there alone as dusk settles in around her, until her breathing slows, and the rise and fall of her chest stills.

Her smile frozen in time forever.

Indistinct conversation stirs Hannah from her dream. It sounds distant and muffled at first. She struggles against the grogginess for several long moments as she gains consciousness and her mind connects the bits and pieces together, recalling what brought her here. Her initial impulse is to run, but she does her best to tamp down the panic as her eyes fly open to focus on the trio in front of her. Rope still binds her wrists, and she tries standing before waves of vertigo wash over her and she collapses onto the forest floor. The voices belong to females, which diminishes some of her fear. She knows they should frighten her regardless of who they are, so she braces for whatever fate has in store. Two young women and a skinny colored boy of about twelve return her stare with wide eyes. One woman gasps and clutches the others arm for support, as if the very image of Hannah is so shocking, she must brace herself to remain upright. The other crosses herself and places her hand over the other woman's grip on her arm.

Her thoughts drift to Malcolm and Jacob momentarily, and the heartache is too much to bear. She has never experienced such unimaginable pain. The tears flow down her cheeks, her sobs echoing through the woods. She doesn't care if these people are a threat. Death would be a welcome escape. She cannot stay here, wherever here is, if her husband and son are not with her. Her entire being is tied to the one she loves, the man who waits for her in 1868, and it overshadows any fear of what might become of her.

"Abraham, help the poor woman sit up!" says one of the women, yanking her out of her reverie.

"Yes ma'am, Miss Johnson."

The boy moves to Hannah and draws her to a sitting position.

"Untie her, quickly," says the other woman.

"Yes, Miss Williams," he responds.

He steps behind Hannah and works on the knots, releasing the binding. She brings her arms forward to examine her bruised and bleeding wrists.

"Oh, poor dear! What has happened to you? 'Twas likely one of those horrible, stewed pirates who ofttimes make their way ashore. Or mayhap one of the Godless savages who roam the forest. 'Twould not surprise me in the slightest. Oh, where are my manners? I am Abigail Johnson, and this is my cousin, Temperance Williams. What is your name and where do you hail from?"

Hannah glances between the two women, not sure how to answer their question. She cannot tell them she is from the future.

Well Abigail, I started in 2071, and it's a long, convoluted story. Perhaps you can just direct me to the nearest time warp portal, where I'll make my way back to 1868, where I am most recently from? Right. That's not going to happen.

She does not know where or when she is. From the look of their clothing, and Abraham, who she assumes is a slave boy, she guesses she is somewhere in the 1700s. A wide range that does not help her present situation. And she still has no clue where she is, even if she could figure out what year they sent her to. She is no history buff, so she goes with the first thing that comes to mind—feigning ignorance.

"I, I don't know," she says, inhaling a deep breath to steady herself.

"You do not recall from where you hail?" asks Temperance.

"I am sorry, but I remember nothing. I may have arrived on a ship. I am not sure. . ." she trails off, not trusting her voice to give her away.

"'Tis sensible, I suppose. You could be from anywhere if you traveled by ship. What is your name?"

"Mary, I think. I am just so embarrassed. I believe they must have hit me on the head."

"Someone had ill intentions. You need only look upon you to see that. They bound you and left you here," she says, her arms sweeping out to the surrounding forest.

Hannah looks down at her wrists again and rolls her shoulder.

"We should not want to abandon you whilst in this condition, you shall come to the estate with us until your memory returns," states Abigail, leaving no room for objection.

"Thank you. May I ask where I am?"

"Why, you are in Alexandria, of course."

"Virginia?"

"I know naught of another. Is there more than one Alexandria?" chuckles Abigail.

"No, no, of course not. I am just so confused."

"Aye. You have suffered quite a scare. Abraham, assist Mary up and help us take her to the manor. Quickly, now! Do not dillydally."

"Yes, miss."

She leans on Abraham until she can walk unassisted, and they reach the house fifteen minutes later. The plantation is a lovely two-story mansion surrounded by immense oak trees. She allows them to lead her upstairs to a modest bedroom where Temperance gives her a nightgown and insists she sleep. After applying a salve to her wrists, she wraps them in cloth, promising to bring her a meal when they serve supper. They shut the door and leave Hannah alone in a household with strangers, in a place she has never been to, and with no idea what timeline she is in.

She glances around the bedroom, her gaze stopping at the four-poster bed. There are thick velvet curtains hung on all sides and several layers of bedding. A dresser lines the opposite wall with a porcelain wash bowl and pitcher on it. A pot sits on the floor next to it. She realizes that must be the chamber pot, and the thought sends shudders through her. They expect her to relieve herself in a ceramic bowl on the floor when she has just grown accustomed to the outhouse at home. She pushes the image from her mind as her eyes sweep over the rest of the room. A rocking chair is positioned in front of the large stone fireplace and a dressing table with a mirror and straight-back chair are in the room's corner. The bedside table holds an oil lamp, a candle and a bible.

She settles onto the bed and falls asleep despite her best efforts to stay alert, and when a knock on the door wakes her, the sun is setting. Abigail and Temperance enter, carrying a tray. They leave the plate with her and instruct her to get more rest after she eats. She realizes they will question her again in the morning, but without knowing the year she is in, it will be impossible to concoct a plausible tale.

"I understand this may sound peculiar to you, but I do not remember what year it is. My mind is still so fuzzy."

"Fuzzy?" asks Temperance.

"I mean addled. I cannot recall things I should know."

"'Tis the year of our Lord, 1790," says Abigail. "Your mindfulness shall return, I pray so. An acquaintance of my father's fell and struck his head. He lost his memory, and he slept for three days. After a fortnight, his recollection returned. Who knows how long you were alone? 'Tis lucky we were on a stroll and happened upon you."

Hannah knows she was not alone in the woods for more than a couple of hours. She also realizes she does not have much more time to stall them with her account of amnesia without a convincing story. However, she says nothing and nods in agreement. At least she has learned where and when she is. Not that the information helps her any. She knows little about Alexandria in 1790. She remembers it is a substantial port city on the Potomac, so her description of arriving on a ship is believable. Other than that, her knowledge of colonial history is scarce, at best.

She sips the tea the women bring her, and picks at the dinner. The sweet potatoes are tasty, and she finishes them, but they undercooked the green beans, and they are hard and stringy, picked too late, after the tough string developed. The bird must be pheasant or quail, as it is too small for a chicken. Either way, after one bite she discovers it is under-seasoned and bland, and she is reluctant to eat more of it because she is not at all certain they prepared it safely. Meat that is raw or has been through unsanitary processing is the fastest means for her to become ill. And without antibiotics, that is not a choice she can afford to take. She does not try whatever the mush is next to the beans. It looks like a cross between grits and wet cornmeal, and her palette is not that adventurous.

She sighs and places the tray on the side table, so tired she can almost feel the weariness seeping from her bones. Resting against the feather pillow, she tries to doze again, but worries about what the next day will bring crowd her thoughts. Will she have to hide in plain sight and build a new life in Alexandria, a stranger in her own country? Or can she find a way back to the man she loves? Both scenarios seem equally insurmountable as she finally drifts to sleep in the unfamiliar house.

TWENTY-NINE

Alexandria, Virginia 1790

Hannah wakes to sunlight streaming through the thin curtains. She blinks and squeezes her eyes shut again, willing the brightness to leave her alone. She has nothing new to share with Abigail and Temperance, who will no doubt quiz her on her past today. There is no choice but to continue with her amnesia ruse until she fabricates a story or finds somewhere else to stay while she figures out her next move. The tap on the door pulls her back to the present, her stomach twisting with dread.

"Come in."

"Good morn, Mary." They walk in together, Abigail carrying a dress and undergarments. "We thought mayhap you wish to wear proper clothing whilst you are here," she says, not able to hide the repulsion on her expression as she glances at Hannah's own clothes on the chair.

"We musn't have a guest of ours dressed as if she is a scullery maid. Cecelia, Bring the fresh wash bowl in," adds Temperance. "Are you still unwell today, a bit out of sorts?"

"I'm exhausted, and my memory has not returned, I'm afraid."

A young colored girl enters the room with a pitcher and basin. She stands in place, eyes downcast. She is stunning, with skin the color of mocha. Her pale brown eyes are large and almond-shaped, with eyelashes any woman would envy. Hannah can imagine her on the runway of a high-end fashion show in Paris or Milan and wonders if she is household staff or a slave. Anyone held as captive to another sickens her, and she forces the thought out of her mind.

"Cecelia will help you wash and dress and then you'll join us for tea and porridge," states Abigail, leaving no room for argument.

"I can do that for myself," answers Hannah.

"Oh, fiddle de-dee. 'Tis why we have staff. Now, let her assist you and you shall come to the veranda aft for brunch."

They leave together, like two cyborgs in perfect step with each other. The door closes behind them and Hannah glances to Cecelia, who still stands holding the basin.

"Really, I can wash myself. I prefer to, actually."

"I ain't never met no white woman wants to do nuthin' fer herself," she responds, her colloquial, broken English confirming she is likely a plantation slave.

"Well, you have now. I need you to help me into all this nonsense, though," she answers, sifting through the clothing.

The corners of Cecelia's mouth turn up in a slight smile. "Yes ma'am."

"Would you mind waiting in the hall for me and I will call you in when I'm done?"

"Yes ma'am, Miss Mary."

Cecelia backs out, closing the door softly. Hannah undresses and rinses her face and hands with the warm water. She has a quick sponge bath using the cloth as best she can, thinking she would do just about anything for some modern-day toiletries. Sitting on the chair in the room's corner, she leaves her own undergarments on, then calls Cecelia in, who helps her into the corset and bustle pad. She pushes and pulls Hannah until she is ready for the skirt and overtop.

"No disrespect ma'am, but you's is actin' a woman who has never worn proper dress in her life."

Hannah turns to face her. "Oh. Well, I, I, oh, never mind. I don't remember who I am. Someone hit me on the head and left me for dead, and I have no memory of my past. I apologize if I've made this difficult for you."

"No ma'am, I's jus sayin' what I's see is all. Now you's is a proper mistress," she says, stepping back to admire Hannah's dress. "Sit an let me fix yer hair, 'tis wilder than a bird's nest, it sure is."

Hannah allows Cecelia to style her hair into a low bun. She looks at her reflection in the hand mirror and hardly recognizes herself anymore.

She does not resemble the person who left Los Angeles all those months ago. Until yesterday, she was the happiest she had ever been. What a difference a day makes. She sighs and studies the shoes Cecelia holds out for her. They are like slippers with small heels, covered in a brocade material. She slips her feet in and puts her weight on each foot to test the feel. They could be a half size bigger, but thankfully, they are not as uncomfortable as she expected them to be.

Cecelia steps backward to examine her. The many layers of clothing are hot, and Hannah shifts uncomfortably, her movement restricted. The stay forces her to maintain a correct standing position and the panniers on the sides serve no purpose other than to make her appear twenty pounds heavier than she is. She would prefer to be in just the shift and stockings, but of course that would be highly improper public dress for this timeline. She must admit they made the stomacher and petticoats with beautiful fabric, but that's the only positive thing she can find. The discomfort far outweighs the beauty.

"You's look real pretty, Miss Mary. You's sure to get men folk courtin'. Gentleman will be callin afore you know it."

"What? I already have a husband! I certainly don't need another one," she replies. Her hand flies to her mouth, knowing the moment it leaves her lips it is a grave mistake. She fusses with her dress while avoiding Cecelia's gaze. She is sure her face portrays her dread, so she concentrates on relaxing the furrow in her brow and inhales a deep breath.

"I mean I may, I do not know for certain. I wear a ring, so perhaps I am married, I, I don't remember," she stammers.

"Miss Mary, I knows there's sumpthin' amiss with you, sumpthin' you's hiding. It don't bother me none. Your secret is safe with me, ma'am. I gives you my vow."

Hannah considers a rebuttal, but realizes Cecelia is on to her.

"Cecelia, please, I do not wish the ladies of the house to discover I have been less than forthcoming with them. I mean them no harm. I give you my word. But I must remain here where I am safe. Just until I decide what to do. I only need time to find my way home."

"Master works Isaac at the docks. Mayhap he could stow you on a ship. After that, yer on yer own. But ships go most everywhere from here."

"I appreciate your offer Cecelia, but it will take more than stowing away on a ship to get me home," she says, tears filling her eyes.

Cecelia crosses the bedroom to her. "Oh, Miss Mary, don't cry. Yer sure to find yer road home soon, I's feel it in my bones. My mama had the sight, and I's do too."

Hannah wipes the tears away. "I hope you're right. Thank you for keeping my secret."

"I's a slave here, but I's got no loyalty to this plantation or the masters who run it. No, ma'am. They has no loyalties to me and mine. Now we each know sumpthin' 'bout each other we don't want them to learn."

Hannah grasps Cecelia's hands in hers. "Thank you. You are the closest I have to a friend right now. I suppose I should go out to breakfast before those two miss me. They might grow horns or howl at the moon if I'm late."

Cecelia giggles and follows Hannah out of the bedroom.

When they reach the table on the wrap-around porch, the cousins are drinking tea.

"Lovely, there you are. Right in time for tea," says Abigail.

"I confess, I am still experiencing shoulder pain, so it took longer to dress than I expected."

"Well, you are here now," replies Temperance, patting the seat on the chair next to her.

"When we finish brunch, we shall visit the city and see if anything is familiar to you," says Abigail. "I wish to have a private audience with Mr. Thomas Martin. He has the ear of the entire city of Alexandria. Mr. Martin 'twill surely be aware if anyone is searching for you."

Temperance snaps her head toward her cousin. "Thomas Martin's foul deeds have blackened his soul, Abigail, and he shall receive no absolution from me. I have naught to say to him. 'Tis best we act alone on behalf of our guest."

"Pray do not behave as if I am helpless, Temperance. Mayhap he can recommend an apothecary for Mary."

"Save for your father, Mr. Martin 'twould be your betrothed!"

Hannah speaks before the argument escalates further. "I was hoping to rest today, perhaps take a tour around the estate property. I am exhausted, and truly not up to a trip of any length. My sincerest apologies. I realize you are only trying to help."

"We shan't have you boguing through the city whilst you remain so weary. 'Twill be nothing but a fool's errand. I beg forgiveness for my cousin. I should not want to offend you. We shall plan for the morrow," replies Temperance, glancing sharply at Abigail, who is clearly disappointed they postponed the trip into town.

"Mary, your accent and language is naught I have heard before," says Abigail.

"I wish I could tell you where I acquired it," says Hannah, eyes downcast. "I seem to have a vague memory of traveling in the far east. Perhaps that is where it comes from?"

"How exciting! I yearn to travel however I fear I shall never be blessed to do so. Father forbids it," says Abigail, pursing her lips in anger.

They say nothing more about Hannah's accent, and she sighs a breath of relief.

It relieves Hannah when they agree to take her on a tour of the land. She needs to know where she is and get her bearings about her. The more pressing problem of how to return home aside, she must learn how to live in this timeline for whatever amount of time she is here.

She does her best to focus as they eat porridge while making small talk, and they tell Hannah about the plantation. Abigail's father and his sister, Temperance's mother, own it. Abigail's mother and Temperance's father are both deceased, so only the four of them live there. The brother and sister are on a buying expedition up the coast to New York, leaving the women here alone, except for the work force and the estate slaves.

Hannah watches them during breakfast and finds it difficult to maintain silence when they interact with the servants. A few of the slave children wander onto the lawn during brunch, and Temperance is not kind to them. Hannah can tell she is attempting controlling her anger with her present, but her disdain for the household staff and slaves is clear. She tries to hide her revulsion, but she knows her sharp glances surely reveal her genuine feelings.

They stroll the property after breakfast, and it takes several hours at Hannah's slow pace, every step labored. The shoes pinch her feet and are horrible to walk in over the uneven ground of grass and dirt. She stretches her shoulder each time the muscles spasm, trying to keep up and be friendly while she steers the conversation away from her amnesia. It exhausts her. Shortly after, they return to the mansion to clean up, and after a nap she is glad it is the supper hour.

The cousins insist they serve dinner in the formal dining room, with its ornately carved furniture and flowered wallpaper. Wool rugs in rich colors cover the hardwood floors. The china is beautiful, and the staff polished the silver tea service to perfection. Hannah is aware they are trying to impress her with their obvious wealth, which she takes as a good sign. If they planned to boot her out anytime soon, they would not be so eager to influence her opinion of them. Or maybe they enjoy flaunting the fact that they have money. Either way, she intends to be a model house guest and remain here for as long as they allow her to—or until she can figure out how to get back to 1868.

She forces herself to eat because of the mixed company, but still picks around the meat, eating as little as possible. After finishing dinner, she excuses herself and wanders into the library. What a grand room. Paneling covers all but two of the walls where bookshelves line them from ceiling to floor. She runs her fingers over the books and pulls one out occasionally. The opportunity to touch texts two-hundred-eighty-one years old in her timeline is thrilling, and she spends the entire evening there, perusing the volumes.

By eleven o'clock she is completely drained and climbs the curved staircase to her room, wanting nothing more than to collapse into bed. The oil lamp is lit when she arrives, her nightclothes laid out on the bedding with a sprig of wildflowers on them. This must be Cecelia's doing, she realizes. Hannah smiles as she smells the flowers, laying them on the night table. She slips out of the skirt and bustle struggling to reach the lace-up back of the overtop with her sore shoulder. Just when she resigns to sleeping in the thing, a soft knock on the door draws her attention.

"Yes?"

"Miss Mary? 'Tis Cecelia. Do you need help with yer clothes?"

"Oh yes, please come in."

Cecelia steps in and giggles when she sees the state of undress Hannah is in.

"I know, this is the farthest I could make it alone. I can't reach the lacing with my shoulder in this shape. How did you realize to come up? It's so late."

"I waited til I saw you finish in the library. Gives you a chance to get out of yer skirt is all."

"You're a gem, you know that?"

Hannah waits while Cecelia loosens the clothing and then wiggles out of the top to flop onto the bed. "That is so much better. That thing is brutal. You're lucky you don't have to wear one."

"They ain't much 'bout my life to call lucky, miss. So's I's reckon 'tis a blessing I don't."

"How old are you, Cecelia?" she asks, sitting up.

"I don't rightly know, miss. Ne'er knows fer sure. Massie says I's twenty years. 'Spose she's right."

"You're too young to do nothing but work. Would you like to accompany me into Alexandria tomorrow?"

"Oh no, ma'am, I's ne'er done that afore. Miss Abigail and Miss Temperance ne'er bring slaves to the city with them."

"You let me worry about that. Just be ready after breakfast."

"Yes ma'am, Miss Mary," she answers, beaming.

"Goodnight, Cecelia," she says, returning her smile.

"I's tighten the ropes on the bedstead afore you get in."

Hannah has no idea what she is talking about, but hops off the bed. Cecelia lifts the many layers of blankets and turns a key-like wrench at the foot of the bed that pulls the ropes tight between the boards.

"There, 'twill help you sleep tight, Miss Mary."

"I shall. Thank you."

She studies the bed for a moment after Cecelia leaves. Sleep tight. She can't help but wonder if this is how the old expression came about. Hannah climbs onto the feather mattress, pulling the covers up around her. She falls asleep dreading another day in this timeline but knowing she is helpless to do anything to change it.

She is awake early the next morning and almost completely dresses herself without Cecelia's help, her shoulder feeling far better. She only needs to tighten the corset lacing for her. As if reading her mind, Hannah hears a soft knock on the door and Cecelia calls her name.

Once Cecelia helps her with the corset, they agree to meet on the veranda right after breakfast. She joins the women for brunch, sipping her tea and choking down the flavorless porridge while the cousins make small talk again. Molasses improves the flavor some, but it is still not anything she would eat every morning.

"How does your memory? Ofttimes a good rest cures what ails us. Do you remember where you hail from or why you were abandoned to perish in the woods?" asks Temperance.

Hannah knows she cannot keep up this amnesia pretense much longer. The women will want information soon, and she needs them to let her stay here while she figures things out.

"No, not at all. I fear it may never come to me unless I find something to spur my memory. I think it is a splendid idea for me to go into the city today, as you suggested yesterday. I would prefer Cecelia join us, though. I depend on her in my infirm state, and I would not be comfortable making the trip without her. I might require support or become too tired."

"You wish for Cecelia to accompany us? She is a slave. 'Tis highly unusual," replies Abigail.

"Do the staff never escort you to town?"

"Staff, yes. Slaves, no," states Temperance, raising her chin slightly and looking away. "'Twould be proper to bring one of the household staff with us. We shall have Elijah escort us in the carriage. I am certain you will be able to make the trip then."

"I'm already comfortable with her. Forgive me for being pushy, however, I feel very fragile, and after my trauma I am experiencing some mistrust. You have both been very generous to me, and I appreciate your hospitality and kindness. I pray to impose on you once more and ask that I take Cecelia with today," she says, glancing between the two of them.

"'Tis fribble, Temperance. Cecelia may attend us, as our guest wishes," says Abigail.

"I suppose 'twould do no harm. We should prepare to leave so we are home afore the heat is too much to bear this afternoon," says Temperance sharply, not pleased to lose the battle.

Thirty minutes later, the four women walk down the lane leading away from the house and wait outside the barn for the buggy. The morning sun beats down on them, and the humidity is already stifling. Hannah realizes a three-mile trek in their dresses and footwear would have been too demanding for her, especially in the heat.

They ride along the path, twisting through the trees and crossing a rickety bridge over a narrow creek. They pass a few cabins and farms, and two large plantations on their journey to town. The women chat about who lives there and offer tidbits of gossip about each person. Hannah nods politely and mutters an occasional comment, but she is focusing her thoughts on how to get home to Oklahoma. The only solution she comes up with is to find a transporter and hijack their transponder. Which is clearly a million to one shot. But the prospect of being stuck here forever makes her stomach roil. She expects the cousins will soon grow weary of her amnesia story and want to toss her out on her own. How could she survive here? She cannot bring herself to think about what living here might compel her to do to stay alive. All her hope hinges on Malcolm somehow getting word to Christine and her making her way here to rescue her. That seems just as unlikely, but she intends to remain near her drop point on the slim chance someone shows up. Please let them come for me, she prays silently, the hope a constant refrain in her mind. Now forced to face the prospect of life without Malcolm, she knows if she must carry on alone, it will destroy her. The thought shudders a fresh wave of fear through her before she pushes the image aside.

As the trees give way to fields and rolling hills, they reach the boundary of Alexandria. The city is enormous by this era's standards with over twenty-five hundred people and is the most crowded place she has been to since her original transport out of Los Angeles. Their carriage stops at the wharf and they wander along the port's edge, inspecting the vessels. The river laps at the side of the dock, rocking the boats as Hannah feigns studying each one, pretending to search for something to jog her memory. Passengers board and disembark up and down the waterfront. She says a prayer of thanks she did not arrive by boat. The crews appear weary and underfed, and even the overpowering stink of the brackish water cannot cover the stench of body odor as she passes by them. She decides she has had enough of the harbor for the day and tries to steer the women away from the area.

"I'm sorry. The ships all look the same to me. Nothing here sparks my recollection."

"The details are of great importance indeed in discovering who you are. We shall continue into the city proper, and pray 'tis more familiar," says Temperance.

Alexandria runs east and west, and Hannah remains aware of where she is as they press on into town, in case she requires the knowledge later. It smells of smoke and something unidentifiable that gives it a sour, almost rotten odor at times. As the buggy passes a row of unremarkable buildings, she sees a man propped up beside the entrance of a tavern, snoring loudly enough that she hears him over the sound of the carriage wheels. The fetor of discarded animal carcasses wafts through the air as they approach the meat market, and she resists the urge to gag.

As they turn onto Royal street from Fairfax, they stop for cider at an inn called Mason's Original. Once inside, Cecelia stands aside, not permitted to sit with them. That angers Hannah. She wants to have their refreshments and be on their way again, so Cecelia does not have to stand in the corner like she is less than everyone else. She does not realize they serve hard cider until she takes a huge gulp of it, only to cough most of it up. Cecelia rescues her from spitting all of it up by patting her back. With only a few patrons in the bar, she does not draw much attention. But her two companions stare at her with wary looks, and she can tell they are waiting for her to apologize for her social gaffe. Which, of course, she does. The last thing she needs to do is offend them.

After a brief rest they rise to leave, Abigail motioning for Cecelia to follow. Hannah blinks and shades her eyes against the bright light of day as they step out of the dark tavern. She does not see the trio of people walking down the lodge stairs, their path missing hers by mere seconds.

THIRTY

Alexandria, Virginia 1790

Christine's eyes flutter open at the sound of a footfall on the forest floor.

"It's only me," says Adams. "Gray left a while ago to do recon, see if he can pick up a lead on the way into town. I don't know about you, but I'd much rather sleep at an Inn than out here in the woods."

"Ditto. I've had enough of camping to last me a lifetime." Christine rises to a sitting position. "How long have I been out?"

"Almost an hour."

She sifts through the supply pack for a pouch of water. "It sure is humid here," she says, wiping beads of sweat from her brow.

"Yeah, I hope it's not a far hike into the city. This outfit isn't helping either. I think I'm chafing."

"TMI, Adams."

She walks behind a thicket of brush for a pit stop when Gray jogs into camp. Perspiration covers his face, and he removes his hat to wipe his forehead with his shirt. "Damn, it's hot here. I found the route to Alexandria, it's less than thirty minutes if we keep up a good pace."

"My hero," says Adams sarcastically.

"Screw you, Adams, don't be a sore loser. Give me the money I won when we get home and move on, pal."

Christine steps out from behind the bushes. "What's wrong with you two?"

"Nothing," says Adams.

"He's just pissed because he lost our bet about you and he owes me a few bucks. Ignore him."

"A bet about me?"

Gray nods. "Yeah. I told him you and the Brit were a thing after you got home. And Frank confirmed it for us yesterday."

"Well, isn't Frank helpful," she says sarcastically. "You know, a year ago I would have told you both what assholes you are. But I've grown since then."

"And now?" asks Gray.

"Now I'll keep those thoughts to myself about what jackasses you are."

"Nice. Way to go, Gray," Adams says, shaking his head.

"Come on, let's start for town and get going. Seventy-two hours isn't much time to find Hannah," she says.

Gray bends over in an exaggerated bow. "After you, m'lady."

The three of them hike through the woodlands to the edge of downtown where they roam the length of the wharves, getting a feel for the area. Schooners are tied to the dock, cargoes being loaded and unloaded non-stop, while they anchor larger sloops further out along the Potomac. Most of them are merchant vessels that appear barely able to stay afloat by modern standards.

It is a bustling, loud place where no one pay them any attention, which allows them the opportunity to take it all in. They had not expected it to be much of a city in this era, so its size surprises them. Even though it is large, it is nowhere near what it will become someday. Christine envisions it in her own timeline, and the comparison is astonishing.

Bare chested slaves carry crates from the holds to the decks, and finally to the docks, where a harbormaster logs them in a journal. The pungent stench of body odor wafts through the air, mingling with potent spices, and captains can be heard barking orders to crewmen up and down the wharf. Alexandria is an official port of entry for foreign ships to complete customs inspections and is one of the ten busiest and wealthiest ports in America—and it shows. It is the shipping and manufacturing center of the Potomac River with wharves, warehouses, ship builders, butchers, millers and distillers, all crowded into buildings along the waterfront. The locals export agricultural products and locally manufactured goods to all the states in the nation and all over the world from here.

After an hour there, they see nothing to lead them to Hannah and move on. They pass homes that range from mansions such as the Carlyle House, the center of social and political life in Alexandria, to small log houses with clapboard roofs where the working class reside. Christine pauses as they approach the now famous Christ Church, unable to walk by without taking a moment to admire it.

"Doesn't Washington live somewhere near here? Wouldn't it be something to meet him while we are here?" chuckles Adams.

"Doubtful, he's already president, so he lives in the White House," responds Gray.

"His place is in Philadelphia. The presidential headquarters aren't finished yet. I don't remember a lot, but I'm sure he spent time in Mount Vernon, which is somewhere close, I think. Even so, the chances of us running into him are slim," says Christine, but secretly wishing they would catch a glimpse of the first president. "Besides, this is not a sight-seeing trip. Let's just find Hannah and go home. All these people make me nervous."

The men nod in agreement and they continue to roam the streets, trying to look like they are out for an afternoon stroll. All three of their gazes continually sweep the crowds, looking for Hannah or anyone who might be a threat to them.

Downtown hums with activity, and again no one pays any attention to them—which suits them fine. Their only goal is to blend in, retrieve Hannah, and go back to Oklahoma as quickly as possible.

They drift over to North Royal Street, which seems to be the heart of the city. Most of the women are in dresses less proper than Christine's, wearing bonnets, which makes her appear overdressed with her formal hat. But as they get further into town, they wear bustle pads and elaborate stomachers, similar to her own clothing. Men are in breeches and boots with loose hanging shirts, or waistcoats and full coats with tights and buckled shoes, but almost all of them sport tri-cornered hats.

Wheels from wagons and carts have etched deep tracks in the road, making them uneven and difficult to walk on. People crowd the sidewalks, so they remain in the roadway, unwilling to have more contact with anyone than is necessary. Some roads are cobblestoned or bricked, but not all of them. Those that are have a thick layer of muck tracked onto them, creating a muddy, slippery mess. Shops and two-story structures line the streets with wood barrels and live animals in pens stacked along the alleyways, even spilling into the streets in places. They pass a tailor shop, an apothecary, and what appears to be a brothel, judging from the women's efforts to entice passing men inside. Taverns are another popular establishment and seem to make up every third or fourth building.

Adams points out an inn just ahead. "There it is, Mason's Original Tavern. That's the place I read about online last night. It's in the middle of downtown and we should be able to rent a room."

"Okay, let's do it," says Gray.

They hesitate for a moment before pushing the door open and stepping into the pub. The first thing to hit them the minute they enter the dim building is the smell—warm ale and spoiling food left out too long. Stifling heat and humidity immediately follow. With no climate control, it almost feels like a sauna, and the perspiration trickles down their backs. There are several patrons, mostly men who appear to be dock workers, scattered at tables drinking from tankards, the din of their conversation and laughter carrying loudly throughout the bar. The Ritz Carlton, it is not. A seedy motel would be a welcome upgrade to this, the foul odor alone enough to make them nauseated. The low ceiling gives the entire place a claustrophobic feel that causes Christine to shudder, despite the sweltering temperature.

They approach the barkeep who is mopping the bar top with the dirtiest cloth she has ever seen. His hands are rough and calloused from years of hard manual labor, unlike their own. Gray takes the lead, all of them apprehensive that none of them speak in the current vernacular, and the less attention they draw to themselves, the better.

"How does it, sir?" asks the barkeep, glancing up at him.

"We wish to let a room for the night. Anything with two beds. It will be my wife and me, and our friend," Gray lifts his chin toward Christine and Adams.

"Only 'ave one bedchamber left with one bed," he says, eyeing them up and down and flipping the grimy bar towel over his shoulder. "Ye fellow 'twill need to sleep on the floor, but we've extra quilts."

"All right, fine. That will have to do, I suppose."

Gray works out a price with him and pushes the silver coins across the counter. The man pockets them into a pouch tied to his belt and then tucks it into the waist of his pants.

"Mayhap ye be comin' to the board then? Meat pottage and cheate bread are ready soon, and all spirits are cash on the barrelhead, no credit."

"No, thank you. We'll be out all afternoon."

"Very well. 'Tis my tavern, if ye require anything whilst here, ye see me." He walks out from around the counter and motions for them to follow him. They exchange glances when they notice his flintlock pistol tucked into the back of his waistband, a reminder that most everyone in this era arms themselves. Everyone but them.

The room is at the end of the hall upstairs, one bed, a table, two chairs and a fireplace.

He leaves the door ajar while he gets the quilts. "No wash tub, no privy for lodgers either. Chamber pot is in the corner yonder," he says, pointing to a ceramic bowl on the floor. "Till the morrow," he says, walking out and closing the door behind him before any of them can say anything.

Once he's gone Adam's puts the pack down, and they all relax for the first time since arriving.

"Well, I guess we should decide who will sleep where."

"I don't care, I'll take the floor. It's probably cooler there anyway," says Christine, fanning her face with her hand and sitting on the edge of the bed.

"I'm not sleeping in the same bed with this asshat," adds Adams, glancing over at Gray.

"Finally, something we agree on. Christine, you take the bed, we'll sleep on the floor. It isn't spacious enough for two people to sleep comfortably anyway," says Gray.

"Jeez, I hope these don't have fleas or bedbugs," says Adams, shaking out the quilts.

Christine rises with a start, peering down at the bed for any telltale sign of bugs. The owner's standards for clean seem ridiculously low as she remembers the state of his bar cloth.

"I just want to find Hannah. I'm not worried about where I sleep," she says, straightening the bedding, still searching for insects.

They eat lunch before picking up the search and settle on MREs and the emergency water pouches. Christine sits on the bed eating, bouncing on it a few times. It seems solid, but is lumpy and hard, and makes a crinkling sound when she moves. Referring to it as a mattress is a charitable term, but she determines it beats wet leaves on the hard ground. Unless it's home to bugs. After some thought, she decides to camp on the floor with the guys tonight, not willing to take a chance. Fleas and bedbugs can transport back to 2071 just like she does.

Gray finishes his MRE and takes out his transponder to search for a signal from Hannah's tracker, frowning as he types information into it.

"All I pick up is that she's east of here, somewhere within five miles. If I could run a complete report, and not this ghost scan, I could pinpoint it."

"It's too risky, Gray, you know that. Hoyt can't cover that in the system. The enforcement team would be all over that in minutes. Especially since she was just sent here a few days ago. East is a starting point. We'll have to go with that," says Christine.

"Okay, let's get to it then," says Adams, hoisting the pack over his shoulder.

"Want me to carry that for a while?" asks Gray.

"Nope, wouldn't want you to break a sweat, pretty boy."

"Get over it, Adams. Nobody likes a poor sport."

"Oh, for God sakes, stop it you two. You're acting like twelve-year-old boys."

The men laugh, and she follows them down the stairs and outside to the sidewalk. The roads are soggy, the humidity almost unbearable. Christine walks gingerly through the swampy street, stepping around a mound of horse manure, wondering what else has mixed with the dirt to form the mud. The animal stops a few yards ahead of them to release a stream of urine on the roadway. And she has her answer. She turns her head only to discover a man relieving himself in an alley behind a building, and she shudders. Before she can look away, a window further down the path opens, and a woman unceremoniously empties the contents of a chamber pot into the alleyway. She will never understand how enough people lived through this era to grow the population without succumbing to a myriad of bacterial borne diseases. Their immune systems must be indestructible.

Looking at the muddy ground again, she tries her best to push aside thoughts of the foul sludge she is wading through. Gray turns and nods his head to her, motioning for her to catch up to them. Sure, it's easy for them to trudge through the rancid liquid. They are both wearing knee-high leather boots with flat heels, she thinks to herself angrily. She is in brocade covered slippers with a kitten heel. Life is so unfair sometimes. She side-steps more horse excrement as she hurries to fall in step with them, considering all the ways she will make them pay for this later.

They walk east in a general direction, no specific destination in mind, away from the four women who left Gadsby's before them. Christine's gaze sweeps the crowds nervously. When they exile prisoners, they send them to sparsely occupied areas always outside of a city. Even when they stranded her, she was never anywhere as populous as this place. She touches her waistband to make sure her transponder is secure—it is the one thing that makes her feel safe. If they run into an emergency, at least they can escape to home. But that would also mean losing their only chance to rescue Hannah, so that would be a last resort.

They reach the edge of town and hike into the forest for a rest, where Gray checks his transponder again and downs an entire pouch of water.

"We're closer. She isn't in the city. The trace shows she's within two miles of us. Southeast of here."

"Crap. They do not create these for hiking," says Christine, flopping on the ground and kicking off her shoes to rub her feet.

Adam's looks between them. "Do you think we should quit and take up again tomorrow? It will be dark in three hours. As mediocre as the hotel is, it beats spending the night out here."

"Let's try for another hour before we call it for the day. If there's any way to find her in the foreseeable future and get out of here, I'm all for exploring the Virginia woods in these frigging shoes a while longer," says Christine.

Their walk yields nothing after trudging through the woodlands for a mile. They pass two houses, but neither reveals any sign of Hannah, and Gray's transponder still shows her a mile or so off.

They continue on, but after hiking for a half hour, they are ready to give up when Gray gives them the signal to stop and crouch. Christine and Adams kneel next to him as he points to a sizeable plantation house. Three women sit at a table on the large porch. They are too far away to catch any detail, and there is no tree cover to allow them to sneak closer. They observe them for fifteen minutes when a branch snaps behind them. They spin around to see a young colored woman peering at them with wide eyes. As they turn, she drops the basket she is holding, frozen in place with fear.

"It's all right, we won't hurt you," says Christine, rising slowly. "My name is Christine. We are searching for our friend, Hannah. We believe she may be lost, and we only want to take her home."

The girl stands still, her gaze cutting back and forth between them.

"Is there a woman named Hannah here who arrived recently? She is shorter than me and has long hair."

She glances to the veranda and then to Christine. A definite sign she knows something.

"Ain't nobody here by that name, miss."

"All right. Has someone come here in the past few days with the description I gave you?"

"I's don't see nuthin', ma'am. I's just a slave here. I's pay no notice to Missus Johnson's new guest."

"What is your name?" asks Adams.

"Cecelia," she answers.

"Cecelia, we only—"

Christine raises her hand to silence him. "Cecelia, can you take a message to Ms. Johnson's guest for me? Will you tell her Christine is here and I'll wait for her here? Can you do that?"

"Yes, miss." She doesn't hesitate, dashing out of the trees and cutting a wide circle around them and across the meadow to the house. They watch her approach the table and pour more tea before standing aside, waiting to serve them again. One woman stands and is gesturing agitatedly at Cecelia. Christine goes to the basket she dropped and peers inside. It is full of wild mushrooms. Maybe she is angry the girl did not bring any mushrooms. Two of the women go into the mansion and Cecelia grabs the third woman's arm, holding her back. She leans in close to her and points toward the tree line. The woman twists, shading her eyes from the sunlight, staring into the woods. She picks up the bottom of her skirt and starts down the steps hurriedly. One of the women appears on the porch just then, and she turns to face her. They have a brief conversation, though too far away for Christine to hear anything. The woman turns once more to look in their direction. She pauses at Cecelia's side, then walks through the door, out of sight. Cecelia rushes down the stairs and through the field.

"Miss Mary says for you to stay here, 'twill be here at dark. I's show her the way," she says, between gasps for air.

"Mary? That's not my friend's name."

"Miss Mary told the masters she don't remember her name. I's knew she was lyin', but I's told her, her secret 'twas safe with me."

Christine sighs with relief. "Thank you. We'll remain here until you return."

Cecelia glances at the basket she dropped earlier, moves to pick it up, but thinks better of it. She kicks it behind a gigantic black oak and runs off toward the house.

"Are you certain it was her?" asks Gray.

"Not at all. We're too far off for me to confirm. She's the correct height, and petite, but who can tell from this distance? I assume it's her or she wouldn't have sent the message to wait for her. These dresses are no help either, the yards of fabric and bustles make us all appear to have the same build."

"I don't know, I think they're kinda sexy," says Adams, rustling through the supply pack for a snack.

"Adams, I really didn't need to hear that. As enlightening as this trip has been in getting acquainted, please stop sharing," says Christine.

Gray laughs and relaxes against a tree, placing his hat beside him, hands behind his head and legs outstretched. "May as well get comfortable. We have a while before the sun sets." He closes his eyes and is asleep within minutes.

Christine tamps down her frustration over waiting for Hannah. The longer they are here, the more risk they encounter. She sighs, knowing there is nothing she can do but to be patient, and before long, she has convinced herself they will be on their way home in a few short hours. She was wrong.

THIRTY-ONE

Alexandria, Virginia 1790

Christine removes her hat and tosses it to the ground near the supply pack, glad to be rid of it, if only temporarily. Adams eats a protein bar and stands watch while she wanders the immediate area, searching for some way to entertain herself. Sheer boredom drives her further into the woods where she discovers a few old grave markers and reads them all before she notices a doe and her fawn feeding. She watches them, enthralled. It never ceases to amaze her, the beauty of nature. She never experiences these things in her normal timeline, and she longs for the simple pleasures she discovered during her extended time in Oklahoma and England. So caught up in the moment she almost misses the leaves crunching behind her as someone approaches. She twists around, startled to see two men leering at her. The dread settles in her stomach as she surveys the sight in front of her.

"Well, well. What do we 'ave here?" one of them says, grinning to reveal several missing and rotted teeth.

"Tis a miracle. Mayhap she waits here for us as a gift from the heavens," leers the other man, scratching his scalp and chuckling.

"Aye, 'tis our lucky day, Ferris. She's ripe for the pickin."

"Sure 'twill be a welcome comfort for the long sail ahead."

Christine tries to quell the rising panic as she stands frozen with fear. Her mind races with thoughts of how to escape as her heart slams against her ribcage. She smells their stench from ten feet away, they reek of body odor and urine, and it is difficult controlling her desire to retch.

"I'm not going anywhere with you. And if you don't back off, my two friends will come and kill you," she says, trying to sound bold, but she hears the fear in her own voice.

The men chuckle and take a step toward her. Her initial impulse is to run, but she is rooted in place with terror and tries to scream. She realizes she is in trouble when it comes out as a weak gargle. It only takes a few seconds before the adrenaline kicks in, and she bolts away. They hesitate briefly but recover quickly to give chase. It is impossible for her to gain any real traction in her slipper-style shoes, and she trips on a branch that sends her crashing to the ground with a thud. The pirates are upon her in under a minute and she battles against their grip. They pull her up and one slaps her, hard. They meant the smack to intimidate her, but it only fuels her fear, and she struggles harder. The toothless man is close enough for her to feel his warm breath on her face as he chuckles, the odor an assault all its own.

"What ye aim to do, scream fer yer mates? Naught can hear ye out here, naught but us," he says, laughing loudly.

He eyes her up and down, and she shudders.

"Ye look to want to 'ave a go at me. Ye shall have yer chance later, don't ye fret," he says.

Christine glares at him but does not give him the satisfaction of a reply as her thoughts drift to something much more sinister in mind for him.

The pirates had been wandering the woods looking for a farm or someone to rob when they spotted her. The ship they arrived on anchored in the river only a few miles away. She is merely a crime of opportunity for them, unlucky enough to be in the wrong place at the wrong time.

She prays her team hears her cries for help, but she does not know how far off she is from them. Frank will not be happy about this. He trained her better than to wander off on her own, and right now she dearly regrets her lack of discipline. She vows if she makes it out of this alive, she will make sure he never knows about it.

The transponder in her waistband digs into her side, reminding her about the option to transport out if she cannot escape them. But Gray and Adams will not know she made it home if she transports alone. They will burn up the seventy-two-hour window hunting for her, causing the enforcement unit to discover they are here. She cannot leave them to twist in the wind like that. Her capture is her mess to clean up, and she must devise a way out without exposing them. Transporting would be a last-ditch effort only if certain death was imminent. She realizes she needs a plan, and she needs it fast. She struggles to snag the device and slide it into her stomacher where she can access it easily, but they grab her arms before she reaches it.

"Stop fightin' lass. Off to the ship with ye," hisses Toothless. She is not sure what makes her want to vomit more, his grin or his stench.

They each grasp an arm and lead her deeper into the forest. She continues to struggle against them until Toothless uses the rope tied at his waist as a rudimentary belt to secure her hands behind her back. The other one vigorously resumes the attack on his scalp while she calls for Gray and Adams repeatedly with no response. Great, he probably has lice, she determines, and leans as far away from him as possible to avoid contamination.

She lets her feet slide out of her shoes without them noticing, hoping to provide a clue when her team searches for her. They walk for another hour, her soles tender, but the thick cover of leaves helps protect her from cuts. Then the trees thin out, and she sees the Potomac. If they hold her captive on a ship, no one will ever find her, she has no doubt about that.

Darkness has fallen when they arrive at their camp. The moon shines brightly, revealing a rowboat on the shore and a larger vessel anchored about a half mile out on the river with its large canons pointing toward land. She wrestles with them as her panic swells and wiggles out of their clutch. Running to the woodlands, she gets a few dozen yards before they tackle her again, and for the first time since being taken hostage, the tears flow. She will die on this beach before she allows them to hold her captive on that floating prison, abused by these men and who knows how many others. Her fear is only outweighed by her determination to devise an escape plan, because letting them take her on that ship is just not an option.

"Get her in the jolly boat," says Toothless, pushing her forward.

They drag her to the canoe as she kicks and fights where they push her inside. One guards her as the other builds a fire while they discuss leaving for the ship at first light. That gives her a small amount of hope, thinking at least she has tonight to plan her escape.

After producing a jug of rum from the boat, they drink until their eyes glass over. Christine is dehydrated but refuses any alcohol. Lice Guy decides he wants her to partake in the spirits, so he pinches her cheeks between his thumb and forefinger until her mouth opens and he pours it in. She coughs and spits it at him, which only angers him, and he hits her again.

Thankfully, Toothless eventually passes out after too much liquor. "One down and one to go," she whispers to herself.

She stares up at the full moon and stars, listening to the surf breaking against the shore. The sound matches the rhythm of Toothless snoring. She thinks she may get out of this without the help of her team until she sees Lice Guy is still wide awake and ogling her. She imagines what lascivious intentions he has in mind for her, and it terrifies her to the core. Where the hell are Gray and Adams? Their seventy-two-hours is wasting away, no thanks to her. By now they must have begun the search for her, which means they are not focused on rescuing Hannah. She prays Hannah and Cecelia made it to them safely, because there is more at stake here than her own survival.

The man forces Christine to fight him off repeatedly, which is easy to do in his inebriated condition, even with her hands bound. Her hand-to-hand combat training turns out to be useful, and her endurance is excellent. When her resistance proves to be too much effort for him to deal with in his impaired state, he finally gives up and takes a break. The outcome was fortunate tonight. But come morning she is certain her good fortune will be nothing more than a distant memory. Maybe she would get lucky. Or maybe she would get dead. Either way, she was not getting on that ship. Or giving up.

* * *

"We've got movement. Two women incoming," says Adams, peering through his night vision glasses.

"It's not fully dark yet," Gray states, eyes still closed from his nap.

"Don't know what to tell you, they're headed our way."

As they approach, Adams recognizes one of them as Hannah. "Yes!" he whispers to himself.

The men stand, waving them in. Hannah stops at the boundary of the trees, glancing back and forth between them.

"Who are you? Where is Christine?" she asks.

"Adams and Gray," says Adams, nodding toward Gray. "We work with Christine. She went for a walk."

"A walk? What are you talking about?"

"Yeah, she left a while ago, Gray, over an hour," says Adams.

Gray's head snaps to Adams. "How long was I out?"

"About the same. She's been gone the entire time."

"Something isn't right, Adams. She knew Hannah would meet us here, she wouldn't stay out this entire time. We need to find her."

"Then we're coming too. Cecelia knows this territory."

"Fine, let's get ready to move out then."

As the sun sets, the trees throw long shadows across the forest, making it hard to see. They rifle through the backpack, removing their flashlights. After they remove the liner from the adhesive strip on the back, they secure them on their chests, so they are hands free. Cecelia gawks at the devices, saying nothing as the men lead them into the woods. They find the area where Christine struggled with the pirates and are more convinced than ever she is in danger.

It is pitch dark after an hour, but for the beams from their lights.

"Shit," Gray blurts out. "How did we let this happen? We should never have allowed her to leave the stakeout location. That was a stupid mistake. She knows better, and so do we. We've been walking around these woods and going nowhere. It feels like we're moving in circles."

"As if we could prevent Christine from doing anything she wants to? Come on, Gray, she would have told us to go screw ourselves if we had said something to her," scoffs Adams.

Gray doesn't respond, pinching his lips together. They continue to search, becoming more discouraged with every minute that goes by. Dawn is a few hours away and the worry and stress show on their faces. Adams puts on the night vision glasses periodically, but he has only discovered forest animals.

"We're wasting our efforts out here," says Adams. "Gray, we should just take a chance and do a full scan on her transponder. Maybe they won't catch the activity at base."

"They'll see it. But I was thinking the same thing. We've been at this for hours and if we don't find her soon, we'll have to do it. We have no other choice. We can't leave her here."

"And your ghost search shows her within a couple of miles from us?" asks Adams.

"Yes, but the signal is weak, and I'm still unable to pinpoint it."

"Okay, you guys, let's just keep looking. She hasn't been missing a full night yet. She can't be too far, I mean—" Hannah's words are cut short by a distant scream.

The group exchange a look and pick up their pace, moving in the sound's direction.

Gray and Adams crash through the woodlands in a jog when Cecelia stops them after covering a mile.

"Look!" she exclaims, pointing to the ground. "I tripped on one."

Adams aims his beam at her, highlighting the shoes.

"They have to be hers, who else would leave these out here in the middle of nowhere?" asks Hannah, picking them up.

"She must be at the river," Cecelia points ahead to the faint glow of a campfire in the distance, barely visible through the woods.

Gray resumes his lead and Adams walks behind the women to provide light as they move closer to the shore. Gray reduces his beam to low and signals Adams to do the same as they reach the edge of the tree cover. Once they see the beach, they turn off the flashlights to allow their eyes to adjust. Before their night vision returns, a bloodcurdling scream emanates from near the campfire. Gray has heard enough and dashes out of the woods, followed by the others. Two people are in a skirmish next to a small rowboat, one of them a woman. They race toward them, and Gray shouts as they approach.

"Hey, let her go!"

The pair stop fighting as the man looks up. Christine pushes him off and sits up. Dirty tears streak her face as she attempts to scoot away, her bare feet kicking sand at him. Her torn dress hangs loosely from her shoulder. The man grabs her with one hand, pushing her onto her knees in front of him, and reaches out with his other. He pulls a knife out of the man's chest in the rowboat behind him, pressing it to Christine's throat as he drags her up, moonlight gleaming off the blade.

"Be on yer way. 'Twas I who discovered her first. And I am not kin to sharin," he replies.

Christine's eyes dart between Gray and Adams. "Get him. Even if he cuts me, take him out."

"Let her go, asshole. This will not turn out good for you," states Adams.

Gray takes out his transponder and punches in coordinates and instructions.

"Gray, no!" screams Christine. "Hannah has her tracker in, she can't transport!"

"We need to leave, Christine, now."

"No! I am not leaving without her!"

"How about if we buy her from you," suggests Adams, quickly glancing at Gray as he steps forward. "We have money. It's all yours. We just want the woman back."

He tightens his grip on Christine, but his eyes narrow. "How much?" he asks.

"I don't know, a lot. Here, take it all." He reaches into the knapsack and holds up a small velvet drawstring bag full of silver. He empties a few coins into his hand to show him.

"She's a mouthy wench, I've no use fer her. Bring me the silver."

"No," says Gray. "You release her, and it's yours."

The pirate stands, yanking Christine up with him. He takes a step toward Gray, who walks to him slowly. Gray extends the money as the man shoves Christine away. His eyes widen as he sheaths the knife and reaches for the silver. Gray pushes Christine behind him and snaps his hand away from the pirate as she runs to the other women. Adams steps forward to stand beside Gray and motions to the women to stay where they are.

Hannah unties Christine's hands, just as the men advance toward Lice Guy. Her wrists burn from the rope cutting into them and her fingers have a pin and needle tingling sensation. She rubs them as the feeling returns.

"Wait, 'twas a gentlemen's deal, you vowed to give me the silver" the man stammers backing up and scratching his scalp furiously.

"Yeah, well, I lied," says Gray, as Adams moves to him.

They subdue him with the rope used on Christine, securing his hands behind his back.

"How do you like it, asshole?" says Christine, as Adams tosses him into the canoe roughly. She watches from the beach as they wade out to thigh high waves, pushing the boat with them, where Gray dumps the coins into the river. The man throws himself at the edge of the jolly boat, watching the silver sink to the river's floor in the murky water. The rowboat rocks in the gentle surf as they give it another shove, helping it to drift further out with the waves. Hurrying back to the shore, they turn the flashlights on and stomp out the dying fire.

"Are you all right?" Gray asks Christine.

"I will be. I'm just shook up. And dehydrated."

Adams jogs over carrying the backpack, handing her a pouch of water. He applies antibacterial spray to her wrists and wraps the wounds in a sterile wrap.

"That was a stupid move to take off alone, Christine," Gray says, shaking his head.

"I'm very aware of that, Gray. I don't need a lecture from either of you," she says, glancing between the men. "And Frank is not to know about this. I mean it. Not one word."

"First medieval England, and now here. Rescuing you is becoming a regular assignment for us, Christine," mumbles Gray.

"Okay, I deserved that. But I'm serious. This will only make Frank feel guilty about sending us here. He is not to hear about what happened on this beach. And thank you for coming for me, by the way. If they had taken me on that ship, no one would have ever heard from me again. That would almost certainly have been a death sentence for me."

Both men nod and sigh.

"Oh my God Christine, I am so glad you're safe, and I'm so relieved to see you!" cries Hannah, hugging her and returning the shoes she left in the woods.

"Me too," she says, shivering at the thought of how close she came to vanishing forever without a trace.

"How did you find me?" asks Hannah.

"Hoyt told us where they transported you, and Gray traced your tracker under the radar. We couldn't do a full scan, but it led us in the general direction. Thank Cecelia, she was the one who made this so easy."

Hannah smiles at Cecelia. "She's helped make my entire stay here bearable, believe me. She also spotted the fire on the beach so we could locate you. It seems we all owe her an enormous debt."

"Yes, so it does," nods Christine.

"So, when do we leave? Can you take me to Oklahoma?" asks Hannah.

"Yes, you can go home. But not with your chip in. The enforcement team will send you elsewhere the moment they see you've moved. That will also raise a massive red flag to them, because obviously you can't transport without an agent and a transponder."

"So, what do I do then? I have to get back to Malcolm and Jacob," she says, her eyes filling with tears.

"We need to extract your tracker, Hannah. Adams is a medic, and he brought the extraction device and the supplies to do the procedure. You can take an antibiotic to prevent infection and never worry about it again. The system will signal you as deceased, then archive and restrict your file. You'll be clear to travel anywhere you choose after that."

"Chad will think I'm dead too, right? And I can live with Malcolm in peace?"

"Yes. We can remove Malcolm's chip too if he wants us to. Neither of you will exist in the eyes of the CCEA."

"I like the thought of being anonymous to the CCEA, although I hate the idea of field surgery. But I guess it must be done. I'm ready, let's do it," she says, taking a deep breath.

Cecelia says nothing through the entire conversation, looking between them as they talk. Her expression is a mixture of confusion and fear.

"Cecelia, I realize this is confusing to you. You have seen much tonight you don't understand. My friend is here to take me home. To Piedmont, Oklahoma, in the year 1868. My husband and son are waiting for me there. I don't want to leave you here, Cecelia, come with me. The government will outlaw slavery in 1865, so you will be a free woman there. I know what it means to be without your freedom, and I want you to have that. Where we are from, people don't keep slaves. And Malcolm can build you a cabin on our property. You'll be happy, I'm sure of it. You can help me sell my baked goods and care for the children at the school. Will you think about it?"

Cecelia looks more confused than ever. "But Miss Mary, the year is 1790. I's don't understand."

"I know, Cecelia, it's an overload of information to consider. When I said I was from a place far away, I meant it. I'm from another era, Cecelia. I realize that sounds impossible, but it's true. I live in the future, and my friends here are from even further ahead in time. There isn't time to explain everything to you now, but I promise I will, once we are in Oklahoma. I only want you to have a better life. Please trust me."

Cecelia dips her chin for a moment and then stands up straighter. "If you say 'tis true, then I reckon 'tis the truth. I don't rightly understand it. But 'tis much I don't know about this world, Miss. I's don't wish to live here, Miss Mary, so if you's willin' to welcome me home with you, I's be mighty glad to go with you. Wherever that is. 'Tis nuthin' holdin' me here. Wherever we go cain't be no harder to stay alive than here."

Hannah looks at Christine, who nods at her. She has no issue with taking Cecelia along. She helped save her life tonight.

"We should contact Frank first," says Gray.

"I'll deal with Frank, don't worry. I'm heading this mission, and I'm allowing it," states Christine.

"Okay then. Hannah let's get you somewhere safe for your tracker extraction," says Adams. "Whoever is on that ship will hear that asshole yelling for help any minute now. I prefer to be nowhere near here when they come looking for us."

THIRTY-TWO

Alexandria, Virginia 1790 / Piedmont, Oklahoma 1868

"We can take Miss Mary to the slave quarters. 'Tis no one there save for the rats," says Cecelia.

Gray leads the group through the woods the same route they came. The sound of the pirate's yells for help fade as they make their way further into the forest. Christine hopes he drifts for days before he is fished out of that canoe. They cannot kill anyone for fear of disrupting the timeline. Although if ever she had wanted to harm someone, it was him. He would have taken her hostage onto a pirate ship to abuse her until she succumbed to disease or murder. When Toothless awoke on the beach from his stupor and demanded to join in the fun with him, Lice Guy did not hesitate to eliminate him, declaring he had no intention of sharing her with him. He did Christine a favor by eliminating one of her threats, but chills run down her arms at the thought of what could have happened to her, left alone with either of them. She fended him off when he was drunk and sloppy, but once sober she would be no match against him, especially with her hands bound.

Two hours later they approach the property, and Cecelia directs them to a small shack. Mats line the floor, but it is otherwise empty except for the rats that scurry away as they step inside. She tells them they no longer use this cabin; all the servants sleep in the larger cottage on the opposite border of the house.

Adams points to a nearby mat as he lets the supply pack drop. "Hannah, lie on your stomach. I need help to remove this clothing, I must access her T6 vertebrae, just below the level of her shoulder blades."

He digs through the supplies, gathering items while Hannah positions herself. Once he applies bactericide to the equipment before laying out a sterile cloth, he sets out the extraction device, liquid bandage and surgical glue, loosening the caps on the bottles. Next, he uses sanitizing spray on his hands and arms up to his elbows. Gray puts on neoprene gloves and opens another pack for Adams. He does not touch them, holding it open as Adams grasps the gloves and snaps them in place. Cecelia and Christine work on removing Hannah's upper clothing, while not exposing the rest of her to everyone, which is no simple task. With her back exposed, Hannah lies still while Adams takes a sterilized drape out. He pokes around, then counts down the vertebrae from her neck, noting the site with a marker.

"Hannah, I'll talk you through this, so you know what's happening, okay?"

"Yes, fine," she says, trying to sound brave, but the fear in her voice is clear.

"The antiseptic is being applied. It will be cold, but that's normal."

He applies the sterilizer around the marked space, all the way to her shoulders, the base of her collar, and down to the middle of her back.

"Next I apply the numbing medication. I'm going to test your feeling in various areas and say start when I begin. When you no longer feel my contact, I want you to tell me. Do you understand?"

"Yes, I get it."

"All right, start." He starts at her neck and it satisfies him when she has no reaction to his touch below her collar. He repeats the process from her shoulder blades and lower back, pleased she is numb in a large enough range. Gray opens the plastic wrap over the surgical drape and holds it out to Adams, who removes the sterile cloth from the package and spreads it over her, the opening positioned over the black mark he made earlier.

"I'm beginning the procedure to extract the tracking chip. Once it's out, Gray will destroy it. As soon as he does, a signal goes to enforcement immediately. As of that moment, you cease to exist as far as the CCEA knows."

He plants the tool over the spot and pushes it gently at first, then with more force, until it breaks the skin slightly. He drags the stopper up and a slight click resonates as it extracts the chip. Adams removes the barrel from the device, and Gray grabs it to take outside.

"The tracker is out, Hannah. I'm closing the wound, using the medical adhesive. After that I inject you with a nerve blocker that lasts for twenty-four hours. You'll have some tenderness at the incision site, but it won't be too bad at all. The final step is to cover the opening with an antiseptic pad and liquid gauze. You need not remove it, it's a long-wear bandage that disintegrates on its own in a couple of days. Avoid getting it wet or that can expedite the disintegration process. There shouldn't be any bleeding, but Malcolm needs to check it tomorrow. If there is any drainage, take an antibiotic immediately. Questions?"

"No, I've got it."

"Good, all done then." He glances up at the two women, nodding and signaling them to dress Hannah. Adams puts all the used pads and equipment into a biological waste bag and seals it, packing it away with the other medical items. He cannot help but notice Cecelia is looking at everything with a mixture of awe and disbelief.

"Miss Mary, is you hurt?"

"No Cecelia, I'm fine. I didn't feel a thing. And please call me Hannah. That's my real name."

"Yes, Miss Hannah."

Gray returns and tosses the cylinder into the pack. "All taken care of. You're officially expired to the CCEA."

Hannah beams and tears fill her eyes. "I'm free."

She turns to Cecelia, "We both will be soon."

Cecelia smiles at her, the prospect of becoming an emancipated woman almost unimaginable. How is it conceivable the country could outlaw slavery, she wonders? She never expected to see that in her lifetime. She had resigned herself to spending her life as a slave, working for the merciless cousins. Oh, they have displayed pleasant behavior since their guest was here. But she has seen them be vindictive and cutthroat in the past, and she knows what they are capable of. She is not sure what to think about what Miss Mary, or Miss Hannah, told her about living in a future year. It sounds impossible. But she recalls the stories her mother used to tell her when she was young. Their ancestors practiced Obeah, although she warned her never to reveal that to anyone. The masters do not allow the slaves to study or worship it. She remembers the legends of far-ago relatives appearing to serve them, and if that is possible, maybe Miss Hannah's story could be true too. She figures she has nothing much to lose. She sees how Mr. Johnson looks at her recently. It won't be long before he forces her to come to his bedroom at night, just as he makes Phibe. And now Phibe is with child. Cecelia is hardly able to take care of herself—a child of the plantation, as they call the master's mixed children, would not be a welcome addition. So, she can stay here where a bleak outlook is a forgone conclusion or choose a leap of faith with Miss Hannah. Into an unknown yet exciting destiny. Her life here will only get worse, so it is a simple decision, and she is thankful to have a choice.

"All right. Let's do this. I've programmed a tandem jump, so we travel simultaneously," says Gray.

"Cecelia, you will be light-headed, and then go to sleep. When you awaken, we'll be in 1868, Oklahoma, together. Some of us will regain consciousness before others. If you are the first one up, wake me or Hannah, okay? Don't be frightened, we'll all be here with you," says Christine.

She nods, but does not respond, her fear beginning to overwhelm her. This is a pivotal moment in her young life, and she does not face it without apprehension. Hannah grasps her hands and squeezes, trying to reassure her as Gray completes programming the transponder.

* * *

Both men awaken before the three women do. They stretch their legs and relax until the others stir. Christine is already awake when Hannah and Cecelia come to. Cecelia scans the grove, passing her hands up and down her chest and limbs, presumably to confirm she is still in one piece. She smiles and raises her face to the sky, allowing the sunlight to warm her. Hannah rises and stretches, eager to start for the ranch.

"Are you ready?" she asks, peering at the group. "I don't mean to be impatient, but I know my capture must worry Malcolm sick. I want to get home as soon as possible."

"I am," replies Gray, yawning.

Hannah crouches next to Cecelia, who is still smiling. "Are you all right? Are you well, or do you need a minute to lie down?"

Cecelia blinks slowly, her hand going to her head. "Your head might feel as though it's spinning a little, but that will pass soon," says Hannah.

Cecelia shakes her head and uses the tree for support as she rises unsteadily. "I's can walk, though I's ne'er felt this way afore, 'tis as if the earth neath me is moving."

"It will clear in a few minutes. Today begins your new life. I give you my word to do all I can to make it a wonderful one for you."

"Oh Miss Hannah, you's put all to rights by bringing me here. 'Tis more than I's could ever hope for. Is I truly free here?"

"You are," she says, grinning.

Adams picks the pack up and is bracing to heave it over his shoulder when Gray swoops in and grabs it from him.

"Nothing doing, pal. I will not hear you complain that you had to carry the load the entire trip. I got it."

Adams opens his mouth to protest but decides against it. "Fine with me. It's about time you picked up the slack," he answers, grinning at him.

Gray secures the knapsack, and they wander out of the trees into the open plains, the women following. They walk for a little over an hour before they crest the last hill before the house. Hannah peers down into the valley at her home, and happiness wells inside her as she gazes out at the familiar countryside. Without a word, she races down the hillside ahead of everyone.

"Let's allow her a moment alone with her family before we converge on them," suggests Christine.

They watch as she rounds the fence and disappears, the rest of them lingering on the bluff for several minutes before they amble toward the property.

* * *

Malcolm and Jacob sit on the dining room chairs he brought to the porch earlier, and he makes a mental note to himself to build seating for the deck. He should have thought of that before, and he chides himself for not doing enough to make the house more livable. But even his self-loathing cannot deter him from noticing what a beautiful summer afternoon it is. The sort of day that has you believe the future is full of hope and possibility. If only Hannah were here. He shakes his head, not permitting the image to develop. He cannot allow himself to think about her because if he does, he may not pull out of the darkness it will bring. And he has Jacob to think about now. He cuts open the first watermelon from their garden and gives the boy a slice. He watches Malcolm eat his melon and spit out the seeds and mimics him. They throw the rinds into the pen with the pigs and laugh as the swine squeal and fight over the treat. Malcolm's thoughts drift to Hannah again when Jacob suddenly sits up straight. He shields his eyes with his hands, staring past the animals to a small hill.

"She's home! Ma!" he shouts, as he leaps from the deck and sprints away at top speed. Malcolm's gaze follows him and then he sees her, his heart jumping around his chest like it is dancing. Hannah runs to Jacob, loose hair flying behind her. Clutching the hem of her dress, she lets it fall at the last moment to scoop him up. She spins him as he clings to her, his small arms wrapped tightly around her neck. The breeze carries the sound of their laughter to him, and only then does he dare trust the vision before him, as a sense of relief surges through him. By the grace of God, and despite all the odds against it to keep them apart, his wife has come back to him. And in an instant, his world is complete once more.

He springs up and rushes to them. She sees him and places Jacob on the ground gently. She remains standing there, tears flowing, as Malcolm races to her. They embrace and cry, while he kisses her eyes, cheeks, lips.

"Oh my God, I was so bloody worried I'd never see you again. I didn't know if you were safe there, or even alive," he cries, Jacob still clutching Hannah's skirt, refusing to let go.

"I'm fine, I promise. I'll tell you all about it later. I'm so glad to be home," she sobs.

John darts across the divide between their cabins. "Hannah, you're here, you're back!"

He stops just short of her, beaming and laughing.

"I'm good, John," she sniffles, wiping her tears away as she hugs him.

Malcolm looks beyond her to the approaching group. He strides toward them, hugging Christine and the men. Cecelia hangs back, unsure of what to do.

"Malcolm, this is Cecelia. She's going to stay with us until you build her a small cottage of her own on the property," says Hannah, pulling the girl forward by her hand. "She saved my life and Christine's."

"It's nice to meet you. Any friend of my wife's is a friend of mine. This is our son, Jacob."

"Hello Ma'am," he says, still clinging to Hannah's leg.

"Oh, you's can call me Miss Cecelia, young gentleman. I's very pleased to make your acquaintance."

"This is our neighbor and friend, John Harding."

John tips his hat to Cecelia as they all walk to the cabin. They remain on the porch for a couple of hours while Hannah tells the group about her days in Alexandria. Jacob plays with Buddy and John's dog, never letting his mom out of his sight. As the day wears on, they drink coffee and eat watermelon and berries from the garden, enjoying the afternoon and each other's company.

"I'm sorry I have nothing better prepared in the way of food. With Hannah gone, I've been cooking only the basics."

"I'll have you fattened up in no time, don't you fret," she says, winking at Malcolm.

"I hate to break this up, but I need to discuss something with you, Malcolm," says Christine.

"Sure, anything."

Christine's eyes dart to Jacob, then back to Malcolm.

"Son, go brush the horses for me, will you please? I'll come and get you later."

"Yessir, Pa." He gives Hannah a peck on the cheek before skipping down the deck to the barn.

"We took Hannah's chip out as planned. Adams has supplies to remove yours too, if you'd like. You would both be clear to travel anywhere then. But also, your tracker would register as expired and the CCEA will log you as deceased and archive and seal your records."

"Brilliant. I want to live here without concern about going into a red zone or having Chad send someone else after us. I do not intend to look over my shoulder for the rest of our bleedin' lives. It's unsettling, to say the very least."

"Great, let's do it," says Adams, standing up and grabbing his backpack.

"John, will you keep Jacob entertained for about thirty minutes, please? He shouldn't be here when we do this," says Hannah.

"Of course."

"I's can help too, Mr. John. I's sure 'nuf ain't keen to see that again," says Cecelia.

"Yes, I'll show you around the land."

Cecelia follows John to find Jacob while the others go inside for Malcolm's procedure. Adams has him lie on the bed as he repeats the surgery he performed in Alexandria. Twenty minutes later he finishes, and Gray takes the chip outside to destroy it.

"Both of you need to inspect each other every day. Any signs of infection, discharge or bleeding, take an antibiotic. Understood? I don't expect any complications, but check the wounds anyway, to be certain."

"Yes, we understand. I will let nothing happen to my wife now that I have her back, Adams. Thank you. Thank you all. Once more you have given me a tremendous gift I can never repay you for. First in England, and again here. I am beyond indebted to you."

"It's not a big deal, don't worry about it," replies Adams as he repacks the survival bag.

"Maybe it's not much to you, but to me it's my entire world," he says, squeezing Hannah's hand.

Adams and Gray stand to leave. "We'll be outside when you're ready, Christine," says Gray.

"All right. Just give me a moment. Will you send John in please?"

He nods, and they step out of the house. A few minutes later, John enters.

"Let's sit down, shall we," suggests Christine.

The four of them assemble at the dining table, and when Christine looks up, her eyes fill. She doesn't wipe the tears away, allowing them to roll down her cheeks.

"I think you all realize you won't see me again. It's too risky. If there are any more manually induced glitches by Hoyt, the IT team might research it. They'll discover all the transports were to this area after they run report after report until they uncover who transported here. We cannot compromise any tampering with the program for a long while. If it's ever safe for me to come back and visit, I'll try. But don't count on it."

Hannah hangs her head. "Christine, is that possible now? Is there a chance they will find out you were here?"

"They won't, I'm protected. Hoyt has the trips buried well, but any more of them and we're concerned it will flag the process."

"I don't know what to say. I'm truly at a loss for words," replies Malcolm. "Call me daft, but I hadn't thought ahead about what would happen now."

Christine stares at John, who is struggling controlling his emotions. She smiles at him and grabs his hand.

"I owe you my future, John, literally. But I must ask for one last favor from you. Two, actually. Look after them," she says, nodding toward Malcolm and Hannah. "I trust you, and I know you'll make sure they stay safe."

"And the second favor?" he asks.

"Take care of yourself. Be happy. I won't ever forget you. I will remember you long after you leave this earth."

He embraces her and then kisses her cheek. "I beg the same of you, Christine. Go home and live your destiny. Marry your Englishman. I will not forget you either."

"How do you know about Ethan?"

He glances at Malcolm. "Just because we are men, does not mean we never talk."

Overcome with emotion, she sobs into his shoulder until he pulls away and grins at her. "Go on now, you have a life to live. We will be fine here," he states, sniffing and working to hide his sentiment. "I have animals to tend to. Malcolm, I'll see you both in the morning."

He walks out without looking back, nodding at Cecelia and the men waiting outside before heading to his ranch. Christine watches him from the doorway until she loses sight of him to the hill that separates the properties, knowing she will never see him again in her lifetime.

Christine removes the wrap from her wrists, stuffing it into her waistband. She stands next to Gray and Adams as Hannah, Malcolm, and Cecelia watch them transport home. Hannah buries her face in Malcolm's chest as they fade away in front of them. Sensing they need some time alone, Cecelia leaves to join Jacob, who is brushing Malcolm's horse in the barn.

They stand on the porch for several long moments, arms around each other's waists, looking out over their property. Hannah is the first to break the silence.

"Do you miss it? Being in our old timeline?" she asks.

"Not really, do you?"

"Sometimes I dream of running water and indoor plumbing. Music and movies are on that list too, and of course my sister and nieces. But other than that, there's not much to miss, is there?"

"No, there really isn't. I'm well suited to this lifestyle," he says, kissing the top of her head. "I say we just build a life here that is convenient and comfortable, doing nothing to draw attention to ourselves."

"Or getting too far ahead of things for this timeline. We need to be sure our lives here leave history unchanged."

"I couldn't agree more, my love."

They remain on the porch as they watch Cecelia and Jacob walk toward the house from the barn. Hannah reaches up to kiss Malcolm and her heart swells with love for the man who spanned time to find her and make her world complete. Malcolm gently brushes the loose hair from her face then pulls her closer, knowing in his soul he is exactly where he was always meant to be.

THIRTY-THREE

Los Angeles, California 2071

Christine wakes in the capsule to Frank nudging her.

"Wake up, sleeping beauty. Let's get you through decontamination and then meet me in my office."

"Okay, see you in a few. Where are Gray and Adams?" she asks, blinking the disorientation away.

"Already in decon."

She steps out of the jump pod, rolling her neck around to work the kinks out, keeping her hands out of sight to hide her wrist burns from Frank. Once through the decontamination showers, she changes into a fresh uniform and puts her costume in a hazardous waste bag. She stuffs it as far down into the container as she can, and starts to Frank's office, satisfied they have pulled off the mission. She tugs her long sleeves down over the bruises on her wrists right before she walks in.

"I sent Ethan, Annabelle and Michael all messages you arrived home safely. They have called me more than once today," says Frank, glancing up at her. "So, tell me about the trip. We waited until you were here to debrief."

They take turns filling him in on the details of the retrieval, but none of them mentions the transported slave girl, the pirates, or the incident on the beach. Christine senses Gray watching her and knows he is waiting for her to bring up Cecelia. She also understands she needs to be the one to inform Frank about her, to spin it with the least amount of impact.

She works to maintain a neutral expression as she looks at Frank. "So, there was one minor glitch. Well, not so much a glitch as an unexpected obstacle. And really, not even an obstacle. More like a__"

"What? Spit it out, Stewart," says Frank, cutting her off before she can continue.

She coughs, trying to stall, because she has to be careful about how she tells him about Cecelia, knowing she cannot mention her capture by the pirates. So, she inhales a deep breath and follows his advice, just blurting it out.

"Hannah brought a friend from Alexandria back to Oklahoma with her," she says quickly, the words running together as she exhales.

Frank leaps from his chair, sending it crashing into the wall behind him, and leans over the desk toward her, hands planted firmly in front of him. "What? Please, please tell me this is a joke. And what do you mean, a friend? She was only there for three days. How could she possibly make a *pal* in that amount of time for God's sakes?"

"No, I'm not joking. I'm serious," she lowers her chin, not meeting his glare.

Frank looks at Gray and Adams, who avert their gazes and say nothing. So much for back-up from her coworkers. Although she can't blame them. It was her decision to allow Cecelia's transport to Oklahoma, and now it is her responsibility to shoulder Frank's wrath.

"Oh, for the love of God," he says, dragging his hands across his face.

"Frank, calm down. She was a plantation slave. A young girl with no future there who was being treated beyond the breadth of human dignity. She helped Hannah, and I made a field decision. It just seemed like the right thing to do. She won't affect history or our timeline. Malcolm and Hannah will see to that. And she is a free woman there, we outlawed slavery in 1865."

"I know when we outlawed slavery. I'm an American too. I graduated from the L.A. school system along with everyone else here," he says, his voice becoming louder with each word, his arms gesturing wildly as he continues to fume.

"Well, it's done now, unless you want me to go back. I'll transport her to Alexandria and seal her death sentence because she's an AWOL slave who has been missing for a few days."

He narrows his eyes at her, his lips drawn into a thin line, and Adams lets loose a chuckle. Frank's head snaps in his direction, rendering him quiet instantly.

"I wish you'd consulted me, Christine. You and your field decisions are giving me an ulcer."

"I considered it, and Gray even suggested it."

Frank looks to Gray, who nods wordlessly.

"But the compromise of communication registering on the system outweighed the danger of taking her with us. With great risk comes great reward, Frank," she says, the last line spoken in a sing-song voice, which she instantly regrets. It was clearly overkill on her part. Frank's face turns a vivid crimson as he paces behind his desk before finally kicking his chair away from the wall and dropping into it.

"You and I will discuss this later, in private, Stewart. Are there any other surprises you need to share with me?"

That is a question she has no intention of answering honestly. Why complicate things any further? Her two teammates realize what she is about to say and want no part of the deception. They both remain silent as Gray fixes his gaze on a spot on the wall, while Adams feigns interest in a piece of lint on his uniform pants. Christine thinks Frank is overreacting, and she regards her next words as a minor fabrication, not a straightforward lie. More of an omission for Frank's own good. If he gets any more agitated, his blood pressure could spike, and at his age that could be dangerous. As his friend, she has an obligation to keep him calm. That's how she justifies to herself what she says next. She feels guilty lying to him, but she also considers it is a necessary sacrifice. One she hopes does not come back to bite her later.

"Nope, not a thing. Everything else went like clockwork, boss," she states, her eyes never meeting his.

"Good. Let's move on, then. Did you eliminate both trackers?"

Adams lets out a heavy sigh, no doubt relieved to push on. "Yes, I removed chips from both Hannan and Malcolm, and Gray destroyed them. I'm sure enforcement is logging them as expired today, if they haven't already done so. By tomorrow they should archive and secure their files."

"Frank, what about Hannah's sister? This will trigger an email to her telling her Hannah is dead. Don't you think I should advise her she's alive and well?" asks Christine.

"No, I absolutely do not. She understood they would notify her next of kin once they declared her deceased. Did she mention contacting her sister?"

"No. But maybe she forgot to. Things were moving so quickly."

"I'm sorry, but no. You cannot disclose that to her. She cannot divulge what she doesn't know, and in order for this to work, no one can learn they survived. Nobody but the individuals involved. That means the people in this room, along with Hoyt, Ethan, Annabelle, Michael and Maddie. Our little group of crusaders, for lack of a better phrase," says Frank, his tone leaving no leeway for negotiation.

The logical side of Christine recognizes Frank is right, but the emotional part of her longs to tell Hannah's sister she is alive and thriving. Perhaps Hannah considered the long-term effects and wants her sister to believe she is dead, hoping it will bring her some closure. Is it worse for her to always wonder? She isn't sure. But Frank gave the order, and she doesn't dare disobey it—at least for the time being. She is in enough trouble with him as it is.

***

The weeks and months after Christine's trip fly by, while she pushes aside thoughts of the friends left behind in 1868. Life slowly returns to normal and her world is tranquil once again. She sees Ethan almost every day since he transferred to Los Angeles, and she and Annabelle take turns visiting, her flying to Illinois, and Annabelle to California. She values her friendship with her now more than ever. Work continues as usual, she transports prisoners back in history and her routine is ordinary, although she keeps smuggling items to her inmates to make their new exiled lives easier. It makes her slightly more hopeful for them and eases her guilt of abandoning them in the past. And after a while, the everyday minutia crowds out any lingering concerns she has about Malcolm and Hannah.

The only occasion she allows herself to speculate about them is when she reads an article online a few months after coming home. Chad Cole is arrested and fired from the LAPD, after they accuse him of brutalizing a female detainee in his custody, causing her serious injuries. The courts convict and sentence him to life in prison for a violent crime. Now that parole is obsolete, he will die in lockup. A fitting punishment for an offender such as him. His career and freedom both snatched from him in an instant seems poetic justice to Christine, and for a moment she wonders if the fact that the news delights her means she is a horrible person. But that sentiment passes quickly as she recalls what he did to Hannah and the helpless inmate in his care. She decides it isn't terrible she does not want him free to hurt the next woman unfortunate enough to cross his path.

But she is disappointed there is no mention of the evidence crime ring. She and Frank sent a letter to the district attorney's office anonymously, detailing all the information Hannah gave them. Maybe the LAPD was keeping it out of the news because of the bad publicity it would generate? But that theory had no legs. Something such as a number of police officers being arrested would be impossible to keep quiet and away from journalists. She can only hope the investigation is ongoing, and the law enforcement involved will be caught, eventually.

Then one day soon after reading that article, on a morning seemingly like any other, fate steps in when she is online to buy a garden hose. Such a normal, mundane task. A purchase she anticipates completing in minutes. But chance intervenes. An internet advertisement banner pops up across the screen, asking if she wants to view land in Piedmont. Apparently, her research for fruits and vegetables that would grow in Oklahoma prompted the computer memory to assume she has an interest in moving there. Or perhaps it really was just destiny. Maybe when she did that search for seeds, the universe tucked the information away, waiting to spring it on her when she least expected it. Not unlike today. A cruel reminder to her they are still out there, and she should not forget them. She doesn't buy a hose, and she doesn't click on the banner, either. But the image refuses to leave her, and that evening she brings it up to Ethan.

"I went online this morning to buy a new hose."

"Hmm. Fascinating. However, if this is your version of dirty talk, you may want to work on it."

"I'm serious, Ethan."

"So am I. Is this normal conversation after only a year?" he asks, chuckling.

"Haha. Very humorous. I have a point. There was an ad asking me if I wanted to invest in property in Piedmont."

"And do you? Want to invest in property in Piedmont?"

"Of course not. What would I do in Oklahoma?"

"I don't have a clue, actually."

"The system used my search history to bring it up, I guess. Months ago, I searched for seeds to take to Malcolm and Hannah. I was checking to determine what would flourish in that soil and climate, and the stupid computer picked today to throw it in my face."

"I'm not sure I understand why it's an issue?"

"I suppose because I don't allow myself to think about them. When they had their chips in, it was an assurance they were alive and well. I could have Maddie check on them anytime I chose to. Now that they have no trackers, I have no way to confirm they are safe. And I never will. After returning from England, at no stage did I ever wonder about Malcolm. And I didn't even know Hannah before this. It never troubled me after I left Oklahoma that I'd never see John again. I don't understand why it all bothers me so much now?"

"It's personal this time 'round, you've seen John a few more times, and he helped Malcolm and Hannah. Hell, you lived with him for months, and he rescued you at your most vulnerable point. You saved Hannah, and you're aware she and Malcolm started a life together. These aren't random people anymore—they are your mates. And you miss them. Do you fancy doing some research to see if you can find out what became of them?"

"Do you think I should? Or would that be a mistake?"

"Well, you gave them the means to thrive, so I'm certain things turned out fine for them. But I don't expect you'll rest until you get this sorted. Once you have it sussed out, you'll feel better."

"I left them with little more than a wing and a prayer. But I think you're right, I'll feel better if I know for sure."

"Uh oh. And there she goes, unleashed," he says, chuckling.

"Hey, this was your idea. I only agreed it might help me move on."

Christine sighs, considering Ethan's suggestion. The only thing stopping her is the fear of discovering something dreadful happened to them. But if she never finds out, her imagination will run wild while she continues to question her judgement. And it will always trouble her. Such is the fickle nature of doubt. Deep down she wants to know if they survived, and how their story ended. She realizes she has to learn what transpired with them, no matter the outcome. Ultimately, the choice to exile was Hannah's, so however things concluded, Christine was only a minor player. She did what Hannah requested—extradite her to the past. Her decision made, she settles on the couch next to Ethan, the laptop open and ready to investigate.

Christine spends hours viewing old census reports and archives with no luck. It only sends her down a frustrating rabbit hole of internet searches. Eventually, she winds up on a site detailing the history of Piedmont. It is a generic website, nothing of actual use, but something near the bottom of the screen catches her eye. It is a reference to a school logged as a historical landmark. The Aldred Schoolhouse. Her heart quickens as she clicks the link. The page opens to a picture of a one-room building with several people posing in front of it. She enlarges the photo and grins, pivoting it toward Ethan.

"Look at the name of the schoolhouse."

"Well, what do you know? There they are!"

She taps full screen, and the image grows. As she studies their smiling faces, she feels relief and happiness overwhelm her, and highlights the title to display the script below it.

Piedmont, Oklahoma residents built the Aldred Schoolhouse in 1871 after a tornado destroyed the original structure. Local pioneers Malcolm and Hannah Aldred donated materials, labor, and student supplies. The school held classes at the town hotel for one month while they constructed the new building, during which Mrs. Aldred assisted the resident teacher, Claire Harding. She continued to support the school after completion by creating an advanced study curriculum for students who would otherwise never receive an education beyond a sixth-grade level. The program was the only one of its kind in the rural mid-west. The Aldred's owned and operated a bakery shop and ran a small farm outside Piedmont. Locals knew the Aldred's as philanthropists, although much controversy surrounded their benevolent affiliation with native Cherokee and other Indian tribes, despite the tension between the cultures. Malcolm and

Hannah Aldred lived in Piedmont until their deaths in 1908 and 1909, respectively.

Pictured left to right, circa 1871 - John Harding and wife Claire with their two children, Benjamin aged 1 and baby Christine. Amos and Cecelia Edgefield with infant son Issac. Malcolm and Hannah Aldred, and adopted son Jacob, thought to be aged 12-13 at the time of the photograph.

Christine reads the article twice. John named his daughter after her. Her name could not be a coincidence, and she beams at the notion. She wonders if he told his wife the story of her living there, and the truth about Hannah and Malcolm. There is no way for her to know, although she believes he would honor their request to keep their secret. Jacob's name is highlighted, so she clicks on that feature next.

Jacob Clarence Aldred, 1858 - 1938. Jacob Aldred survived a severe childhood bout with Cholera at age 14 when an epidemic swept through the rural Oklahoma area where he lived. He was an alumnus of St. Joseph Hospital and Medical College in St Joseph, Missouri, class of 1880, where he graduated with honors. A physician specializing in the study of infectious diseases and antiseptic surgery, he followed in the footsteps of British surgeon, Dr. Joseph Lister. Dr. Aldred was an avid promoter of wound sterilization and sterile surgery practices.

Rumors swirled for years he manufactured his own medications, however, he denied those reports, citing gossip and hearsay. Innuendo extended throughout his career as many of his patients recovered from late-stage infections with no apparent explanation. Some infirm he treated reported being given medication and recovering almost immediately from illnesses such as whooping cough (pertussis), influenza, and tuberculosis. He practiced in New York and Chicago before relocating his family to his childhood homestead in Piedmont, Oklahoma in 1908, following the death of his father, Malcolm. Dr. Aldred continued to practice medicine in Oklahoma up until his death in 1938, at age eighty.

Christine reads with fascination, pausing at the remark that some of his patients recovered from serious diseases without explanation. She smiles, realizing it must have been his parents' supply of antibiotics passed down to him. Between their stock and what she smuggled to them, they would have had several hundred capsules. With both Malcolm and Hannah vaccinated against common illnesses, they would only need to use them for infection caused by an injury. They surely educated him about sterile practice and hygiene based on his specialty. They had all done well and lived long lives, and she is overjoyed to learn that. Ethan places his hand over hers, and she looks over at him, happier than she has been for months.

"They were okay. All of them were safe. Even Cecelia. I can't wait to tell Frank and the guys tomorrow," she says, putting the laptop aside and snuggling closer into him.

"I'm sure they will be properly chuffed to hear it."

She giggles, accustomed to his British phrases now, and stays cuddled against him for a minute before she bolts upright, startling him.

"Sorry, I just thought of something," she says, grabbing the laptop.

She pulls up the website again and shares the link, composing a note from her untraceable message center with it. It sure is handy to have an almost-daughter-in-law who is an IT specialist. Maddie set up the account so they could all communicate about the mission freely without fear of discovery.

Hello Heidi,

See the attached article, but please do not share. It is important that I maintain anonymity. Your sister would want you to know she had a wonderful life. Hannah was happy in Oklahoma. I saw this firsthand; she was my friend. Please delete this message once read.

Best Regards,

A friend

Ethan smiles as he peers at the screen. "You're a softie, you know that?"

"I'm an insubordinate, traitorous, crap employee, is what I am, defying Frank's orders like this. But it's the right thing to do."

"Yes, it is. And it's brilliant news about them. Our plan with Hoyt to help people and do wonderful works for the world seems to have panned out well. I loathe to ask you, I truly do, but I need you to say it."

"Say what?"

"Oh, no you don't," he laughs. "Weren't you the one who said, and I paraphrase here, that I had better bloody well be right about Hoyt? I'm so rarely accurate, I really must take the opportunity to bask in the glory whenever possible.

"You hate to ask, my arse," she says, laughing. "Fine. You were right about helping Hoyt and doing good things. Happy now?"

"One-hundred percent, categorically, yes. But I confess, my happiness has little to do with you telling me I was correct. Although truer words were never spoken, and I am rarely given the opportunity to hear them from you. So, excuse me for taking such pleasure in it when I am right about something."

"You're very romantic when you apply yourself, Mr. Ward. But you're only right sometimes."

"Sometimes being the operative word here. I'm at least smart enough to realize you are far cleverer than I will ever be. But I accept that."

"Cleverer, huh? You can't just say I'm smarter? You Brits are so formal. And if you utter one word about your perfect Queen's English or colonizing half the world, I swear I will kick you out of my house," she says, laughing.

"I wouldn't dream of bragging about my British heritage and proper speech. I trust it goes without saying."

Christine rolls her eyes and slugs his arm playfully before resting her head on his shoulder.

"Are you ready for the next challenge, then? Our next mission?"

"You mean our next adventure?"

"Yes, I guess that's more accurate," she replies, grinning.

She lifts her face up to kiss him, knowing her life will never be the same. She realizes none of their lives can ever be the same. And she is fine with that. Circumstance brought them together, and now their destinies lie in navigating humankind to a better place. One small triumph at a time.

THIRTY-FOUR

Piedmont, Oklahoma 1868

Malcolm tries one last time to convince Kanuna to stay. They've packed his horse with supplies and the rifle Malcolm bought him, and his wife's pack carries blankets and their baby. The other natives in his clan wait for him by the river, ready to leave. After the battle at Washita Creek, they fear another attack and are traveling further south to Slipdown Mountain, across the Texas border into Comanche territory.

"Kanuna, please don't go. You are in no danger here. We are over a hundred miles from Cheyenne. General Custer does not launch an assault in this area, I promise you. You know we come from a future time. We are aware of what will happen here, and I'm telling you it's safe. Besides, it's almost Christmas, and snow will be here soon. At least wait for spring before you leave."

Kanuna only grunts and embraces Malcolm as Hannah stands with tears in her eyes, watching them. The Indian territory is dwindling, settlers claiming more of the land each day. Malcolm knows Kanuna and his tribe are safer moving to the mountains, but he selfishly wants him to stay. He wishes life to continue as before. Before Chad's henchman kidnapped Hannah, before the massacre at Washita made Kanuna feel like a refugee in his own homeland. But time marches on, and change is inevitable, no matter how badly he craves it to remain the same.

"Higinelii. Malcolm. You are my friend." He hands him a neatly folded beaded buckskin jacket and places his hand over Malcolm's for a moment before turning to mount his stallion and ride away. Kanuna nods to John but does not move to embrace him. He never warmed to him the way he has to Malcolm, maybe because John was so quick to shoot at him the first time they met. And John's distrust of Indians is deeply ingrained in his character. Whatever the reason, they tolerate each other, but no more, and Malcolm is certain even that much is mostly for his benefit. John tips his hat at him and walks into the cabin. Malcolm realizes he will never see his native friend again, and his sorrow over that is profound. Jacob settles next to Malcolm and slides his tiny hand in his, the small gesture pulling him into the present. Back to his world and the people he loves.

* * *

Piedmont, Oklahoma, 1869

Malcolm and Hannah stand beside John and Claire as they recite their marriage vows to one another. It is a beautiful ceremony filled with love and laughter. Malcolm cannot help but remember his own wedding to Hannah, when Kanuna married them. He would not change that detail for anything. He misses his friend and hopes he and his people found a new home where they can live in peace. Maybe someday they will go to Slipdown Mountain to visit him. He knows the chance of that happening in this lifetime is slim, but if he ever has the opportunity, he intends to find him.

There are many families attending the service in their Sunday best. Hannah has mastered sewing and made Malcom, Jacob, and herself new clothes for the festivities. Anne crafted Claire a beautiful bridal gown with ivory lace and a veil to match. After the wedding, the children run and play while the adults enjoy music played by locals. The liquor flows and they eat the persimmon flavor cake with layers of strawberry preserve filling Hannah baked. It is a huge hit, as usual, and several women ask her for the recipe. She playfully declines, telling them they will have to buy some from her bakery in town. She and Malcolm dance and drink whiskey until her feet cannot take any more. As she sits next to the large bonfire holding Malcolm's hand and watching Jacob, her heart is full, and she thinks her world could not be any more perfect. Things turned out exactly as they were meant to. And she would not trade anything about her life. Not even Chad. She has learned to trust destiny, for if not for his abuse she would never have exiled and met Malcolm, never adopted Jacob, and would not be the woman she is today.

Malcolm looks at Hannah, following her stare to Jacob playing. He glances down to the ruby on her wedding ring dancing in the firelight. She catches him staring and smiles at him. He raises their entwined fingers to his lips, kissing the back of her hand while he watches Jacob laugh, chasing a girl, while trying to pull her pigtails. They could not love the boy more if he were their own biological child. That he isn't makes no difference to them. He is their son in every way that matters. Malcolm's gaze wanders across John's ranch, taking in the townspeople who have grown to be their friends. It amazes him how good his life is here. What began as an exile to medieval England as punishment for a cyber-crime has evolved into a world far more fulfilling than he ever believed possible. His story. Her story. Their happy ending.

* * *

Piedmont, Oklahoma 1871

Cecelia stands perfectly still while Hannah fusses with the finishing touches on her wedding dress. She cannot believe she has a proper bridal gown complete with lace trim, the satin material silky smooth under her touch.

"There, all finished, Cecelia. Turn around and let me look at you."

Hannah gasps as Cecelia turns to her.

"What is it, Hannah?" she asks, worried she has damaged the dress somehow.

"You are so beautiful, Cecelia. Honestly, a vision in this ensemble. You could grace the runway of any fashion show in Paris or Milan. Amos will faint when he sees you!"

"Oh my, I hope not. A groom who cannot say I do does me no good at all. And I am not sure what a fashion show or a runway is," she replies laughing, accustomed to being confused by something Hannah references. She embraces her as her eyes fill. "I cannot thank you enough, Hannah, for all you have given me."

"Oh, don't be silly, I have done nothing any other person wouldn't have," she says, waving her hand in a dismissive motion.

Cecelia dips her chin and raises her eyebrows. "That is not true, and we both know it. But I realize how humble you are."

"Well, this is not the occasion to discuss it. It's your wedding day. Let's get you married!"

Hannah hands her the bouquet and straightens the train of her gown a final time.

"Okay, see you out there," she says, beaming at Cecelia.

Cecelia watches her walk out of the cabin, knowing beyond the door her soon-to-be-husband waits for her. She owes Hannah everything. She brought her here from Alexandria, where she is free. Three years ago, when Hannah revealed she came from the future, she was uncertain what to think. But she had spoken the truth. All she told her on that fateful day has come to fruition. Malcolm built her a small cottage of her own on the far side of their property, and then she found Amos. He is a kind, respectful man who she fell in love with almost immediately. Malcolm employs him as his ranch manager, and he is helping to rebuild the schoolhouse destroyed in a tornado last month. She works with Hannah in her store, baking and selling cakes, breads, and cookies. They expanded to sell savory goods too, and she has learned to cook as proficiently as Hannah. She also taught her to read and write, and how to speak properly. Cecelia spent the past two years studying while Hannah coached her and Jacob in English, geography, basic math, and history. She is an educated woman now, and for the first time, she is proud of who she is. Malcolm and Hannah insist she and Amos move into their very own home, the house that was once Jacob's maternal grandmother's. She never envisioned life turning out this way, and she thanks the heavens for bringing her guardian angel, Hannah, to her.

She takes a deep breath as she reaches for the door, ready to push it open and step into the rest of her future.

* * *

St Joseph, Missouri, 1880

Jacob stands behind the curtain on stage. He waits nervously for the administrator who is reading graduate names in alphabetical order, to announce his name.

"Samuel Albright," the dean's voice booms over the murmur of the crowd.

Jacob's heartbeat quickens. He is next in line. He runs his hand through his wavy black hair, and shakes his hands, trying to release the anxiety like his mother taught him.

"Jacob Aldred," the voice thunders.

He steps out onto the stage and heads across the expanse to meet the administrator's outstretched hand and accept his diploma. He glances out to the audience and sees his parents in the front row. They are difficult to miss. His father pumps his fist in the air and whoops, as his mother raises her hands and claps, then places her fingers in her mouth and whistles loudly. Beaming down at them, he walks off the platform, clutching his degree. At twenty-two, he has the world at his feet.

He loves his parents more than they will ever fathom, and he owes them so much. They took him into their home after his grandmother passed, welcoming him as if he were their own. They never treated him as if they adopted him, and now only vague memories of his biological family remain with him. He was so young when they died, but he remembers how distant and aloof they were. The Aldred's are the exact opposite of them. Growing up, they showered him with love and affection and never mistreated him. Hannah instructed him about many subjects they did not teach in regular school. She is so smart, and he has such admiration for her. When he was sixteen years old, they sat him down and explained the story of how they met and where they are from. The future time, as Cecelia and John refer to it. They are aware of his parent's history, but only because they were a part of it. It was difficult to believe initially, but they know things. Things they should not. They predict impending events that consistently come to pass. And they are knowledgeable in matters common farmers should comprehend nothing of.

Then there is the medication. It is like no other. It saved his life when he contracted cholera as a child, and now he holds his parent's supply. His mother insisted he bring the stockpile with him to college. Just in case, she said. They cannot fall ill from the diseases that rampage through today's population as they received inoculations against them while in the future time. Even if they had not, he knows his parents would still insist he hold the medicine for himself. They love him that much.

It was his mother who tutored him early on about infections and sterile medicinal practices. And his father told him about Doctor Lister, who practiced in England, where his dad was born. He always had an intense interest in science and the healing arts they encouraged, and it is because of them he stands here now, about to receive his medical degree.

It could not have been easy for his parents to travel three hundred fifty miles on a passenger locomotive. And to be here to watch him spend only one minute on the graduation stage seems hardly worth it to him. Yet they sent him a telegram saying they would be here, and true to their word, they made it.

As soon as the dean dismisses their graduating class, he looks for them. His father spots him first and shouts his name. He waves and jogs toward them, both waiting with open arms. They beam with pride, and he thanks God once again for bringing him the best parents he could have hoped for.

"Son, we are so proud of you," Malcolm says, embracing him.

"Mom, don't cry, this is a joyous occasion," he says, hugging his mother.

Hannah smiles at him, swiping at the corner of her eyes. "These are tears of joy, son. Jacob, I promised myself I would wait until today to tell you something."

"What is it?" he asks, frowning.

Hannah grasps his hands in hers. "You have your entire career ahead of you, and you will accomplish wonderful work. I'm certain of that. One day you may have a visit from a woman named Christine. You saw her twice when you were young, but perhaps you don't remember her. If she finds you, you can trust her, just know that."

"Is she from the future time? I have a faint memory of her. Why are you only telling me this now? It seems an odd occasion to bring this up."

"I wanted to make sure I got the chance. I can't be certain when we will see each other again, travel being what it is, and your dad and I are getting older. The ranch and bakery require most of our attention, so we may not be able to visit you as often as we'd like to. You'll soon find a wife and have your own life. And remember, we told you the first coast to coast telephones won't be operational for another thirty-five years, so communication is, well, spotty. Plus, I preferred to wait until you were a man to discuss this. And now you're grown. So, yes, she is from the future.

Call it intuition, but I think at some point she'll look for you. She might need your help, or maybe she'll just show up to check on you. Either way, your father and I trust you'll do the right thing if she needs something."

"I will, I promise. Surely you know I would do anything you ask of me? Now, what of that celebratory dinner at the restaurant of my choice you two assured me I would receive upon my graduation?"

"Just like your father, constantly thinking of food," Hannah says, laughing at him.

"Damn straight, that's my boy. Come on doctor, I'm starving," says Malcolm, grinning at them.

Jacob has a feeling his mother is correct. She usually is. Someone or something from the future is bound to traverse his life at some point. He can only pray for the strength to manage whatever or whoever it proves to be. But for now, he pushes the thought from his mind to focus on the present.

He hooks an arm around each of them, unsure where his journey will take him, but excited about his future as he walks off the campus and into his destiny.

THE END

ABOUT THE AUTHOR

Christy Cooper-Burnett is an award-winning author based in California with a degree in Administration of Justice. After retiring early from the new home construction industry, she now divides her time between northern and southern California. She has one grown son who inspires her to write.

She began her writing career later in life, but once she started, she couldn't stop! Her work focuses on creating relatable stories and characters that transcend genres and encourage readers to imagine what they would do if thrown into the unique, imaginative situations her protagonists end up in.

Finding Home is the sequel to her award-winning debut novel, *No Way Home*.

NOTE FROM THE AUTHOR

Word-of-mouth is crucial for any author to succeed. If you enjoyed *Finding Home*, please leave a review online—anywhere you are able. Even if it's just a sentence or two. It would make all the difference and would be very much appreciated.

Thanks!
Christy Cooper-Burnett

Thank you so much for reading one of
Christy Cooper-Burnett's novels.
If you enjoyed the experience, please check out our recommended
title for your next great read!

No Way Home by Christy Cooper-Burnett

"Immersive science-fiction and a moving character drama."
-Brian Carmody, author of *Hellish Beasts*

View other Black Rose Writing titles at
www.blackrosewriting.com/books and use promo code
PRINT to receive a **20% discount** when purchasing.

www.ingramcontent.com/pod-product-compliance
Lightning Source LLC
Chambersburg PA
CBHW01072910726
47899CB00009B/2991